DRAGOS
VAMPIRE WARLORD

L. A. LEWANDOWSKI

DRAGOS
VAMPIRE WARLORD

ALSO BY L. A. LEWANDOWSKI

The Ghost on Swann

I'm Not Old I Have Patina

Born to Die: The Montauk Murders

A Gourmet Demise: Murder in South Tampa

Bacon Aporkalypse

My Gentleman Vampire

Thirty Days of Work from Home Style

UNDER PEN NAME NELSON Q. LEWIS

Waste Management

SHORT STORY

Passage to Belize

Print ISBN 979-8-9911006-3-2
ebook ISBN 979-8-9911006-2-5

The Orchid Madame
A publishing lifestyle brand

To Sister Leo Veronica who told me my story about Vincent Van Gogh was too fanciful.

CHAPTER ONE

He walked through his garden, an echo of footsteps following him respectfully at a distance. The crunch of the freshly laid gravel path pounded in his sensitive ears; his hunter instincts distinguished a rabbit's paw snapping a twig miles away. No matter. The time for seclusion had ended and he would endure the discomfort of entering the modern world—for her.

This had been Natalia's moonlight garden, the luminous glow enhancing the shine of the leaves, the shapes of the flowers, the outlines of the garden statues. . . and of her, his lost love. Only candlelight had rivaled the glow of the moon, and the memory of her touch still tormented him.

Could their doomed love have miraculously overcome a century of death's shadow, its strength birthing a woman to fill the hole in his heart? Yes, he was certain of it. His beautiful Natalia had returned to him . . . reincarnated? Wishful thinking on his part. He had grudgingly accepted that Natalia's DNA flourished in the flesh of another woman.

Dragos ran his hand along the top of a Japanese boxwood hedge, checking the precision of the cut, ensuring the work he knew would be perfect. Toma was the best sculptor and landscape architect in all of Transylvania, and he was paid well to fulfill the fantasies of his reclusive client. They had never spoken. The detailed drawings Dragos provided were impeccable. No adjustments were allowed.

Dragos paced the interior of the lattice and stone structure, an elaborate folly, which stood high on the hill closest to his castle. From its elevation the layout of the newly planted garden revealed the maze of intricate paths and layers of shrubbery which he knew in daylight would be a verdant ocean of green. The folly would provide a shelter from the harsh Romanian winter. He wondered—could the new Natalia learn to love the night? Could she trade the scorching rays of the sun for a softer light, a sweeter breeze, and a moonlit sonata?

No woman had interested him in over a century. With his mind and body exhausted by war and responsibility, Dragos had retreated to his castle, alone with his music and his books, immersing himself in philosophy and chess theory. A twice-weekly game, played with a local chess master, satisfied his need for socialization.

Then one stormy night his brother, the vampire Bogdan, visited. Years of peace had dulled the animosity, but they still watched each other warily across the mahogany desk of Dragos's study. Bogdan related how there had been a change in the balance of power in the dark world: a powerful alien had established a network of followers. This new warlord was a shapeshifter who had quietly amassed much land and a great fortune in a suspiciously short period. The brothers parted with an agreement to share any intelligence gathered.

For a year, Dragos tracked the alien through the eyes of other minions. Then one day, she appeared. He momentarily doubted his senses—the young woman was the image of his Natalia. His shock turned to joy, an emotion he had denied himself long ago. Natalia's twin lived in America and made her living as a writer. The thought of looking into her eyes, hearing her voice and her laugh . . . only this miracle could persuade him to leave the comfort of solitude and re-enter the world he had renounced, a world where his exploits were legendary, and she had been his greatest loss. Natalia.

He was no longer tired. Dusting off the cobwebs of complacency, he jumped onto the top of the folly. The centuries had not affected his quickness or strength, and it would be foolish of any dark creature to underestimate him. If there was to be war with the aliens, then so be it. He would risk the confrontation and go to her. Natalia had been his one true love, and he had to confirm the existence of her descendent and fulfill his obligations as Natalia's executor.

His enemy remained hidden and had beaten him in the last confrontation with their aggressive move—Natalia's murder. A century had made Dragos wiser, and The Sicilian Defense was in play. Pawn to e5.

CHAPTER TWO

The shopping bags brushed my legs as I hurried up the suspended staircase. I'd completed the Caribbean beachwear list the bridegrooms, vampires David Fanning and Ian Westwood, had given me, purchasing most items from a posh tourist boutique in Montego Bay.

I had also bought myself several treats not on the list—a macramé bikini, reminiscent of the seventies, two silk negligées, and two sets of matching lace bras and panties. I couldn't wait to model the black negligée for Slade Suit, my new . . . boyfriend? We had several hours to spend together before David and his future husband rose from their temporary resting place in an adjacent stone bunker. I yearned to feel Slade's arms around me, and the memory of his kiss left me weak at the knees.

Slade had promised to appear when I asked,

and he kept his word, showing up this morning despite the reek of garlic in my room. He shook his head and threw open the balcony doors.

"Garlic could never keep me from you, darling," he'd said with a shrug. "We're meant to be together." The challenge would be convincing my friends, the vampires who had become my true and most loyal pals, that I was ready for a new relationship. That would not be easy.

I flung open the door to the bedroom David and Ian had generously assigned to me in the fabulous mansion they were renting for their nuptials in Jamaica.

"Slade, I'm back!" Silence. "Slade?"

The voile curtains billowed in the ocean breeze flowing through the open balcony's sliding door. I crossed the threshold and scanned the room. A wily shapeshifter, he could replicate anything. Had he morphed into the bamboo chair angled in the corner? I dropped my shopping bags next to the bed and fingered the seat cushion. There was no tingling sensation like the last time I'd touched a form he had taken. Where could Slade have gone?

Then I saw the note in the middle of the cream tufted duvet on the bed. The bed was huge, and I lay across it to reach the envelope. How sweet. He didn't want me to worry. I ripped open the envelope and would have marveled at his elegant handwriting if the message hadn't wrecked my afternoon plans.

Dearest Natalie,

I hope you have had a lovely day with Arabella. I regret important business requires my immediate attention. Please believe, my darling, that only an issue of utmost urgency would convince me to leave you.

Until we meet again,

Slade

I crumpled the note and threw it on the floor. Cad, jerk, womanizing shapeshifter. Did I have a neon light over my head that read, "gullible dope"? I fell backward onto the bed in utter frustration. What was wrong with me?

I lay there, listening to the laughing cry of the seagulls. Even they knew I'd been ditched, and they found it hilarious. I stared at the ceiling, my disappointment whipping into anger. It was high time I learned to differentiate between a narcissist and a man who actually wanted a relationship. My soulmate had to be out there.

After I'd thoroughly beaten myself up, the relentless pounding of the surf drew me onto the balcony. The waves rolled in and out, hypnotic and calming, and I recalled the warning David's close friends, Tomasina and Jerrilyn Fish, known as Tom and Jerri, had given me. They were the oldest vampires of David's social circle. They were also enforcers, charged with keeping the vampire population from rogue behavior.

"Slade's not at all like I thought," I had insisted. We were at my home in the States, and they had just rescued me from Slade's kidnapping after my best friend David and I won the tango competition. Slade's attempt to seduce me had nearly succeeded. "Yes, I know he imprisoned me in his castle, but he was a considerate host, and we have many common interests. I have to admit, he is the most intriguing, sexiest man I've ever met."

Jerri had gotten up and paced the length of the room. "It's a ruse, Natalie. Shapeshifters are manipulative and notoriously frisky. Slade was stalking you for weeks, and he used that knowledge to appeal to your...sorry...weaknesses. Shapeshifters can read minds. Our informants confirm he is bored with Selena, a woman who became a vampire to stay with him forever. He wanted to seduce the pure princess."

"I'm not pure and I'm not a princess," I'd replied, and Jerri had smiled.

"Just a figure of speech, no harm meant. In our world, a world of dark creatures and bloody deeds, you are as pure as driven snow."

My spotty track record with men should have made me consider the advice, but I wanted . . . what? Slade was an enigma, and although I had heeded my friends advice, I hadn't been able to get

8

him out of my head. He had promised to come when I summoned him, and he had been true to his word, but he had disappeared as quickly as he had arrived in Jamaica.

Now I dropped onto the chaise lounge on the balcony and leaned my head back. The ocean smelled fresh and salty, and if I could lick it, would it taste like those big pretzels you bought from a New York City street vendor?

"I want to be in love," I whispered, closing my eyes and letting the tranquilizing murmur of the ocean ease my exasperation. My conscious mind let go and I drifted into a sweet repose.

In my dream, I was in a garden lit by moonlight. The familiar gravel path led me through an archway heavy with the scent of night jasmine to the folly where my true love awaited me. The heat of love and lust tugged at my soul. In the garden of my dreams, the reflected light cast a becoming glow that masked the blush of desire on my cheeks. I reached out . . . and awoke to a brisk knocking on my bedroom door.

Unsettled, I felt woozy, perhaps from the sun or jetlag from the plane flight from the States. I rose carefully and, resting my hand on the doorjamb, staggered inside to the bedroom door.

"Natalie, my pet, were you napping" Arabella Bishop, my dear friend and roommate, reached out to cup a cool palm on my forehead. "Are you unwell? Your forehead is warm." Arabella was a

Jamaican witch who had recently returned to human form upon the death of a malevolent sorceress. Her bronze beauty glowed, and her aura of kindness was her greatest gift. She had lived with me in America while under a spell in the form of a black cat, and was responsible for introducing me to David Fanning, my vampire pal. When I replay the chain of events of my life over the past six months I have vertigo.

She followed me to the bathroom and hovered while I splashed cold water on my face. My pink and blotchy reflection bore out her concern. The whites of my eyes were red even though I had forced back the tears over Slade. I studied my face, the fine-boned features I'd always thought ordinary and the angled deep brown eyes, until recently, a personal disappointment. It had taken my gentleman vampire, David, and a frisky shapeshifter to convince me my beauty was elegant and aristocratic.

"I fell asleep on the balcony. I think I overheated. What's up?"

"It's almost sundown, sweetheart. The caterers sent helpers ahead to begin the set-up for the rehearsal dinner. You need to get ready." Arabella had changed into a formal caftan, her head wrapped in an elaborately twisted dupsie. The glimmer of the gold and bronze fabric complimented her skin tone and brought out the gold flecks in her eyes.

I checked my watch and gasped.

"My goodness, I was asleep for over two hours! Let me hop in the shower and change. I can be ready in a flash."

Arabella laughed. "Text me when you've finished your make-up, and I'll put your hair up. I can supervise the workers until then." She planted a kiss on my cheek, left the room, and closed the door behind her.

I wouldn't share my dream. It felt deeply personal, and I pushed it to the back of my mind as I stepped into the shower and felt the cool water course over my body. Slade's abandonment was no surprise, really. In romance, I excelled at attracting hot but unsuitable men. The night I met vampire David Fanning, however, was the luckiest day of my life.

CHAPTER THREE

When Arabella had invited David into my home, he'd revealed that my rescued cat was actually a witch under an evil spell and able to communicate with him, a vampire. Shock had quickly turned into skepticism. A non-human-blood-drinking vampire wanted to live in my basement to hide from his horrible ex, Antonio. David's assured me that his sustenance was V cocktails, the chic drink of the sustainably conscious vampire. I was still reeling over the betrayal and exit of my live-in boyfriend and competitive dance partner, Mike Endicott. My self-image dashed, I desperately needed what David promised—a style update and a social life that challenged my introverted tendencies.

I jumped into the deep end of the pool and every day since has been full of surprises.

David didn't hesitate for a second once I flashed the green light, and the Natalie Crisan makeover, long overdue, seeped into every part of my being. He even encouraged me to dance competitively again. Before our doomed relationship ended, Mike and I partnered in many dance competitions.

"Most people have a closet stuffed with clothes for a fairy tale lifestyle," David said when he'd attacked my disorganized closet. "They have nothing to wear for their day-to-day life, and we are going to empty your closet and build a functioning wardrobe."

"You're bossy," I'd answered as he made three piles of my clothes. He ignored my protest.

Most of my existing wardrobe was donated, a few items were brought to a tailor for tweaking, and I had just enough to not be naked. We bartered for David's styling services, and I let him live rent-free in my basement. I'd highly recommend hiring a personal stylist; it is well worth the expense

I smiled at my reflection. My relationship with David had brought me to this gorgeous mansion in Jamaica and bestowed the honor of supervising his upcoming nuptials. I couldn't think of a better way to show him what his friendship meant to me. We had forged a bond, and he'd sprung a fresh, confident Natalie from her chrysalis. He deserved the best and Arabella and I were going to give him his dream wedding.

I texted Arabella and she arrived promptly.

"Wow, you look beautiful, Nat." Arabella stood back to admire the low chignon she had twisted at the nape of my neck. "It's a shame Andrew couldn't come. You two were a cute couple."

Andrew was the warm-blooded nephew of the vampire who owned Nuit Boutique, the shop where David and I created my capsule wardrobe after the closet clean-out. With assistance from the owner, David had chosen elegant pieces to form the core of a fabulous wardrobe. I had also found an iolite necklace which, according to Arabella, held protective powers.

Andrew was nice, available, and interested in me, but beyond friendship, there was no attraction for me. No spark. Andrew's uncle, Ralph— pronounced Raif—Hornblower, would marry the two lovebirds.

"David asked if I wanted him to invite Andrew, but I don't want the pressure of a date," I said. "David and Ian are the story, and I want to celebrate them."

Arabella watched me shrewdly, but didn't contradict the white lie nor mention Slade and Mike.

"It's going to be a fabulous rehearsal," she said. "Sunset is within the hour, and the doorbell keeps ringing with more deliveries. How many orchids did David order?"

"According to David there are never enough orchids," I quoted. I held my arms open wide pretending to stumble under the weight of the orchids. Giddy with party anticipation, we "vogued" down the floating wood and plexiglass staircase of the mansion, striking poses as we went.

"Hey, where do you want these?" a guy in cutoff shorts yelled, burdened under the awkward pot of enormous white moth orchids.

We ushered him and the other florists to the ocean-facing terrace.

I cast a critical glance across the terrace and sighed happily. The décor was romantic and magical, perfect for David and Ian. Their reconnection and enduring love gave hope for those of us drawn to unsuitable men. While Arabella inspected the rows of chairs lining the back terrace, I made sure the Doric columns at the end of the main aisle would support the immense candelabra.

Strands of white lights hung with polished crystals framed the area where my friends would exchange their vows. Statues of cherubs sporting bowties punctuated the end of each row, their hair encircled in tiny white lights. Lush palms and native greenery surrounded the terrace space, making it a private haven.

Sunset that evening was a wash of orange, pink, and purple against a turquoise sky, colors made famous by The Highwaymen. I had admired a stunning painting by Alfred Hair in a Manhattan gallery and thought the colors he'd chosen were impressionistic rather than realistic. Was I ever wrong.

Arabella and I had completed our tasks, and the

only missing piece was the presence of the well-rested grooms.

"Natalie, Arabella, my favorite mortals, where are you?" David called from inside the house.

"Out here!" I called back.

The bridegrooms stepped, arm-in-arm, onto the terrace. David clapped with glee.

"Oh, this is gorgeous. Ian, my darling, we are getting married under the stars in a moonlit garden." I jumped.

I hadn't shared my dream with anyone, and the mention of a moonlit garden had to be a coincidence. The terrace was exactly what David had described to me, but it wasn't the moonlit garden in my dream.

"I'm dying for a V cocktail, aren't you?" David turned and guided Ian back toward the door, calling over his shoulder. "Come inside, peeps. Ralph should be here any minute." I had guzzled a gallon of water in preparation for a well-deserved glass of champagne. Arabella winked at me, and we followed the lovebirds inside.

The attendees at the rehearsal were an intimate selection of David and Ian's pals. Tom and Jerri Fish and other sophisticated vampires mixed with a gang of werewolves ready to party. Ralph and his boyfriend Peter Spearmint finally made an entrance wearing matching agate-colored gabardine suits. They were like unmatched bookends—Peter a slim, pale foil to Ralph's dark good looks. As the owner of Nuit Boutique, Ralph equaled David's acumen in the style department. He made a beeline for me and pulled me to the side of the room whispering conspiratorially into my ear.

"I know you were suspicious when you saw your gown for the wedding, Natalie, darling. Ian confided he was going to propose, and I took the liberty of asking Iris to weave a gown for you. We both kept Ian's secret. Isn't love marvelous?" He pirouetted away before I could respond.

The musicians arrived, and I guided them to the terrace. A jazz band would play inside the house during the reception, and I escorted the members to a corner space inside the enormous marble tiled foyer. The open floor plan with easy access to the kitchen was perfect for the wedding reception. How had David and Ian known that the rental would be so perfect?

"Natalie!" David called and waved from across the floor. I excused myself from the jazz band leader and hurried to my gentleman vampire's side. His cold lips pressed a kiss on my warm cheek.

"Darling, you and Arabella have worked a miracle. Are you ready for the wedding of the century?" I hugged him and gave him a quick peck on the cheek. His chiseled facial features contrasted with his soft brown eyes and thick mop of hair he'd slicked back per usual.

"Yes," I said, straightening his bowtie. He and Ian had matched bowties and socks—completely adorable. "I think you and Ian should rehearse before Ralph drinks another V cocktail."

"How shocking! Yes, we should get the ceremony stuff over with." David's witty remark was met with silence.

"Get it over with? Did I hear you correctly?" Ian had edged into the group without David's notice. David slid his arm through Ian's and leaned his head on his fiancé's shoulder.

"Oh, my love, let's rehearse the ceremony, which will bind us forever." Ian narrowed his eyes but wisely let the gaffe go without drama. A loud whistle made me spin around and Ralph took charge.

"Okay, folks, Ian wants to rehearse. Follow me."

The practice ceremony lasted ten minutes, and then we drifted inside to enjoy a spread of hot and cold hors d'oeuvres. Vampires don't eat food but that didn't stop David and Ian from providing stellar hospitality. The vamps stuck with their mysterious V cocktails, and while I sampled the sushi and sashimi, Arabella and the werewolves popped the sweet and sour meatballs appreciatively into their mouths. The werewolves wouldn't be able to come to the wedding because of the impending full moon, and David and Ian invited them to the rehearsal so they wouldn't feel left out

While we shared stories about the bride and groom, soft jazz floated amongst the close circle of friends who had traveled with their boxes, a polite term for coffin. The chic vamp never says coffin or casket. At midnight, the vampires agreed to visit a famous underground vamp-only club.

"I hope you're not upset, Nat," Ian said. "We've heard stories, and don't want to put you or Arabella in any danger. Jerri has posted two guards here at the house. You should be safe, okay?"

I nodded. Arabella would be in the room next door, and the enforcers would prowl the property until David and Ian returned.

"Have fun, peeps. And be safe." Frankly, I was still curious about Slade's abrupt disappearance, even though my compass now pointed in the direction of narcissistic creep. What would I say to him if he did appear?

I climbed the stairs with Arabella, and we exchanged goodnights in the hallway.

"Do you want me to sleep on the pullout sofa in your room?" Arabella asked.

"Thanks, but no. The florist brought additional garlic garlands and a potted wolfsbane plant with the orchids and I'll drape the new garlands across the windows and doors. I'll wear my iolite necklace, too. I might not smell fabulous by morning, but I'll be fine."

"Okay, pet. I'm taking the same precautions, so if we stink, we'll hang out together. Sleep well." We hugged and retired to our rooms.

I undressed, removed my makeup, and debated using a blue hydrating sleep mask—a benefit to sleeping alone. I scooped the blue goo out of the container and piled it on thickly. The bobby pins came out of my hair easily and I swept a brush through my tresses, the fullness and wave requiring careful brushing. My hair had grown like crazy in the last few months. Pulling my hair into a ponytail, I slid the black silk nightgown over my body. It moved with me like a luxurious shadow as I crossed the room.

After switching off the bedside lamp, I padded to the sliding door under the guiding light of a bright moon. I opened the slider a crack despite the stern warning from David and Ian. The night breeze slipped over the ocean, caressing my Blue Man Group cheeks. I closed my eyes to breathe in the delicious luxury of fresh sea salt. Refreshed, I closed and locked the door.

The cool sheets provided a sensual welcome and propped up on my back to allow the mask to settle, I remembered the trip my ex-Mike and I had taken to Mexico. We had strolled along the rolling surf, hand-in-hand, blissfully in love, or so I had thought. The full moon had lit our path, and the foam of the surf tickled our feet.

I drifted on the edge of sleep.

"Natalia." My eyes flew open. I had limited my alcohol; I wasn't drunk. Had Slade come back?

"Slade? Are you here?" I flicked on the lamp and got out of bed to check the bathroom and closet. Nothing. I drank a tumbler of water, refilled the glass, and put it on a coaster beside my bed. Had I imagined the voice?

I pulled back the curtains to recheck the locks on the balcony sliding door. What the . . . I jumped back: ten feet from the door a huge bat flapped and hovered under the moonlight. Performing a smooth turn, it disappeared into the night.

I staggered back to the bed and perched on the corner of the mattress, my hand straying to my iolite necklace. It was cool to the touch, a good sign. Did Jamaica have bats? I knew they had black rats and snakes. A quick search on my phone confirmed the existence of a Jamaican red bat. Relief flooded my senses.

The door was locked, and I was safe, but . . .

A voice had whispered my name. I sat bolt upright. No, not my name, exactly.

It had whispered, "Natalia."

CHAPTER FOUR

The dream crystallized as the mist lifted and the garden view sharpened. Specific details were oddly familiar; the four stone cherubs representing winter, spring, summer, and fall, which marked the main paths, the abundant night jasmine arbor, the intricate shapes of the boxwood topiaries. I knew this garden. I had spent many days and nights meandering through its intricate paths.

But as I strolled toward the folly, it shrunk and receded. I stretched out my hand.

"Yes, Natalie. Go to him."

The pillars of the folly distorted, swayed, and expanded, then shrank in rhythm with my breath, ragged even to my own ears. The dark shadow of a man loomed in the distance, and I was sucked back to the garden gate, its scrolled iron cold in my hand. It stood between us, and the man came towards me.

"Trust him, Natalie."

I flipped over to my side and opened my eyes, groggy with sleep. My hand grazed something—a note! I sat up and ripped it open.

Good morning,
I used the spare key. Hope you don't mind.
It stinks in here. I had to wear a mask.
You will be VERY unpopular at the wedding if you smell like garlic.
Thank you for all you and Arabella have done for us.
We love you both, David and Ian
P.S. Check your bathroom vanity for a present from us.

A present! I hopped out of bed and trotted to the bathroom. In a gilt box tied with a red ribbon, a beaded black Versace wristlet sparkled. It was just big enough to hold a lip gloss, my phone, and a few tissues for wayward tears. It was the perfect accessory for my gown.

The beauty mask had performed as promised. My skin was plump with hydration, and as soft as a baby's bottom. After a quick rinse off, I heard a tap on the door and donned a cotton robe.

"Natalie? I brought you coffee." Arabella, my savior. I opened the door, and she set the tray on a round table.

"How did you sleep?" Arabella reclined on a nearby chaise longue, stretching her arms over her head like the feline she once was. Her eyes sparkled with delight, and I guessed the proximity to her extended family was the cause. Jamaica had been an unsafe island for her after she had been placed under the witch's spell. Her aura of contentment was palpable, and I would not tarnish it by interjecting my strange dreams or odd voices whispering names.

"Fabulously. David and Ian left me a note, and a present."

"Me, too. The most stunning handbag I've ever owned." She brandished a purple evening bag from a hidden pocket of her maxi sundress. "It won't hold much, but who cares."

"They gave me a black wristlet. It's perfect with my gown."

We moved to the balcony and drank our coffee. The wedding area would receive the finishing touches today, and tonight our friends would vow eternal fidelity.

The sun was a round yellow ball hanging in the perfection of a clear azure sky. I cradled my coffee and recalled the cryptic words of Slade's note.

"Has Slade communicated with you?" My head whipped to the right. Arabella calmly gazed at the ocean.

"Arabella, are you reading my mind?"

"Not totally, pet. But you are radiating a vibe—

expectation mixed with maybe sexual tension. It was a guess." I exhaled.

"Well, I admit he was here yesterday. He kissed me until my brain oozed out of my ears, and then disappeared, leaving behind an obscure excuse. 'A business emergency'. I have not heard from him since then. I guess shapeshifters don't text." Although I hadn't intended humor, the situation was ridiculous, and I giggled.

"It's probably better he isn't here for the wedding," she said. "His presence would stress David and Ian, and who knows what Tom and Jerri would do. I sense a territorial animosity. The dark world has its own caste system. Vampires and witches are at the top. They won't include aliens easily."

"I'm confused. Are shapeshifters aliens? Like from outer space?"

Arabella placed her empty coffee cup on the rattan end table.

"I think certain shapeshifters are from outer space. There are many species—I guess 'species' is the best way to refer to them. I overheard David and Ian discussing the conversation they had with Tom and Jerri about Slade. Slade's specific powers are those of an alien species. He possesses abilities they haven't come across. For a reason I don't quite understand, he poses a threat to the vampire world. And they don't think he chose you randomly . . ." Arabella froze mid-sentence. "What dream?"

"You're reading my mind, and I would like you to stop. With regard to Slade, I get it, okay? He's not just a cheating jerk like my ex-boyfriend; he's a dangerous outlier. No one has to hit me over the head." I rose, grabbed Arabella's coffee cup, and before she could object, stalked off the balcony and into the bedroom.

I was famished and frustrated. Why did my love life require a microscope and interference from everyone I knew? My innermost thoughts were an open book to vamps and witches alike, and I had to learn to block the prying.

But first, breakfast.

Downstairs in the kitchen, I pulled out eggs, butter, chives, bread, and a bowl. Arabella joined me, chastened, and silently cleaned and cut strawberries for a fruit salad. I scrambled the eggs and made the toast, and we carried our respective contributions out to the terrace. We ate in silence.

"I apologize for invading your privacy," Arabella said once we had finished. "I meant no harm. The vampires are concerned—for you and the threat the aliens pose."

"Thank you." I reached out to squeeze her hand. "Let's not argue. The wedding and reception tonight will be memorable. But I have to learn to shield my thoughts from mind readers."

"I know someone who can teach you," Arabella said as we carried our dishes to the kitchen. "Blocking mind readers takes lots of practice, and it doesn't always work." I washed the silverware and dishes, and Arabella dried the knife she was holding and inserted it in the knife block. She faced me. "So . . . you aren't going to share the dream with me?"

The doorbell rang.

"We don't have time. It was a dream, not a nightmare, anyway. Let's finish making this place the most gorgeous wedding venue we've ever seen." I needed to set a boundary, and I wasn't rewarding her intrusiveness.

Iris Lavender, the fairy fashion designer, breezed in the front door, a garment bag slung over her arm. I'd met the diminutive fairy when David introduced us at Nuit Boutique. She'd volunteered to design my costume for the tango competition David, and I had entered. My ex-boyfriend and his new partner and Slade and the vicious vampire Selena Sidwell had competed against us. I liked Iris a lot. We air kissed and she draped the garment bag over a nearby chair.

The ethereal Iris wore an emerald sheath of raw silk, and her bobbed auburn hair and bright green eyes captured every detail of her surroundings. The most striking part of her ensemble, her signature style, was the cream hand-painted peau de soie kitten-heeled pumps she wore.

There were advantages to inhabiting a world filled with alternative people. Those who shrank their world and led lives full of judgment and fear missed out.

The extensive social circle David and Ian belonged to enabled Arabella and I to involve their friends in unique ways. Rather than being put out with the impossibly short timeframe to complete their tasks for the wedding, their pals were honored to be part of the craziness.

Iris had volunteered to fulfill David's wish for an exploding confetti flourish when he and Ian walked down the aisle after their vows. Iris had her own ideas about the requested confetti.

"In the fairy world confetti is pollution. I have come up with a brilliant alternative. It will be my wedding present to them." Iris raised a finger to her lips. "It's a secret."

"I have a present for you, Natalie. I made a gown for a new client and when she tried it on, it didn't fit her waist. It surprised both of us because I measured her myself. It turns out she is pregnant and is due in seven months. With a few tweaks, it will fit you perfectly." Another Iris Lavender original in my wardrobe? I unzipped a corner of the garment bag and took a peek. The sheen of the weave of the fabric broadcasted Iris's handiwork.

"It's gorgeous, Iris." I zipped up the bag and gave her a hug. "Thank you for thinking of me, but I insist I pay you for it.

"Nonsense," she said. "In payment, you can introduce me to the hot guy over there holding the saxophone. I'm single again."

I lowered my voice dramatically.

"Jayce is Arabella's cousin, and she told me he's single. I'll arrange an introduction." I heard my name called and moved quickly to the terrace where two florists held the elaborate orchid and ivy garland aloft.

"Should this be higher?" The serpentine garland was strung with tiny white lights and wrapped around a rope that extended between two queen palms.

"Yes, maybe ten inches." A white aisle runner would be released after the guests were seated. The florist had added an orchid crown to each of the stone cherubs and tied poufy taffeta bows on the back of the regal gilt chairs. The entire space was exactly as David and Ian had envisioned.

Back inside, I perused the impeccable details of the dance floor and cool conversation pit in the living room. The sunken living room featured a crescent shaped sofa upholstered in pale green linen. When David had first seen the sunken living room, he'd been thrilled with the intimate space. He'd stretched out on the couch.

"A sunken living area is to a vampire what a beach chaise is to a sun worshipper," he'd purred.

A low candle-lit succulent display on the coffee table was the perfect accent, and after performing one more glance around the room I moved on to check the food service.

"All under control," the sous chef assured me. He'd handled the tasks to be completed during daylight because the vampire caterers, Jon and his brother Ricky, had become my go-to chefs since David introduced us at my housewarming party. The reception guest list included a large group of fairies and other magical creatures, and the menu reflected the specific dietary preferences of the guests. The vampires in David's social circle drank what they called V cocktails. I had no idea what was in them, and I certainly was not drinking from the intricately decorated black goblets.

"Arabella," I called from the kitchen, where I sampled a caviar-topped deviled egg. "Try one of these. I thought my aunt made the best deviled eggs, but these are insane." Arabella took a bite and nearly swooned.

"Incredible." The sous chef smiled and returned to arranging a six-foot-long charcuterie board.

"I'm going to get dressed," I said.

Arabella nodded.

"Me, too. We have about two hours before David and Ian are awake. Text me and I'll put your hair up when you're ready."

"Thanks, I will." We climbed the stairs to our bedrooms.

I stripped in my bathroom and stuffed my hair under a shower cap. David had taught me squeaky clean hair was difficult to put into a chignon, my favorite style. I donned a silk kimono robe and prepped my face with a primer. While it set, I arranged the plethora of recently purchased cosmetic products in a row. Perched on the tufted vanity chair, I carefully applied the products in order. After playing up my dark eyes, I retrieved the lipstick that matched my gown. Lipstick was always the last cosmetic applied, and only after I was dressed. I texted Arabella, and she popped her head around the doorframe.

"Ready for Arabella, hairstylist to the stars?" Arabella stepped into the room, and I gasped. "Arabella, your dress is glorious! You didn't tell me Iris was making your outfit." The purple and gold material flowed with a lightness that should have made it see-through, yet it was modest. It complimented her warm skin tone, and she held herself like a queen. The ensemble was unmistakably an original by Iris Lavender.

"I didn't think Iris would have enough time to make my dress," she said. "But when we spoke on the phone last week to discuss the confetti burst, she said it wasn't a problem. It is the most beautiful dress I've ever worn." She leaned toward me. "Your make-up is very glamorous."

"Yup. I put on three coats of mascara to make David happy. He would have me in foundation and extravagant eye makeup every day if I would agree."

We chatted and Arabella expertly slicked my thick hair back and twisted it into the chignon. I hugged her, and she went to see who had knocked on the bedroom door. I moved to the closet to get dressed.

I flicked on the overhead chandelier in my closet. The light danced through the faceted prisms, and I paused a moment to admire it. The gown Iris had sewn for me hung on an ornate valet's hook on the far wall. I padded across the thick carpet and admired how the fabric caught the light refracted through the chandelier crystals. I ran the tips of my fingers across the woven material.

Who had I become? Orphaned with grainy memories of my parents, I had been raised by a kind aunt who had focused my energy on cultural excursions and education. Her wardrobe was built around a core of classic pieces meant to last a lifetime. She believed couture was frivolous and she would keel over if she knew what I was up to.

The bespoke gown of blood red shouted to the sky that my future would be filled with a panoramic rainbow of adventures, and I hoped, true love. I unzipped the dress and removed the hanger. Stepping into it, I slid it over my body and turned to admire my reflection. The spectacularly gowned woman smiled at me. Slade's loss. The revenge gown shouted confidence.

The gown needed a zip up the back, and I called to Arabella, who arrived with Iris in tow.

Arabella carefully pulled up the zipper and stood back to admire the spectacular effect of the Iris Lavender gown.

"Wow," she said. "Every time I see your latest creation, Iris, I am convinced it will be my favorite forever, and then you make another miraculous one."

I gathered up handfuls of the gown and turned toward Iris. "Thank you so much for this incredible gown. I love Arabella's, too. I knew immediately that you had sewn it."

Iris curtsied. "I treasure the compliment, my friend. The caftan shape was fun. I've never designed one before but being here for a day I can see why women wear them. Jamaica is far too warm for a woodland fairy." Iris spun around appreciatively. "I love this bedroom, Natalie. I would get lost in such a huge bed. How did David manage to rent it on such short notice?"

"I have a cousin who found it for us," Arabella said. "We needed a bunker for the vampire . . . luggage. There is a large very secure out-building which sealed the deal."

I leaned on Arabella and stepped into my stiletto heels as the sun dipped below the horizon. The sunsets in Jamaica defied description. I never thought a sky could layer shades of purple or pink. Layers of blue morphed into turquoise and a painter's palette of happiness.

"Lipstick!" I teetered on my high heels to the bathroom. While my friends watched the rainbow of colors progress, I lined my lips and applied a classic red lipstick. According to David, "Life is too short not to wear red lipstick."

Downstairs, the string quartet was tuning their instruments on the terrace. It sounded discordant yet harmonic. The front doors of the mansion were open to the night, and the guests meandered in, mostly dressed in black. Jon and Ricky were busy in the open kitchen, and waiters in white dinner jackets passed out V cocktails and champagne. I went in search of the bridegrooms and found them with Ralph, the officiant, in the servant's wing.

"Well, it's about time!" Ralph tried to feign annoyance but erupted in a fit of giggles. "Doesn't everyone look fabulous?"

David and Ian resembled two movie stars from the Golden Age of Hollywood. Peter Spearmint, Ralph's assistant, clicked away on his cell phone as the bridegrooms attached the boutonnieres to each other's tuxedo lapel.

"The cell phone is a marvel. We never would have been able to capture this moment with the old cameras unless we wanted to end it all. Thank you, Steve Jobs." David gave Ian a peck on the cheek, sashayed to me, and twirled me smoothly.

"Magnificent, Nat. Red is your color. How's it shaking out there? Are my groupies prepared for the commitment Ian and I are about to forge? Is there weeping?"

"You make me sound like a horse," Ian said. "We're ready whenever you are, Nat."

"Awesome. We'll shepherd the throngs of your admirers to their seats, and then I'll come back."

A border collie would have helped Arabella and me push the guests onto the terrace. After ten minutes of prodding, we closed the front doors, and I click-clacked my way across the tile floor to the grooms' hideout.

"Knock, knock," I called. The door flung open, and David presented me with a spray of white calla lilies.

"Oh, David, how gorgeous. Thank you."

"You deserve the best of everything, love. Ian, let's do this."

Ralph brushed imaginary lint from David's shoulder, and Peter hurried to his seat while Ralph stood in position under the orchid garland. Arabella had closed the doors to the terrace, and when she saw me, opened them and nodded to the string quartet. The processional, Vivaldi's Concerto No. 4 in F Minor, "Winter" Il Largo from *The Four Seasons* began, and Arabella floated down the aisle to appreciative sighs, her mahogany beauty on display, the folds of the caftan drifting around her in the cool ocean breeze. She clasped one magnificent bird of paradise flower.

When she was halfway down the aisle, I stepped onto the white runner and blushed at the perceptible intake of breath from the assembly. The gown clung to my curves without constricting my movement, and the power of feminine mystery flooded my senses. We took our places to the left, and David and Ian crossed the threshold of the French doors and stopped for maximum impact. Tom and Jerri awaited their arrival at the right side of the orchid garland. Arm-in-arm, the grooms strode proudly up the aisle. Ralph addressed the guests.

"Good evening, friends. We are here to celebrate the joining of our dear friends, David Fanning and Ian Westwood.

"I have known David for many years, and I have admired his ability to forge friendships wherever he traveled. Most recently, I joined him at a housewarming party he organized at Natalie's home in the States. It was here I met Ian, the love of his life. My experience told me it would not be long before I would be standing in front of them and their friends, joining them in matrimony. The grooms have written their own vows. David, will you begin?" The bridegrooms faced each other.

"Ian, I will go first because it is the last time you will have the final word. Darling man, you are the love of my life, and . . ."

Snide laughter blasted from a microphone inside the house. "That's not what you told ME, Davey darling. Remember the night when . . . ow!" Instantly, I realized what had happened. Antonio, David's former boyfriend, had commandeered the jazz band's microphone and attempted to ruin the wedding. Jerri must have intervened. I hadn't seen her move, but the spot beside Tom was empty.

"Please, everyone, stay in your seats," Ralph instructed. "It's been handled."

David and Ian hugged, and I reached for Arabella's hand. Jerri returned in under a minute and Tom plucked a blond hair from her sleeve.

"Obstacles are small mountains and meant to be climbed," Ralph announced. "David, continue your vow."

David cleared his throat. "Ian, darling man, life with me will be an adventure. You are my captain, my true love. Luck has brought you back to me, and I will spend every day thankful to show you what you mean to me."

I pulled a tissue from my wristlet, placed conveniently on my seat before the ceremony.

"Ian?"

"Dearest David, you may think from this day forward you will have the last word, but that's incorrect." Laughter. "We are a team, a couple, equal partners in immortality. You are the light in my world, a beam of dancing moonlight I will follow for all my days. Together, we will do amazing things. I love you forever."

I dabbed at my eyes with a tissue amid the applause and cheers. Ralph patted his hands in the air.

"Love, my friends, is the panacea to the ills of the world. Gentlemen, face each other. David, repeat after me. I, David Fanning, take you, Ian Westwood, as my lawful husband." The grooms repeated the vows in turn, and once again I used a tissue to blot my tears.

"The rings, please." Jerri reached into her pocket and produced two rings, which she handed to Ralph, and he chose one. David slid the yellow gold band onto Ian's finger and Ian followed, sliding a matching band onto David's finger and repeating the promise of fidelity and commitment.

"By the powers vested in me by the Organization for Vampire Happiness, I pronounce that David Fanning and Ian Westwood are married. You may seal your union with a kiss." Ian grabbed David and dipped him backward in a photo-op smooch.

They turned to the congregation, but before they began their walk down the aisle, a surreal sound of wings and celestial singing descended from the sky. From overhead, fairy dust fell in iridescent rainbow ripples. The fairy dust clung to all present for a few seconds. I could see it on the tips of my calla lilies and then it evaporated.

The jubilant congregation cheered, and the unfazed string quartet, plus the horn section from the jazz band, swung into action, playing the requested wedding recessional, the Allegro from J.S. Bach's Brandenburg Concerto Number 3.

"Magical! What a surprise." David and Ian

engulfed Iris, the clever fairy who had engineered the surprise dusting, in a group hug. Iris beamed.

"You have done so much for me, and what good is it to be a fairy if you can't add a bit of glitzy magic to a special event?"

Inside the mansion, the guests were served an array of V cocktails, champagne, or fruit nectar cocktails, the requested libation of fairies and other magical guests. Much to the delight of the chefs, the throng descended upon the Pinterest worthy buffet.

Our dance coach, Ron De Jamme, had asked to propose a toast. Ron, a talented dance instructor and vampire, had trained David and me for the tango competition and choreographed the first-place routine we performed. We'd trounced my ex-boyfriend Mike Endicott and his new girlfriend and Slade Suit and the vicious vampire Selena Sidwell. Ron De Jamme's brilliance equaled his perfectionism, and although several of the dance rehearsals were torture, I'd never experienced the deep feeling of confidence he forced out of me.

"To David and Ian," Ron proclaimed. "May you both tango through life with joy and love!" Glasses and goblets were raised, and I gulped a generous mouthful of the ice-cold champagne.

Whispers about the ramifications of Antonio's stunt and his fate hung in corners. The popular notion that vampires led a reckless, rogue existence was incorrect. The alternative world David and Arabella introduced me to contained rules and structure. Without enforcers like Tom and Jerri, vampires like Antonio could harm many humans. The vampires I knew valued integrity and restraint.

"It's the third major transgression," a stranger pontificated. "First, Antonio stalked a human and forced him to become a vampire. Then he taunted David and threatened Natalie. And today, well, if he ends up in The Pit, it is his own fault." I hurried away from the gleeful judgment and pulled Ron De Jamme to the side.

"Oh, dear, where did you hear about The Pit?" Ron clamped his hands on his hips and glared.

"I overheard Antonio may be sent there."

Ron wagged his finger at me.

"Charming. Conversation at a wedding should be cheerful."

"Please just tell me what The Pit is."

"It is where naughty vampires are eliminated. It's a pit, outside in an abandoned bullfighting arena. Vampires who have one or two strikes against them are made to watch a video of it. A rogue vampire is tied to a pole and exposed to the sun. Horrible."

I shivered. Antonio was malevolent. How could I forget the night at Nuit Boutique when an innocent shopping trip had turned into a dangerous stand-off? Antonio had blocked our exit, and if David hadn't been there to protect me . . .

"You two look like you're up to no good." David

and Ian had snuck up behind us. Ron was slick in his deflection.

"Hello, newlyweds! I am trying to convince Natalie to return to my studio. It is a crime to deprive the world of our collaboration."

"True, true," Ian said. "And now it is time for me to dance with my husband." They sashayed away, and Ron whispered in my ear.

"Saved by the first dance. Let me know when you're back in the States. I'm serious about a new competition. If David isn't up for it, I have a fabulous partner in mind for you."

CHAPTER FIVE

My final duty as wedding planner was a command performance of David and my first-place tango routine.

"This choreography may be my masterpiece," bragged Ron De Jamme to anyone and everyone. David escorted me to the center of the tiled floor as the guests moved to the perimeter of the room.

"Okay, partner, let's show'em what champions can do." David raised his hand to cue the music, and we danced with the joy of friends bonded over a love of movement. I managed to get through the routine without ripping my gown, a major victory.

It was time for the cutting of the cake, and although vampires didn't eat cake, the bridegrooms would never deprive their guests of the yummy tradition. The caterers wheeled a spectacular four-tier dark chocolate fondant creation crowned with red roses to the center of the room.

"Death by Chocolate," the caterer announced.

After the ceremonial cut, I carried my piece outside onto the terrace with a glass of port. Chocolate and port were a favorite pairing. My responsibilities were completed, and tomorrow I would force myself to return to healthy eating and open my laptop. I'd ignored my current manuscript for days.

When I was finished eating my cake, a waiter swept by and gathered my plate. The moon's reflection on the sea pulled me toward the beach, and I had no reason to disoblige the invitation. I slipped off my heels and meandered to the edge of the terrace. A few moments of rest would be welcome; the final sips of the twenty-five-year-old tawny port which remained in my glass would be savored under the silver glow of the moon.

I craved a few moments of solitude to reflect on the success of the day. No one would miss me for fifteen minutes or so, and then I would return to the chaos of my friends' wedding reception, centered and fortified. I stepped onto the cool sand and sank onto a lounge chair.

The sounds of the party traveled with the night breeze. True love had won, and Arabella and I were thrilled David's and Ian's wedding had been the dream they'd envisioned. The glamorous shindig would last until an hour before sunrise. Strains of New Orleans jazz, a favorite musical genre of the sophisticated modern vampire, competed with the swoosh of the surf, a snare drum supporting the seductive saxophone.

The vampires, my newfound circle of undead pals, had traveled from many countries to celebrate with David and Ian, and would dance until impending daylight required them to return to their boxes. The moon was bright and its near full stage had nixed the werewolves from the guest list, unfortunately.

I breathed in the salty freshness, my shoulders relaxing. The sand was soft under my aching feet. I'd danced with every person who'd invited me, and most had behaved. The presence of Tom and Jerri, the enforcers who had declared themselves my protectors, kept the crowd on their best behavior. Antonio's uninvited appearance and swift ejection were an additional warning. I dug my toes in the sand and leaned back on the lumbar pillow. Tomorrow, I would summon the energy to record the details of the wedding. Goodness—had we only arrived in Jamaica three days ago?

Footsteps approached. They stopped, and then restarted, completing their final trespass into my Zen. I didn't acknowledge the intrusion on my reverie. I felt a strong presence, and an icy déjà vu washed over me. The stranger sat without my invitation to do so, and we rested on the lounge chairs without speaking. His voice broke the silence.

"Natalia."

Why should the syllables of a name I had no association with accelerate the beating of my heart? The voice was familiar. Slowly, I turned to where the man reclined, his face bathed in shadow.

I was momentarily lightheaded, wrapped in a vortex of vertigo. As suddenly as it began, the wooziness ceased. Perhaps the generous pour of port had put me over the edge.

The stranger seemed content to sit with me and watch the surf. A couple strolled along the breaking waves, holding hands, and paused to kiss. Maybe it was time to walk back to the house. I didn't own the beach, but the stranger had deprived me of the privacy I craved. Witty conversation was the last thing I wanted.

"It is a lovely evening, don't you think, Natalia?"

"My name is Natalie, not Natalia. And how do . . ." The thudding of multiple pairs of feet pounding across the sand cut my question in half. Great. Obviously, if I wanted privacy, I would have to sneak up to my bedroom and lock the door.

"Natalie, are you alright?" Jerri asked, concern in her voice. She and Tom halted between the stranger and me, feet planted firmly, ready for a fight. The stranger chuckled softly.

"Hello Jerrilyn, Tomasina. What a delightful evening. Have the festivities concluded?" There was a moment of shocked silence and then Jerri bowed formally.

"Voivode," she said, "how nice to see you again. I'm certain David and Ian would have welcomed you to their event if they had known you were in Jamaica. They are entertaining their guests inside; would you like me to escort you to them? I would be honored to do so."

I picked up my shoes and stood, nearly tripping over the edge of the chair. Did I hear correctly? Jerri had addressed the stranger as voivode, the ancient warlord title. Were we in the presence of Dragos Dracul, the supreme ruler of the vampire world? The man rose from his chair.

Months ago, in the States I'd had an unsettling vision in which a man appeared to me as I worked in my office. The man sat behind a huge mahogany desk and his eyes bored into mine, his apparent disbelief quickly morphing into an expression of obsession. He was handsome; bald with elongated black eyes, and I'd never seen a man who possessed his features or his air of regal self-confidence. When I relayed my daydream to David and Ian, they'd quarreled about how much I should be told about the dangerous warlord, Dragos.

After I insisted upon knowing who the man was, Ian had relayed the history of the Romanian vampire wars and had assured me that Dragos hadn't been seen in a hundred years. I was safe with them if I exercised a few precautions. How wrong they had been. Dragos, the vampire warlord had tracked me to Jamaica and stood within ten feet. My arms erupted in goosebumps.

Had Dragos's legendary temper mellowed in the last century? My first instinct was panic—to run like a frightened rabbit back to the mansion and hide under the bed. I couldn't pretend to be ignorant of the tales of murderous rage and the annihilation of scores of the undead after his wife's death. Instead, my body felt paralyzed, and the port glass slipped from my hand, landing with a soft thud on the sand.

"I have been quite well, thank you." Dragos's voice was tinged with impatience. His manner of speaking was clipped and formal; a king addressing his subjects. "I will, of course, congratulate David and Ian on their nuptials when they have a moment." He cleared his throat. "I believe it is still a social convention for those who know all parties to introduce those who are unacquainted."

Jerri hesitated. She had urged me to walk the dark world with caution, and the infamous vampire warlord was insisting on a formal introduction. Would an introduction place me in danger? Could Tom and Jerri defend me against this uber-powerful vampire?

She had no choice. It was clear Dragos's request was a command. Jerri turned to the king.

"Your Majesty, may I present Natalie Crisan. Natalie, His Majesty Dragos Alexandru Dracul."

Immediately the voivode rose, approached me, and bowed.

"Miss Crisan, I am pleased to make your acquaintance," he said.

I nodded and pressed my lips together. We were caught in a moonlit spotlight, pulsating with uncertainty. He retreated one step, allowing a respectful space between us. He studied me, and I returned his gaze, unsure what I should do next.

"Sir, may I ask what brings you to Jamaica? We are a long way from Transylvania," Jerri asked.

Tom, Jerri's wife and fellow vampire enforcer, had not uttered a word but remained glued to my side. Dragos appeared unperturbed by the question.

"I am here on business, Jerrilyn. Perhaps we should move this conversation to the terrace. I have two important topics to discuss. The first concerns Miss Crisan. The second requires a meeting with the Westwoods and the vampire guests."

"With respect, sir, this is a happy occasion. What possible business could be important enough to disrupt a wedding? Can it wait until tomorrow evening?"

Dragos took a step closer to Jerri, and she stepped back.

"I will overlook your brashness. I decide what is important and what is a trifle. Let us sit on the terrace and I will discuss the first part of my business, which as I told you, concerns Miss Crisan. The second topic, when I reveal it, will make you rethink your reluctance to interrupt mere frivolity." Woah. Jerri had apparently overstepped protocol, and if the warlord chastised an enforcer like a child, I had no choice but to listen to whatever announcement concerned me. His arrival had wrecked my evening, and I felt the slow burn of anger at his ill-timed visit.

The four of us trudged over the sand to the veranda. Dragos strode to table furthest from the laughter and music spilling through the open doors of the mansion. Without a glance at the couples mingling on the terrace, he seized the chair at the head of the table and sat. Several guests gawped at his entrance and retreated to the periphery of the terrace, mouths hanging open with shock. A stunned waiter slunk backwards into the house.

Tom and Jerri flanked the voivode, and Tom motioned for me to sit next to her. The stranger who had appeared to me in the States had traveled from Transylvania to meet me, somehow knowing I was in Jamaica. There was nowhere to hide, and I sensed my life was about to pivot, perhaps a triple pirouette ending in a perfect fifth position—or on my butt.

Dragos leaned back in his chair. He had said our conversation was to begin immediately, yet he seemed to relish the luxuriant garden surrounding the terrace. His gaze skimmed over the lush palm trees and exotic flowering plants.

"I have never visited the Caribbean," he said. "I am fond of gardens, as was my wife."

The word wife struck me, and I felt the fleeting wisp of an odd ache in my heart. His black oval eyes, mesmerizing in their intensity, gripped mine. His head was hairless, his skin color swarthy, the same as in the vision. His attire, a dinner jacket and tailored tuxedo pants, was of an old-fashioned cut, but he wore it as easily as David wore jeans and a T-shirt.

"Miss Crisan, I will first address a matter of grave importance that concerns you. Do you wish Tomasina and Jerrilyn to bear witness to our personal business?" A massive ruby ring on the third finger of his left-hand glowed blood red in the candlelight.

"Yes, I would like them to stay," I said. He nodded.

"I have only become aware of your existence recently, and I apologize for my ignorance. I plead a broken heart as my excuse. I required solitude and shut myself off from the world for over a century. I am compelled to correct a grievous oversight, and I am here in Jamaica to ensure you receive your inheritance, or should I say, legacy." He tilted his head and studied me.

"Were your parents unaware they were of Romanian ancestry?"

Did I hear him correctly? A substantial inheritance? Romanian ancestry? My dear Aunt

Loretta had talked about my parents, but the family stories may as well have been Grimms' Fairy Tales. My questions were often deflected, and I gave up pestering her.

"I am not Romanian, I'm American with German ancestry," I stammered. "Why would you be giving me an inheritance? We don't know each other."

Dragos drummed his fingers impatiently on the table, and once again, the ruby ring flashed, and I sensed his impatience at my question.

"I would not expect you to understand," he said curtly. "There is much I need to explain to you about your ancestor and the topic is not a conversation for this meeting. Simply put, you are the only living descendant of Natalia Crisan Dracul, my deceased wife. The information I am about to reveal is personal and sensitive in nature." He allowed the revelation to sink in.

I did not know I had Romanian blood. My parents died when I was a child, and I was raised by sweet Aunt Loretta. We were as American as grilled hotdogs on the Fourth of July. I sat up straighter in my chair.

"I was never told I had Romanian ancestors, and I don't care if Tom and Jerri know about my ancestor or my family history. I want them to stay." I'm not sure where my strength came from, and Dragos was momentarily silent. I trusted my friends and there was no way they were leaving me alone with the infamous warlord.

He considered my request and raised an eyebrow.

"My wife's stubborn streak is evident in your response, Miss Crisan. You are not related to me, but to my deceased wife. Natalia wished for a child, and as a vampire, I was unable to create a life. Together we chose the man who would fulfill Natalia's desire to experience motherhood. Your male ancestor was a soldier—a great warrior.

"There were no other children from the utilitarian union. This information would only serve to fill in the branches of your family tree if there were not a considerable inheritance you are entitled to. I have protected the legacy my wife left for over a hundred years." He leaned forward. I was spellbound by the weight of his words as he unraveled the story of my family history.

"You own a mansion in Romania and many other objects of significant worth. I have carried one item of great sentimental value with me from Transylvania." He extended a small black velvet box to Tom, and she passed it to me. I turned the black velvet box in my hand. Slade Suit, the randy shapeshifter, had given me an identical black box when he had kidnapped and hidden me in his castle after David and I had beaten him in the tango competition. Despite his horrid behavior, I was wearing the black Tahitian pearl and diamond earrings he had given me before I was rescued. Had expensive jewelry become my Achilles heel? Dragos was behaving like a gentleman, but perhaps he hoped, like Slade, to appeal to my newfound weakness.

I opened the box.

"Oh, heavens." The mate to the ring Dragos wore winked at me in the light. The enormous ruby glowed, the meticulously cut facets highlighting a deep red stone with a pinkish undertone. It was encased in a heavy yellow gold and diamond setting. "I . . . have never seen anything . . . it's like a crown jewel." The fire of the stone was mesmerizing, and although I felt drawn to it, I did not touch it. I would wait until Arabella had inspected it.

Dragos acknowledged the assessment, dipping his chin like the punctuation mark at the end of a sentence. "It is a crown jewel worn by my wife, and your ancestor, Natalia Crisan Dracul. The ring is part of a parure of rubies I gave her when we married. We chose the rubies together. The set is precious to me—and priceless."

David and Ian, arm-in-arm, burst onto the terrace.

"Peeps, where have you been? It's not nice . . ." David froze, and a hand flew to his mouth. Ian patted David's arm, stepped forward, and bowed.

"Voivode, you honor our event. May I present my husband, David Westwood? David, His Majesty, Dragos Alexandru Dracul." Dragos inclined his head and David managed a bow. He glanced at me, eyes bulging. Behind him, more incredulous vampires drifted onto the terrace. From beyond the potted palms, two vampires in formal military attire stepped forward.

Dragos rose from his chair and glancing briefly at the rapidly filling terrace, assumed an erect military posture. He was about David's height, just shy of six feet.

"Miss Crisan, I fear our first evening together must end. I do not wish to worry you, but the business we will discuss is not your concern. I must ask you to leave us, but I will return tomorrow evening to continue our discussion. The ruby ring is yours should you wish to keep it per the stipulations of my wife's will. I have posted guards to protect the jewel and you, and the security detail will change in the morning. You must indulge my precautions. A piece from the parure went missing the day my wife died."

He strode to my chair. I got to my feet a bit shakily, perhaps a combination of the long day, the decadent glass of port I'd drunk, or the news that I owned a home in Transylvania. Could I trust that Dragos was telling the truth? The king extended his hand. With the box in my left hand, I held out my right. He barely touched my fingers as he bent over my fingertips, sweeping the whisper of a kiss across them. His gaze latched onto mine—then he quickly returned to his seat at the head of the table.

Arabella called my name from somewhere at the back of the throng of guests, and I trailed after her into the house. The French doors closed behind us.

Inside, a few remaining guests mingled and munched. The jazz band announced their final set, and several couples hurried to the dance floor. Iris was dancing with Arabella's cousin Jayce, and she winked mischievously.

"Iris said she'll usher the last few guests out. She and Jayce have hit it off. Let's go upstairs," Arabella said, guiding me to the staircase.

We climbed the stairs, and she pulled me into her bedroom.

"Nat, what is going on? Was that Dragos? He's in Jamaica?" I plopped onto a chair and tossed my heels on the floor.

"Yup, all the way from his castle in Transylvania. He came here to tell me I am Romanian and to give me this." I opened the box and Arabella gasped.

"That is a serious ruby, pet. Wait . . . you didn't put it on, I hope?"

"No way. Can you tell if there is a curse on it?"

Arabella took the box from me and placed it on a table. She retrieved a piece of stationary from the desk and used it to remove the ring from the velvet box. Then, she cupped her hands over it and closed her eyes. She remained in a near trance for a few minutes, mumbling an incantation. Finally, she opened her eyes.

"The ring is not cursed. In fact, it may possess happy memories. Would you like to put it on while I'm here?"

"No, not yet. I need to think about the implication of accepting it, along with a house which I'm guessing is a mansion, and the rest of Natalia's bequest." I relayed Dragos's apology regarding my inheritance, and the ruby par—something that included the ring.

"You own a mansion in Romania?" Arabella's expression mirrored my own bewilderment.

"Apparently. My upbringing was decidedly middle class, with no hint of castles and jewels. Aunt Loretta didn't work, and we lived well if simply. She assured me she paid my college tuition from the insurance money my parents had left me. I barely remember them now."

I did remember craning my neck to look up at my dad; he must have been very tall. When they disappeared from my life I'd longed for my mother's lap, the sweet songs she would sing to me, and soft jasmine scent she would leave behind after my bedtime hug. Those were the few memories I still held, and whether they were real or imagined I'd never been certain. We'd moved several times, and I'd never had the opportunity to form a close friendship with children my age. One of the homes had an upright piano, and I'd loved the feel of the keys under my fingertips. Our final relocation was, even to a child, cloaked in mystery. My parents had packed the house seemingly overnight, the piano was left behind, and Aunt Loretta came to babysit while my parents went on a "business trip."

"Aunt Loretta stayed after my parents died, and I don't remember meeting her before then. She'd hugged me hard and told me about my parents' accident. She never shared details of where she'd lived before. We traveled a bit—London, Paris, Florence. She said she wanted me to be 'finished,' but in a modern sense. Culturally sophisticated and well-read. She said the modern woman had to be able to pay her own bills. The house in America was paid for from an insurance policy my parents had, and I received a small inheritance from Aunt Loretta when she died. I've been lucky to get freelance work and to sign a contract for my next book." Arabella had listened to my soliloquy with a concentrated frown of incredulity.

"It's all rather mysterious. Dragos is the king of the vampire world. I wonder what they're discussing? He kicked me out—in a classy way."

"Speaking of kicking people out," Arabella said, "I'll go downstairs and make sure the guests have left. Do you want anything? I'm making a cup of herbal tea."

"Can you please unzip me first?" The zipper descended smoothly down the back of the gown, and I turned to my pal. "Thanks. I would love a glass of water if you can manage it—I'm definitely dehydrated."

"Sure thing." Arabella left and I dropped my gown to the floor, stepped out of it, and crossed to the closet to hang it up. I slipped a nightgown over my head and returned to the table where the ruby ring glinted in its box. I wasn't certain what Dragos was up to, and I didn't trust him to place my interests before his own agenda. I would proceed with caution.

CHAPTER SIX

On the terrace, chairs scraped across the pavers as the vampires assembled. Tom and Jerri had vacated their places, and two vampires unknown to the wedding guests claimed their seats. Dragos waited until the last undead had huddled in before rising to face his audience.

"Gentleman, the information you are about to hear is of grave concern to our world. As one who has led armies, I state we are at the beginning of a war. I became aware of this situation because of the vigilance of my brother, Bogdan Michael Dracul, Duke of Transylvania." The man seated to the left of the voivode rose and inclined his head in greeting. Resplendent in full military regalia, he surveyed the assembly with the critical eye of a general inspecting his troops. Medals and ribbons covered the left side of his jacket, and a sword in a golden scabbard hung at his hip. Letting out a deep sigh, he sat down and swung his attention to the king.

"To my left is Count Marius Ardelean, my personal secretary and longtime advisor." The count rose, nodded sharply, and dropped quickly to his seat. "After much discussion, we have concluded that the threat is strong enough to warrant action.

"The duke will provide the specifics, but here are the crucial takeaways. A group of alien shapeshifters have established themselves on Earth. Their aim is nothing less than dominance of the dark world long ruled by vampires and witches. My responsibility as your voivode is to continue the peace that has reigned for over a hundred years. My brother and I are sworn to congenial coexistence. The threat from these unnatural creatures will disrupt our world and expose the mortals of the earth to unspeakable danger." Dragos waved away the V cocktail offered to him. He purposefully made eye contact with each vampire, acknowledging their presence. He would not forget who had heard his analysis of the threat to their world.

"Our concern comes not from prejudice, but from the actions of the man who styles himself as their leader. Bogdan." Dragos returned to his chair at the head of the table and Bogdan stood again. He was slightly taller than his brother with a full head of dark hair. His ramrod posture was the only physical characteristic he had in common with his brother. Where the voivode was swarthy with oval, deep set eyes, Bogdan was pale with cheekbones set high under wide-set brown eyes.

"Good evening. The voivode has explained the situation we face, and I will provide details of what my spies have seen. But before I do so, I will second His Majesty's words of inclusion. The dark world we walk includes many alternative creatures who live in peace and harmony.

"My first suspicion arose when an entire village in Italy, including the castle, was purchased by a shapeshifter. Imagine the wealth necessary to buy vineyards, homes, the village, and the four-hundred-year-old castle. The disruption was seamless. Where did the families relocate to? Who moved into the homes left furnished by the former occupants? What individual could organize these logistics without a word from local authorities or media?

"What we discovered was a cunning plan of bold genius. Where did the wealth come from to purchase the castle and environs? For this band of thieves, the removal of precious artifacts, jewels, and art was child's play. The ability to melt and ooze through the smallest of spaces enabled the brazen thieves to breach Swiss bank vaults, private art collections, and we suspect the British Museum. The Swiss are known for secrecy and deny the secret vaults of Nazi possessions and other wealth acquired from spurious means. If a diamond choker stolen from a Jewish heiress during WWII goes missing, does one report it to the police?"

The scream of an animal cut through the silence and David reached for Ian's hand. Tom and Jerri listened; stony expressions etched on their faces. Bogdan continued.

"The thievery and outrageous behavior of the leader of the shapeshifters crossed a line of civilized conduct. We believe this shapeshifter became aware of a direct descendant of the voivode's wife. How he came by this information is a mystery my agents are working to solve. He kidnapped the young woman, and through his manipulative mind powers, nearly succeeded in seducing her. It was only through the swift action of four brave vampires and a witch that the young woman was saved." Dragos and Bogdan sought out Tom, Jerri, David, and Ian. Bogdan returned to his seat and Dragos spoke to the flabbergasted vampires.

"The solution begins with a concerted offense. Our first job is the dissemination to all vampires of the alien threat. Each of you will receive a list of vampires to contact. There is a script as well as counselors to assist you in accomplishing your task. Every vampire must help if the plan is to succeed." The horizon had changed from black to dark gray, and Dragos suddenly sprung from his chair. The spellbound audience awaited his final command.

"It will soon be dawn. I will return tomorrow evening and answer any questions to the best of my ability. Your participation is not voluntary. We are under siege. Goodnight." Bogdan and Marius rose, and the three men walked across the terrace and onto the beach. In the distance, the sound of flapping wings receded into the night.

"I thought he was dead," Ralph Hornblower said, hugging himself.

"Obviously, he's dead. He's a vampire." Ron de Jamme rolled his eyes.

"You know what I mean. Wasn't he killed in the Romanian wars? By his brother?" Ralph raked both hands through his thick black hair.

"The brothers are presenting a united front, and we will have to do as we're told," Ian said softly.

Jerri cleared her throat.

"Friends, Dragos is our voivode. If he has traveled from Transylvania, this is a very serious matter. We must accept the tasks we are given. The shapeshifter of which he speaks is extremely sly and has powers we cannot fight against unless we are united. We need to retire and rest. Let us consider what we have heard and meet tomorrow evening when we rise."

CHAPTER SEVEN

While the vampires hunkered down with their leader, I was overjoyed to get into comfy clothes. My feet ached from the high heels, and my make-up felt like a balaclava. Standing barefoot in the bathroom, I doubled cleansed my face until every scrap of make-up was gone. My nightly beauty ritual of serum, eye cream, and night cream was automatic and a naked face with glossy skin stared back at me. Beautiful or boring? What had my ancestor been like? Did I really look that much like her? A Romanian queen would have had formal portraits painted. The mystery of my family history might finally be solved because of this bombshell.

I should have been exhausted, but the conversation with Dragos had pumped my adrenaline to an insane level. Letting the light catch the fire of the facets of the pebble-sized stone, I turned the box right and left. Suspicion flooded the logical side of my brain. It was quite a weak excuse to say he had only recently become aware of my existence. Did he know what had happened to my parents?

The curious side of my brain, however, wanted to know more about my ancestor Natalia and my inheritance. The fire of the ring danced a hypnotic solo, and Danse Macabre popped into my head. How appropriate.

Dragos insisted the ring belonged to me as Natalia's rightful heir. He had been respectful and kept his distance, but the announcement of his return tomorrow evening to discuss details of my inheritance filled me with dread. He hadn't asked for my permission. I left my bedroom and knocked on Arabella's door. I heard the patter of running feet and the door swung open.

"What's wrong?"

I carried the ring box in my hand. I did not want to be the person who lost Natalia's cherished ring.

"Arabella, you have to help me. Bring me to the person who can teach me how to block mind readers. Any defenses are better than nothing." Arabella hugged me and I plopped down into an overstuffed chair.

"I will send a text to a healer—a friend of my auntie. If she is on the island, she will see you."

I exhaled.

"Thank you, I feel better already." Arabella leaned toward me.

"Are you sure you don't want me to sleep in your room?"

"Thanks, but no." The skin under Arabella's eyes was smudged a deep purple. She needed rest and so did I. "Dragos said he has guards watching the house. Why that makes me feel safe . . . I have no idea. Let's get some sleep."

In my room, I was startled to find the newlyweds perched on the edge of my bed. David popped up and ran to me.

"Natalie, will you ever forgive me? Jerri gave us a rundown of Dragos's revelation about your inheritance. I had hoped you and I could be besties, and, well, that I could protect you from the dark side of my world. I've failed miserably. What do we do now? Dragos is coming back tomorrow night . . . are you going to accept your inheritance?" David's eyes strayed to the box clenched between my fingers. "Is that the ruby ring? Did Arabella check it?"

I sat on the bed and extended the box toward him.

"The ring is amazing, so don't drool on it. The ruby is . . . as big as my ex's ego," I joked. "Anyway, I need your advice because I haven't a clue what to do."

David opened the box and showed it to Ian,

who had moved to the open balcony door. The sky had lightened, and they were late to their boxes.

Ian glanced at the ring and shook his head.

"If Dragos brought a ring of immense value to Natalie, he has decided she will accept her inheritance. We will, with Natalie's permission, act as her agents. I'm not sure Tom and Jerri can commit to a trip to Romania which will be required. The voivode might be amenable to our involvement if it means Natalie will comply with the will." He pulled David toward the door.

"David, it's almost sunrise. We have to go. There is a person below your window, Natalie. Close and lock the doors. He is one of Dragos's security guards, and per the voivode's promise, you and the ring are under very high security."

The sky continued to lighten, and David reluctantly snapped the lid on the ring box shut.

"See you tomorrow, love," he said as they hurried from the room.

I pushed back the curtain and peered out the slider. Directly below, a dark-haired person perched on a straight-back chair.

Following Ian's direction, I rechecked the lock on the balcony door and slid two chairs in front of it. I rearranged a garland of garlic across the chairs, then hung the remaining spray of garlic from the entry doorknob. Crawling into bed, I stole one more look at the priceless ring, snapped the box shut, and slipped it under my pillow. Sleep grabbed me at the exact moment the first rays of dawn crept over the horizon.

CHAPTER EIGHT

Romania filled my dreams. Mountain vistas, woodlands where wolves howled, and castles dusted with snow flashed through my mind's eye. In the first frame, I glanced down at leather boots climbing over dead tree stumps and navigating the uneven forest floor. An animal panted loudly at my side. A dog? Perhaps a large hound.

The second frame focused on a woman's hand raising an ornate goblet in response to a toast. On her left hand, the ruby ring's fire blazed in the glow of candlelight. She laughed; a joyful sound of silver bells draped on a winter sleigh. A man's baritone laugh joined her.

When I awoke, the sun was high in the sky, the scorching rays ensuring my undead friends were resting comfortably. I smelled coffee, slipped on my robe and searched for the delicious aroma.

Dearest Arabella had brewed a full pot of high-test coffee, and she smiled when I made a beeline for the pot.

"I was just about to wake you. We have an appointment with Myrna in an hour. There's tons of yummy leftovers from the wedding if you're hungry."

I settled on a high-backed chair at the island counter and slurped my coffee with epicurean gratitude. The earthy roast smell filled my lungs. It would take days to fully recuperate from the previous night's shenanigans and Dragos's startling revelations. The caffeine jolt hit me, and I jumped down from the chair.

"Thanks for making the appointment and the coffee. I'll shower and snag a couple of those caviar deviled eggs. They were decadent."

I was dressed in a half hour and relaxed on the balcony while the sun worshippers set up for the day. Despite my initial disbelief, the conversation with Dragos the previous night began to make sense. My parents' backstory as imparted by Aunt Loretta was hazy at best. Only a photo album and one framed photo of the three of us in a wood provided evidence of my parents brief involvement in my life. In the photo my father cuddled me in his arms and my mother grinned, her head resting on my dad's shoulder, an arm wrapping around my body. Those two precious mementos had disappeared during a burglary. Who would have wanted an old photo album?

Aunt Loretta said we were a mix of German, Norwegian, and Polish DNA; Romanian ancestors never entered the discussion. When she died, I was broken hearted and completely alone in the world. As the sole heir of her estate, I was shocked to find my home had no mortgage and that my frugal aunt had a tidy investment portfolio. I was able to follow my dream, to become a writer without the worries of an initial income.

Slade Suit had said my beauty was aristocratic, beyond modern comprehension.

I had never contemplated the genetics that had given me high cheekbones and nearly black angled eyes. My skin tone was deeper than most of my friends, and if I wore a clear lip gloss at school, the Catholic nuns would escort me to the restroom to 'wash off your lipstick.' Sister Margaret didn't like me and would stand next to me while I rubbed a tissue across my crimson lips, turning over the tissue to show it was clean. She was disappointed my 'devil's pout' couldn't be whitewashed.

The girls at school went crazy over my hair, which was chestnut brunette and luxuriously thick. David had helped me to style it to my advantage and encouraged me to wear make-up to complement my bone structure. Mike had been stingy with his compliments, and until Slade had come into my life, I was unaware of my classic beauty, admired by the mysterious shapeshifter with a connoisseur's eye.

Arabella's cousin arrived in a burst of Bob Marley to drive us to the healer. We hadn't rented a car because Arabella had left a vehicle behind when she had escaped to America to avoid the witch who had cast a spell on her. When we arrived in Jamaica several days ago, she discovered a different cousin had crashed her car, and to keep the peace the family promised to chauffeur us anywhere we needed. Arabella had an extended family that rivaled a Roman Catholic woman I knew from elementary school.

It was a white-knuckle ride. We bumped along rutted backroads, finally making a turn into a narrow path crowned by a balcony of palm trees.

If Arabella hadn't been with me, I would never have ventured inside the cottage. The wide porch was hung with fisherman's nets, and seashells covered the ground on either side of the path to the front door. Potted plants dotted the front lawn, and on the porch next to a turquoise hammock, an old woman repaired a fishing net. She could have been seventy or a hundred.

"Arabella, hello! I am happy you asked for my help." They embraced, and Arabella introduced me.

"Myrna, this is my dear friend, Natalie. Natalie, this is Myrna." Myrna held my arms aloft in a sort of hug, and although her eyes held mine, I did not feel she was trying to read my thoughts. Good start.

"Welcome, Natalie. Come inside, my lovelies. Let's have a cool drink."

Inside her cozy kitchen, Myrna poured lemonade into three glasses, and we followed her into the backyard. The Garden of Eden flourished in the tropical paradise, where we each chose a chair and settled in the dappled shade. After a brief catch-up, Myrna placed her empty glass on the moss-covered table beside her chair and faced me.

"Arabella tells me you want to block people from reading your thoughts. Mind reading and blocking the mind reader are advanced skills. Tell me about your awareness when someone is accessing your thoughts." Myrna spoke like a psychiatrist, and I wondered at her reclusive lifestyle and home.

"Several of my friends, present company included, can read my thoughts. It feels like I'm being drained, and more importantly, it invades my privacy. Can you teach me to raise a shield or something to stop them? I'd be grateful."

Myrna laughed.

"I can teach you, of course. You will have to practice, but often the initial rebuff to the mind reader will discourage them." Arabella set a white envelope on the table.

"Thank you, my dear. Old age is expensive." I opened my mouth to ask about the payment, and Arabella brought her finger to her lips. Myrna had closed her eyes, and we sat silently amidst the birdsong and the rustling of the palm fronds. The sound of her breath calmed me, and my gaze was drawn upward to a colorful bird calling to its mate. When I brought my attention back, she was watching me.

"You are aware when someone is accessing your thoughts, which is the first step. There are a variety of ways to block others from accessing your mind. A simple but effective technique is to choose an animal you have known, or one you believe to be strong and aggressive. Like a tiger, an ape, or a bear. The type of animal will make itself known to you. Breathe and count. Now close your eyes."

Exhausted from the wedding and reception, I sat with my eyes closed counting through my inhales and exhales and lingered close to sleep. And then it happened.

In my vision, a wolf lay at my feet. I reached down to pet it, and it rolled onto its back. Its golden yellow eyes held mine with a protective love and family bond. Startled by the clarity of the vision, I blinked. The back of my neck felt warm, but my hands were ice-cold.

"A wolf," I offered. "With golden yellow eyes and a mostly white-gray coat."

"Your description is very specific," Myrna said. "You know this animal."

"I think so. I had a dream where I was walking in a forest . . . I can hear a large animal panting by my side. Maybe the animal in the dream is the wolf

I saw when I was meditating." I felt a calm familiarity while petting him in the vision. The wolf made me feel safe.

"Good. Concentrate and bring the wolf to you. See the wolf clearly. Ask it to protect your thoughts. Command it to be your protector."

Once again, I closed my eyes and summoned the wolf. He sat before me. His handsome, familiar face warmed my heart, and I reached out to stroke his head.

"Protect me," I asked silently via my mind. "I need you to protect my thoughts from those who would read them. Block them, my true and loyal friend."

The wolf bowed his head, and my eyelids fluttered open.

"Did the wolf agree to help you?"

"Yes, he did. What will it look like when he helps shield me?"

"He could rebuff the mind-reading intrusion in different ways, maybe a howl or growl."

Myrna motioned for us to lean forward.

"Let's practice. Think of something, then call the wolf. Arabella, you will try to access Natalie's thoughts." I closed my eyes and took a deep breath.

I thought of the gall of my ex-boyfriend Mike coming to my house the morning after he and his new girlfriend and dance partner had lost to David and me at the Calypso Fever dance contest. His plan to win with a "better and lighter" partner backfired when he'd nearly dropped her during a routine lift. I pictured his smug face . . . and felt an intrusion into my recollection. Arabella was in my head.

The wolf's handsome face came to me. I made a silent appeal. "Wolf, protect me." He sat, intently watching me, but he did not move. Giving in, I opened my eyes.

"He's watching me but not responding to my request. What am I doing wrong?"

Myrna rubbed her hands together and then let out an exclamation.

"Ah! If you knew him as a pet, he has a name! 'Wolf' will not make him obey your command; the request must appeal to your relationship. Close your eyes again."

I did as instructed, returning to the deep breathing that delivered me to the edge of sleep. I concentrated on the memory of the wolf's triangular face, his luxuriant fur, the muscles beneath, and his wide, powerful chest. My breath slowed, and the vision of a woman's back sharpened, her body curled on the floor next to a wolf cub. She rubbed his belly, and he was in rapture. The roaring fire blazed, and they snuggled —warm, safe, and content. She pulled a blanket over them, lay her head on a pillow, and with one arm around the wolf cub, sang a song in a foreign tongue.

"Lupu." The word simply appeared in my mind. "His name is Lupu."

My hands were shaking as I drained the last of my lemonade and tried to avoid looking at Arabella. This was heavy stuff. Myrna clasped her hands in her lap.

"Let's try again."

What safe memory could I think about which, if revealed, Arabella already knew? I recalled the time after our break-up that Mike and his girlfriend, Alix, showed up at my favorite restaurant for lunch. The sweet suburb of Bedford, New York where I live was thirty miles from Manhattan, and my literary agent had come into town to discuss the book I was writing. She had nearly thrown the breadbasket at him. He had posed confidently, holding Alix's hand and wearing a designer polo shirt I'd bought for him.

I felt something, possibly Arabella reading my thoughts. Good, I had learned to identify it. Now, to block her.

I fought to find the full-grown wolf, imagining the chill upon his fur after a run in the woods. I held out my hand to scratch behind his ears, and he appeared.

"Lupu. Protect me, block the intruder." He lay down and emitted a low warning growl. A surge of strength caused me to sit up in my chair.

"You blocked me," Arabella cried. Myrna clapped her hands.

"I didn't block you. My faithful protector Lupu did." Exhausted from the effort, I fell back into the softness of the cushions. Arabella finished her lemonade, and finally, Myrna spoke.

"Is there anything else you wish to ask me? Something about a ring?"

I nearly choked. I had brought the ring in my handbag and hadn't told Arabella.

"I was given a ring as a gift, but I don't know if I should keep it." Myrna perceived I was holding back, and she may have guessed that the priceless gem was in my handbag. I hadn't respected Dragos's security precautions; I'd taken a priceless crown jewel away from the posted security guards at the mansion. I arranged my face in an innocent expression and waited for Myrna's prediction. She stared into the distance.

"I see a woman in a vault. A man stands next to her, and they discuss jewelry . . . there is a party. The woman wears a tiara and red stone jewelry, including an enormous stone set in diamonds. A quartet plays music and people dance. Snow blankets the ground around the castle. The sky is black and hung with stars and the man escorts the woman to a garden gate. They kiss. The wolf is on the porch. That is all." I stared at her, open-mouthed. No one knew about the garden gate.

"If the ring is the same one worn by this woman, you will have to decide if you want to travel to the cold place. I feel there are answers there—adventure and danger. Yet, I sense no threat from the man in my vision. Something protective surrounds you."

"Thank you, I am grateful for your help," I stammered. Myrna reached out her hand and held mine a minute longer.

"I wish you safe travels, Natalie. Trust your instincts and be wary of people who want a quick friendship. Trust the wolf. He was a loyal friend in a past life; your past or an ancestor's past, I cannot tell you for certain. Lupu will send a new protector to you if he can."

Arabella's cousin rounded the turn with a screech of tires to chauffeur us back to the mansion. In a couple of hours, Dragos would continue the story of my ancestor, Natalia. Would I need to use my newfound skill to block his mind-reading powers?

Arabella went to her room and I brought a glass of water and a snack onto a shady area of the terrace. Myrna's reference to a past life confirmed my recent dreams, and rather than becoming anxious, I felt relaxed. I slid the ring box underneath the lounge pillow and drifted off to sleep with the handsome face of Lupu floating before me.

CHAPTER NINE

"Blood! I must have fresh blood!" There was a crash of glass, and several servants scurried through the open door. The voivode's younger brother stifled a chuckle and entered the bedchamber of his wife, closing the door behind him.

"Dearest darling O, are you abusing the servants again? Dragos will not be pleased."

The ostentatious vanity dripped with ropes of crystals, the better to reflect the hazy image of the vampiress Olenka Dracul. She brushed her silken hair with conceited concentration using a precious boar's head bristle brush. She had finished her maquillage, applied perfume between her breasts, and all that remained was to choose among the magnificent gowns hanging in the closet. She replaced the hairbrush on the onyx surface of the vanity and turned to her husband.

"But darling, it is so frustrating," she cooed. "It is common knowledge that once a week I require fresh young blood. You have indulged my preferences for a century. Would you want to spoil a masterpiece? The young man has agreed and is waiting for the jitney to bring him to me. Preparations have been made, and I am hungry! It would mean so much to me, my lord, if you would arrange with our gracious host to let me have a guest for the return journey."

Olenka rose and untied her robe, letting the gleaming silk cascade to the floor. Her perfect body, braless and clad in lace panties, received the reaction she sought. Bogdan came to her, traced his palms down her body, and nuzzled the intoxicating scent between her breasts.

"My darling O, you are my moon and stars. I will personally see your thirst is quenched. And perhaps later . . ."

"And later, my lord, we will quench your thirst as many times as you wish."

Bogdan bowed.

"Done. I look forward to receiving my reward, dear one." He exited quickly, closing the door behind him.

Olenka stepped over her robe and crossed the padded rug to an immense closet. She would wear the low-cut black gown. It highlighted her décolletage, and the last time she wore it, Dragos's reaction was one she cherished. The voivode had been without a woman for a century and more. Perhaps he was ready for a diversion. He had been blindly faithful to the usurper, Natalia Crisan.

Olenka strolled to the full-length mirror and appraised the perfection of her body. No one could rival her beauty. If her plan of seduction succeeded, her revenge would be complete, and her power consolidated. Both brothers would bend to her will. She would, however, need help distracting Bogdan, who, even after centuries of intimacy, had not tired of her charms.

"Dotia!" she hissed. The closet cupboard creaked open, and a washed-out bone thin woman ran to her, dropping a curtsey.

"Oh, get up, you dolt," she said. "Help me into the V-neck black gown. I am leaving my hair down, but I will wear the bat tiara. I will not require you after dinner."

Dotia fussed around her mistress, adjusting the gown, expertly taping Olenka's breasts to increase their roundness and height. Once dressed, Olenka pivoted and lunged toward the surprised woman, grabbing her by the back of the hair.

"Tomorrow, you will bring me a virgin. I am sick of excuses. You have all night to work on it. If you do not accomplish this, well, do not plan on a return trip to Romania on this ship. Can you swim?" Olenka traced a red varnished nail down the jugular vein of the woman's throat and pushed her away with contempt.

Dotia shuddered. Olenka returned to her vanity and picked up the diamond-encrusted bat tiara.

"Tell me, Dotia, have you ever had a lover?"

CHAPTER TEN

The screech of an argument between children interrupted my dreams.

"It's my turn to hold the spool," yelled the small boy. The taller boy, perhaps a brother, danced with the kite spool over his head.

"Jump higher," he shouted. "If you touch my elbow, I'll let you fly the kite."

The determined sibling took a running leap and instead of touching his brother's elbow, knocked him to the ground. Face in the sand, the older brother relinquished the spool, and the precocious lad darted away while his brother spat sand from his mouth.

"Just wait 'till I catch you!" Getting to his feet, he sprinted after his brother.

Bleary-eyed, I traipsed into the house. I filled a thermos with water and ice and retired to my room for a cool shower to wake me up.

Myrna's visions and my discovery of Lupu added another layer of intrigue to the recent events. I decided to mull the new information in the tub instead. After filling it up, I dropped two coconut bath bombs into the water.

There was nothing like a bath to relax the muscles and reset the mind. I reached for a loofah mitt and massaged my body. Then I leaned back on the bath pillow and meditated.

I must have dozed because my skin had pruned. Not a problem. I slathered on body cream and sprayed my face with a rose hip spray. Wiping the mirror wasn't necessary to see I looked refreshed, a big improvement from parched, hungover Natalie. There was a text on my phone from Arabella an hour earlier.

Arabella:

Hey, Nat, I just got off the phone with my auntie. What are you doing?

I tapped a response quickly.

Me:

Lol, I was rehydrating. Drinking gallons of water. If you want to hang out, let me know.

Arabella responded.

Arabella:

I napped. The bed is comfy.
Pulling myself together, it may
take hours. 😔

I'd carried the ring box with me, and I flipped it open to make sure the precious jewel hadn't disappeared. What was I going to do about the alleged Romanian inheritance? Had Aunt Loretta known my ancestor had been a queen in the vampire world and kept the secret from me?

I trudged to the balcony and unlocked the door. The warm ocean breeze ending a spectacular beach day swirled around me. Under the late afternoon sky, the sparse population of beachcombers was ignorant of the fabulous vampires who rested in the rented glass and steel mansion. The two young boys were nowhere in sight. A naughty idea occurred to me. What would happen if I yelled: "Hey! Lots of hungry vampires are going to be up in an hour or so . . . lounge at your own risk." I chastised myself for the mean thought—my friends didn't hunt humans, and my bet is that Tom and Jerri would be angry with the prank.

Below me, there had been a changing of the guard. A blond man paced along the rear of the mansion. Clad in head-to-toe black, the guard could have been FBI or private security for Beyoncé. Dragos was taking my protection seriously.

What was the appropriate attire for a tête-à-tête

with a vampire warlord? I flipped on the light in the spacious closet and sorted through the dresses David and I had picked out. A floral pink and blue maxi sundress was a possibility. It was sophisticated without trying too hard. Rope wedge espadrilles would allow my feet to recover from the sky-high heels I'd worn for the wedding.

I slicked my hair back in a ponytail and applied minimal make-up. Dressed in the sundress, I went downstairs and joined Arabella on the terrace. She had made fresh lemonade and poured me a big glass.

"Hello, pet. I was hoping you would join me for a talk before David and Ian rise."

I sipped the lemonade and placed the ring box on the table between us.

"Thanks. I haven't a clue how to approach the inheritance situation. I desperately need to discuss it with David and Ian. What if the inheritance promise is a trick? I won't go to Romania alone. Ian mentioned he and David could act as my advocates —is it fair for me to beg for their help?"

The sun was only half visible on the horizon, and shafts of butterscotch and raspberry sorbet washed across the deepening blue. Arabella refilled my glass, and I twirled it in the wet ring on the table. We let the silence lengthen and watched the sun sink into the horizon. Solar landscaping lights in the shrubs glowed, and Arabella went to flick the switch for the terrace party lights.

"They won't consider it a burden, love." Arabella settled back in her chair and reached out to squeeze my hand. "You don't know how to safely socialize with the vampires on Dragos's ship. It is in the harbor, and it's huge. My guess is he brought courtiers, staff, etc. The ship is the size of Britannia." She examined her cuticles and casually asked,

"Do you want me to go with you?"

"Yes!" I jumped up and hugged her. "I'm not sure how many people I would be allowed to bring on the journey. But. . . Dragos seems intent on fulfilling his wife's wishes, and I'm convinced there's more at play. I mean, Slade disappeared and Dragos shows up? Dragos may allow me an entire entourage to guarantee my journey to Transylvania."

"Who has an entourage?" David and Ian had arrived on the terrace, a V cocktail in their grips.

"Well, good evening, Westwoods. How's married life?" Arabella and I got up and hugs were exchanged. The happy couple pulled two chairs to our corner, sat, and leaned toward each other.

"Dreamy, my darling. I've never been so content," David said. Ian leaned over to kiss his cheek. "But we interrupted. Were you discussing Dragos?"

I checked to ensure no one was eavesdropping and lowered my voice.

"Yes, we were. Arabella says there is a

humongous ship belonging to him in the harbor. I'm nervous. If I get onto the ship, I'm his prisoner."

"Hardly a prisoner—an esteemed guest and a wealthy heiress of Romanian ancestry would be a better description." My plan to get input from David and Ian had imploded. Dragos stood in impeccable evening attire, flanked by the same two men from the night before. I blushed with embarrassment, and without further comment, he snapped out a formal bow.

"Good evening, Miss Crisan," he said, acknowledging Arabella and the Westwoods with a nod. "I am pleased to answer any questions or concerns you may have about your inheritance. We have brought the documents and, after the reading of the will, are happy to provide additional details to allay your fears. May we move to the larger table?"

"Good evening," I said. "Um, yes, the big table would be more comfortable, I think." I sat next to the personal assistant and placed the ring box on the table. Dragos leaned back and crossed his arms.

"You are not wearing the ring." It was not a question. Annoyed by his tone, I inhaled deeply and met his gaze. No one spoke and I called Lupu in my mind. Dragos's incredulous expression confirmed my suspicion; he was attempting to access my thoughts. He recovered himself quickly and raised an eyebrow.

"Marius will read the will of my late wife," he said.

Marius cleared his throat.

I, Natalia Crisan Dracul, being of sound mind and body, leave my estate in its entirety to my son, Dragos Alexandru Bogdan Michael Dracul. Should he not reach the legal age of inheritance per Addendum C, the entirety of my estate, listed below, will be held in trust by my husband, His Majesty Dragos Stephan Dracul. Only a person, or persons, who is a direct descendant of my son by blood, is entitled to claim my estate.

The attorney looked up at Dragos for permission to continue, and Dragos waved his hand impatiently.

"These specific items are described per the wish of Her Majesty," Marius said.

My gold is in the vault in the castle. My investments include the deeds for buildings in Europe and England and several active farms. There are certificates of ownership for a steamship company and other business ventures, as detailed in Addendum B.

The mansion I named Le Refuge Bleue includes one hundred and twenty-three acres of wood. All of the contents of my home are included in the inheritance. The following are some of the more valuable items.

The Vermeer in the drawing room was a wedding gift from my husband, your father. The portrait with my darling Lupu is the work of Romanian artist Emilian Lazarescu. My bedroom has a charming Fragonard series. There are drawings by Botticelli, Raphael, and a jewel of a painting by Canaletto in the music room.

The Ming Dynasty temple jars and the jade Buddha in the drawing room are extremely valuable.

My jewelry collection is extensive. The sapphires, emeralds, and Burmese ruby parure are kept in the vault in the castle, as are the diamond tiaras. There are two: the Flower of Romania, and Mintaka, the star of the Orion constellation. The Dracul diadem is a crown jewel and therefore I do not own it.

My horses are superior stock and are stabled on the castle grounds. Percy is my loyal steed of impeccable breeding.

My library contains many rare volumes and incunabula; however, it is largely a collection of my favorite novels. Your father's library is unparalleled, and you will hopefully share a deep love of reading. The music room contains instruments of the highest quality and several rare, handwritten composer musical scores. Note the Vivaldi and the Mozart.

Finally, my dearest Lupu, my most loyal and devoted friend, will mourn my loss. He may or may not accept my death by becoming your guardian. If he chooses to protect you, then you are fortunate. Treat him as you would a brother.

My darling son, I wish you a long life filled with love, like the love I have found with your father.
Natalia Crisan Dracul

The voivode's secretary folded the will and deposited it on the table.

No one spoke. I pressed my nails into the palms of my hands, and the pain helped me focus. Lupu had been Natalia's pet wolf, and he had come to me when I summoned him to protect my thoughts from mind readers. My hands began to shake, and I quickly hid them under the table.

According to my ancestor's last will and testament, I was an heiress. My break-up with Mike and my vulnerable emotional state had led to meeting vampire David Fanning and entering an alternate world I didn't know existed. Questions swirled in my head. Had Slade Suit known my connection to Dragos and the incredible wealth that awaited my discovery? Was his motivation for getting close to me beyond the deep attraction he'd declared?

"Miss Crisan," Dragos said. "The extent of your inheritance, and therefore the change in your situation, is, I'm sure, quite shocking. We will leave this copy of my late wife's will with you. I think it is best for you to discuss the particulars of your legacy with your friends or seek legal representation within the vampire world.

"Please note the final addendum of the will.

You must move to Romania for a period of no less than one year in order to claim the inheritance. No items mentioned in the will can be transferred or moved out of Transylvania permanently. If you decide to accept, we will travel in two days' time aboard my ship, *The Natalia*. Accommodations have been prepared for you and four guests." Dragos stood and his eyes traveled from the ring box to my frozen expression.

"I give you my word that I will do everything in my power to protect you. No matter where you reside, you are of great interest to those who would use you to get to me. The highest level of protection I can guarantee you until the . . . other business is sorted out is to provide you with safe housing and bodyguards. Romania is a beautiful country, and you should understand the great woman from whom you descend."

I nodded and stood awkwardly, reaching for the ring box.

"Thank you for traveling to Jamaica and informing me of my ancestor's legacy. I am not sure . . . it's too much too fast . . . I have no idea what to do. And the ring makes me nervous." He walked to me and smiled.

"You need time to consider the enormous change this will make in your life. I will leave two of my most trusted men behind, and if you send for me, I will come." Once again, his gaze rested on the black velvet ring box.

"The ring is yours as part of the Burmese parure, and I hope you will wear it. My late wife adored it and would be happy to see it worn by a relative. Good night, Miss Crisan." He bowed, pivoted, and retreated toward the beach, followed by his brother, who hadn't spoken a word, and the private secretary.

I dropped into my chair and, leaning forward, covered my face with my hands.

Three sets of footsteps faded, and I raised my head.

"All I needed was a place to rest after breaking up with Antonio," David said. "This is all my fault. If you hadn't met me . . ."

"You forget, I invited you to stay in Natalie's basement." Arabella shook her head. "If anyone is to blame for exposing Natalie to Dragos, it is me."

"Stop!" I didn't exactly shout, but I was loud enough to silence my friend's mea culpas. "No one is to blame for my ancestry or Natalia's murder. If Slade Suit is as wily and dangerous as Dragos believes him to be, he would have found me, anyway." David's incredulous expression confirmed my suspicion.

"Wow, do you think I am a simpleton? FYI, Slade showed up in Jamaica the first day and promptly disappeared, leaving a cryptic note. Then Dragos appears like a Tim Burton Father Christmas, hands me a priceless ring, and reveals that the vampire world is threatened by aliens.

Slade is a shapeshifter from another planet, right? And he figured out who I was in relation to Dragos. Did I miss anything?" Ian had gone to the kitchen to retrieve a bottle of wine.

"Bordeaux my dear?" Ian's calm could be unnerving. He filled two wine glasses, handing one to Arabella and the other to me. I took a tentative sip and nodded approval. Without thinking, I flipped open the ring box. The pink undertone of the Burmese ruby matched the Bordeaux perfectly.

"What the heck," I said. "Aunt Loretta used to say, 'in for a penny, in for a pound'." I extracted the ring from the box, weighing it in my hand. Before my pals could prevent me, I slipped the ring onto the middle finger of my right hand.

Everyone stared, and Ian was the first to speak.

"Kids, Dragos is not moving from the port until Natalie is onboard. Can we hide her somewhere where Slade and Dragos won't find her? Unlikely. A better plan would be for David and me to negotiate for your safe passage to Romania and accompany you to ensure he holds to the specifics, including securing your sizable inheritance. If there is to be a war, Slade may try to kidnap Natalie again. I guess the question is, who is Natalie safer with?"

David combed his fingers through his hair.

"I need another V cocktail." Everyone laughed and Ian tapped out a message on his cell phone. Raised voices reached us. People were arguing on the beach—then silence. The crunch of footsteps on the sand announced Tom and Jerri.

"Hello, all. Sorry for the commotion, one of Dragos's guards was being overzealous. He tried to block us from coming up to the house and made us explain our business here. Newbie." I had never seen Jerri anything except calm, and Tom looped her arm around her shoulder.

"It's okay, hon. Let's have a seat and explain why you almost smacked Dragos's employee." Jerri scraped out the chair Dragos had vacated and dropped heavily into it. Through the glass doors, I saw our loyal caterers, Jon and Ricky Pate, laying out hors d'oeuvres and furtively filling black goblets from an ornate pitcher. I didn't remember asking them to come tonight. Was I going crazy? Pressing my head back on the chair, I stared at the night sky. The full moon had risen, its glow gloriously brushed onto a midnight canvas.

Jerri spoke.

"Tom and I have done our own recognizance, and Dragos's allegations are supported by suspicious facts we've unearthed. An alien army has been forming for the last ten years, but the aliens have been on Earth longer than that. Slade Suit is at the top of the earthly power pyramid, but we're not sure if he is the actual leader." Jerri's tone carried a hint of empathy. She had been there the night I was rescued from Slade's Italian villa. It was becoming crystal clear that I wasn't chosen randomly.

"Where is the safest place for Natalie? That has to be our primary concern," Ian said.

Jerri steepled her fingers.

"Dragos has promised to guard Natalie, and the presence of two zealous security guards on the property appears to back up his commitment. He has given her his wife's ring, an item of personal significance, and traveled to inform her of her ancestry and inheritance." She took a sip of her V cocktail.

"As our king, it's in his interest to rally the vampire world. So, beyond making sure Natalie receives her legacy, we must extract other . . . promises."

"You mean; A, he won't make me a vampire and B, that I won't be murdered like my great-great-great-grandmother," I said. "David, tell Jerri what we were discussing before she and Tom arrived."

David glanced up, having spent the last ten minutes staring intently at his goblet and twirling it clockwise. Guilt etched his handsome face. I cared for him so much and couldn't bear to see his self-recrimination. If I was at the center of a power struggle it was only a matter of time before I ended up in my current predicament.

"We were discussing the safest place for Natalie to live," David said. "If Dragos found her here, he can find her anywhere. Maybe it's better to control the narrative, i.e., receive a promise of security and safe passage to Romania, and 24/7 security from now on." His goblet must have been empty, because the caterer whisked it away and replaced it with an even more elaborately painted vessel.

"Yes, it is prudent to accept the security and to, respectfully, get specific details of what Natalie's living arrangements are to be," Jerri said. "Unfortunately, Tom and I cannot travel to Romania. Dragos has tasked us with rallying a select group of prominent American vampires. It is an honor. Ian, David, I know you are due to leave on your honeymoon . . ."

"Ian and I will travel to Romania on the yacht," David interrupted. Ian leaned over and patted his husband's hand. "It will be a different vibe than we planned, but an experience we'll never forget. Do we know who else will be on board?"

"Bogdan's wife, several courtiers, Dragos's personal secretary, and his wife, security, and staff. There is a special section for your boxes. It's a floating palace." Jerri stood.

"We have an appointment with several vampires on Dragos's list tonight. I suggest you draft any questions you can think of, and we'll do the same. Don't worry, Natalie, your friends have your best interests at heart. Good night."

"Night Jerri, Tom." It was unnerving to have so

little say in my future, but I knew my friends meant well.

Arabella pushed a pad and a pen toward David.

"The mortals haven't had dinner, guys," she scolded. "I'm starving. You two start the list of Natalie's concerns, and we'll be back after we've eaten something."

In his study onboard *The Natalia*, Dragos and his brother occupied matching leather chairs on opposite sides of a mahogany desk. The sliding doors to the balcony were open to the night, the lights of the island shining like a constellation of hope. Dragos drank silently, his thoughts filled with the serendipity of the moment. Natalia had protected her son, the heir to the throne, placing Prince Dragos's welfare above her own life. Even at the hour of her death, she was impressive. Her actions had hidden the infant and provided a chance for the Dracul dynasty to continue. From her grave, she had outwitted evil and sent her superb genes to her biological descendants.

Natalie Crisan was the image of his murdered queen. Having seen Natalia's heiress in the flesh with her flat American accent and manner gave him pause. His hope that Natalia had come back to him after a hundred years of heartbreak was fantastical. Still, Natalie had summoned Lupu to protect his attempt to penetrate her thoughts. Lupu had allegiance to no one but Natalia. The connection between the two women was strong. He rubbed his thumb across his lower lip. He had to move carefully. Natalie Crisan must be convinced to accept her inheritance. Perhaps, once in Romania, he would understand the correct path to take with the mortal.

His besotted brother, however, was unconcerned about Natalia's heir and Dragos's happiness and as determined as ever to run interference for his spoiled wife. Olenka was Bogdan's Achilles heel as Natalia remained his own obsession.

Dragos knew of the ceremonies Olenka held at his brother's castle, and he had ignored her fetish for decades. An agent had assured him the 'guests of honor' were willing and content to donate blood in exchange for an eternity of luxury and pleasure. He needed his brother at his side to fight off the alien threat, and Bogdan's only blind spot was Olenka. Dragos drained his cocktail and returned the chalice to the tray.

"I will permit Olenka's guest, but there is to be no drama, Bogdan. Olenka's plaything is required to behave himself. The ceremony will not take place on my ship. Olenka can sample the new blood, but she must suspend gorging herself until we reach Lisbon."

"Thank you, Voivode." Bogdan inclined his

head, but Dragos saw the hint of a smile he quickly buried.

Dragos refilled the jewel-encrusted goblet and held it up to the light. Natalia had teased him about its opulence. Only she could make him see the humor in drinking death from the glittering vessel.

"Do you think Miss Crisan will agree to return with us, sir?" Bogdan's question annoyed him, and Dragos banged his goblet heavily on the table.

"Why do you ask this? Have I not guaranteed her safety?" Bogdan bristled at his brother's tone.

"Olenka thinks she might hesitate. After all . . ." Dragos flung his hand outward, his anger and exasperation accidently knocking over the goblet. Vermillion liquid exploded into the air, and the half-filled carafe on the silver tray toppled onto its side. Splotches and a rivulet of crimson streamed over the side of the table. Both men stared at the blood as it trickled over the table's edge and onto the carpet.

"From this moment, I request your word that no negotiations, contracts, or any movement of Miss Natalie Crisan are discussed with your wife. Swear it." Without hesitation, Bogdan stood and dropped to one knee.

"Voivode, I give my solemn word that no details regarding Natalie Crisan will be discussed with my wife. This includes her security, wealth, etc." Assurance delivered, he rose, returned to his seat, and tipped his goblet back to drain the final drops.

"Good," Dragos said, mollified by his brother's response. "Let's join the others. I have asked the musicians to play Schubert's *Death and the Maiden*. I believe it is a favorite of Olenka's."

"It is. She will be pleased you remembered."

"I forget nothing, especially the shared pleasure derived from beautiful music." The men left the room, and the manservant who entered gave a yip of glee, bent over the table, and lapped up the spilled blood.

Seated in the darkened theatre later that evening, Bogdan brought Olenka's hand to his lips and kissed her open palm. The oath he swore to Dragos was demeaning, but he would suffer much for his spectacular wife. Olenka was picky about her blood diet, and although she would drink V cocktails to fulfill basic dietary requirements, it was her search for living donors to enhance her youthfulness that he found exciting, for she was demonstrably grateful when indulged. In bed, before joining the other guests, he had held her cherished body in his arms.

"Darling, I am no different from the fabulous mortal, Victoria Beckham," she had murmured in his ear. Her finger traced the muscles of his chest, and he felt a thrill of possession. "She only eats steamed vegetables and fish. No fat or processed food. She grows more stunning with age. My goal is identical, and to achieve the results, I must drink blood directly from the source." She offered her body once more, and he gloried in their shared passion.

Bogdan existed in his brother's shadow, always the spare to the heir, and it was demeaning to have to grovel so Olenka could access the blood she desired. Dragos had bent to the politically correct climate and weakened access to the traditional manner of attaining the fresh blood Olenka craved. She was an exquisite jewel, his alone to protect, and from the beginning of their relationship, her need for fresh blood was unquenchable.

Within days of rescuing her from the forest, she became his wife and a glorious vampire. As a wedding present, she begged to visit the village of the peasants who had murdered her mother and grandmother.

"Darling, bring me there and let me have my revenge. Later, we will celebrate . . . in private." Her words thrilled him, and they had traveled by horseback, alone on their mission of murder.

"First, the mayor's home, then the doctor's home." After drowning her hatred in the blood of her enemies, they had galloped back to his castle and made love until the impending dawn sent them to their coffins.

In the village the next morning, shrieks of terror and fear shrilled through the streets as the corpses of the two prominent families were discovered.

"Strigoi!" The word through the grief-stricken town, and the morticians gathered the bodies, exposing them briefly to the morning light. Once certain the victims were deceased, they performed their grim tasks.

Remembering the viciousness of Olenka's revenge aroused him, and as the other guests concentrated on the intricacies of Shubert's *Death and the Maiden*, he traced his tongue from her palm to her dainty wrist. His message succeeded, and Olenka pulled her attention from the stage. Her eyes widened, and she leaned forward, pressing her full lips onto her adoring lover's mouth.

He would never tire of her, and Bogdan had accepted long ago that his enduring passion for his wife was a weakness she would seek to exploit. In her vain quest for physical perfection, however, she failed to fully comprehend that her fetish for blood would never sway his absolute loyalty to the house of Dracul. He hated to admit it, but his brother was correct; Natalie Crisan's welfare trumped his wife's curiosity. Olenka's inquisitiveness about Natalia's heir could be innocent, but he would hold true to his promise of secrecy and enjoy how hard Olenka would try to wheedle the information from him.

CHAPTER ELEVEN

"I think we've covered the important issues." David stretched his arms over his head and walked to the edge of the mansion's terrace.

For the last two hours, the four of us had hammered out the details of the next year of my life. Security and protection, domicile, legal representation to review the terms of my inheritance, strategies to meet my writing contract commitments without travel to America, and the accessibility of excellent health care professionals should I get sick. I would need to close my home in the Bedford, New York, and hire a management company to take care of the property. Vivian my agent would know a company I could hire. I was disappointed to leave my newly redecorated home.

"David did such a fabulous job on my house," I said. My makeover and redecoration of my home had been the start of our friendship. Lamenting the loss of my posh digs and home office, I pouted. "And I finally have a piano. When I got home, I planned on hiring a piano teacher."

"Well, that's a simple problem to solve. We'll ask Dragos to provide a piano. My guess is there is at least one on *The Natalia*." Ian added this to the list.

"What about my wardrobe? Should I have my clothes shipped to Romania? What is the climate like in Romania?"

"I def think someone should pack and send everything in your closet." David had returned to the table. He wasn't behaving like my normal bubbly pal, the confident stylist and interior decorator who had taken me in hand. "My guess is you'll need more gowns and formal wear. How many gowns do you have with you?"

"Three." A knot was growing in the pit of my stomach. The thought of dressing for dinner, wearing an evening gown and dripping in jewels and a tiara might seem ideal to a little girl dreaming of meeting a handsome prince, but what would happen to my favorite comfy sweatpants?

"I'm keeping my yoga pants and comfy sweatpants. I'll wear them with a tiara if I have to." My friend's laughter burst through the stillness. I was lucky to have friends who would rearrange their lives to protect and support me. Yet, I yearned for solitude to process the cataclysmic changes in my future and decided to make a break for it.

"That's all folks," I said, mimicking my favorite

childhood cartoon. "If you think of anything else, add it to the list. Arabella, do we have any appointments tomorrow?"

"No, pet. I will be at the botanica in the morning if you need me." She held my elbow, guiding me to the doorway, and we hugged. "Text me when you get up tomorrow morning, okay?"

"I will. Good night." I blew David and Ian a double kiss.

In my bedroom, I changed and inventoried the clothes hanging in the closet. Planning to return home after the nuptials, I had packed light. I would need to shop before I boarded *The Natalia*. I flicked off the light and moved to the sliding doors. Should I leave the door to the balcony open? The night air was delicious, and the crash of the surf was better than a sleeping pill or a hot toddy. I slid a chair in front of the open door and draped two garlands of garlic across the opening. I brought my hand to my neck to check my iolite necklace. It was cool to the touch, a good sign. Arabella had cautioned that if it grew warm, I was to tell her or David immediately. The warning reminded me of the swords glowing blue in The Hobbit when orcs were nearby. When Tolkien created orcs had he considered adding vampires to his world?

How would my ex-boyfriend Mike react to the seismic change in my financial status if he found out? During the years we were together he'd obsessed about money, fashion, and living up to other people's expectations. No doubt he would have proposed immediately if he knew about my windfall. Were he and Alix still together? I bet not. Thank heavens I'd changed the locks on my house.

And what about Slade? Was his duplicity worse than Mike's intrinsic selfishness? At least Mike didn't want to take over the world.

Crawling under the cool sheets, I summoned Lupu.

"Protect me, my faithful friend."

A vision of Lupu crystallized. He raised his head from a pillow in front of a roaring fire. The intensity of his yellow eyes acknowledged my request, and with a sigh of contentment, he returned his head to the pillow. I surrendered to sleep.

CHAPTER TWELVE

"Is he handsome?" Olenka brushed her hair with long strokes. It fell in a golden waterfall down her back.

"I have a photo, Your Grace." The agent bowed, stepped forward, and placed the photo in the outstretched hand of the duchess. Olenka leaned it against a glamorous photograph of herself wearing the diamond bat tiara and resumed brushing her hair.

"Hmm, he looks like the Hollywood celebrity the fans go mad for. Ryan something. Is the man fit?"

"Yes, ma'am. Fit and strong. His skin will meet your exacting standard. His hair is thick. He is just under six feet tall."

Olenka returned the hairbrush to the mother-of-pearl vanity tray. Cupping her hands under her chin, she leaned forward to better study the young man in the photo. She could tell an American mutt from across a crowded drawing room. Chaotic DNA sometimes created a fine specimen. His arrogant smile aroused her: here was a man who needed to learn his place.

"He is acceptable. Is he in Jamaica?" Olenka dabbed her wrists with a heady fragrance.

"Yes, ma'am. I took the liberty of flying him to Jamaica. I would have paid for his flight myself had you disapproved." The agent bowed low.

"Excellent. You have proved useful. The agreed-upon amount will be wired to your account when the banks open. Bring him to the yacht and put him in a mid-level guest room . . . the Green Room. My husband indulges me, but the voivode will intercede if we are not discreet." She waved her hand in dismissal.

"Thank you, Your Grace."

The agent had scarcely left when there was a knock from behind the door of Bogdan's adjoining dressing room.

"Come in!"

Bogdan, barefoot in black silk pajama bottoms, padded to the glowing vanity, lifted his wife's hair, and nuzzled her neck.

"Are you pleased, my darling angel?" The advent of the aluminum backed mirror allowed all vampires to have a reflection, and Olenka's vanity boasted a three-sided jewel-encrusted fantasy. Mirrors and portraits of herself in formal dress covered the walls of her boudoir. She swiveled in her seat and extended both hands.

"You spoil me, darling," she cooed. "I know Dragos is set in his ways, and yet you continue to satiate my elevated palate. My new prize appears promising. America is teeming with opportunity." She draped her arms around his neck.

"Before we rest, I thought we might spend time together? The concert pleased me. Did you suggest *Death and the Maiden*?"

"No, Dragos did. He recalled it was your favorite." She pulled back to search his face.

"How interesting. I must remember to thank him. His memory is remarkable." Bogdan took her hand and led her to the four-poster bed.

"It's what makes him most dangerous. Enough talk; time for bed."

CHAPTER THIRTEEN

Dragos's mouth curved, the muscles lifting into a seldom used expression—a smile. Natalia's heir had agreed to sail to Romania but had proven a tough negotiator. He reread the sheet of paper, her list of requirements, delivered by a messenger to his yacht. He had sent his agreement immediately and instructed Natalie and her guests to be ready to sail the next evening. The addition of her friends would add joviality to his staid social circle. It would also make Miss Crisan less anxious. Her comfort and security were uppermost in his mind.

The newlywed's accommodations were impressive, and he had instructed the staff to see that the Westwoods' smallest wish was fulfilled. He had hired a personal maid for Natalie, and a bodyguard would shadow her when she was out of her suite. Another guard would be posted outside the door to her bedroom.

As the host of *The Natalia*, he would greet her personally when she boarded the super yacht and escort her to her chambers. She was reserved with strangers, an attribute he admired. How would she react to the lavishness of her suite? He had personally chosen the museum quality furnishings, bespoke fabrics, and elegant accessories to guarantee her comfort. Entry to the suite of rooms was forbidden to prevent Olenka from spying, but he suspected she had disregarded his instructions. How he treated his prized guest was not her business, but he had to tread carefully. Bogdan's support was crucial, and he was unreasonable when it came to his wife.

From behind the immense mahogany desk Dragos surveyed his study, an updated replica of the one in his castle. He adjusted the miniature of Natalia, framed in gold, and glanced at his watch. *The Natalia* was the brainchild of Marius, and his trusted secretary had performed his duties with the highest professionalism.

"Voivode, a second home, particularly one which can be moved strategically, would be useful if we were to go to war. It will be of battleship standard but retain palatial qualities for you and your guests." As usual, Marius was ahead of the enemy, excelling at a living game of chess. But even he had not anticipated the discovery of Natalia's great-great-great-granddaughter.

It had given Dragos much joy to surround his

wife with music, art, books, and precious jewels. He would drape silk, satin, or velvet fabric, brought back from his travels, across her lap, and her dressmaker would be called to design a new garment. What vicarious pleasure he had felt watching her delight in his gifts. Perhaps Natalie Crisan was his second chance at happiness. A knock at the door broke his reverie.

"Come."

One of his most trusted and efficient operatives entered. Danior Winn's years of service to Dragos were a testament to his political savvy, and his preference to work in the shadows in support of his king suited them both. He bowed and approached.

"Have you information for me, Danior?"

"Yes, Voivode. My information concerns the shapeshifter known as Slade Suit," he said.

"Continue."

"There is talk he may try to secure her."

Dragos reached for the jeweled letter opener, a cherished gift from his wife, and gauged its weight in his open palm. The pointed instrument had more than once been used to dispatch an enemy.

"Ah. Where is the alien located?"

"Three of the alien's agents have arrived in Jamaica. She may be at risk."

Dragos rose.

"You shall be rewarded for your service. Send in my valet and then exit through the secret door."

The asset did as he was told, and a moment later, the voivode's valet hurried into the room.

"Bring the Duke and the Count to me."

"Yes, Voivode."

Dragos was still holding the jeweled penknife when a brief knock admitted his brother and secretary.

"Voivode." It was apparent Bogdan had been enjoying Olenka's charms. He had dressed hastily. Marius stood to his right, paper and pen in hand to record his king's instructions.

Dragos carefully replaced the treasured penknife on its engraved holder. The two men remained at attention before Dragos's desk and observed the purposeful movements of their king, movements which historically precipitated a military action. Dragos sat and indicated the chairs positioned in front of the huge desk.

"I have received alarming information from a trusted informant. An attempt to kidnap Natalie Crisan will take place tonight. This is intolerable, and we must intervene. Bogdan, you will travel with her maid and a dozen trusted soldiers to the mansion. Immediately. The Westwoods are to be made aware of the alleged plan, and every precaution must be taken.

"You must persuade Miss Crisan to come aboard the ship tonight. She is no doubt packing and organizing for the trip to Romania. Her maid will finish the task. Miss Crisan's accommodations are prepared, and her safety is imperative."

"Yes, Voivode," Bogdan said. "I will gather the soldiers immediately and depart."

Dragos nodded dismissal and swiveled the chair toward the sliding door, open to the night and the lights of the port town. He would not lose her to a slimy alien.

* * *

Marius headed to his office while Bogdan returned to his dressing room to retrieve his sword. His wife's giggle startled him, and he whipped his head toward the sound. Olenka lounged naked on his bed, a mischievous grin playing on her stunning features.

"Why are you taking your sword? Do you wish to play a new game?"

"I cannot answer your questions, O. It concerns Natalie Crisan. I have sworn an oath."

Olenka rose and strutted to her lover.

"Husband, Dragos's obsession with the new Natalia will be useful, don't you think? I guess that you are suddenly required to bring her aboard tonight. Excellent. We will arrive in Romania on schedule to conduct the ceremony." Bogdan attached his belt and slid the sword into the scabbard.

"My darling O, make sure your new toy understands the rules. He is to remain hidden and eat dinner in his room until we are underway. He may have to stay in his room for the entire voyage. If he is invited to an event with Dragos and the court, which I sincerely doubt, he is to be charming to Miss Crisan and will not engage her in conversation if she doesn't want to speak to him. If he annoys Dragos's honored guest, he may find himself tossed overboard." Bogdan moved to the bed and kissed his wife's neck.

"I hope his flavor profile will meet your standard, my gourmand. Be careful. Remember, you walk a tightrope." Olenka pursed her lips seductively.

"Come back soon, my love. I will wait here for you." When the door closed behind him, Olenka covered her mouth to muffle a hoot of glee. Perfect, she thought. The ship will leave before dawn and the American mongrel will finally be where I can befriend her. My beauty is eclipsed only by my brains.

Grabbing an ebony silk kimono robe, Olenka twirled, letting the folds of the robe fly about her. Blissfully breathless, she paused to tie her robe. It was time to move forward with the next stage of her plan.

"Dotia!"

The maid scurried in, eyes downcast. Torturing Dotia brought her daily doses of entertainment.

Yesterday she had thrown a shoe at her, and Dotia's cry of pain had amused her.

"As unhappy as I am with your failure to secure what I asked for . . ." Olenka delayed her words until Dotia's shoulders trembled with fear. "Your continued underwhelming performance concerns me. I expect loyalty and creativity from my staff.

"You are, however, in luck. Kronid has brought me a man who will travel with us to Romania. We will put him in the Green Room. I hope I do not have to ask if it is prepared per our previous conversation?" Olenka strode to Dotia, lifting her chin and leaning toward her until their faces were inches apart.

"You will go to the lower deck and await Kronid's direction. You will do exactly as he tells you. You will not speak. You will see my guest is comfortably settled in. You are permitted to ask if he requires food or drink. Then you will insist he lock his door and return directly to me to report.

"If anything goes wrong, you will demonstrate your loyalty by a small donation." Olenka ran a finger down Dotia's jugular vein. "A word of warning: you will discuss his presence with no one. Now go."

CHAPTER FOURTEEN

"This is ridiculous," I called down from my perch on the staircase landing. "You expect me to leave with you immediately? I was sleeping, and I'm not packed. I'll be ready tomorrow evening, as we agreed."

I had awakened from a deep sleep to the sound of a wicked disagreement somewhere in the house. David and Ian faced off against Dragos's brother and a platoon of armed soldiers. Heads swung in my direction and Bogdan bowed.

"Did I overhear you have plausible information of a kidnapping attempt by alien forces? Is your source reliable, or is this a trick?" I stomped down the staircase, tying my robe tightly around my waist. Adrenaline had cleared the cobwebs of sleep, but a knot had formed in my stomach and the snack I'd eaten hours earlier threatened to make an unwanted reappearance.

"Miss Crisan," Bogdan said. "His Majesty has sent me and a dozen of his most trusted soldiers to escort you to *The Natalia*. Here is the maid he has hired for you. She will remain here and pack your wardrobe and other personal items."

A young woman of perhaps seventeen or eighteen stepped forward. Her hair dark brown hair was smoothed into a low bun and her dark eyes held an expression I guessed was nervousness coupled with excitement. She was petite, and a bit shorter than me, and her simple dress of navy blue was professional and classy. I swung my attention back to Bogdan.

"The voivode hired a personal maid for me?" Dragos was taking liberties, and another frank discussion loomed in our future.

"His Majesty is conscious of your comfort and rank in his court. A personal maid is to be expected." Bogdan pressed his lips together. "We do not have time to discuss domestic arrangements," he said. "Westwoods, if you are to accompany Miss Crisan, you will need to move your boxes. Staff can move your personal effects after we have departed for *The Natalia*."

Arabella placed her hand on my shoulder. They had woken her too, and I was relieved to have her beside me.

We hugged, and I whispered,

"They're saying I'm in danger. What should I do?"

We turned to David and Ian, and I said, "Help me decide. Please."

David glanced at Ian, who held up his hands in surrender.

"I think you should go to the ship and bring Arabella with you. We will coordinate the movement of our boxes. We are almost packed, and the maid can finish packing for you. Change, grab a coat, and take your pajamas. Arabella, do the same. We will sort this out tomorrow evening when we have more time."

Ian was logical, and if he thought we should relocate, then I would accept his assessment.

"Okay, give me ten minutes." Arabella and I went to our rooms, and I changed quickly, stuffing pajamas, a robe, my laptop, and jewelry in my carry-on bag. There was a knock at the door. The young woman Dragos had hired waited with a shy smile.

"Oh, hello," I stammered. "What is your name?"

"Ana-Maria, Miss." She curtsied. "I will stay behind and pack your things. Is everything in here or are there other items I need to gather from the house?"

"I think my stuff is all here, but if you could look around, I would appreciate it."

"Of course. Whatever you wish. I will be quick."

Arabella exited her room, and we descended the

stairs to where the soldiers awaited. Our overnight bags were taken from us.

"Excellent. Men, positions, please. Andriu, text the voivode's valet that we are on our way."

Bogdan led the way. Three men armed and dressed in camouflage positioned themselves on either side of Arabella and me. We went out the front door of the mansion and were assisted into a black Humvee. A similar car led our vehicle and one followed close behind.

When we reached the dock, three jitneys awaited, and we were put in the center one with Bogdan and three armed guards. Too terrified by the military operation to speak, I squeezed Arabella's hand. The jitneys flew across the water toward a cruise ship in the distance, and I suddenly realized *The Natalia* was enormous.

I closed my eyes.

"Lupu, my faithful friend, protect my thoughts." I saw a vision of boot-clad feet running in the snow and a ball sailing through the air to a leaping gray and white wolf. "Thank you." It had become easier and easier to call him to me.

I opened my eyes as we pulled up to *The Natalia*. An open flap let down from the side of the ship provided a platform we could step onto, and Bogdan extended his hand to help me. The ice cold of his fingers sent a chill up my spine, but it was too late to change my mind.

We were guided through a labyrinth of

corridors until we came to an elevator. Once inside, Bogdan pushed a button, and the doors closed. The elevator sped upward past several levels resting in semi-darkness, the glow of emergency lights the only indication of passenger safety provisions. The elevator stopped and Bogdan gestured.

"After you, Miss Crisan."

"Arabella comes with me." I reached for her hand, and she squeezed mine in solidarity. Whatever craziness was in play, I needed her by my side.

"As you wish."

In the hallway, a liveried servant bowed.

"This way, Miss Crisan, and . . ."

"Arabella Bishop," she said with confidence. He pivoted and strode down a hall carpeted in plush burgundy. Our muffled journey seemed to go on forever. Finally, we stopped in front of a ponderous wooden door. A royal crest and shield had been expertly carved into the gleaming surface. Our escort knocked.

"Come."

"Voivode, Miss Crisan and Arabella Bishop."

"Thank you." The heavy door closed softly behind us. Dragos left his position by the open sliding doors and approached us. He regarded me for a moment, no doubt gauging my mood. His gaze traveled to Arabella but quickly returned to me. He bowed.

"Good evening, Miss Crisan, Miss Bishop. I was

hoping to welcome you to my ship in a more celebratory manner. It is unfortunate you have come aboard under these dramatic circumstances."

"Dramatic is an understatement," I said. "I was asleep when the Duke and my friend's loud voices woke me. Is the kidnapping threat from a reliable source?"

Dragos bristled.

"I would not have conducted a military operation and inconvenienced you if I thought otherwise. The intelligence is from a trusted source. You will be safe here on my ship."

He gestured to a seating area. "Would you prefer to rest a minute, or shall we move to your suite?" He acted like the perfect gentleman, and although I wanted to grill him more on the reason behind our hasty exit from the mainland, I preferred to hunker down with my friend and hopefully sleep.

"I would like to retire to my room. Do you agree, Arabella?" She nodded.

"I will personally escort you both to your suite. Your bedrooms are located on either side of the shared living and dining area." He advanced to the door, and upon ushering us into the hall, the waiting servant snapped to attention. Dragos waved him away and, as we retraced our footsteps away from his office, he educated us on the ship's specifics —her size, speed, theatre, and the string quartet he had hired for the journey.

"Music is a passion of mine. I play the violin for my enjoyment. The string quartet has an extensive repertoire, and I hope you will choose a few favorites for them to perform." We passed many doors, eventually arriving at a glossy white double door with a posted sentry who saluted Dragos and stepped smartly to the side. Dragos unlocked the door, and after taking one step over the threshold, motioned for me to enter.

"This is your bedchamber, Miss Crisan."

The siren song of an Art Deco fantasy pulled me into a dreamy boudoir tastefully decorated with exquisite, museum-quality furnishings. Pale pink silk covered the walls, and my feet sank into the plush padding of the thick, pearl white carpet. A massive, skirted vanity was topped by Venetian mirrors and blazed with the soft light of petite crystal lamps set on either end. Its mirrored surface reflected the crystal perfume bottles arranged on an alabaster tray. The vignette glowed in a celebration of feminine mystique.

In my wildest Art Deco visions, I had imagined myself in such a room, and the reality of its existence floored me. I brushed my hand across the quilted satin bedspread.

"Art Deco is my favorite," I said. "How did you know?"

Dragos had remained near the doorway during my perusal, and he appeared pleased with my reaction.

"My goal is to provide for your comfort as my honored guest, and one of my agents made inquiries. An antiques dealer in the city by your home in America remembered your distress over a table you lost to another buyer. We located the table, purchased it, and it will be shipped to your home in Romania."

The piece he was referring to was a round inlaid table on fabulous hand-carved legs. I swooned when I saw it and wanted it desperately for the foyer of my home in New York. I had begged my ex-boyfriend Mike to chip in and he'd declined. We'd lived together for two years and he'd never even paid utilities, the freeloader. The delay proved disastrous. Another Art Deco collector had snapped it up, and I'd cried.

Dragos opened a door. "Miss Bishop, on the other side of the sitting room is your bedroom."

We followed him through a lovely living room filled with more Art Deco treasure and several vases loaded with calla lilies. He led us into another room, and an ice blue color palette greeted my friend. The four-poster bed was hand painted with curling ivy and cobalt blue morning glories.

"This is lovely, thank you," Arabella said.

Dragos inclined his head and walked to the window where the sky was no longer ink but had lightened to a deep gray.

"I must leave you. Thank you for coming

aboard with haste and have a restful sleep. I will see you tomorrow evening." He bowed and was gone.

"Arabella, I'm wiped out. I am not undead, but I am keeping their hours."

"I'm beat, too. Let's leave our bedroom doors open to the sitting room and lock the other doors. The vampires have to get back to their boxes. I'll see you in a few hours and we'll talk."

"Sounds good." I yawned. "My room reminds me of Nick and Nora Charles and *The Thin Man* movies. I might get lost in that huge marshmallow of a bed and not climb out for days." We air-kissed, and I strolled through the sitting room to my bedroom.

Upon second glance, the bedroom was even more luxurious than I'd realized. Dragos had been gauging my reactions, and I hoped I'd expressed enough admiration for his efforts. Would a poor staffer go to the guillotine if I didn't clap and jump up and down with glee?

Once dressed in my pajamas, I whispered, "Lupu. Snuggle with me." The wolf appeared in my mind's eye, ever watchful, his stately head resting on crossed paws. His handsome face was my final vision as my body sank deeper into the sumptuous mattress. The drama of the night melted away and I was transported to dreamland.

* * *

On the other side of the ship, Olenka tracked the tip of her nail down her husband's muscled chest. She threw back the sheet and slunk naked across his bedroom, well aware of the leer which followed the seductive movement of her lithe body. She had relished the delicious taste of the American man's blood, and her doting husband had been well rewarded.

The American had winced when her canines pricked his neck, a reaction which excited her. Causing pain and stirring drama were her favorite hobbies outside of maintaining her magnificence. She retrieved her silk nightgown from the chair where she had discarded it before their lovemaking. Raising the garment over her head, she held her arms up in the air so the descent of the material would highlight her curves. She knew how to seduce her husband, and his pleasure in watching her redress after bed gratified her narcissism.

"My darling, I am the luckiest man in the world. I love you in red. You don't wear it enough." Bogdan pulled himself to his elbows on the bed. "We will need to go to our boxes soon." She did not answer; rapt with concentration, she posed in front of the modern mirror he had installed for her. The gift of the mirror had strengthened their marriage —and their sex life. Her lust for blood and pleasure would soon be quenched at the ceremony in Romania. Bogdan would disappear to satisfy his own needs, and these conquests only increased their passion for each other.

Olenka reached for the matching silk robe and slipped her feet into the heeled slippers. A long rest would enable the fresh blood to repair and enhance her physical form. She hadn't aged a day since her husband had rescued her in the woods and mixed his royal blood with hers. She would do whatever was necessary to maintain her plump and radiant youth. Her soul would remain a dry and wrinkled husk, cracked, and forsaken, but she and Bogdan would live forever, and her soul mattered not.

"Come darling," she said. "I am ready for my beauty sleep. I must look my best when standing by the side of my handsome duke. I will charm Dragos's guest and encourage their relationship. This should be our mutual goal, don't you think, my love?"

Bogdan rose and slipped on a pair of monogrammed velvet slippers, black slacks, and a satin smoking jacket.

"Yes, you are right, O. Tomorrow you will meet Dragos's new obsession and indicate your desire for friendship. Tread carefully."

CHAPTER FIFTEEN

I awoke to a throbbing purr coming from the bowels of the ship. The sun shone from high noon. The uber-padded bed seemed miles from the floor, and no step ladder was in sight. I rolled onto my side and hopped onto the floor. I slid open the doors to the balcony and, leaning slightly over the railing, watched a faraway mirage of land receding into the distance. The ship cut smoothly through the ocean, leaving a substantial wake to lap against the sides of the massive ship. Dragos had wasted no time exiting Jamaica.

I went in search of Arabella and found her on the phone and in obvious distress.

"Yes, Auntie, I know I said I would be here for at least a month. No, I'm not angry with Cousin Dwayne. I wasn't using my car anyway, but he has to pay the insurance. I am on a trip to Europe and then I will return for a long visit. Yes. Okay. Love to the family." Arabella tapped her phone off and sank onto the sofa.

"Families are full of drama. My aunt is convinced I left Jamaica because my cousin crashed my car while I was living with you in the States. Of course, my family knows little about the curse and my years spent as a feline. My cousin is a loser, and it was a piece of junk." I heard a noise behind me and Ana-Marie, the maid Dragos had hired for me, hovered in the doorway.

"Good morning, Ana-Maria. Is there somewhere on the ship to get coffee and breakfast?" The lack of sleep had my brain screaming for caffeine.

"I will bring it to you, Miss. Should I bring the coffee first or do you know what you would like for breakfast?"

"Coffee first, please." Ana-Maria left to retrieve it, and I settled on the sofa next to Arabella. I reached for her hand.

"I'm truly sorry you didn't have more time with your family. When we dock, you can fly back if you want. I'd be happy to pay."

"Tsk, tsk. I invited David to live in your cellar when you rescued me. I was in bad shape from the curse, remember? You fed me and were the sweetest owner. Your kindness and friendship with David has blossomed into an exciting adventure. I appreciate your offer, but I am intrigued by Dragos's description of your legacy from Natalia.

And when will I have another chance to visit Romania?"

A few minutes later, Ana-Maria delivered a large tray with a china coffee pot and matching mugs. On the tray, fresh fruit and a basket of warm croissants reminded me I hadn't eaten in over twelve hours.

"This looks yummy," I said.

Ana-Maria poured coffee for me and Arabella and stepped back to wait. I focused on slurping the excellent java and forgot she was there until she cleared her throat.

"Oh, gosh, sorry to make you wait," I said. "I would love a salad. Lots of veggies, and an apple cider vinaigrette dressing on the side, please."

Ana-Maria glanced at Arabella.

"That sounds delicious. I'll have the same."

The maid smiled and left.

"Arabella, what am I doing with a personal maid? Who am I?" My friend refilled her mug and reclined on a plump throw pillow.

"Nat, your fortune has changed. You are wealthy and related to Romanian aristocracy. You have a personal maid, and we are on a luxury ship sailing to . . . Lisbon? Romania is landlocked, and once we dock, we'll need to fly there. I say we eat, clean up, and explore the ship." I refilled my cup and considered my friend's words.

"*The Natalia* probably has a pub with a dart board," I mused. "If we find it, I challenge you to an afternoon of Killer to distract me from the thought of a year in Romania with Dragos and the world of vampires as my primary social circle."

"You're on." Arabella leaned back and her eyes twinkled. "Did I ever tell you I was my high school dart champion?"

* * *

Arabella swabbed the deck with me, clinching our darts competition with Ted Lasso's confidence. *The Natalia* was more than a floating palace—it resembled a buoyant village whose sole purpose was entertaining its guests.

"Tomorrow we'll try bowling," Arabella said as we parted in our sitting room. "Did I ever tell you . . ."

". . . That you were on your high school bowling team?" We laughed, and I closed the door separating my bedroom from the sitting room.

My room had been tidied in my absence and several petite bouquets of fresh flowers dotted the tables. Dinner would be a formal affair, and I scanned the room for the logical place Anna-Maria would have hung my gowns and the rest of my wardrobe. The first armoire was an enormous Biedermeier which matched the vanity. It dominated the wall, measuring perhaps ten-feet wide, and nearly grazing the ceiling. Its pale glossy wood was impeccable. The cabinet was unlocked, and upon opening it I made an unnerving discovery.

The armoire contained the gowns from the wedding and rehearsal and the bronze and black gradient gown Iris had gifted me. But the inventory did not stop here. Sliding the padded hangers slowly to the left, I discovered ten more gowns hung in the lavender-scented space. Black velvet, bottle green taffeta, gold lamé, cream satin, and more—it was the evening wardrobe of a socialite accustomed to black tie affairs. I flipped over a hem and confirmed that it had been altered. At the bottom of the armoire, the high heels I had worn to David and Ian's wedding were joined by three additional pairs of evening heels—black, gold, and silver. I had plenty of money to buy my own clothing, and I didn't appreciate anyone other than David choosing pieces in my wardrobe. I shut the armoire doors and commenced a search of the bedroom.

Stalking to a closet near the bathroom, I found my robe, pajamas, and linen pieces hung on pristine white wooden hangers. The garments were impeccably laundered and arranged by color like a fancy boutique on Fifth Avenue. To the left of my own wardrobe hung several pairs of slacks and several blouses. These pieces were also my size, and the slacks had been hemmed

Was I once again a prisoner in a gilded cage? Nauseated, I ran for the bathroom and held a cool washcloth to my face. Slade and Dragos might be enemies, but their habits were remarkably similar. Slade had filled a closet with lingerie and feminine lounge wear, and he had never hidden his intent to make me his lover when I was his prisoner. Were Dragos's intentions as honorable as he claimed, or had I walked into a trap?

I twisted the taps in the tub, adjusted the flowing water to the correct temperature, and threw in a lavender bath bomb. A warm bath always cleared my head.

While I soaked, I wondered how long it had taken Dragos to prepare the ship for my friends and me. The bathroom was a perfect replica of one from the Carlyle in Manhattan that I'd saved on Pinterest. The walls were papered in white and gold Art Deco chevrons on which whooping cranes glamorously posed. I resolved to open every door and drawer when I was finished bathing and then lay down for a nap.

My search raised more questions than answers. My entire Jamaican wardrobe was stored in drawers and closets, but it had been supplemented with additional garments in my size and preferred color palette of black, navy, teal and creamy white. Bewildered, I poured a glass of water from the pitcher next to my bed, chugged it down and crawled under the covers for a long nap.

"Miss Crisan? It is four-thirty." Ana-Maria stood at the bottom of my bed.

"Really? I've slept for hours." I performed my

new dismount; an Olympic side roll out of bed landing on my feet without a hop. Ana-Maria stifled a grin with amazing self-control. "Would it be possible to get coffee for Arabella and me?"

"Of course, Miss. Miss Bishop told me to wake you. She is on the sitting room balcony."

I found Arabella on a lounge chair watching the sun's reflection on the ocean, its final descent toward the horizon promising to be a glorious event. Balcony is a catch-all designation that didn't do justice to the expansive space. A row of four rattan lounge chairs with adjustable umbrellas faced the sea. A hammock swung in the far-right corner, and to the left an outdoor bed covered in a crisp cotton fabric was protected by a sun defeating canopy. Arabella patted the arm of the lounge next to her.

"Well, hello, sleepyhead. You napped hard."

"I would have slept until tomorrow if Ana-Maria hadn't woken me." I stretched my arms over my head and settled in to admire the view.

We sat in silence, relishing the soft evening breeze. Behind me, I heard Ana-Maria and the clink of china. On a coffee table in front of the sofa, she had poured two cups and brought us a selection of finger sandwiches.

"Cocktails are at 6:30 and dinner is at 7:00," Ana-Maria said. "When you need me, press the button on the wall by the door. If I don't hear from you, I will knock on your door at 5:45." With a sweet smile, she left.

The hot coffee cleared the cobwebs and as I breathed in the aroma, I pushed my anxiety aside to confide what I had found in the closets of my bedroom. Arabella listened intently while she sipped.

"The clothes inventory is different from Slade's kidnapping me, but not completely without similarities," I said. "Let's review the chain of events: As soon as I agreed to return to Romania, there is a threat of another kidnapping requiring me to rush to Dragos's ship. How convenient. And our incredible accommodations are ready for immediate occupancy with a tailored wardrobe of clothing for the trip to my homeland? Am I being paranoid?"

Arabella placed her cup in the saucer and set it on the tray.

"Our instincts developed over millions of years. You are suspicious and you have a right to be. Dragos has been spying on Slade Suit, and he knows you were kidnapped. Fear of kidnapping could be used to manipulate you." Arabella's words rang true.

"Do I confront Dragos with questions about the clothes in the drawers and closets?"

She shrugged.

"Hm, no, I wouldn't anger him," she said. "I would thank him for his hospitality. Ana-Maria is the person to question. Maids have loyalty to their mistress. Dragos may have hired her, but if she is to keep her job, she will want to make you happy."

"You're brilliant, Arabella. I'll tell Dragos how pleased I am with her and gently inquire how she is compensated to make sure she is properly paid. An insider on *The Natalia* would go a long way toward making me feel less anxious."

Arabella rose and pointed to my bedroom.

"Let's choose the gown you'll wear tonight. I'm dying to see the new one from Iris on you." She hugged me. "I think I'll hint that I don't have the correct clothes for the transatlantic trip just to see if the wardrobe fairy visits me in my sleep."

* * *

After we selected my gown and accessories, Arabella went back to her room to change for dinner. I buzzed Ana-Maria to style my hair. The woman reflected in the mirror was the Natalie Crisan I knew, but different in a subtly significant way. The lift of my chin and the confident posture of the new Natalie would have made Aunt Loretta proud. She had given me the foundation of a well-bred woman with a bright future. Had I forgotten the nuggets of brilliance she shared in her unassuming way? I smiled to myself, recalling one of her soliloquies in a café in Paris.

"Try to learn something new each day and

relish even the repetitive, simple activities. In fact, my dear, strive to elevate every day. Life is full of experiences to cherish." She had picked up her pastry and taken a delicate bite. "And when in Paris, eat the pastry!" My aunt's life lessons were gems, and I wondered what wisdom my parents would have shared had they not disappeared from my life.

Perched on the padded satin seat at the Biedermeier vanity, I adjusted the strap on my lace bra. Time for the new make-up ritual. Since meeting my gentleman vampire, I had learned to apply my make-up with an expert hand. David had convinced me to experiment with more products than I ever had.

"Make-up is to play with, darling. When are you going to use foundation? When you're ninety and it sinks into your wrinkles?" The visual was disturbing, and I reached for a foundation sponge.

It was nearly sundown, and I had pulled the blackout curtains and diaphanous sheers across the curtain rod for privacy but neglected to close the slider to the balcony. The cruising speed of the ship had picked up, creating a strong breeze, which whipped the sheers into a frantic tango. Wind and fabric embraced like long-lost lovers desperately intertwining arms and legs to prevent separation. The result was a spectacular tangle. My attempt to undo the mess was futile, and as I reached to close the door, I heard the guitar chords of a familiar country rock song.

I froze. Throwing open the sliding door, the chorus of the ballad I knew well rode the wind like a bucking bronco. Was I hallucinating? I poked my head through the open door and listened.

I wasn't losing my mind. An American rock classic at full volume rose from the deck directly below my balcony. Whomever was blasting Tom Petty's *Refuge* didn't care about disturbing his or her fellow passengers. The wind would make a bird's nest of my hair, but what the heck. *Refuge* held too many memories to count. Forgetting I was clad in only my bra and panties, I stepped onto the balcony to search for the offending source. Gotcha. I leaned to the right and . . .

One deck down, a man sunbathed naked. I could only see him from the waist down, which was good, otherwise he could have caught me spying on him. Slowly, I backpedaled into my bedroom and slid the door closed. Sundown was an odd time to work on one's tan. *Refuge* was psyche-up music, the kind a marathon runner would add to a playlist. Who was he? I pressed the buzzer for Ana-Maria. She arrived promptly, carrying a pitcher of water.

"I, um, went to close the sliding door and my hair got a little messy, sorry. I love how it looked . . . can you fix it?" The sweet young woman had created an intricate braided chignon with ease, and more than a few pieces had come loose.

"I'm happy you are pleased. We'll leave these two pieces down to frame your face. See? You have beautiful hair, and my mother taught me lots of styles. Have you decided on your gown?"

"Arabella and I decided I should wear the new gown from Iris Lavender, a fashion designer we know. It was a gift!" I removed the gown from the armoire and laid it carefully on the bed.

Ana-Maria beamed approval. "It's amazing. Are you ready to dress?" I nodded and Ana-Maria carefully placed the gown on the floor so I could step into it. My jewelry would remain the same: the iolite necklace, the black pearl earrings from Slade, and the ruby ring from Dragos. Black satin pumps and the wristlet handbag from David and Ian completed my ensemble.

The gown Iris designed deserved more than an aside. The deep V-neck was a discreet cut, my preference. A silver bodice melted into a bronze skirt which changed to black at the knees. It had a short train, a glamorous touch I didn't think I would like, but Iris had mastered the elegant flow of the colors. I stared at myself in the full-length mirror, once again recalling Slade's comment praising my aristocratic beauty. The compliment couldn't make up for what he was—a dangerous alien intent on world domination according to Ian and David.

A rat-a-tat on the door announced my gentleman vampires.

"Come in!"

Both had donned their formal tuxes and David pretended to faint into Ian's arms.

"Lord have mercy, who is this beauty who stands before us. Is that the gown Iris gave you?"

"Who else could create a gown like this?" I turned to Ana-Maria. "Thank you for helping me. Enjoy your evening."

"Thank you. I am available when you come back to your room. Just press the buzzer." When Ana-Maria was gone David teased me.

"So, Miss Fancy Pants," he said with a wink, "how does it feel to have a maid? You'll never have to do laundry again. Or anything else you don't want to."

Arabella, resplendent in a purple caftan and dupsie, had entered through the open sitting room door. We gushed over her outfit, and she returned the compliment.

"Nat, you look stunning. Are these handsome men our escorts? Aren't we lucky ducks."

From somewhere, the sound of a gong rang out.

"A gong?" David snickered.

"Watch your manners, David. You are in the presence of the aristocracy." I poked him in the side with my finger. Ian jumped in to add an additional warning.

"Behave, husband. No snide remarks or eye-rolling." David shrugged and threaded his arm through mine as we exited my bedroom door.

"Arabella and I have lots to tell you about our

day poking around the ship," I whispered in his ear. "We played darts, and found a Happy Days bowling alley, a Hollywood-style movie theatre . . . "

"Like I said," David interjected, interrupting my list. "*The Natalia* is a floating village."

* * *

Dragos paced the drawing room, eager to host his first evening with Natalie as his guest. She was unaware that her explorations with her friend were observed, and doors had been unlocked in anticipation of her walkabout. Her amusement was what mattered now that she was safe from the alien threat.

His chef had prepared a feast, a range of delicacies fit for a queen, none of which he or his inner circle could eat. A vampire's diet was strictly blood, be it from an animal hunted in the woods, or the plethora of recipes for V cocktails. His sommelier did not share the ingenious recipes he created for the enjoyment of the king and his courtiers. There were rogue vampires who stalked and drank their fill from the source, like Olenka. They tried his patience. Years ago, he had issued a decree against a vampire sucking from an unwilling human. Although Bogdan insisted Olenka's never ending source of blood conformed to the letter of the law, Dragos doubted it. Olenka's youthful bloom could only mean one thing. Eventually she would make a mistake, and he would insist that she curtail her addiction. No one was above the law.

His thoughts were interrupted by his brother's entrance. Bogdan strode into the drawing room, shepherding Olenka as he always did, reveling vicariously in the reverence her beauty inspired. Her ice-cold splendor was not to Dragos's taste, he had preferred the burnished warmth of his late queen's coloring.

Beneath the shimmering chandeliers, Olenka's skin glowed like a votive flame; plump, poreless, and smooth as a newborn. The blue of her eyes shone unnaturally bright. She had fed before her rest; Dragos was certain of it. Her devious obsession with her exquisite appearance, and the lengths she would go to maintain it was not a secret in elite vampire circles.

He knew that Olenka had proclaimed herself a connoisseur of the blood. She'd bragged to her adoring cronies that her voracious appetite for blood drawn directly from a vein allowed her to choose her victims by specific physical attributes. Her agents carried an ordered list of criteria for her donors. Dragos had repeated the conversation to Bogdan who had called it jealous gossip and insisted the donations were voluntary.

Dragos was also aware of the ceremonies, Olenka's euphemistic name for the blood-soaked orgies she hosted when one of her supposed volunteers wished to become undead. Loyal

Marius handled the oversight for these events, and he no doubt indulged himself. Despite the king's standing invitation to the ceremonies, the gilt embossed notes were tossed into the trash. Dragos had evolved since Natalia's murder. He was content to remain in his castle with his books, music, and chess, and turn a blind eye to the flouting of his decree. He needed his brother by his side.

"Good evening, Voivode." Olenka curtsied and then brushed an air kiss over each of Dragos's cheek.

Bogdan inclined his head. "Voivode."

"Olenka, the sea air agrees with you. Did you have a good rest?" Silent communication passed between husband and wife. She smiled coquettishly.

"My skin soaks up the moisture like a sponge, Voivode. Romania can be dry, don't you think?"

Dragos opened his mouth to reply but swallowed his response as Natalie stepped into the room. Conversation halted, and disbelieving eyes bulged at the heiress's likeness to Natalia. Dragos, momentarily overwhelmed by the living homage to his dead wife, gathered himself quickly, and chest held high, greeted his honored guest.

"Good evening, Miss Crisan, Westwoods, Miss Bishop. I hope you are enjoying the journey so far."

David responded, "The accommodations are excellent, Voivode. Thank you for your hospitality."

The small talk was brief as liveried waiter

presented flutes of champagne to the living, and V cocktails to the undead.

Dragos proposed a toast. "To Miss Crisan, the descendant of my deceased wife, Natalia Crisan Dracul. Welcome to *The Natalia*. I look forward to introducing you to your homeland."

*   *   *

The champagne was ice cold and crisp, and I balanced the flute close to my body to control the quiver of my hand. A man and woman came toward us, and I recognized the man as the voivode's brother. The exquisite woman leaned in for the traditional two cheek air kiss greeting.

"Miss Crisan, may I present Her Grace, The Duchess of Transylvania." Dragos stepped to the side. "You have already met my brother, The Duke of Transylvania.

"Miss Crisan, I am excited to finally make your acquaintance," the duchess gushed.

I was momentarily dumbstruck by her beauty. A sculptor's dream, her features deserved to be cast in marble. Her cheekbones rose high under slanted eyes, a violet blue with thick lashes and arched eyebrows. Her skin was perfection; a blemish would have been a sacrilege if found upon her milky complexion. Her golden hair, twisted high upon her head, shone, and her hands, spotless and veinless, were accented by pointed nails varnished a deep shade of red.

"How kind," I replied, managing to sound composed. "This is my dear friend, Arabella Bishop." Arabella submitted to the air kisses and stepped back quickly. Was something amiss?

Olenka poured on the charm.

"How do you do, Miss Bishop? How wonderful it will be to have more ladies to divert the conversation from drab masculine interests." The duchess smiled, revealing teeth appropriate for a toothpaste commercial.

"Do you like music, Miss Crisan?" she asked. "We have a marvelous quartet performing tonight."

"I adore music. What a treat." A tray of canapes was presented to me, and I plucked one of the salmon puff pastries. While I chewed, the other ladies in the room joined our group, and Olenka's witty banter enthralled the gathering.

"The program is a surprise, Miss Crisan. But first we must not forget dinner—you will be hungry." She twirled in a smooth quarter turn toward Dragos and waited. No words were spoken between them, and it was obvious Olenka confidently functioned as his hostess.

He stepped toward me.

"Let's go through to the dining room. We will eat and then move to the music hall." He offered his arm, and I slid my hand over his elbow.

Underneath the fabric, the stiffness and cut of his muscles was apparent.

While the vampires drank from their embellished goblets and chatted about music, fashion, gardens and horses, Arabella and I were served a delectable feast. I was seated to the voivode's left, across from his brother. Arabella sat next to the duke, and Dragos's personal secretary, Marius, was to my left. Although Dragos did not eat a morsel, he watched me closely and commented that the mushrooms were from his property in Romania.

"They are delicious. The risotto is perfect. Don't you think so, Arabella?"

I brought Arabella into the conversation whenever possible. Normally she was a bubbly, active participant no matter the venue, but tonight, she dined behind a quiet veil of reserve. Had I missed a faux pas or snide comment? I would ask when we were alone.

After a creamy vanilla crème brûlée, my favorite, we rose and walked through a row of rooms ending in an intimate amphitheater. Acoustic paneling lined the walls, and red velvet seats faced a raised stage appropriate for a small orchestra. The heavily corded stage drapes were drawn back, and four gilded chairs and music easels awaited the musicians.

"Miss Crisan, if you would oblige me by sitting here," Dragos said, gesturing to the plush seat on his right. "Mr. David Westwood, would you sit to her right. Miss Bishop, to my left, and Mr. Ian Westwood, to her left. Thank you."

As I settled in my chair, I wondered at the high level of protocol. American culture was relaxed, perhaps to a fault. The formality kept Dragos at a discreet distance, which I appreciated.

Once we were seated, the lights dimmed, and the musicians filed onto the stage. They bowed and seated themselves, playing a few notes before launching into the program. The airy opening of Vivaldi's *Four Seasons* filled the hall. Aunt Loretta and I had attended a performance in London at the Barbican Concert Hall. The memory comforted me, and I closed my eyes to savor the notes I knew so well. Aunt Loretta had ensured her love of Vivaldi passed to me. Had Dragos somehow known the cherished memories the music held for me?

The first violin was incredible, and I resolved to inquire about him after the concert.

When the last strains of *Winter* faded away, I jumped to my feet with the rest of the audience, applauding enthusiastically. I felt momentarily elated—and then the unexpected urgency of last night's exit from Jamaica gave me pause. This was my first night aboard *The Natalia*. Had Dragos researched my favorite composers and instructed the musicians to be ready to play? Should I be suspicious or politely inquisitive? It was obvious he wanted to please me. Emboldened by the power of that realization, I asked the billion-dollar question.

"Vivaldi's *Four Seasons* is one of my favorite pieces from childhood. How did you know?" The room became eerily quiet. Was it bad form to question the voivode?

Dragos looked down at me and held my gaze. "I am pleased you enjoyed it; it was my wife's favorite. She often said it depicted the seasons of Romania perfectly, as if Vivaldi had written it while in Transylvania. We listened to it many times, and through its genius I was able to recall the last time I physically experienced the seasons in sunlight.

"We were fortunate to secure Bela Banfalvi and a few others from Budapest Strings," he added. "They will join us for refreshments if you wish."

"Oh, I would love to meet them, thank you." He seemed sincere in his response, and I squashed the doubt lurking in my mind, even though he hadn't actually answered my question.

"We will go to the rooftop lounge. I don't think you have been there yet." Hmmm. Staff must have been reporting on Arabella and my exploration of the ship.

"No, I have not." My friends and the rest of the entourage walked a short distance to the elevator, and Dragos, Arabella, and me ascended to the top deck. Several steps brought us to a glass enclosed, domed bar. The stars glittered and an infinity of blackness surrounded us.

"The night sky is breathtaking," I said. "I've never seen so many stars." The music had been like a hug; although I had questions and concerns, I felt relaxed and less on guard. I slid my arm through Arabella's.

Dragos was quiet for a moment. "The night enhances what the daylight washes away," he said softly.

My response was interrupted by the entrance of the sedate musicians and the rest of our elegant group. After a glass of port, and pleasant conversation with the first violin, I made an apparent misstep.

"Does someone here like Tom Petty? He was a favorite of an ex-boyfriend, and he played *Refuge* on repeat. The song was playing on the deck below mine."

I'd dropped a bombshell. The vampire courtiers went silent, and the lead violin player chuckled.

"Tom Putty? I dislike American country rock. It is rude to force one's musical taste on another. I am more considerate and wear earbuds when I blast Beethoven's *Fifth*."

I observed Dragos discreetly shift his attention from our circle to the table where Olenka dispensed her opinion on an artwork the couple were purchasing. Bogdan looked up, and he and Dragos communicated silently. Bogdan placed his hand over his wife's. I pretended I hadn't noticed the interaction and wisely changed the subject. The response to my innocent comment was intriguing and I wondered what Tom Petty had done to deserve such disapproval.

* * *

Olenka's guest in the Green Room had overstepped, and Bogdan knew he had to get his wife out of the line of fire.

"It is time to retire, don't you think, my dear?" Olenka frowned, an expression she took care to avoid whenever possible. She wasn't finished giving her advice on an upcoming auction in Paris, and Bogdan knew better than to interrupt when her sophisticated opinion was sought by her inferiors. Despite her husband's rudeness, she presented a united front.

"If you wish, my lord. I must confess I am . . . tired." Marius's wife tittered.

"My, you two are like newlyweds. How marvelous to require alone time after so many decades."

The quick escape almost worked. Olenka dropped a deep curtsy and swept an air kiss across her brother-in-law's cheek, and her husband bowed. But before Bogdan could pivot toward the door, Dragos said, "After you walk Olenka back to your room, join me in my study."

The command was demeaning, and Bogdan

was stiff with rage. Once the door of Olenka's bedroom closed behind them he gritted his teeth.

"Tom Petty? What have you brought into our circle? Didn't you explain to him that he was to be invisible?" Olenka removed the diamond choker from her throat with care and considered her possible responses.

Bogdan was no fool, and the new acolyte had misbehaved. There would be hell to pay if the American minion upset Dragos. Manners and breeding mattered to the voivode. She pulled the clips from her hair, and it cascaded over her shoulder in a ripple of liquid gold.

"Darling, I will be very stern when I visit him tonight. In fact, I will drink a bit extra. He will feel unwell tomorrow and will learn his lesson." She wrapped her arms around her husband's neck and pressed her lips to his.

"Dragos will be easier to manage if his relationship continues to progress with Natalie Crisan," he said as he traced his lips down her elegant neck. "She is the key. If he becomes besotted and determined she replace Natalia, the distraction will be useful. He will release his stranglehold on military operations. Your new toy must not disrupt the peace between Dragos and me. The encroachment of the aliens is a considerable threat and requires a united kingdom."

Olenka kissed his neck, and he drew her closer. "Natalie is no Natalia, although her sly compliment paid to the insipid Vivaldi piece touched Dragos," she murmured into his neck. "As to my new courtier —I will visit him now and chastise him. Good luck, my darling. Remember, Dragos knows as well as you do that your alliance is the key to success against the aliens."

He traced his finger down her backbone, resting his palm on her bottom.

"Loyalty is at the core of my relationship with Dragos, my love. Any other sentiment would be suicide."

* * *

"Thank you for a lovely evening, um, Voivode." I sounded awkward at best. In my wildest fantasies I'd never imagined that the royalty I'd meet would be a vampire king and his court. A crash course in protocol was imperative—I would not make a fool of myself in front of this powerful man. "I have never heard *The Four Seasons* performed in such an intimate venue. It was an incredible treat."

"It is my intention to make you accustomed to elevated experiences. Glorious music is certainly one of them." Dragos bowed and my friends said goodnight.

In the sitting room, Ana-Maria had left a pitcher of ice water and a pot of herbal tea. Arabella poured herself a cup of tea and settled in an armchair. I filled a glass with ice-water and took the chair closest to her. I hadn't asked her to provide V cocktails, and the Westwoods talked while we sipped.

"I wonder who was playing Tom Petty," David said. "It seems a weird choice for a Romanian ship with the vampire elite."

"Where are you going with this?" I asked. My question about *Refuge* was apparently a big deal. Did the king despise country rock? Did he object to my reference to a past boyfriend? Or was he annoyed that another guest had disturbed me, the heiress to his wife's estate?

I observed that David and Ian maintained a singular focus on each other, and knew they were having a silent conversation.

"David is being protective, which is understandable." Ian shrugged. "Tom Petty did perform internationally. Maybe the person in the room below you saw him in concert." I sensed disagreement. David was sensitive and would continue to blame himself for putting me at risk. I had to reassure him.

"Hmm. I appreciate your watchfulness," I said. "It did seem a strange choice of music. Oh, and the guy was stark naked. I decided not to mention the nudity to Dragos. I don't want to be responsible for someone being chucked overboard." David gasped and received a stern look from his husband.

I finished my glass of water and poured another. "The chef uses too much salt. Between the sodium and the sea air, I'm going to blow up like a balloon up and my eyelids will swell shut."

"Tell Ana-Maria you need low-salt," Ian said. "She can handle the request directly with the chef without Dragos knowing."

"I'm still stuck on a guy sunbathing naked on *The Natalia*. Was he hot?" Ian smacked David's arm.

"Natalie is keeping the details to herself," Arabella mused. "He must have been impressive." I threw up my hands in mock surrender and wandered to the open sliding door. If I stretched out my hand, could I pull the moon toward me? Dragos had said, 'The night enhances what the daylight washes away.' There was an introspective almost poetic side to the warlord. Could I trust these sensitive reflections or was I being played?

Behind me, David whispered into Ian's ear while they cuddled on the sofa. They would want to spend time alone before retiring. Babysitting me wasn't exactly a romantic honeymoon.

I crossed the room to them.

"Dragos mentioned at dinner that the ship will dock in the Lisbon port, and tomorrow night he wants to review the logistics of flying from Lisbon to Transylvania. I'm going to ask him if I can spend a day sightseeing before we fly to Romania. I'd like to see the Museu Gulbenkian, Rossio Square, and maybe San Jorge Castle. I may need help negotiating, guys. I don't want to give the impression of a lack of cultural curiosity or set the precedent of blind obedience."

David hooted with laughter.

"No one who knows you could accuse you of blind obedience." He rose and stretched. "We'll be happy to assist you in manipulating the voivode." Ian jumped up and steered David to the door.

"Good night, my protectors." I blew them a kiss.

'Night, peeps. Have fun tomorrow." They closed the door behind them, and I locked it.

"Good-night, Nat." Arabella gave me a peck on the cheek and headed toward her bedroom, leaving me to develop my plan of attack for a day of sightseeing in Lisbon.

I had told Ana-Maria not to wait up for me. Contrary to David's comments, I didn't plan on becoming a helpless princess. My maid kept the same hours as any other non-vampire and she needed to sleep. These thoughts ran through my head as I undressed and hung up my gown

Cruising aboard *The Natalia* was my maiden voyage, and I wondered if people became complacent after many cruises. There was an old-fashioned luxury to the slow pace, the sea air, dressing for dinner, and conversing with fellow travelers.

I yearned for one more deep breath of sea air before sliding beneath the silk sheets on the humongous bed. I slid open the balcony door and stepped barefoot onto the outdoor carpet which covered the balcony. The dew from the sea air enveloped me, and beyond the guardrail, a pancake shaped circle of gray fog wafted over the peaks of the rolling ocean. The slap of the water against the side of the ship added a meditative rhythm to our transatlantic passage. Perhaps I could sleep on the balcony one night before we docked in Lisbon. Would it be safe? I'd ask Arabella her opinion tomorrow.

Voices drifted from the balcony below mine. I could not identify the male voice, but the female who berated him was undoubtedly Olenka. The circle of fog maintained its shape and floated closer to the voices—a chill crept down my spine. Olenka's tirade had to be coming from naked Tom Petty guy's room. The fog dropped lower until it was parallel with the balcony. The slider to naked guy's room must have been open. I heard her screech 'obedience', and the murmured response must have displeased her because a crash of something hitting a wall was followed by a loud slap and Olenka's cry of triumph. Then, total silence except for the sound of the ocean's wake against the side of the ship.

I tiptoed backwards over the slider threshold and into my room, sliding the door shut and engaging the lock. Whatever had just transpired in the room below mine wasn't my business, but I would tell Arabella about it in the morning.

CHAPTER SIXTEEN

The frigid air whipped my hair back, and I soared above a winter forest dusted in snow. I didn't flap my arms but glided, riding the wicked currents. Down below, a sprawling mansion was home, and I descended, my landing muffled by a thick blanket of snow.

The familiar bark of a trusted companion jolted me. Stepping onto the porch of the blue house, I reached for the doorknob. . . it hovered beyond my outstretched fingers. My hand slid across a soft surface, and I opened my eyes.

Surrounded in silk on the marshmallow soft mattress, I inhaled deeply, reluctantly abandoning dreamland. Performing my perfected dismount, I grabbed a robe and buzzed Ana-Maria. A brief knock heralded her cheerful face, carrying a tray laden with coffee, orange juice, and a basket of fresh croissants. I followed her into the sitting room and sat on the sofa. Arabella was nowhere in sight.

"Heavens, you anticipated what I want perfectly," I said as she poured a steaming cup of fresh coffee. Arabella suggested I ask her about the wardrobe additions this morning, so I'd waited until we were alone.

"Ana-Maria, I keep forgetting to ask you about the additional clothing in the closets and drawers in my room. I'm a little confused. Can you please explain?"

Her face wore a worried expression.

"I was waiting for you to ask me, Miss. When I packed your clothing in Jamaica, I was instructed to send measurements to the voivode's valet. There is an area of the ship stocked with a large inventory of garments should a guest forget something, like a jacket. Items were pulled from the inventory. Did I miss something?"

"Oh no, you chose well. Thank you, Ana-Maria."

She exhaled in relief.

"Miss, my friends and family call me Ana, except my mother who insists on the Maria."

"Well then, I shall call you Ana. And you must call me Natalie."

Shock resonated on her face, and she blushed.

"I couldn't, Miss. I would get in trouble." Before we could explore the topic further, Arabella arrived dressed and ready for breakfast.

"Care to share your treasure?"

Ana had anticipated my guest and filled a second mug. I gulped down the perfect brew and settled against the sofa pillows.

"I will refill the pot, and when I come back, I will be happy to take your breakfast order if you're ready." She closed the door behind her, and I whispered to Arabella.

"My latest dream was amazing. I was gliding over a forest. It would be so cool to fly." We giggled.

"Flying is a positive sign of working out a problem. I was in the bathroom playing Caribbean music. Did I wake you? I'm sorry. I've never been able to sleep in."

"Don't worry, hon, I didn't wake to Bob Marley. But this really weird thing happened last night in Naked Guy's room." Arabella was my sounding board, always logical and calm.

I told the story of the previous evening with as much detail as I could remember. I described the odd formation of the fog and how it moved like a singular entity.

"The fog was creepy," I said. "And I think Olenka smacked Naked Guy hard—I mean I could hear it from my balcony."

"Vampires can morph into different forms." Arabella returned her coffee cup to the tray and slowly went on. "Bats, wolves, rats; and I have heard of very powerful vampires who are able to travel as a thick mist. Perhaps Dragos is keeping tabs on the guest? If so, Olenka's behavior is not a good look. You're positive it was Olenka's voice?"

"Absolutely. She was furious. Do you think my comment about the music was the cause?" I didn't want to be responsible for the slap.

"Hmm, maybe. It appears Naked Guy is a mystery guest—he wasn't at dinner. And I think the staff is usually housed on a deck below the water line. If he's Olenka's guest . . . I don't know." Arabella stopped mid-sentence when Ana returned with another pot of coffee and left with our breakfast requests. We sipped in silence for a few minutes.

"Arabella, was something bothering you at dinner last night? You seemed distracted."

Arabella cradled her empty cup in her hands and knitted her brow. "I wasn't going to mention it unless I noticed it again, but your story about Olenka yelling at Naked Guy has changed my mind." She sighed. "Olenka has bad energy. Evil energy. Her smile and her beauty hide a malevolent nature. She couldn't take her eyes off the ruby ring. Last night's drama confirms my fear that she is dangerous."

"My friend, you are sensitive to jealousies and threats, and I appreciate the warning. She didn't comment on the ring, which is odd since she has stated how close she and Natalia were. I'll be less nervous tonight, and I'll pay closer attention, especially since I know she was in Naked Guy's room."

Ana returned with our breakfast, and while we ate, we discussed what amusement we would try.

"Shuffleboard," I said. "Maybe I'll have a chance."

"Nat, did I ever tell you I was on my high school shuffleboard team?"

"I'm determined to find a sport I can beat you at." Arabella could place a shuffleboard disc like a pro. If I couldn't beat her at sports, I'd beat her talking smack.

"How about skeet shooting? Jenga? Pick-up sticks? Hopping backward on one foot?" My stomach hurt from laughing and we raced back to our suite. Lunch was waiting on the balcony, and I put on the macramé bikini I'd bought in Jamaica. Stretching out on a lounge chair next to Arabella, I meditated for a few minutes. I'd gotten into a regular habit of yoga and meditation at home, and it helped with worry and the anxiety I'd felt after my break-up. A short meditation also became my daily pre-writing routine. There was no reason I couldn't return to my practice, and to the manuscript. I had plenty of free time.

"What I need is a yoga class," I said. "I'm not

centered. Should I ask Dragos about it tonight? Maybe someone on the ship is a yoga instructor."

Arabella put down the book she was reading.

"Dragos has tried to anticipate your comfort," she said. "He might be annoyed if he thought staff hadn't done proper research on your hobbies."

"Hmm, good point. I'm not sure he would react well to a mistake or oversight. I'll ask Ana if she knows of a yoga instructor on the ship. I've decided to ask Ana about her family's relationship to Dragos. If they are mortal, it's a good sign that they trust Dragos with their daughter."

Arabella stuck a bookmark in her novel and swung her legs off the lounge chair. "Ana is a sweet woman. If Dragos's promise of protection is valued by Ana's family that is a checkmark in his favor."

The afternoon sun's heat had worn me out and a nap in the cool comfort of my bed would prepare me for another late night with Dragos's court. I stood.

"I'm going to lie down," I said. "I decided on the red gown this evening, a strong color for negotiating an extra day in Lisbon."

"Great idea. See you in a few." Arabella shuffled off to her room and I padded barefoot to my bedroom and lay down on top of the silky comforter on the bed. I drifted, but my curiosity regarding Ana's situation, blocked the deep nap I'd sought. After two hours of tossing and turning, I pressed the buzzer on my nightstand.

Ana entered bearing a tray of cut-up fruit and a frosted pitcher of ice-water. She filled a tall glass and handed it to me.

"Thank you, Ana." I drank, wondering how to bring up her current employment and how she had been hired. She stood, patiently waiting, aware there was a reason she had been summoned.

"Ana, I don't want to appear nosy, but I am confused. You aren't a vampire. How did you find out about the maid job and how do you keep yourself safe on a ship filled with vampires?" I pointed to a chair, and she sat, folding her hands in her lap.

"I am glad you asked. My family has taken care of the Dracul stable for decades, perhaps centuries. You could call us horse whispers. My family is not undead and is protected by His Majesty. The voivode asked my father if he would permit me to travel with him, and my father agreed. The pay is excellent, and I have a wonderful apartment across the hall from you. The other staff are jealous, but they are not responsible for your comfort, which was the voivode's uppermost concern. You are gentle and kind, so the job is easy."

I refilled my glass and relocated from the bed to a chair close to her.

"Your father trusts Dragos with your safety. That says a lot." Ana smiled.

"As an additional precaution, I have an ointment from a gypsy my grandmother knew. One dot on my neck, and it absorbs quickly. The potion is powerful. Vampires keep their distance." Interesting. I would have to ask David and Ian if they noticed Ana wearing anti-vampire ointment.

"I hope you don't think I'm nosy."

"No, Miss, not at all. My parents were hoping I could travel before settling down with my fiancé. I am returning to the local university in the fall. I am majoring in languages. I speak five; English, Romanian, French, Spanish, and I'm learning Portuguese." I sat bolt upright. Serendipity?

"Excellent! We dock in Lisbon in two days. How about a day spent touring with me and Arabella? Wouldn't that be fun?"

Excitement lit up Ana's face.

"I would be grateful to see Lisbon and practice my Portuguese. Thank you!" Treating Ana to a tour of Lisbon made me feel less guilty about prying into her reason for being on *The Natalia*.

Arabella knocked on the door, and I called, "Come in!" Ana left us, and I filled Arabella in on my invitation to Ana and her prodigious language skills. Now all I had to do was persuade Dragos.

"Lisbon, here we come," Arabella cheered. "The stars are aligned, and the only missing piece is Dragos's blessing. The high-stakes negotiations will require charming Natalie. Let's work on your talking points."

"Charming it is. I will hide my independent

core and captivate him with my cultural curiosity. Talking points sounds like a TED talk."

"Exactly, Nat. I listened to a podcast recently called How to Get What You Want In Ten Easy Steps. Pretend I'm Dragos."

"Should I bat my eyelashes or whine in a little girl's voice?" Arabella was pushing it. I didn't think it was necessary to prepare as if Dragos and I were debating. I exhaled impatiently.

Arabella rose and walked toward the door to the sitting room.

"Fine. I can see you aren't taking me seriously. Do you want to see Lisbon or not?" Wow. Arabella was being bossy. Did a visit to Lisbon mean as much to her as it did to me? She had placed my welfare and safety before remaining with her family in Jamaica. I was being pettish.

"Sorry, you're right," I said. "A few clear reasons will convince Dragos I'm not catching the next plane to America. I wonder what he would do if I tried to escape." Arabella nodded and returned to her chair.

"We must make him see the side trip as another show of his trustworthiness and appreciation for your position as Natalia's heir. Maybe you start by saying . . ." From my chair I admired the vase of white calla lilies, my favorite flower, on the table to Arabella's right. They hadn't been there yesterday. Dragos had done his research.

Arabella's voice receded.

I was tethered to Dragos through Natalia's will. I couldn't contemplate his anger if I was to renege on our agreement. But cancel it I would if he nixed a girl's trip in Lisbon.

* * *

Bogdan scanned the drawing room of *The Natalia* and congratulated himself for the millionth time on his good fortune.

In a room of beautiful women, Olenka eclipsed the fairest, rendering feeble the synonyms a poet might use, when he could simply utter 'magnificent.' His wife preferred the word, as did her husband, who watched proudly as she outshone the admirers surrounding her. She was his greatest possession, the jewel with no equal in the vampire world.

Her features, cut like the facets of a precious gemstone, became more extraordinary with age. Her cheekbones were legendary, and the spectacular ruby earring which dangled from her perfect earlobes had been payment for the protection given to a debt-ridden landowner. Olenka adored rubies, and he knew she coveted the ruby parure his brother had secured for Natalia.

Across the room, Olenka's gaiety enchanted him. Her laugh's charming tone drew outliers to her orbit, and he enjoyed observing the pull of her magnetism. If their eyes chanced to meet across a crowded room, she would secretly acknowledge his admiration with a touch of a fine-boned finger to her left earlobe.

The dinner gong sounded and broke his reverie.

He could not abide the dinner gong used in fashionable aristocratic homes. A gong reminded him of war, and he wished his brother understood his aversion to the sound and the horrible memories it conjured. Perhaps when the American became the voivode's hostess, Olenka could suggest it.

The peace he had brokered with his brother was critical and allowed him to concentrate on his favorite hobby—spoiling his wife.

The woman who enthralled him, the duchess clothed in finery and decked in jewels, was a different person from the unkempt young woman he had stumbled over, asleep in his wood. Dirty and near starvation, he had leaned closer for a taste of her sweet blood. Her eyes flew open, a bright violet blue unlike any shade he had ever seen. It was love at first sight, and he had to have her.

This miraculous woman, unlike dozens before her, had continued to captivate him. He watched her dazzle a cranky general in his army, and he replayed his luck in finding her before her purity was spoiled.

In the wood the first night, she drew back, hugging the ragged shawl around her shivering shoulders.

"What is your name?" He had tried not to sound gruff, but she shuddered.

"Olenka," she whispered. "The villagers burned us out of our home."

One of his guards had reported to him of the burning of witches in the village.

"Are you a witch? Tell the truth." The innocence of her expression when she spoke was entrancing.

She raised her chin and clutched a burlap sack to her chest. "The women in my family are witches. Witches are revered when we save a life and hunted and burned when an illness strikes a village. My mother and grandmother were blamed for the death of the mayor's son. I know my family is dead. I hid in the forest where the villagers would not track me because they believe the wood is evil. I am alone in the world, sir."

"This is my land. If you are a homeless orphan, you are not safe in the forest." He picked up Olenka and carried her to a hunting lodge hidden behind a thicket of trees. Decades of smoke stained the roof timbers and deer trophies covered every inch of the interior walls. He dismissed a servant and placed a tray of bread, cheese, and wine before her. She stuffed her mouth while he stared.

"You are the most beautiful woman I have ever seen. What is in your carryall, Olenka?"

"The family bible of healing spells, tinctures, and incantations. My mother gave it to me and pushed me out the back door when she saw the villagers approaching with torches. My grandmother barricaded the front door while my mother kissed my forehead and whispered, 'Run.'"

"Ah. My guard reported there is a reward for the missing daughter. This is you?" Bogdan scrutinized the young witch. "You are eating too fast."

"How do you know about the reward?" Her eyes filled with tears. "Please don't turn me in."

Bogdan reached forward and pushed a goblet of wine toward her.

"I will not turn you in, but sunrise is imminent, and we must return to my castle. You will be safe there. Come." Fear flashed across her face, and he knew that Olenka realized who he was. He knew the villagers spun tales of the bloody wars fought by the powerful vampire brothers who lived in the castles on top of the mountain. He stretched out his hand and she took it meekly.

They mounted an immense horse, Olenka in back, her arms circled around Bogdan's waist.

"Hold on tightly."

* * *

Olenka felt the pull of Bogdan's stare across the drawing room and preened inwardly at her continued power over him. Slowly, with a seductive caress, she traced a fine-boned index finger up her neck, over her ear, and along the setting of the priceless ruby drop earrings. The response, a secret sign of their lustful alliance, aroused them both; the seductress's promise of physical pleasure yet to come.

Olenka owed Bogdan her life, but she'd paid her tab long ago. The night he had whisked her onto his horse she had gripped his waist in fear. He was the only hope she had of avoiding the horror of her mother and grandmother's murders. What did this mysterious man want of her? Was he one of the two fabled vampires whose castles looked down upon the village where she had been born?

He had commanded her to hold on tightly, riding with a frenzied pace through forest paths, jumping his steed over rotting stumps. Cloaked riders joined them from behind the trees as they galloped higher and higher. The pounding of horses hooves and the cry of night creatures were a cacophony of foreign music, and she tightened her grip around his waist. She had never been this close to a man, her mother had protected her innocence, running several suitors off their property. Olenka knew she was on her own; Mother could no longer protect her.

They passed through a towering iron gate and there before her, the hulk of a stone castle loomed, dark and foreboding. Bogdan drew his horse to the front door and dismounted and lifted her from the saddle.

"Follow me quickly, Olenka." He'd grabbed her hand and dragged her up the steps he took two at a time. His ice-cold hand squeezed her delicate one, and they hurried through a massive hallway with a vaulted ceiling and up a soaring staircase to a wide landing.

On the right, they entered a drawing room, more cheerful than the dreary starkness of the reception hall. A fire roared in a black marble fireplace. The room was masculine, with carpets, heavy dark wood furniture, and paintings of horses and huntsmen. Chilled from the brisk ride to the castle, Olenka ran to the fireplace and held out her hands. Bogdan reached for a black goblet on a small table and drank deeply.

"I do not have enough time to enjoy your company this evening, Olenka. I must return to my resting place. My servants will care for you. You will be safe; you have been marked as my own. We will talk tomorrow." He bowed and exited with great haste. From the shadows, a man stepped forward.

"Miss, if you follow me, I will bring you to your room. Your maid awaits." Olenka had no choice but to do as she was told, and she trailed behind the stiff back of the butler. He stopped at a gleaming ornately carved door, opened it, and stepped to the side to let Olenka enter. The ragged orphan, momentarily dazed, breathed in a splendor beyond her wildest dreams. Her head swiveled right and left, awestruck by the luxury of the sumptuous bedroom. An ancient woman dressed in a grey shift which matched her pallor, stepped forward and curtsied. Olenka dropped her carryall and cautiously tiptoed to the immense canopy bed hung with corded damask. Her entire family could have slept comfortably in the bed. It could be her bed, or if the vampire desired her, their bed.

She needed protection and her decision was immediate. If the vampire who had saved her was lord of the castle, she would marry him and become a vampire. He would introduce her to a life filled with luxury and pleasure, and she would gladly surrender her soul. She pivoted from the bed and addressed the waiting maid.

"I would like a bath."

CHAPTER SEVENTEEN

After dinner that second evening, we were once again entertained by the superb quartet, this time performing a selection of pieces by Debussy and Ravel. The impressionistic music was complicated to follow, and my attention drifted. To my left, Dragos maintained a military posture throughout the performance, his palms resting on his thighs. The emotion of the music rose and fell, and I fought to focus on it and not overthink my plan for a sightseeing adventure in Lisbon.

When the concert was over, Dragos dismissed everyone except me and my friends.

"Shall we proceed to my study? I assume the Westwoods will be joining us?" He turned to Arabella. "And you, Miss Bishop?"

"Thank you, sir, but I would like to return to my room." She winked at me. We'd rehearsed how I would tell Dragos I wanted to tour Lisbon, and had agreed it might be better if he didn't feel outnumbered.

"I'll take you," Ian said. "David, you go with Natalie."

I was glad Arabella wasn't traveling the halls of *The Natalia* unaccompanied. We joined Marius in Dragos's study at a circular conference table, and he passed out several copies of legal documents.

"We will wait for Mr. Westwood to return before we begin," Dragos said. I took a deep breath and boldly scanned the room. You can tell a lot about a person by the books they read and the ornaments they surround themselves with in their private space. On the wall behind the mammoth desk, a shield with the Dracul crest centered an impressive collection of polished silver swords and gruesome weapons. I declined the port I was offered and asked for water. Ian returned quickly, and Marius opened the discussion.

"Miss Crisan, I have prepared copies of the addendums of the Last Will and Testament of Her Majesty Natalia Crisan Dracul for your records. I have also listed separately the items not mentioned in the will. As you know, your receipt of these items is dependent upon your residing in Romania for one year. No items, or currency, can be transferred out of the country. We wish to protect the heritage of our great country."

I raised my hand to display Natalia's ring.

"Yet, I was given the ruby ring of my ancestor.

In Jamaica. You have not explained how I am related to Natalia. I am assuming because of my last name we are related on my father's side?"

"You are correct," Dragos said. "Male ancestors were dominant, and that is how you retain the name of Crisan. We are researching and assembling a family tree for you, but that will take some time. I hope you will be patient; we want it to be accurate. Natalia's heir, the heir to my kingdom was hidden as was his son."

The answer sounded plausible. A family tree would answer a lot of questions Aunt Loretta had deflected. Was she protecting me or did she not know the answers?

"A family tree would be marvelous, but you haven't answered my question about the ruby ring. If I do not agree to fulfill the contract, will I have to return it?"

Had it not occurred to these powerful men that I might refuse my inheritance? Dragos set his jaw.

"Once you have fulfilled the terms of the contract, you are free to travel wherever you please with the ruby ring. However, it is a priceless gem and historical artifact. It would be foolish to walk about without security while wearing it." His eyes dropped to my hand, where the massive ruby glowed in the lowlight of the study. "I am glad you are wearing it. It suits you." Ian cleared his throat.

"Voivode, if we can proceed with Natalie's concerns," he said. Dragos nodded and Ian continued. "What type of security will Natalie have? And who will be allowed to enter her home in Transylvania?" David opened a small notebook, and with pen poised, awaited these crucial answers.

"Miss Crisan's safety is of the utmost importance. Security guards will be stationed day and night on her property. Security cameras are installed around the property, monitored twenty-four hours per day. There are no blind-spots. The staff was vetted with my final approval. Ana will be returning to university in the fall, but we will find a suitable replacement."

"I have no say in my security detail?" I asked.

Dragos pursed his lips.

"The men and women responsible for you are my employees. If you are uncomfortable with anyone or anything seems . . ." He searched for the correct word. ". . . odd, let me know immediately."

"Listen carefully, Miss Crisan. No vampires other than David and Ian should be invited into your home. Vampires require an invitation to cross the threshold of the Refuge Bleue because you own it. This is different from the mansion in Jamaica because you did not own the home. I understand you protected yourself with garlic boughs, an excellent precaution. Your home is protected from other dark creatures who attempt entry. We have developed sensors to alert us to alien trespassers. You do not have to fear Slade Suit or his slimy followers. Your in-house staff is limited to only those necessary to maintain your residence, and they have also been thoroughly checked."

Woah, he'd thought of everything, including protection from his arch enemy, Slade Suit. David and Ian exchanged glances.

"Basically, if I flush a toilet, the entire security staff will know? Are there cameras inside the house?"

David snickered and Ian shot him a stern reprimand. Dragos maintained his reserve. Our misbehavior had no effect on him or his secretary.

"Excellent question," he said. "There are no cameras inside your home. There is a security panel inside your bedroom that controls the main house alarm and a separate motion detection network on the second floor, where the music room, guest suite, and your bedroom and dressing room reside. There is also a main alarm panel on the first floor, but it does not control the second-floor motion detection. Some of the artwork is attached to the main house alarm. When you move in, we can review the security to ensure you feel it is adequate." Dragos sat ramrod straight, and he drummed the fingers of his right hand in a repetitive pattern which reminded me of soldiers on parade. Was this his tell? We weren't playing poker, but it was time for me to go all in.

"I have a small request," I said. "I understand we will be docking in Porto de Lisboa in two days' time. I would be grateful for a day to explore the city with Arabella and Ana, who is studying Portuguese at university. Can this be arranged?"

Dragos relaxed slightly in his chair and folded his hands.

"I anticipated your request, Miss Crisan. I have reserved several automobiles for you, and security has been awaiting my direction. Let Marius know what attractions you would like to visit. He will see to a tour and full access."

Why had the ease of his agreement annoyed me? Did he maneuver the people in his life like pawns on a chess board? I blurted before I played the question in my head.

"Do you play chess, Voivode?" The simple question produced a bizarre effect. Dragos and I locked eyes, and I would not give him the satisfaction of dropping my gaze. Around us, the room receded as if a camera aperture had opened, blurring the periphery of the space. Dragos and I were alone. The heat of resentment rose in my body. He had outmaneuvered me, still controlling with ease my journey to his castle. His anticipation of my desire to tour Lisbon was maddening. Even more annoying was the calm, contemplative expression on his face as he rubbed his thumb across his lower lip.

"I enjoy a good game of chess. Do you play?"

I pushed my irritation aside.

"I played with my Aunt Loretta. She was quite good. It took me years to beat her."

"Then I look forward to a game when we reach Romania." A knock at the door admitted Bogdan. Dragos frowned and got to his feet.

"Please excuse the abrupt end of our meeting. My brother and I have important matters to discuss. Review the documents at your leisure and formulate any additional questions. I bid you good evening." He bowed and his valet escorted us to the hallway. The door closed firmly behind Bogdan.

The burgundy carpet of the ship's hallway muffled the sound of David, Ian, and my retreating footsteps. I had nearly lost my temper with the king of the vampires, and I was embarrassed at my lack of self-control. Dragos had, so far, been a perfect host. Arabella had told me to trust my instincts; I was convinced that I was at the center of a power struggle.

"What's with the 'Do you play chess, Voivode' question? Were you baiting him?" David knew me too well to have missed my tone. Perhaps I had been rude, and I stalled and pretended to admire the artwork on the walls as we walked back to my suite.

When we were inside my sitting room I answered.

"You're right, I was baiting him a bit. It is infuriating that he is always one step ahead of me. How did he know that I'd ask to tour Lisbon?" Arabella came out of her bedroom in her pajamas and robe, carrying a mug of tea.

"What did Dragos say about Lisbon?" She took a big slurp of her tea.

I had pulled out the pins holding my updo and raked my fingers through my hair.

"He had already made plans for cars and a tour guide. Does he have the sitting room bugged?" Do we need a security sweep?" I was getting riled up again. What was wrong with me?

"Dragos is a brilliant tactician," Ian said. "He has survived as king because he observes and anticipates the moves of his rivals. In your case, he is determined for you to be comfortable and entertained. I think his intentions are honorable, Nat."

Honorable. Ian was logical and perceptive. I looked at David.

"I am not discounting your feelings, hon," David said. "But maybe dial it back a bit. We're here to protect you. And we know for a fact that the entire ship has been put on high alert to make every day your best day ever."

"I feel like I'm the birthday girl at The Magic Kingdom."

"You are Dragos's honored guest," Ian said. "Let's have fun with it. Seriously, I think he would lasso the moon if you asked him."

After David and Ian had left and Arabella had once again retired to her bedroom, I slipped onto the balcony and made myself comfortable on the huge lounge outside my sliding door. The moon's reflection rippled on the inky ocean and the sky was strewn with a necklace of stars. I had always been an early to bed gal, preferring the glow of the sun to the mystery of the moon. But as I lay there, listening to the silence broken only by the sea washing against the side of the ship, I admitted to myself that the night had its advantages.

I slept.

CHAPTER EIGHTEEN

Dragos picked up the exquisite miniature portrait of Natalia from his desk. She had been an amazing woman, and as queen consort had served his kingdom well. Only once had angry words come between them. But her master plan had proved correct. Natalia's insistence in the face of his stubbornness had produced a son and heir who's descendent was safe and traveling to Romania on Dragos's ship. Even after a century, the memory of the conversation and his capitulation to her logic annoyed him.

As was their habit, they had bathed together, the warm water lapping over Dragos as Natalia leaned back into his arms. His fingers massaged the lavender shampoo into her scalp; slowly, seductively, the firm pressure following the bones of her skull in a lather of foreplay. His hands were strong, and with practiced skill they knew where to rub and kneed as they moved down to the nape of her neck.

His attention to detail showed his care and desire, but the same loving hands could be cruel, meeting out harsh discipline when necessary. He knew she had heard stories of the punishments exacted upon those who displeased him. His loyal Natalia refused to believe the tales and banished the messenger of the rumors. It was gossip; evil words designed to separate them, she had said.

"My darling, I know you could never be the cold-hearted villain of the horrible stories," she'd whispered in his ear. Her loyalty to him had been absolute.

Dragos was her angel, and his hands knew her body from her scalp to her toes. Natalia moaned softly when he pressed the stress knot on her left shoulder. He alone succeeded in eliminating it, kneading it firmly until it released and gave way to tender kisses. She tilted her head back, and he poured a cascade of water and then another over the thick mane he adored. As wet and fragrant as the flowers growing in their garden, she would turn and settle in his muscled arms.

The deep tub of heated water was their personal space. Only in this claw-foot tub in front of a roaring fire did his skin absorb the warmth drained from him centuries earlier. Yet, as he held her in his arms, he knew she sensed his displeasure.

There was one subject on which they disagreed, and Natalia was intent on having her way.

In the past, if Natalia desired something she had only to ask. Land, jewels, gowns, Arabian horses—she had only to hint, and it was hers. Her latest obsession was a different matter. She ached to welcome motherhood and produce Dragos's heir. Her own baby to rock in her arms. Creating life, however, was impossible for a vampire. The physical pleasure she and Dragos enjoyed could not bring a child into their world.

Dragos's obstinacy had driven a wedge between them.

"There is only one way for me to get pregnant, and I have devised a plan," she said. "It is no difference than breeding horses, Dragos. I require a stud for the job, the same way I chose an animal to impregnate my adored broodmare."

For her plan to proceed, however, Dragos's ego would have to accept her planned infidelity. The sperm donor, a young soldier who served on the human side of the regiment, waited in his study. He was handsome, smart, and willing. How had she chosen him? Had she fluttered her eyelashes and brushed against his body? The thought filled him with rage.

Natalia traced her lower lip against Dragos's and then pulled back to stare deeply into his eyes. He drew her closer, firmly kissing her on the mouth. She responded passionately, bringing him to the brink of surrender. When the kiss ended, he searched her pleading eyes. Could there be a minute chance of bridging his barricade of pride for his beloved queen?

"Pleeease darling. I can predict my cycle exactly and we will only couple once," she begged. "If the pregnancy does not happen, then it was not meant to be. You know how I adore you, worship you, love you with every ounce of my life and breath. I desire no other man, but I, we, don't have a choice. Can't you see that the child will be ours to raise and love? You will have an heir." She'd caressed his cheek and continued her plea.

"We've discussed this so many times, and I give you my solemn vow that when the baby reaches adulthood, I will join you as a vampire and we will spend eternity together."

Dragos had pushed her gently away and stepped from the tub. He dried himself and dressed in his military uniform. There was to be a secret meeting that evening and he would inspect the soldier she had chosen in spite of his disapproval. The soldier was a strapping young man. Hatred filled Dragos's heart. He burned with jealousy at the thought of the carnal act that would place the interloper's seed in her womb. Could he permit the intimacy? He pivoted to her as she reclined in the tub.

"Natalia, I have an important meeting. When I return, if you are awake, we will resume this conversation. We both have much to consider." He turned and exited with the proud posture of one who led thousands of men.

Dragos descended the grand staircase and marched to his study where the soldier was waiting. Natalia had asked his permission, an action which ran contrary to her pithy refrain that it was easier to ask for forgiveness than permission. He had banished the soldier to the Russian front after the carnal act was completed, where the biological father of his son had distinguished himself in battle before losing his life in a freak accident.

Dragos replaced Natalia's portrait on his desk and rose. It was time to rest, but he had much to consider. He had never investigated the soldier's death, in hindsight a costly error. Perhaps if he had put his ego aside, Natalia would not have paid for his mistake with her life.

CHAPTER NINETEEN

I awoke at nine o'clock.

The intense sun glittered from a cerulean sky over a sea of navy blue, bursting color like the vivid blues used by Henri Matisse, my favorite Impressionist painter. Stepping onto the balcony, I wondered what area of the ship Arabella and I should explore.

A loud crash came from the deck below, and I leaned over the railing to see if the mysterious man who had incurred Olenka's wrath had resurfaced. The railing was slick with moisture, my hands slipped, and my body was flung forward. Strong hands grabbed me from behind. If Ana hadn't arrived to check on me, I might have toppled into the ocean. She sat me down in a deck chair.

"Miss Crisan, are you alright?" I put my head between my knees. Finally, I found my voice.

"Ana, you saved my life. I leaned over too far. Thank you."

"Can I get you something? Water? Coffee?"

"Coffee, please." She sprinted into the bedroom and returned with a mug of her amazing coffee. It was hot, and I sipped loudly, willing the coffee to clear the vision etched in my brain.

A few minutes passed, and I felt my breathing stabilize. I wanted to doubt what I had seen on the balcony below mine, but . . .

"Ana, what do you know about the man who is in the room below mine?"

She averted her eyes.

"I am not permitted on the deck. Dotia, the duchess's maid, told me he is a special guest of her employer. He hasn't left his cabin. Only Dotia and the duchess have visited him."

"Who else is on the deck?"

"The quartet is at the other end of the ship. The man in the Green Room is alone on this end."

I made a snap decision. Arabella would have talked sense into me, but I had to know if what I'd seen was true.

"Ana, I am going to change, and then I am going down to the Green Room. If anyone asks you had no idea I was exploring that deck. Okay?"

Ana blanched.

"I cannot stop you, Miss. Please be careful. I have heard stories about, well, Dotia had a bruise on her face, and it lasted for a week."

Poor Dotia. I had seen her scurrying next to the wall like a frightened mouse. Who would have hit the vulnerable young woman?

I changed into jeans, a top, and a black hoodie. Arabella hadn't poked her head in like she normally did; she was probably power walking around the ship. I asked Ana to tell her I was sleeping in. I tucked the hood tightly around my face and gave her a thumbs up.

I took a left out of my room, and at the emergency stairs at the end of the hallway, descended to the lower level. Three doors down on the left, poor Dotia snored in a straight-back chair. Hair askew, she needed a meal and obviously a good night's sleep. I tiptoed past her to the door marked Green Room and tried the handle. The door was unlocked, and I slipped in silently, closing it softly behind me. I hadn't been hallucinating when I'd nearly fallen overboard.

"Hello, Natalie. Fancy meeting you here." Mike Endicott, my ex-boyfriend, lounged on an upholstered chair, feet resting comfortably on an ottoman.

The Green Room was an apt description for the layers of verdant color on the walls, fitted carpet, and bedspread. The green was punctuated by expensive mahogany furniture, gleaming under a fresh coat of beeswax. The room reeked of old money, exactly the kind of luxury Mike admired.

Mike's pale complexion contrasted with the

deep tones of his elegant ensemble, an homage to Cary Grant. A Hermès equestrian scarf was tied around his neck. He didn't get up.

"Mike, what the heck are you doing here?" It was a redundant question—the scarf at his neck told me what he'd done. But why?

"Darling, there's a coffee maker in the bathroom. Is it rude if I ask a guest to make her own refreshment? As you can see, I'm under the weather."

"Sure. Then you're going to tell me what is going on."

Despite how shabbily Mike had treated me, he looked ill, so I brewed coffee and brought the pot with me. I poured his, adding a dash of milk, and handed it to him. He cradled it with trembling fingers, and I took the closest chair.

"Thanks, dearest Nat. You know, you were the best thing that ever happened to me." A pain shot through my heart. Why should the words of a cheating ex-boyfriend who humiliated me affect me? Mike drank and I waited for an explanation.

"Nat, I wasn't honest with you about Alix, and I'm truly sorry for the hurt I caused you." His back was to the open sliders, and I scanned his face for the narcissist I had loved. He took another sip of his coffee and continued, "I took your love for granted, but I hope we can be friends. It seems we've ended up in the same social circle."

"Are you stalking me?" I couldn't help but

accuse him. "Did you follow me to Jamaica? How did you know I was on this ship?" He set his coffee cup on the table next to him and adjusted his scarf.

"Hon, I'm sick. Right before I left you, I started feeling weird. Like I was drugged. Tremors in my legs, weakness in my hands. After I nearly dropped Alix in the dance competition, I went to a specialist at the suggestion of my doctor. I have a neurological disease with a long name. There is no cure, and it has a rapid onset. I could be in a wheelchair in a couple of months." How had I not noticed these symptoms? Why hadn't he asked for my help?

"The night after I got the death sentence, I was leaning on the bar at Ryan's place, on my way to tying on a good one, when a gorgeous blonde woman slides up to me. She knew about my unfortunate health problem and claimed she could offer a solution. A solution? I was all in. We left the bar together, and she took me back to her swanky penthouse apartment. Her name is Selena Sidwell."

"OMG, is Selena on *The Natalia*? Is she making you a vampire? Mike, she hates me, she's taking her revenge on you." Mike snickered. Selena Sidwell was Slade Suit's ex-girlfriend—ex because of me.

"I am never a victim, Nat, you should know better than anyone." He smirked, the old Mike briefly surfacing. "And it amazes me that the woman I thought was the pinnacle of naïve would be on *The Natalia* hanging with aristocratic vampires." He wagged his finger at me and although the insult annoyed me, I let him continue.

"Selena explained she was an agent for a very rich powerful vampire. Royalty. It turns out that the vampire is the Duchess of Transylvania, known to many as Olenka the magnificent leech who you are socializing with each evening. Selena passed my resume to the number one agent." He adjusted his neckerchief.

"Olenka has ceremonies where several mortal humans submit to a little bit of bloodletting. All voluntary, supposedly, and the titillation to me—the main event. Olenka will drink my blood and then reverse the process, giving me an infusion of her own ancient blood. I will become a vampire and live with her in her fabulous castle until she releases me into society. I will be very wealthy and super popular." Mike leered at me. He had always needed the upper hand when we were together. Did Dragos know about these ceremonies? When was this taking place? My head was spinning.

"Mike, have you gotten second opinions on your medical condition? I've come into money—long story—and I'd be happy to help you. If what you were told about these ceremonies is true, then Selena and Olenka are malevolent. Please don't do this."

Mike chuckled.

"And Dragos is a monk? Your dance partner, David what's his name from the tango competition is a vampire, too. That's cheating, you know. He's had decades to practice." The coffee had perked him up and he was enjoying himself. There was a knock at the door and Mike yelled.

"Do not enter! Do you hear?" A sob could be heard from the other side of the door.

"Nat, go lock the door. Secure the deadbolt." I did as I was told. Someone was weeping loudly in the hallway.

"It's Dotia, she's in trouble," Mike said. "The duchess won't be pleased I had a visitor. I'm her cherished prize. If Olenka finds out the visitor was Dragos's 'honored guest,' well, I can't be responsible for other people's problems. I have enough of my own." His eyes were bright with anticipation of Dotia's punishment. My concern for Dotia could be addressed later; I had to persuade Mike to reconsider his decision.

"Mike, be honest with me. You want to be a vampire?" He shrugged.

"I don't want to be a cripple. I'm not strong enough to handle the blow to my ego. The duchess has promised me eternal life, riches, and access to the elite of the vampire world. She requires absolute loyalty and obedience. The stunning Olenka confined me to this lavish room, but she did not forbid me to receive guests. She forbade me to blast my music. I am here for her . . . indulgence. Be careful, my darling. I don't think she likes you."

"Thanks for the warning." What else could I add? He'd made up his mind.

Mike watched me with a fond expression I barely remembered from the early days of our dating. "You haven't asked me why I'm onboard *The Natalia*?" Goodness, did I want to know? I sighed.

"When we were hanging at Selena's place, she was working a full court press," he continued. "She was drinking from this black goblet she filled from a pitcher in the refrigerator, and she got a bit tipsy. She changed the subject and started raving about a woman on board *The Natalia* who was the long-lost heir of Dragos's wife. 'Wait until the mousey boyfriend thief gets to Romania and sees the pile Dragos lives in. She'll be undead before you can say Renfield.' You know, Nat, since we split, your fortune has swirled upward and mine plopped into the garbage can. Because of my deteriorating health, I couldn't handle my clients at the real estate office—I quit before they fired me. I have to admit I wish I'd never left you."

I'd heard enough. He'd broken my heart and now he was refusing my help. It figured. Money, power, and the promise of a life of luxury had blinded him to what he would become.

"Well, you did dump me; rudely, I might add. My offer of financial help stands. I would not want to be beholden to Selena or Olenka."

"Precious, the vampires have united in a mission

to retain their wealth and supremacy. Selena told me there are powerful aliens determined to usurp the vampire hierarchy, and alliances are forming. Sides must be chosen. Whose side are you on, Natalie?"

Without a word, I marched to the door. In the corridor outside his room, I froze in front of an ashen Dotia. Her tear-stained face confirmed my suspicion that it was she who had knocked and been driven from the door. I patted her shoulder and trotted down the hall to the staircase. I hoped she'd be okay. Mike had clearly accepted the harsh realities of the vampire world. By traveling with Dragos and his inner circle to Romania, had I unwittingly chosen sides?

Arabella was showered and waiting for me in the suite, absorbed in the latest Donna Leon mystery. I was afraid to tell her Mike Endicott was the naked guy who had blasted Tom Petty, and she didn't ask where I'd been. My rash solo visit might have repercussions, both for Mike and poor Dotia. I should have sought Arabella's opinion, but it was too late for self-recrimination.

"Ana gave me directions to a library," I said. "She knows one of the stewards who practices yoga, but not if they're certified. She'll let me know when we get back."

The ship's guest library was a ten-minute walk from our deck. Fitted bookshelves housed an impressive collection of classic novels, poetry, history, biographies, and a few modern best-sellers. In the corner, a window seat boasted a fabulous view of the ocean. Here and there deeply cushioned armchairs encouraged the visitors to relax in the solitude with an old or new story. The rich smell of leather-bound books added to the aura of relaxation.

I chose a comprehensive history of Romania and set it aside. *The Wind in the Willows* caught my eye. I pulled it down from the shelf and a piece of paper floated to the floor. I retrieved it and read, *"Aliens will triumph. Be forewarned."* How peculiar and unsettling after my conversation with Mike.

"Arabella, look what was in my book." I handed her the slip of paper.

She read it and pursed her lips.

"No one could have known you would choose this book. Didn't you read it in school?"

I shook my head.

"No, we were given a choice, and I chose to read *A Wrinkle in Time.* The placement of the note is weird, don't you think?"

"Definitely odd. The fancy dinners and late hours have sapped my energy, and I'd be thrilled to just read on the balcony. Maybe Naked Guy will sun himself."

I forced a laugh.

"A quiet afternoon sounds perfect."

Back in my cabin, I changed into the macramé bikini I'd bought in Jamaica. Ana had located a woman who knew yoga and gave me her cabin number. Ana seemed distracted, but when I asked if she was okay, she lifted her chin.

"Yes, Miss. I'll be right across the hall when you want lunch." She curtsied, something I had stressed made me uncomfortable, and hurried away. I wouldn't find out until later that evening the wretched chain of events I had set in motion.

Besides Dragos, Bogdan, Olenka, Arabella, David, Ian and me, the guests aboard *The Natalia* included Dragos's secretary Marius, his self-absorbed wife Camelia, and two other couples who were part of Olenka's exclusive entourage. These women, all vampires, spent hours dressing and focusing on how to preserve and ideally enhance their beauty. Their evenings involved discussing said beauty treatments, comparing their jewels, castles, staff problems, and gossiping about any vampiress who was showing her age. I avoided their shallow conversation, and it was by chance I overheard the gruesome news.

"Really, Your Grace, you are incredibly generous to share your access to virginal blood from the source. A female virgin is always the best. My skin hasn't been this plump in years." Leaning forward Camelia whispered. "Darn all these rules and regulations. Thank you, darling friend." Olenka preened and patted her perfect coiffure.

"My pleasure, Camelia dear. The recent regulations are tedious and inconvenient. The aristocracy shouldn't have to abide by rules designed to control the peasants. We understand moderation and free-will."

They giggled and raised the jewel encrusted goblets in a toast to their benefactress.

"Did I detect a touch of Timisoara? Green and floral notes." The comment caused an ear-piercing shrill of laughter from a large-busted woman. The men glanced in their wives' direction and Dragos frowned.

"Shush, Margareta. The voivode is frowning. We've been naughty, but our beauty is an ornament to their elevated positions in our world. Men don't need to know how we maintain our allure."

I pleaded a headache, a flush on my cheeks. Injustice and cruelty would always defeat my ability to conceal my emotions.

"Miss Crisan, has something upset you?" Dragos observed me closely. What would happen if I repeated the conversation I'd overheard? I lied out of self-preservation.

"No, I sometimes get headaches if I am out in the sun too long."

He nodded.

"The sun is strong on the water. I hope you feel better."

I grabbed Arabella's arm and hurried back to my room. As soon as we entered, I pressed the buzzer for Ana. She arrived immediately. Her bloodshot eyes and red nose could only be the result of crying.

"Ana, what's wrong?" I asked even though I knew the answer.

She crumpled to the floor, her hands over her face.

"Oh, Miss. Dotia is missing since . . ." She burst into tears. I squatted next to her while Arabella watched us suspiciously.

"Natalie, what haven't you told me?" I avoided her stern gaze and attempted to comfort the distraught young woman.

"I was going to tell you tonight," I said. Ana wiped her tears with the handkerchief she held.

"Tell her what?" David and Ian had knocked on the sitting room door and David's head peaked around the door jam. I waved them in and, closing the door behind them, they looked at the drama before them; Ana red-eyed and distraught, me, terrified and squirming with guilt, and Arabella, arms crossed and prepared to pounce.

"Dotia, Olenka's maid is apparently missing." I had no idea how to soften the news of my clandestine visit to Mike and his plan to become a vampire.

"And we are involved in the maid's disappearance in what specific way?" Arabella's tone reeked of suspicion. This was going to get very messy.

I steered Ana to a chair and kicked off my high heels. "Ana, do you want to hear what I found out? If not, you can wait in my bedroom."

I poured myself a glass of port from the recently restocked bar cart and explained. The deeper I got into my tale, the more foolish I felt. Arabella was fuming.

"You knew the naked guy was Mike, and you didn't tell me? You didn't think Dotia could be in serious danger from your actions?" Hearing it spoken, by a true friend, made me deeply ashamed.

"Natalie, we have explained to you multiple times that all vampires aren't kind like David and me." Ian loosened his bowtie and paced the length of the sitting room. "Even Tom and Jerri, because of their job, have a dark side. How could you endanger yourself and other people by visiting a guy you'd guessed might be Mike, the self-serving jerk who jilted you? This is an awful predicament." He moved to where Ana sat and knelt before her.

"Ana, I know this is difficult for you, but in order to help Dotia, we need to know how you came by your information and what was discussed. Please." David had remained silent and perched on the sofa next to a smoldering Arabella.

"One of the other staff, Elena, said the duchess rang for Dotia directly after sundown," Ana sniffed. "Dotia was steaming the duchess's lingerie, and when she heard the request, she started shaking and crying. She wouldn't tell Elena what was wrong. After a few minutes, she calmed down, left the laundry room, and no one has seen her since. A maid from one of the duchess's friends finished Dotia's task and took the lingerie with her. Dotia is particular about the duchess's lingerie and always washes and presses it herself. Something bad has happened to her."

The conversation between Olenka and her friends would have to be revealed, but I feared for Ana's safety if she knew too much.

"Ana, I need to speak with my friends. Can you wait in my room . . . please? Don't go back to your cabin." Ana rose and Ian escorted her to my bedroom. I was horrified at what I had instigated but had to come clean. When Ian returned, I repeated verbatim the pithy gossip of Olenka and her cronies. When I was finished, I hid my face in my hands.

"The poor child," Arabella said. "Do you think she's dead?"

I shivered.

"If four vampires drank from one emaciated woman, she might well be dead," David said. "Or she might be—changed."

"Changed? Well, that's a nice way to reframe

the result of Natalie's carelessness." Arabella glared at me.

I searched David's face, and he grimaced. My stomach lurched because even my gentleman vampire couldn't shield me from the repercussions of my negligence.

The immediate concern was how to protect Ana. Could she be in danger?

"We will negotiate on Ana's behalf." Ian straightened his bowtie and took charge. "David, you and I will go to Dragos and request a private meeting. We'll say Natalie is extremely concerned about a friend of Ana's who was supposed to meet her for dinner, and no one can find her. I'll call her Dotty or something. Then, we'll say how pleased Natalie is with Ana, and politely if she is under his protection . . . I'll know what to say by the time we get to his study." David got up from the sofa and followed Ian to the door.

I thought about stopping them and speaking to Dragos myself. But I was a coward and let my gentlemen vampires advocate on Ana's behalf.

"Lock the doors and keep Ana in the suite," Ian said. "If we have time, we'll return. If not, I suggest Ana sleeps here. Keep her with you tomorrow until we can update you on our conversation with the voivode." They left quickly, and Arabella and I went to my bedroom.

"Ana, you will sleep in my suite tonight. We must ensure your safety, and Ian and David have gone to see the voivode. Would you like to use the bathroom to get ready for bed? You can borrow a pair of my pajamas." Ana didn't argue, and I knew she was scared to be alone. When we had her comfortably settled on the large sofa in the sitting room, Arabella followed me back to my room and closed the door. She was beyond furious.

"You were reckless, Natalie. You should never have been on the lower deck or visited another passenger alone. Mike is becoming a vampire—and as dangerous as a stranger, for heaven's sake. And you lied to me. That's the worst part."

"I'm sorry, I . . ." I searched for an explanation and came up dry. I had screwed up big time and put myself and others in peril.

Arabella raised her hands and shrugged off my apology.

"Dotia is the one who requires an apology. Yesterday may have been the last sunlight she will ever see." With those ominous words, my friend stormed across the sitting room and the light went on in her bedroom.

If you Googled simpleton, a photograph of yours truly would pop onto the computer screen.

CHAPTER TWENTY

The next morning, I lay in bed staring at the ceiling, replaying the events of the previous day. Conversation drifted in from the sitting room, but as the resident pariah, I didn't attempt to join. Eventually I slid open the door to the balcony and stood at the guard rail, letting the cool morning breeze awaken me. I'd never seen Arabella angry, and I'd gladly suffer caffeine deprivation rather than be the recipient of another tirade.

Someone cleared their throat behind me, and I turned, surprised to see Arabella standing in the doorway. I was not getting off easy.

"I'm going with Ana to her suite so she can get a fresh change of clothes," she said. "I grabbed a couple of DVDs when we were in the library yesterday. We'll watch TV and lie low until David and Ian report back." Arabella had taken control of the disaster I'd created.

She glared at me and said, "Natalie, you will have sway with the kitchen. You can call in our orders and ask for them to be delivered. Ana is under the weather. Apparently, there is a flu going around." Her words cut and I hung my head. She pivoted and returned to the sitting room. I slid the balcony door closed and followed her into the sitting room.

"Ana, let's get your clothes. Natalie, lock the door behind us and do not leave the suite."

I did exactly as I was told. The ladies came back with clean clothes for Ana, and she hid in the bathroom when breakfast and lunch were delivered. We spent a quiet day in the sitting room watching movies and taking naps, and I turned down the offer of a yoga class. I only spoke when addressed and tried to disappear into the furniture. My impetuous actions may have cost Dotia her life. How does one atone for such a huge mistake?

Ana fell asleep on the sofa while we were watching *Laura*. I seized the opportunity to shower and lay out my ensemble for the evening and Ana woke up in time to save me from a lopsided updo. I didn't dare ask Arabella to help me. I was halfway done with my make-up when Ian and David knocked on the sitting room door.

David smiled sympathetically at me when I joined the group. Arabella caught the supportive interaction and pressed her lips together. I blurted.

"Guys, I was in shock last night, and I

compounded my poor judgement by letting you plead my case to Dragos. I should have gone myself. I'm the one who messed up." Ian shook his head.

"I appreciate the intention, Nat, but you might have made Dotia's plight worse. If David and I are to be your sponsors and protectors in vampire society, you must let us represent you in tricky circumstances and teach you how to interact in various situations. Safely. And you have to promise to tell us in the future if you have—suspicions or sudden impulses."

I hung my head. "I promise."

Ian filled us in.

"So, David and I spoke with the voivode last night, alone. He listened, and I admit I was nervous at how intently he watched me. When I finished speaking, he picked up a silver jewel-encrusted penknife and rose from behind his desk. He balanced it in his hand and then deftly tossed it back and forth several times before replacing it on its gilded stand. It was terrifying.

"He was cagey about blaming anyone within his immediate circle for Dotia's disappearance, but he assures me he will verbally restate the strict protection protocol of Ana and our party. As for Dotia, he will make inquires." What a relief. I glanced at Arabella, hoping for a small reprieve, but she ignored me.

"He asked me why I became a vampire," Ian

continued. "When I hesitated, he waved his hand and said I was not required to answer, but I think he guessed." The truth is that Ian had become ill and disappeared from David's life. Several months ago, he'd shared that his conversion to vampire status was conducted in a ceremony with a rich duchess. Just like Mike, he had become a vampire to cheat death. Olenka had shown no interest in him or David, but I suspected Ian had been one of her volunteers. I was in the doghouse and in no position to question him to confirm my suspicions. When David was diagnosed with a terminal illness he had been solicited by a vampire's agent—not unlike Selena's stalking of Mike. David's conversion had been a private affair. Ian and David's reconnection at a housewarming party at my home in Bedford, N.Y. was memorable.

Was Dragos aware of the black-market profiteers who assisted vampires desperate for fresh human blood? My insides squirmed.

I was relieved that Ana was under Dragos's protection. If anything happened to her, I would have run amok.

"Natalie," David said. "You are not entirely to blame for this mess. It took me a decade to grasp the intricacies of the vampire world. We neglected to delve beyond the basic precautions because we didn't want to scare you. From now on, you can never go rogue like you did with Mike. Ever." Wonderful David, kindhearted and my true friend.

"I promise. And I am deeply sorry for what I've done."

Arabella got up and walked to her room and closed the door.

"Give her time," Ian said. "She's angry and probably feels a bit guilty because she knows more about our world than you do. She'll forgive you when she forgives herself."

"Thanks, I don't know what to do."

"You can't do anything," Ian said. "Just let her be."

I hugged them and went back to my room to finish my make-up and get dressed.

Fifteen minutes before we were due at dinner, Ana answered the furtive knock at my bedroom door. In the vanity mirror, I was shocked to see a dazzling Olenka step into my bedroom foyer. Dripping in diamonds, she inclined her head to acknowledge Ana's respectful curtesy. She did not wait in the foyer to be announced but sauntered into my bedroom, posing briefly to gauge my reaction to her magnificence.

Satisfied with the effect of her glorious entrance, she turned to the full-length mirror to inspect the drape of her gown's train. She dismissed Ana with a wave of a beringed hand and confided, "Natalia and I were opposites; she of raven hair and jet-black eyes. Her complexion was tanned by the sun, and swarthy even in winter. We meant to sit for a portrait together, but the darling woman died too soon." She glided several steps further into the room, taking stock of the luxurious chamber. She frowned.

"Good evening, Your Grace." How dare she enter my bedroom as if the intimacy was a common occurrence. "Did you need something? I am not quite finished dressing." I touched-up my eyebrows and replaced the makeup brush into a crystal vessel.

"I hope you don't mind if I complete my makeup," I said. Ignoring her, I popped the top off my lipliner and outlined my lips. I observed her in the reflection of the vanity mirror. Mike had said she didn't like me, and Arabella said she had bad energy. Considering Dotia's disappearance, her invasion of my personal space was unsettling. She studied the painting of a moonlit garden that hung over my bed.

"The painting is a lovely homage to Natalia's garden. She and the voivode designed it together. Did you know?" Surprise must have registered on my face, and she smiled. Score.

"My dear, Miss Crisan, have I done something wrong?" Her voice oozed with the charm she used to captivate her inner circle. "I hoped we would be friends. Natalia and I were like sisters. Being married to brothers, military men who occupied senior positions in our superior world, we shared our deepest hopes, dreams, and the odd disappointment. You and I will be spending many hours together, and frankly, you are unschooled in the protocols of Romanian aristocracy."

I composed myself by applying a deep magenta lipstick. I didn't trust her offer of friendship. One deck below mine Mike reclined in his cabin waiting for her to show up for another sample of his warm blood. Dotia was missing. A direct approach was best. I rose slowly, and with a smooth swish of my train faced her.

"My ex-boyfriend is on the ship, and he told me he is to become a vampire at an elaborate ceremony?"

She laughed, a pleasant sound, like the tinkling of a dinner bell, more appropriate to a charming anecdote than a direct question.

"Your ex-boyfriend; what fruitful serendipity." She stepped toward me and her eyes traveled to the Tahitian pearl earrings Slade had given me. "My dear child, how can I answer you without shocking your guile-less sensibilities? The truthful answer will, perhaps, change your opinion of Michael."

"Impossible. I am well aware of his narcissism and vanity. We lived together. He was the worst sort of boyfriend."

Olenka continued her inspection of my bedroom, eventually balancing herself daintily on the edge of a satin slipper chair, her posture a credit to her breeding.

"Marvelous, this is what I hoped for . . . a sharing of memories closest to our hearts," she purred. "I would confide our plan to you, but I know you have already visited Michael. I did not seek him out, Michael was brought to me by an employee, and I was initially unaware of your association. He is unwell, news he has found out most recently, as you know. Terribly sad. He does not wish to deteriorate and die horribly, and I can help him there. Michael will become undead, and I will receive blood the old-fashioned way." Before I could interrupt, she waved her hand imperiously.

"Dragos frowns upon draining human blood to death. My fetish is human blood from the source. A V cocktail only whets my appetite for the prick of the skin, the pulsing of the vein, the sucking of the life force. Dark bliss, Miss Crisan." Shocked into silence by the sheer evil of her soliloquy, I felt fear rise within me.

"Michael is young and virile, and his blood has a fresh masculine musk with a hint of chocolate. He offered a sample taste to seal our deal and offered his firm neck to my discerning palate. He wants what I can give him—eternal life, wealth, luxury. He has even picked out the sports car I will give him after he is . . . mine." My stomach lurched, and I drew a deep breath to calm myself. Had she made a similar offer to poor Dotia?

"There will be a glorious ceremony in Transylvania at my castle followed by pleasure of every kind. My ceremonial gown is made of solid gold mesh cloth studded with diamonds. Bogdan indulges me even if the voivode disapproves. After his conversion, our darling Michael will have entry to the most elite vampire circles. By offering an illicit taste here and there as his body acclimates, he will become the new society darling. Aren't you pleased for him?"

I thought I was about to vomit. Olenka continued, a malicious glint in her eyes.

"And what about Dotia? Where is she?"

Olenka frowned but quickly raised her left hand and smoothed the skin between her brows.

"Dotia was an abused orphan I rescued. She owes me her life. I do not tolerate mistakes from my employees, nor do I explain my private affairs to outsiders. Dotia was given a choice, and she chose wisely. Stay out of my business . . . darling. Our friendship will work much more smoothly if you concentrate on Dragos's obsession with you. You have realized he is . . ."

Through a brain fog of despair for Dotia, I barely heard the rapping at my suite door. The door to the sitting room flung open and Ian and David entered. I had collapsed onto a chair.

"What's happened? Nat? Natalie?" David knelt in front of me and Olenka rose calmly from her seat.

"Goodness, we were discussing an upcoming celebration in Romania. Events encouraging our glorious culture and social networking are one of the voivode's pet projects. Could Miss Crisan have eaten bad food? I will speak to the chef. I hope to see all of you at dinner." She sauntered toward the door.

"Do not repeat what I told you, my dear friend. Girl talk is strictly confidential." She was in my head! A rush of adrenaline shot through my system, and I summoned Lupu. He growled, blocking her access.

The sequins of her train swished as she pivoted. Anger flashed across her face. She recovered her composure and raised her eyebrows.

"Lupu? The devil's spawn. Excellent choice." The door closed softly behind her.

"Natalie, what just happened? Please answer me." Ian brought me a glass of water and I took a sip, spilling a little on the carpet. I handed the glass back before I gave myself a shower. Then I relayed the conversation with Olenka.

"So Olenka is still conducting the ceremony," Ian said. "It would be useful to know the vampires who attend, but also dangerous to be a guest and not take part in the . . . festivities. Abstinence would be noticed."

I inhaled a ragged breath.

"When Mike and I were together, he shared that the men in his family died young. Different ailments, but none lived past fifty. He has a progressive neurological disease. Is it a coincidence Olenka's agent found him? I don't think so. And I couldn't get a clear answer from Olenka about

Dotia's disappearance." I crossed to my vanity and opened a crystal bottle of perfume. A soft blend of white flowers and amber greeted my nose, and I dabbed it on my wrists. I breathed it in and searched for calm in the turbulent waters of Mike's impending conversion.

"Olenka is rich and has agents who troll the world for blood donors," Ian said. "The practice isn't much different than sex trafficking. Children are kidnapped; sisters are sold. It's a horrible situation. All the victims don't become vampires. Olenka is a connoisseur of blood and will drink until she is satiated, which can mean death to the person. If she has agreed to make Mike a vampire, she favors him or has a plan for him. Rest assured there will be attendees who will not survive her event."

I shivered.

"Mike is petrified of old age, illness, and especially death. I won't judge him, but it is typical of his greed to find a wealthy duchess and trade blood for lavish immortality." A knock at the connecting door interrupted our conversation, and Ana told us that it was time to visit the main salon.

I grabbed my evening bag and slipped the ruby ring onto my right middle finger. David and Ian noticed and exchanged a glance.

"Okay, you two, don't read into my wearing the ring. The jewel is priceless, and it makes our host happy for me to wear it. More importantly, I suspect it annoys Olenka no end."

David grabbed my hand and spun me in a circle.

"You've taken sassy to a whole new level. I am holding onto the hope Dotia can be saved. Let's be careful tonight." We hugged and linked arms.

Ian and Arabella followed close behind as headed toward Dragos's drawing room and the night's entertainment.

"What is the subject of your manuscript, Miss Crisan?" Bogdan had been extremely attentive all evening, while Olenka had expended minimal energy in my direction, which suited me just fine.

"The story begins with an emphasis on the greed and entitlement of multiple generations of an Alaskan family and the Native American tribes they coexist with. I hadn't initially planned on a romance theme, but I've decided to integrate one, perhaps a doomed relationship."

"What prompted you to add the doomed romance?" Dragos inserted himself into the conversation.

"I suffered through an awful break-up recently. The man and I lived together for over a year, and I thought we were to be married. He left me for another woman. Writers never waste the words that flow from firsthand experience."

"I am sorry to hear you have been hurt. We share the pain of heartbreak."

The room went quiet. Was this a rare admission from the voivode?

"Yes, quite true," I said. "Oh, and I keep forgetting to thank you for sharing the painting of Natalia's garden. It is mesmerizing."

Dragos frowned and replaced his cup on the table.

"How did you know it was Natalia's garden?"

"Why, the duchess told me when she visited me before dinner." With exquisite control, the voivode's head swiveled toward where Olenka sat, a frozen sculpture of chiseled perfection.

Ah. She had broken a directive from Dragos; perhaps my suite was off limits to the other guests. I decided to use her apparent misstep. By allowing her to save face I could demonstrate to both her and Dragos my intention to play their game.

"The duchess has kindly offered to assist me with Romanian protocol and culture. I gratefully accept." I caught her eye and grinned like the Cheshire cat.

Olenka paused for a split second before raising her goblet high. With a serene smile, she faced me.

"What superb news. A toast, my friends, to Natalie Crisan. Together, the family Dracul will instruct you in the richness of your Romanian heritage."

Dragos raised his goblet to my wine glass.

"I have no doubt, Miss Crisan, that you will quickly acclimate to our world," he said elevating an eyebrow quizzically. "You will be a worthy chess opponent."

When playing The Sicilian Defense, Aunt Loretta had always stressed that white should aim to control the central squares. By rescuing Olenka I had done just that, and I'd slowed the pace of the game to one which suited me. If Olenka proved to be an enemy, I needed to keep her close.

CHAPTER TWENTY-ONE

Before the night was over, Olenka made a great show of securing a private meeting with me the following evening. Patting the seat next to her on the settee, she embraced the role of senior royal and chosen mentor of my entry into her elite world. Arabella sat down on a chair close-by. My negligence had not overshadowed her self-appointed responsibility toward me.

"Now, Miss Crisan," Olenka said. "I must declare what an honor it is for you to accept my offer to assist you with your future duties as the queen's direct ancestor." She preened and glanced briefly at her cronies, who sat in rapt admiration of her new service to the voivode. "Shall we meet tomorrow evening? In your suite or mine?"

"Perhaps in my sitting room?" I preferred to have our private discussions on my home turf.

"Excellent. An hour after sunset? Your maid

should be present to hear our discussion. She has a significant responsibility." The other women nodded.

"What an excellent idea," I said. "Ana is a sweet and helpful woman. My hair would never look this elegant without her skill."

The ladies giggled.

"I don't know what I would do without my maid," Camelia said. The ladies murmured in agreement. With a smile, I stood.

"I look forward to our meeting, but it is late. Good evening, Your Grace, ladies." I crossed the floor to where the men huddled in a circle. When I approached, they abruptly ended the conversation and got to their feet.

"Voivode, thank you for a lovely evening," I said. Behind me, Arabella repeated my words like an echo.

"It is my pleasure, Miss Crisan. Sleep well." The men bowed and only David left with Arabella and me. In the suite, David closed the door and paced to the sitting room.

"The voivode has asked Ian to join his advisors," he exclaimed. "Bogdan is skeptical, but the voivode said he is out of touch with current events and requires the calm logic of a modern, sophisticated man. Ian couldn't say no. It is an honor."

"The voivode is perceptive," Arabella said. "Ian

will add a touch of kindness and inclusivity. Congratulations to him."

Arabella had barely spoken all evening. She turned toward her room. "Good night," she called over her shoulder. David and I watched her stride across the sitting room. The light switched on and the door closed softly.

"I don't know what to do," I said. "She hasn't spoken two words to me since Dotia disappeared."

"There isn't anything you can do. Perhaps if we can get information on Dotia's whereabouts, she'll forgive you. She's as upset about Dotia as she is about you keeping Mike's presence on the ship from her."

I shook my head.

"I made a terrible mistake, and I can't undo it. I don't know how Olenka found out I'd visited Mike —maybe he told Olenka to curry favor. I don't put that past him in his current state. We've protected Ana. Should I ask Dragos about Dotia? Maybe follow-up on your conversation with him?"

David's expression was thoughtful.

"Nat, I know your intentions are good. Let's give it another day. Has Ana heard anything?"

"No, she hasn't. But, since Olenka and I are becoming besties should I try a second time?"

David snickered.

"Olenka is best friends with herself, but you charitably covered her faux pas with Dragos. It was obvious your rooms were off limits. Maybe ask if

Dotia can give Ana lingerie pressing lessons. These ladies prize their maids. Olenka may share positive news." David crossed his arms.

"Do you think I'll have to walk several steps behind Ian? The voivode favors him." I stifled a giggle and hugged him. "I'm sure the voivode is thrilled to have two sophisticated, modern vampires in his camp."

The compliment smoothed David's ego, and he ran a hand through his thick hair.

"Thanks, darling. I'll say goodnight. Lock up behind me and I'll see you tomorrow."

I held open the door.

"I'll have lots to report after my first lesson in Romanian protocol." We air kissed, and I bolted the door behind him.

I slid open the balcony door and breathed in the fresh sea air. No lights shone from the room below. Was Mike sleeping, or had Olenka arrived for a midnight snack?

There had been several brilliant chess moves this evening. Shielding Olenka from the voivode's wrath was, I must say, an inspired move on my part. But the voivode's action, enlisting Ian to advise him on modern vampire matters, was clever. If Ian and David, my friends and protectors, became a part of the voivode's inner circle, the odds of my remaining in Romania for at least the full year increased dramatically. Well played.

* * *

Ana blanched the next day when I told her Olenka had requested her presence for the evening's lesson. Arabella, despite her coldness, was more concerned with logistics.

"I'm not sure how she entered your bedroom without an invitation. Perhaps she had been in the room before. I will place a protection spell at the doors to exclude her." Arabella said. "I wouldn't allow her in your rooms again."

"What do you suggest?" I maintained a respectful posture and direct eye contact with Arabella. She was a loyal friend, and I had betrayed her trust.

"Meet in neutral territory. How about the sky bar on the top deck where we met the first night after the music program? Send a note to Olenka's room and let the ship's staff know you require privacy." Arabella rubbed her hands together, preparing to cast a protective spell. She hadn't used her spells recently, but I knew her intuition was always spot on.

"Super idea!" My response was a bit dramatic, and Arabella narrowed her eyes. I wasn't getting off the hook anytime soon.

* * *

Olenka was waiting for Ana and me in the sky bar. A ceiling of skylights provided an unobscured view of the twinkling stars which filled the inky sky. Low tables with small, shaded lamps shone soft rings onto the polished marble surfaces. We were not late.

Olenka was dressed for dinner in a claret-colored gown that shimmered with tiny crystals scattered across the fabric. I had chosen to wear the midnight blue gown Ana put in the closet, and although it fit perfectly the fabric did not flow with movement like the gowns Iris had made for me. Olenka did not rise but concentrated on our entrance. When I reached her, she extended her hand.

"Good evening, Your Grace."

"Good evening, Miss Crisan. I insisted the staff bring us proper chairs for our first meeting. There is no need for discomfort." She did not acknowledge Ana, who retreated to a far corner and awkwardly hunched on a straight-back chair.

Olenka pressed her lips together with disapproval.

"Staff should never sit in the presence of their employer, unless given permission." Ana rose nervously from her chair, and I motioned for her to sit.

"I gave her permission before we arrived." If she dismissed questions about Dotia, then she was not entitled to comment on Ana. "Thank you for sharing your time and experience with me. Your insight will remove stress from the formal events."

Olenka accepted my gratitude with a dip of her head and lowered the black goblet she was holding to a side table.

"Miss Crisan, have you considered becoming a Romanian citizen?" I hadn't and it was not a condition of my inheritance per Natalia's will.

"Is Romanian citizenship necessary? It hasn't been mentioned to me before now."

She smoothed the skirt of her gown and considered my response.

"Romania allows dual citizenship. The voivode would consider it an honor if you requested this. If you are a Romanian citizen, he can bestow a title on you. Titles are crucial to elevating one's position.

"When you become a Romanian citizen, you curtsy to him upon entering a room before beginning a conversation. Depending on your title, you will be curtsied to or be required to curtsy to senior aristocracy. We can revisit the protocol in the future." She reached for her drink and studied me over the rim.

A glass of water sat on the table next to me, and I sipped for a moment to buy time. Dual French citizenship had always been a dream of mine, but Romanian dual citizenship made more sense in light of my inheritance.

"Your Grace, where would you like to begin?" I asked.

Olenka smiled.

"There is a lot to cover. We will start with appearance and bearing. The aunt who raised you did an adequate job of finishing you, by which I mean elevating your cultural experiences. Dull people are intimidated by travel and cultural exploration.

"You carry yourself well and walk gracefully. Your conversational skills are fine and with my help, you will charm a room. You are educated and well read. Do you play a musical instrument?"

I had anticipated a discussion of protocol, but it would be useful to have a clear picture of Olenka's opinion of me.

"No, but I intended to study the piano. I was hoping there was one in Le Refuge Bleue."

Olenka drew her hands together.

"Excellent. Natalia played the pianoforte, and I understand there is a music room in Le Refuge Bleue." The fact that she knew the musical instruments in Natalia's home was interesting.

"And I understand you are an award-winning dancer." Ah. She had picked Mike's brain.

"Yes, Mike Endicott and I met in a ballroom dancing class. We competed together until our break-up. I also studied ballet as a young girl and attended lessons whenever I could in my hometown."

"Perfect. The voivode will certainly announce a

ball to introduce you to vampire society. Your dance skills will be an asset. Do you ride?"

"No, I don't."

"Riding isn't strictly necessary, but I'm sure you own horses. The voivode will have taken care of the equine stock after Natalia's death." Olenka stared at the darkened windows, deep in thought. She resumed her instruction.

"One final comment. Your appearance and wardrobe must be impeccable. Americans are casual and often sloppy with their attire. Casual for you from now on will mean skirted suits for luncheons, bespoke slacks and cashmere sweaters, elegant dresses with matching jackets. I understand David Westwood is your stylist, and his work is satisfactory. Your style is quietly sophisticated, but for evening events, you need more glamour because you will be wearing jewels and eventually a tiara." Her gaze dropped to the ruby ring. When she lifted her eyes to mine, envy shadowed her expression.

"The ring you wear is part of an exquisite parure. If the voivode bestows a title on you, you will wear a tiara in his presence. It is a sign of respect. Natalia had a magnificent collection of jewels and tiaras. Jewels are the ultimate status symbol." She brought her hand up to her head to the diadem she wore.

"Your Grace, it is time for cocktails."

Ana gasped. Dotia had silently entered the room from a hidden staircase. She stared straight ahead at her mistress; Ana and I might not have been in the room. She didn't look ill, but her pallor and calm confident bearing obliterated the spark of hope I'd held in my heart.

Olenka rose from her chair.

"Thank you, Dotia. Miss Crisan, we are in port tomorrow. Perhaps we can continue our conversation in Romania?"

"Yes, thank you for your time and insight," I said. "I will walk with Ana back to my suite. Miss Bishop is waiting for me."

"Of course. I will see you in the drawing room." Olenka's gown swished as she exited, Dotia bringing up the rear.

Ana leaned against the door, and I rested my hand gently on her shoulder. She whispered.

"Dotia is . . . is . . ." I pulled Ana into my arms. She trembled as I searched for words, but I found nothing but the truth.

"Undead," I said. "No one can help her now." We exited the bar and braved the sea wind on the short walk to the indoor elevator. Ana's ragged breath negated conversation. My room was a few steps from the elevator, and I fumbled with the card key.

"Well, here they are! My goodness, your hair looks like a tornado hit it." David, Ian and Arabella were dressed for our last night aboard *The Natalia*.

"How did the first lesson go?" Ian was always the man to put our group on track.

"Olenka was helpful, in a bossy duchessy kind-of way. I require an entirely new wardrobe, apparently. My Aunt Loretta did an 'adequate' job educating me on the finer things." The condescension of the word adequate produced the desired response. Now for the bad news.

"We saw Dotia." At my words, Ana stifled a sob. "She is a vampire."

Arabella brought her hand up to her mouth and dropped it abruptly.

"How does she look?" A strange question to ask, but Ian had to have a reason.

"She appeared calm and not malnourished. Pale but healthy."

"Ah." Ian rose and stopped in front of Ana. He leaned forward and hugged her.

"If Dotia is undead, then Olenka gave her a choice. In the vampire world, a choice is not extended unless there is a reason. Ana, has Dotia reached out to you?"

"No, she wouldn't even glance at me when she spoke to Olenka. We've known each other for years. She was like. . . sleepwalking." She began to cry, and Arabella put her arm around Ana's shoulders.

"Ana, Ian and I are vampires," David said. "There are tons of reasons why the lifestyle works for people. Do you think it's possible that becoming a vampire is a what Dotia wanted? There are thousands of vampires who live fulfilling lives. Look

at Ian and me. We get to spend eternity together."
He glanced at Ian.

"For all eternity, my darling," Ian said as he
reached out his hand to David. Ana swallowed hard
and blew her nose with a tissue. Could Dotia's life
as a vampire be an improvement?

"Miss, I need to fix your hair." She held her
head high and moved through the door into my
bedroom. She was handling her friend's vampire
status better than I had dealt with Mike's
impending conversion. She adjusted my hair in
silence, and her composure returned. Just as she slid
the last bobby pin into place, the dinner gong
sounded. We walked Ana to her cabin door.

"Don't open the door to anyone," Arabella said.
Ana nodded.

"If you need us for any reason, don't hesitate to
call," I added. "We'll check in when we return.
Okay?"

"Okay. Thank you." I heard the dead bolt click
as Ana locked the door.

Ana removed her dinner from the fridge and
popped it into the microwave. A wonderful bonus
of being on *The Natalia* was access to the yummy
leftovers from the previous night's dinner hosted by
the voivode. She stripped out of her clothes and
donned a terrycloth robe, tying the robe as she

dashed to turn off the beep of the microwave in the pristine galley kitchen. Using potholders, she pulled out a steaming plate of an epicurean feast and set herself up at the kitchen table to eat. She had borrowed the novel *Persuasion* from the library and hoped it would relax her after the awful news about her friend. Poor Dotia . . . was becoming a vampire truly her choice or an ultimatum from the horrible duchess?"

The ring of the housephone startled her. Had Natalie forgotten something? She set her fork on the floral placemat and reached for the phone.

"Hello?" Someone breathed on the other side of the connection. "Hello?"

"Ana." One word, and she felt the bile rise from her stomach.

"Dotia?" Ana couldn't find words of comfort to console her sweet friend.

"Don't grieve, Ana. I chose my fate," Dotia said. "I could not return to my foster family a failure. The duchess treats me differently, now. My precious gift to her, virgin blood from the source, is what she cherishes most. My position as the vampire maid of the Duchess of Transylvania has elevated me in our world. There will be other opportunities for me to better myself. The duchess has promised me a proper education. I was removed from school to work as a laundress when I turned thirteen."

"So you are. . ."

A soft laugh like an exhale came from the other end of the line.

"My friend, I am undead, and I have never felt better."

* * *

The shadow of a smile threatened to break the stoic expression Dragos wore like a shield. Conversations halted mid-sentence. The uncharacteristic reaction of the voivode warranted complete attention.

"You wish to become a Romanian citizen?" His pleasure was apparent, despite his superior self-control.

"The subject came up when the duchess and I were chatting about Romanian protocol. Our conversation was enlightening." Dragos shifted his gaze for a second to acknowledge Olenka, and she inclined her head gracefully. "We were having such a lovely chat, and I forgot to ask for recommendations of books about Romanian history and culture. I also love poetry and would love to read Romanian authors."

The subject of poetry and history delighted Dragos even more, and he rattled off a few titles.

"I will lend the volumes to you from my private library. Keep them at your leisure."

Conversation resumed, and I wondered if our discussion would be dissected behind closed doors.

Did the vampires wonder about the Dragos who admitted to heartbreak? When Arabella and I were finished eating, the guests proceeded to the music hall for the last performance aboard *The Natalia*. We took our customary seats.

"Your Majesty, I know that the Westwoods spoke to you of my concern about Dotia and Ana. I saw Dotia this evening. Unfortunately, she is a . . ." He looked down at me and the words stalled and jumbled in my mouth. The intensity of his gaze perplexed me, but I refused to blink. I held a measure of responsibility for the situation, and it was about time I showed him I was capable of asking my own questions.

"I have spoken directly with Dotia," he said. His eyes dropped briefly to the ruby ring I wore and then lifted to meet the challenge in my eyes. "She told me that she wished to become a vampire. She has many logical reasons. There will be incentives for her in my brother's household, and there is a binding contract between her and the duchess. I am satisfied that she was not forced." He delivered his comments like a proclamation. Had Dotia told the truth?

The heavy drapes retracted, revealing a gleaming pianoforte elevated on a center stage platform. The audience applauded as the pianist entered and bowed. I leaned toward Dragos and asked, "Isn't the pianist one of the violinists of the quartet?"

"You are correct, Miss Crisan. His first instrument was the violin, and years later, he added the pianoforte and piano to his repertoire. He plays other instruments, as well, but those three are ones he has mastered."

I was not familiar with the piece played, Mozart's *Piano Quartet No 1*, nor had I ever attended a performance of a piano quartet. Besides the pianoforte, the other instruments were a violin, the larger viola, and a cello. Energy, emotion and joy were evident in the performer's faces. I adored Mozart, and listening to the pianoforte, I remembered Olenka's comments about Natalia's pianoforte. Natalia's will had mentioned a music room. These happy thoughts were immediately crushed by Dragos's revelation; Dotia had choosen to become a vampire. I would have to decide what to share with Ana, but there was no way to remove her pain.

The concert lasted less than a half hour. The men withdrew to Dragos's study, and the women reclined on the satin chairs in the salon next to the concert hall. V cocktails were served to the vampires, and Arabella and I each held a petite glass of port.

"How fitting," Olenka commented as she observed my choice of libation. "Port in Portugal. Miss Crisan, what plans have you made for tomorrow?" The other ladies politely awaited my reply.

"We have a couple of historical sites to visit, and I was hoping to inspect the boutiques. I would love a handbag made by a local artisan. Or shoes."

"Ah, an excellent idea. It is preferable to purchase bespoke and handmade over mass produced." A murmur of concurrence from Olenka's friends encouraged additional coaching. "Supporting local crafts is a pet project of His Majesty. He will approve of your gesture."

I glanced at Arabella, who sipped her port and studied Olenka. My agreement with Olenka had apparently emboldened her to bestow feedback whenever she chose. Although I wanted to encourage our alliance, the constructive criticism grated on my nerves, and I preferred to relax in my bedroom. Getting smoothly to my feet, I handed my empty glass to waitstaff.

"It was a pleasure to sail with everyone, and I hope to meet all of you soon in Romania. The concert was sublime and has put me in a dreamlike state. Goodnight, ladies."

Arabella got up.

"Good night," she said. "It was a lovely passage."

Olenka feigned disappointment. "My dear friends, the last night on board is my favorite celebration! I am sad you will miss the festivities. Sleep well."

A chorus of "goodnight" sent Arabella and me

out the door, where a burly security guard appeared to walk us back to our suite. Not a word passed between us on the journey back, and once again I wallowed in self-recrimination.

CHAPTER TWENTY-TWO

Arabella went directly through the sitting room to her bedroom. How long would I be punished for my impetuous visit to Mike's room? I closed the adjoining door and kicked off my shoes. The room was in deep shadow, a shaft of moonlight slicing through the darkness the only illumination.

I slipped off the gown and hung it in the closet. In the bathroom, I performed the nightly beauty rituals. The transatlantic crossing had been swift, and the conversations blurred in my mind. The chef had continued to use too much salt in the food, and I poured a big glass of water and carried it to my vanity. My intention was to peruse the book of Romanian folklore I had borrowed from the onboard library and winddown so I could sleep.

I had left my silk pajamas on the vanity stool, and dressed only in my lace bra and panties, I switched on the light to reach for them. A sound, the intake of breath, startled me and I pivoted. Mike lounged on my bed, clad in a white T-shirt and pajama shorts.

"God, what a fool I was. Look at you. You're gorgeous, Nat."

I found my voice and tried to keep my cool.

"Mike, how did you get in here?"

He slid off the satin bedspread and crossed to me.

"I climbed from my deck. It wasn't too difficult; I've gotten stronger recently. Listen. . . I love you, Natalie, and always have. I told you I made a mistake with Alix, but I knew my life would be short and . . . I'm truly sorry for hurting you."

"You've already apologized, and I forgave you." He reached out and stroked my shoulder with his hand, and then I remembered I was in my underwear. I backed up and grabbed the pajama top.

He sighed.

"Can we talk?" Mike wanted something, and I was curious.

"Sure." I pointed to a chair, and I sat safely out of arm's reach on the vanity tuffet.

"Nat, I know you don't owe me anything. You were a peach when we were together, and generous with your success. I didn't deserve you, and I never will." There were two welts on Mike's neck that he had attempted to hide with makeup.

"What do you want, Mike?" My voice held the

exasperation I felt. "Your cheating upended my life. I'd never felt so low and alone."

"I know, I know. The breakup was completely my fault." He exhaled loudly. "Nat, tonight is my last free night before they take me to Olenka's castle for the ceremony. I don't want to spend tonight solo. There is one parting gift you can give me—we can give each other—even though I was a lousy boyfriend." He was exasperating.

"I'll ask again, Mike. What do you want?"

He knelt in front of me.

"I love you, Natalie Crisan, and want to spend the last night of my mortal life making love to you."

I choked on my surprise.

"Seriously? What a nerve you've got." I crossed my arms.

"Have you been with anyone else since we split up?" I blushed, and he smiled. Slade Suit and I had kissed passionately, but he had disappeared from Jamaica before anything else happened. It would have been nice to say, "of course", and wipe that grin off Mike's face.

"That's none of your business," I answered.

"You're right. But after the ceremony I'll be undead, and I want to remember us together, the way we were. Please, Nat."

I pushed him to the side, and he landed on his bottom. I stalked to the slider and slammed it open. The wind had picked up and a strong gust whipped my hair off my face. He came up behind me and gently rested his hands on my arms. I felt his breath, then a soft kiss on my neck. My insides lurched. We had been good together . . . once upon a time.

Mike still had magic in his touch, and I weighed a night of bliss against the excitement of a chapter of Romanian folklore. There would be plenty of time to read about wood nymphs and wars. Tonight was about Mike and Natalie. Releasing the grudge I had brandished like a torch; I fell into his arms.

The next morning, the ship's aura had altered. It took a minute, but I finally realized the engines of the ship were silent. The hum and vibration of a large ship became comforting to its passengers. The ship was in port and Mike was gone from my bed.

I didn't regret my actions. I felt light and deeply rested. Mike had snuggled until I fell asleep, but he told me he had to be in his room before sunrise.

"Olenka and your royal benefactor would go ballistic if they knew we were together," he'd whispered. "Thank you for being with me. I'll always love you." He was right. It was better if the intimate encounter was our secret. My pals would put me under house arrest if they knew what I'd done.

The sound of an outboard motor roared, and I picked my pajama top off the floor, slipped it over my head and rushed to the balcony.

A sleek cigarette boat sped away toward the dock. Several men were in it, and one turned and raised his hand in farewell. I let out a sob. My Mike was gone forever.

* * *

Before we left for an eagerly anticipated day of touring Lisbon, Arabella came quietly into my bedroom and closed the door. She didn't greet me but simply launched into the latest update on Dotia.

"Natalie." Arabella wore a grave expression. "To confirm, Olenka made Dotia a vampire. Dotia called Ana last night and said she was content with her decision. She says Olenka gave her the choice, which I don't believe. Before we socialize in Romania, we must discuss the dangers of our situation again with Ian and David . . . and how a poor decision could endanger you and others." I felt the heat in my cheeks. Sleeping with Mike was yet another poor decision on my part, and one I wasn't going to admit unless tortured. I didn't want to start the day with tears, and Arabella was right. I needed advice from my vamp friends, and the inner strength to follow it.

"We can try to ask them tonight when we fly to Transylvania," I said. "Dragos will be on the plane, and probably the rest of his guests from *The Natalia*. I am deeply sorry for making such a huge mistake." Arabella shrugged. Before she could say another word, there was a knock on the door."

"The jitney is here to take us into the port." Ana

wore a sweet linen dress and an adorable straw hat."

"Ana, your outfit is perfect! We're going to have so much fun."

"You look so cute, Ana," Arabella agreed. "Lisbon here we come!"

The quick ride across the harbor stoked my excitement. It was a clear day, the bright blue sky studded with cotton ball clouds. The typical port stores lined the plank walkway, but we weren't interested in imported souvenirs. Two black SUVs waited across the street and as we reached the curb a door opened, and a man stepped out to greet us.

"Hello and welcome to Lisbon. My name is Salvador, and I am pleased to be your guide for today."

Salvador was the best advertisement for Portuguese men. His dark brown hair was swept off his face, curling at the nape of his neck. He was long and lean and wore a crisp button-down shirt open at the neck and creased khaki slacks. On his feet, a brand of luxury sneakers completed his attire. I guessed his eyes were brown, although he didn't remove the wire frame designer shades.

We piled into the SUV and I turned around to confirm the second black SUV would follow. Ana sat up front with Salvador, and Arabella and I clicked our seat belts in the spacious second row. Our first stop was the Praca do Comercio. While we admired the triumphal arch, Salvador explained the rich history of the site. The security guards hung slightly back, and I nicknamed them Bert and Ernie.

We dipped into a few stores, and Salvador apologized for hurrying us through the shopping district.

"We have a secured a private tour at the Museu Calouste Gulbenkian," he said. "Then I thought we would have a snack and head to Old Town in Porto. Porto has luxury shopping, if you are interested, and we should have enough time to visit the Clerigos Church and Tower. Miss Crisan and her party have been invited for a private port tasting at the home of a local aristocratic family. It is a noble family, and quite an honor."

"It all sounds wonderful," I said. "I was hoping to buy a belt or shoes. Made in Portugal, of course. Maybe gloves? My guess is Romania is chilly."

"Excelente," Salvador said. "We will go Rua Augusta for shoes and Rua do Carmo for gloves. I will call ahead to stores I know." Ana said something to Salvador in Portuguese, and his surprise at her language skills was evident.

"We are in your hands," Arabella murmured. The quaint scenes outside the car window, washed with the pastel palette of the city, held her attention, and we sped toward a day of sightseeing and hopefully shopping.

Our second stop was the Museu Calouste Gulbenkian. An imposing rectangular cement structure contained a sleek open floor plan designed to highlight the impressive collection of Armenian born businessman Calouste Gulbenkian. Our docent greeted Salvador warmly in Portuguese and switched easily to English. Bert and Ernie had entered with us, and Bert hung with us while Ernie did recognizance.

"Good morning. My name is Raquel, and I will be conducting your tour this morning." Raquel, an attractive woman with a head of abundant curly hair, beamed a welcoming smile.

"We could not close the museum, so please stay close to me while we walk. Let me begin with a brief background on our great benefactor, the collector Calouste Gulbenkian. He was born in Armenia but moved to England because of persecution and became an English citizen."

Museums are a passion of mine. I never hurry a docent along. I was determined to absorb every detail. My Aunt Loretta would have loved the collection and its curation. She had a discerning eye for art and had stoked my interest.

"From an early age, Senor Gulbenkian admired art and began collecting," the docent said. "His interests were widespread, and he educated himself on the artists or period which caught his attention. We are lucky that at the end of his life he chose Lisbon as his home and ensured his collection remain together in this museum." We followed Raquel into an open space with sleek wood-paneled walls and cases filled with Asian vases.

"Typically, we explain the collection by beginning with the Pharaohs of Ancient Egypt, then through the Middle East and Far East. The collection includes European masterpieces by Fragonard, Boucher, Manet, and many more. René Lalique was a close friend of Senôr Gulbenkian, and we have fabulous examples of Lalique's craftmanship. Do you have a preference?"

"I would love to see the European paintings, but everything sounds amazing. Perhaps if you show us your favorites?" Raquel nodded her approval.

"Perfect," she said. "Let us start with the Pharaohs. There is a statue from the 26th dynasty 660-610 BC. A marvelous piece."

". . . Madame Camille Monet was quite beautiful, and Renoir's portrait pleased her. Renoir and Monet were lifelong friends and often painted together. Camille's eyes mesmerized Monet when they first met."

While we listened to the docent's description of the marvelous features of the painting, Arabella had strayed to a far wall. I heard her exclaim, 'What the . . .', and saw a tall man run from the area, and disappear around a corner. Arabella jogged to my side, and I felt her arm circle my waist.

"What's wrong?" She shook her head, but something had occurred to stress her. Bert and

Ernie registered the situation, and Bert sped in the direction of the stranger.

"Nothing, pet. I made a mistake, is all." I overlooked her odd outburst because she had called me pet. She hadn't used the affectionate nickname in days.

No museum tour was complete without a visit to the museum store. The Gulbenkian shop displayed a well-curated assortment of books, stationary, and other gifts. I bought a book on the history of the Gulbenkian museum collection and a biography of Calouste Gulbenkian. Ana cheerfully accepted a gift from me of a book on the Impressionist collection, but Arabella shook her head and insisted on paying for her tome on Islamic Art. We said goodbye to Raquel, thanked her for a fabulous tour, and piled in the car with our treasure.

We lunched at a tiny restaurant where Salvador knew the owner and ordered for us in musical Portuguese, stuffing ourselves with bolinhos de bacalhao, croquete de batatas and pastel de nata for dessert.

"I can't eat another bite," Ana laughed, holding her stomach once we were back in the car. "I want to learn how to make the bolinhos."

"I don't," Arabella replied. "If I knew how to make them, I would eat a bucket-full several times a week and gain a hundred pounds!"

"I will be sure to repeat your compliments to my friend." Salvador maneuvered the SUV smoothly around a corner. "There are two parking spots right in front of the store. How lucky we are!"

Standing on the sidewalk outside the well-known Ruo do Carmo, Arabella considered the window of the famous glove shop. Ana appeared more interested in the fine linen store across the street. Arabella followed Ana's hopeful gaze.

"I want to buy a present for my parents, Ana said. "My mother would never treat herself to fine linen."

"Go ahead you two, I'll check out the glove store." Ana jogged happily across the street with Arabella in tow.

"Miss Crisan, may I make a phone call to my office while you are in Ruo do Carmo? I will stay exactly here." Salvador pointed to the sidewalk, and I laughed.

"Please make your call. I don't think I'll get lost in the store. Bert and Ernie are scanning the street for criminal activity, and will no doubt follow me inside." I pressed the buzzer of the heavy glass and wood door, and a loud pop told me the lock was released.

The world-renowned glove store displayed exquisite merchandise behind sparkling glass cases. The store was the size of my walk-in closet in America, and Bert stationed himself at the doorway. Salvador warned the store could get busy, but luckily the only other customer in the shop was a man admiring a pair of black riding gloves, his murmured conversation into a cellphone undiscernible.

I found what I wanted quickly, purchasing cashmere lined leather gloves in four different colors. I had zipped up my handbag and turned to exit the store when I heard his seductive greeting.

"Hello, darling."

My body erupted in goosebumps. The customer who had kept his back to me during my purchase was none other than shapeshifter Slade Suit.

"Slade, why are you in a glove store in Lisbon? Are you stalking me?" In the reflection of the glass case, I saw Bert's body pivot in our direction, and he spoke into his headset.

"Stalking has negative implications. I am aware of the drastic change in your situation, my love. I hope you enjoyed your transatlantic journey. Were you treated well?" His eyes devoured me with a gleam of lust.

"The crossing was first-class, and the voivode was charming and attentive. He would never write a cryptic note and disappear."

Slade frowned. Bert took a step toward us.

"Oh yes, Dragos is known for his kindness and gentility. I would have explained my necessary absence, but before I could utter a syllable, the ancient vampire warriors descended on Jamaica like a horde of locusts. I'm surprised to find you are still mortal."

My face grew warm with anger.

"Dragos is obviously a touchy subject for you. Frankly, I am late for an appointment. Our final destination is Romania. Please write." He blocked my exit, and the door opened to admit Ernie. They moved to either side of Slade, and Ernie's hand slid underneath his jacket. Slade sized them up and snickered.

"Be careful, Natalie. The last human Dragos bestowed his favor on met a painful end. The vampires are a greedy bunch, and my business plans may make Dragos's world messy."

Ernie held a small shiny object in his hand, and it had a perceptible effect on the shapeshifter. His eyes lost their attractive silvery green and grew murky.

"Thank you for the warning," I hissed. "Now get out of my way." He moved backward and opened the door, stepping onto the sidewalk. The bodyguards rushed past me, separating us. Ernie was ready to pounce. Slade raised his hands in the air in surrender.

"Of course, my darling. I hope we can . . . talk in the future." Grinning, he took three steps backward and performed a smooth dance reverse turn. The cocky alien sauntered down the sidewalk like a wealthy local searching for a present. Salvador was at my side immediately.

"Is everything okay?" He clocked the defensive position of my security detail and the abrupt exit of a stranger. He wisely chose to comment on the shopping bag.

"I see you had success," he exclaimed. "Maravilhoso. Here comes Arabella and Ana. If we leave immediately, we will be perfectly on schedule for the port tasting." Ernie replaced the object in his pocket and held the door while we settled back into the car. I leaned back on the headrest and closed my eyes.

Slade had stalked me to Lisbon. His obsessive behavior was dangerous, and I was thankful Dragos had thought ahead to provide bodyguards. Slade knew I was an heiress and on my way to Transylvania. My friends would need an immediate update, and I'm sure Dragos would learn of the encounter. Slade and I were finished, but other than clueing in my close friends, I would not discuss his horrible behavior, past or recent, with Dragos. The less said, the better.

The menacing encounter aside, the day had fulfilled my goals of a quick trip to Lisbon filled with cultural immersion and fruitful shopping. Salvador chattered and navigated the streets of Porto to our final destination in the city. Rights and lefts disguised the rise in elevation until he negotiated a sharp turn through an ornately scrolled gate. At the end of an unpaved road, the ancestral villa of the elite port dynasty declared its eminence.

We exited the vehicle slowly, speaking in low

voices as if in a church narthex. Our security detail exited their vehicle but made no move to accompany us. Salvador lifted the knocker, but before it could fall, the door swung wide, opened by a woman dressed for a garden party. Her black hair and the aloof bearing contrasted with the warmth which we had experienced from the locals. She did not wait for an introduction.

"I presume you are Natalie Crisan's party?" Her gaze swept our faces, and I stepped forward.

"Good afternoon, I am Natalie Crisan. This is very kind of you. I am a huge fan of port."

She reached out her elegant hand.

"How do you do? Please follow me, we will be tasting in the conservatory." She led us into the hush of a terracotta tiled foyer. Suits of museum grade armor gleamed in the low-light, and overhead the mounted animal heads, trophies of the skilled marksman, heralded the excellent results from centuries of hunting expeditions. Our steps echoed down the shadowy passage ending in an enormous glass enclosed garden room filled with brilliant light. A long table held several bottles of port and multiple glasses.

"My husband will be conducting the tasting. I will tell him you are here." Without a backward glance, she rushed from the room.

"Salvador, did we do something wrong?" I whispered.

"No, the Coros-Sousa family is very private.

They are an old noble family. Our presence in their home is an honor." The tap of quick footsteps announced the arrival of the current keeper of the castle.

"Hello, welcome to my home. I am Pedro Coros-Sousa, but please call me Pedro." He shook our hands and listened attentively to our names. Salvador made a slight bow, and our host responded in kind.

"We are honored to meet friends of the Dracul family. My uncle was quite pleased to show hospitality to an old friend. He sends his greetings to you but is unable to join us."

Ah.

If Pedro Coros-Sousa's uncle knew Dragos, then he was undead or tapped into the Fountain of Youth. Maybe port was the elixir of life? If it is, count me in.

"Thank you for hosting the port tasting in your incredible home. Arabella and I adore port." Pedro brought his hands together with delight.

"Are you aware of the history of port?" Thankfully, I had read a primer in the car.

"I understand only wine made in Portugal can be called port, and the English and the French fought to control it." Pedro's smile widened into a devilish grin.

"Quite right. During The Hundred Years' War, each country fought for access to our wine. Excellent. Let's begin the tasting with a recent, fifteen-year wine. Port is, of course, fortified with brandy, originally used to stabilize it during shipping." He expertly poured an inch into each glass and handed them to us. He held his up.

"Our port must satisfy exacting standards of color, bouquet, and of course, taste. Let's try."

"Delicious," Arabella said. "Raspberry?"

"Yes! One will most often taste fruit in port."

We were each given a glass of water to rinse our mouths.

"Now this one." An inch was poured into fresh glasses, and we sipped.

"The flavors are more concentrated, mellow. I taste cinnamon," I said. Pedro smiled and nodded.

"Correct. You have an exceptional palate. Cinnamon it is. The wine was crafted by my father and is a thirty-year-old tawny port." We rinsed again and moved to the next bottle.

"The flavor profile of this bottle was specially crafted for the wedding of a friend of my uncle. My uncle personally oversaw the entire process—from the grape choice, to crushing the grapes in lagars, and of course the fermentation process. The slow addition of brandy to quiet the yeast is an art he excels at." We brought our glasses to our lips, and I nearly lost my balance. I reached my hand out to steady myself and the wine resting on my tongue provoked a vision.

"How sublime," a woman's voice observed. The perfection of her elocution defined her as a cultured, educated woman. "Chocolate sauce with hint of blackberry. Don't you agree, husband? You must thank the count when you write to him." The woman's hand raised the crystal glass in response to a resounding cheer.

"Long live the King! Long live the Queen!" A diamond and ruby cocktail ring and matching bracelet flashed in the candlelight. From the elevated platform the panoramic view of the grand ballroom revealed the jubilant guests and their ecstatic reverie. In the distance, a wall tapestry heralded the house of Dracul.

Arabella's faraway voice called my name.

"Natalie, Natalie, are you okay?" Four sets of concerned eyes observed my effort to refocus my vision.

"Chocolate sauce. And a berry—blackberry." Pedro raised a quizzical eyebrow.

"It is obvious you have a discerning palate, Miss Crisan. Further tutelage from me is unnecessary. Let us enjoy the bottle on the terrace with a refreshment."

Arabella slid her arm through mine. Our host picked up the bottle of port and exited the open doors to an expansive paved terrace. Ana asked him a question in Portuguese, and with apparent delight, he, Ana, and Salvador chatted amicably.

Arabella and I hung back.

"What happened? I thought you were going to pass out."

Poor Arabella. Proximity to me presented continuous danger and daily encounters with menacing outliers. I leaned toward her and whispered in her ear, "I had the strangest response to the taste of the port—a vision of a celebration at a castle, I think Dragos's. Natalia was there; I repeated her description of the port to Pedro. Did you see his reaction?" She nodded.

"What's happening to me?" I stared into the glass of port and recalled the vision, still fresh in my mind. "Am I dreaming or . . ." A nascent idea crystallized and with it, anxiety and uncertainty.

"Could Natalia be communicating with me from the grave?"

Her jaw dropped.

* * *

I wasn't sad to leave the villa. On the terrace, I noticed the tiniest shift in Pedro's treatment of me. A bit of deference, perhaps, as if I was royalty. When we parted on the steps outside the huge front door, our host leaned over my hand to brush an air kiss across it.

"Miss Crisan, it has been a pleasure and an honor to meet you. Please extend my uncle's best wishes to His Majesty."

"Thank you. I will tell the voivode how kind you were in entertaining my party in your home." The response pleased him.

On the trip back to *The Natalia*, I stared out the window and considered Pedro Coros-Sousa's final words and the requested greeting to Dragos. My relation to Natalia, and the favor shown to me by the voivode, had spread quickly through the vampire world and its environs. My dreams and visions were no longer something I should keep to myself. David, Ian, and Arabella were participants on my journey, and I had to prioritize honesty. No more secrets.

CHAPTER TWENTY-THREE

We had barely enough time to change and finish packing before a steward knocked on the door to gather our luggage. My odd dizzy spell at the villa had softened Arabella's attitude toward me. I did a quick tour of my bedroom.

"If anything is left behind, it will be sent to your home, Miss Crisan." The steward stacked our suitcases onto a luggage cart and pushed it quickly down the corridor. I grabbed my handbag, and we three ladies boarded the jitney to the dock. A black SUV idled at the end of the pier.

"My goodness, we are on a military timetable," I muttered.

My eponymous security detail, rode in the front seat, Bert negotiating the rush hour traffic with precision. At the airport, we were directed to a separate terminal reserved for private planes. The sun had dipped below the horizon, and the day settled into twilight.

Dragos's plane, painted in the colors of the Romanian flag, was at least the size of Air Force One, which I had seen parked at Newark International Airport. We were briefly questioned, and our passports were inspected before we walked onto the tarmac and made the long climb up the steel steps into the plane. Ana left us to sit with the rest of the staff in the rear of the plane.

Inside, the flight attendant escorted us to a curtained area in the middle of the plane. A faux wood wallpaper and ivory leather padded seats gave the creepy impression of the inside of a coffin, perhaps comforting décor for those who spent their days resting. The window shades were shut, exacerbating the claustrophobic atmosphere, and I broke out in a cold sweat.

Arabella reached for my hand.

"Natalie, what's wrong?"

"Can you please put up the blind? I need to see light, even if it's artificial." Arabella pushed up the shade, and the black clad flight attendant pursed her lips. Other guests were boarding, and she hurried toward the front of the plane without instructing us to close the shade.

"This plane is like a coffin," I said, clicking my seatbelt.

"It's like a man's study. Obviously, it was decorated without a woman's input." Arabella settled across the aisle, checking the placement of her bookmark. I hadn't told Arabella about Slade's appearance in the glove store. She had a right to know he was stalking me. I cleared my throat.

"What?" She closed her thick book with a thud.

"Arabella, Slade was waiting for me in the glove store." I recounted the tense conversation and his thinly veiled threats.

"I thought I saw him in the museum, and now I'm certain of it." So that was why Arabella had hurried to my side. His skulking about was further confirmation of Slade's sinister intentions.

Arabella reached for my hand.

"There is a bad current swirling around you, like you are in the vortex of a battle. I wonder if Slade is interested in your inheritance or because you are a descendant of Natalia? He obviously hates Dragos and the other vampires. What did he call them?

"He said 'the ancient vampire warriors descended on Jamaica like a swarm of locusts.' And that's why he left. Maybe I'm just irresistible."

"Darling, you are irresistible." David and Ian had arrived, and relief and comfort washed over me.

Arabella moved to the window seat in my row, and the newlyweds settled into their seats across the aisle.

"David, I need to tell you what happened today. I saw . . ."

"Miss Crisan, Miss Bishop. I hope you enjoyed your day in Lisbon." The voivode had appeared to greet us—or perhaps ensure I hadn't run away. He was dressed in black, sporting a tailored blazer and pressed slacks. Did he know about Slade's appearance in Lisbon? He had probably insisted on a full report of my activities. Was that a bad thing? His precautions had paid off; Slade was definitely stalking me.

A shadow of a smile crossed his lips. Perhaps his protection was necessary. Natalia had loved him. Were the visions a communication from her to trust his concern for my welfare? It wasn't the time or place to explore these possibilities, so I made small talk.

"Yes, thank you. Pedro Corso-Sousa asked me to extend the best wishes of his uncle."

"Ah. And you enjoyed the port tasting?"

"Oh, yes. Pedro was gracious, and the tasting was very informative."

"I am glad the day met your expectations. If you'll excuse me, we need to be underway, and I must speak with the pilot." He swiftly exited through the curtains separating our party from the forward cabin. How would he react if I told him about the visions? Our relationship was so new, and it would be a disaster if he thought I wanted to take Natalia's place.

Before I could update David and Ian about Slade's reappearance, the curtain was flung open, and Mike stepped through. He was dressed for the cover of GQ magazine, and his eyes strayed to mine briefly, but he said nothing as he passed to the next curtain which separated us from the staff and the restrooms. He looked well-rested. No one spoke until he retraced his steps up the aisle and pulled the forward cabin curtain closed.

David whispered, "I've heard the ceremony is scheduled for two days' time. Invitations are the ultimate status symbol, and vampires are assembling from all over the world. Mike is not the only person who will be. . . featured."

Arabella changed the subject.

"Tsk-tsk. Let's use our time productively. It would be helpful if you could clarify for Natalie, again, the precautions of letting people into her home—in detail. Like vampires, for instance."

"Sure." David unbuckled his belt and adjusted the curtain, taking a quick peek. Once again in his seat, he laid out the basic rules I should follow for my safety.

"Let's review the rules. A vampire can't enter a home he or she hasn't been invited into by the owner. Once invited, we don't have the ability to invite others. So, if you want Ian and me to live in your home we can, and we can't invite others."

"But Arabella invited you into my home in Bedford. She wasn't the owner. I'm confused, that doesn't make sense."

"It doesn't, totally," Arabella agreed.

"Technically, I wasn't a guest, but a permanent resident, maybe that's why. Also, David has nonaggressive energy. If you had told David to leave when he was in your kitchen, he would have been blocked from reentering."

Ian was adamant.

"We must ensure the boundaries of Natalie's home. Olenka visited her bedroom on *The Natalia* without an invitation. That can't happen in Romania."

"What about Ana or other staff?" There were apparent nuances to the rules. I was determined to control who could get into my house.

"Approved guests, mortals, are free to come and go but should be forbidden to allow other mortals in without your permission," Ian said. "I also think cameras and modern technology will add a level of safety."

The plane engines engaged, and we sped forward, smoothly lifting into the air current. Below, the lights of Lisbon blinked their farewell.

"If my home has a basement or other area you are comfortable with, you're going to live with me, right?" David reached his hand across the aisle and patted mine.

"Of course, darling. I'm sure there is a wine or root cellar. We'll check it out when we arrive." He had a mischievous look in his eyes.

"Do you think we'll drive through Borga Pass?" He stage whispered. "How cool would it be if a creaky coach on wooden spoke wheels was waiting to take us the rest of our journey?" David bounced wildly in his seat, imitating the jostling carriage ride.

"I hope not." Bram Stoker's *Dracula* was a fantastic book, but I preferred an SUV to an ancient coach. "How long will it take to drive to the castle?"

"Not sure, hon. The uncertainty makes me a wee bit nervous—we'll need to settle our boxes. Ian, do you know?"

"I understand there is a contingency plan if we get delayed. David, you were in the meeting. Didn't you pay attention?"

"I forgot that part. I was mystified as to how the voivode could be completely bald."

I choked on my water, and some spurted from my mouth.

"David, my mouth was full." David's banter always had the ability to distract and relax me.

He shrugged.

"I can't help it if I'm hilarious."

"If you comedians don't mind, I am going to close my eyes for a bit. My book can wait." Arabella adjusted the seat back, raised the footrest, and slid her travel pillow around her neck.

"Me too," I said. "We were running around Lisbon since early morning."

I settled into the plush comfort of the ample seat for a nap. Maybe people wouldn't behave poorly on flights if the configuration of Air Dracul became the standard for all commercial airplanes.

* * *

I woke with a start. One cold finger laid on my arm still had the ability to shock.

"Sorry to wake you, hon." David leaned across the aisle. Next to him, Ian had his tray table down and was reading. "We are about forty-five minutes from the airport. Right on schedule." I rolled my shoulders back and rotated my neck right to left. Next to me, Arabella was absorbed in her novel.

The captain came on the intercom and announced we were beginning the descent for our landing in Bucharest Otopeni (OTP).

"I need to use the restroom." I unfastened my seatbelt.

"Me too," Arabella said.

Pulling back the curtain at the rear of the plane, I was happy to see Ana on the right side of the aisle, earbuds in, enjoying a movie. Several other staff were spread out within the four rows. On the left side of the aisle, all the rows were filled with paler, silent individuals engaged in industrious duties. One gentleman polished a pair of black boots, while a woman knitted a sweater. Dotia sat at the end of the last aisle, closest to the bathroom. Head down, she had a stack of paper on which she wrote carefully. She did not look up when we passed.

"Hello, is everything okay?" Ana had pulled out her ear buds and paused her movie.

"Just using the restroom. We'll be landing soon."

"Let me know if you need anything." She twisted the ear buds back in and resumed her movie.

Arabella used the toilet first, and I relaxed on a cream cashmere covered sofa. The area was a comfy nook with an interesting library stored behind closed Plexiglas doors. The curtain at mid-cabin opened, and Mike stepped carefully down the aisle, drawn to me like steel to a magnet. He dropped onto the sofa next to me, threaded his arm around my shoulders, and pulled me toward him.

"Last night was incredible. Thank you." Leaning forward, he kissed me passionately. The door of the lavatory opened, and he jumped back. The one secret I hadn't shared with my friends was Mike's sleepover last night. I wasn't ready to admit I'd broken my promise to them in less than twenty-four hours. I didn't want to think about their reaction if they knew what I'd done.

"Natalie, do you want me to wait for you?" Arabella spoke to me, but her stern expression fixated on Mike.

"No, I'm fine. Thanks." She raised her eyebrows, and I thought she might stay despite my response. Did she suspect something? Thankfully, she swiveled slowly and went back to her seat.

"I need to use the restroom, Mike. I drank a lot of water." He pushed a lock of hair behind my ear and kissed my cheek—the old charm was back. I scolded myself; why had I slept with him? Had I forgotten his terrible treatment of me? Mike had teased me once that I was like an egg; the hard shell on the outside was easily cracked and the inside could be scrambled without much effort.

"You were always hydrating," he said. "Smart. This is the last chance I'll have to speak to you before—you know. I love you, Natalie Crisan. Send me good thoughts, please."

"I will. I hope you're making the right decision." I didn't say I love you, a small victory for my battered self-esteem.

"I'm making the best choice for me." He would always make the best choice for himself.

Resting my hand on his warm cheek, I searched his eyes for his humanness and the intrinsic characteristics he might lose in two days. I didn't want to cry, and I got to my feet. He stood.

"The duchess says there will be a ball in your honor. Will you invite me? We can celebrate with a dance."

"I'll make sure you're invited, Mike. Good luck."

"Thanks, Nat. One more kiss for good luck." His lips brushed mine, and he left me standing alone.

The Sicilian defense continued . . . Another pawn lost to the black queen.

* * *

Upon disembarking from the airplane, Olenka sought me out while the customs inspector reviewed my paperwork.

"Miss Crisan, I must apologize for not visiting you on the plane." Olenka wore her travel suit with panache and carried a fabulous crocodile handbag with a diamond clasp. "Airplanes are a modern necessity which I detest. I am occupied for the next several days but let us coordinate our calendars to continue our talks." We air-kissed. I shielded my thoughts with a quick call to Lupu. Did Olenka suspect Mike and I had reconciled our friendship? For both of our sakes I accepted her invitation with grace.

"I will contact you as soon as I organize myself. Thank you for reminding me."

"I look forward to it." Mike stood off to the side, and when Olenka concluded the social niceties, he followed meekly in her wake.

Satisfied with my documents, the official returned my passport.

"Welcome to Romania, Miss Crisan. Have a pleasant stay."

"Thank you."

The voivode's valet came forward and handed me a pair of headphones.

"The headphones will help with the noise. His Majesty suggested you put them on in the helicopter. They have a microphone for communication." Helicopter?

Four helicopters awaited our arrival. Two were military style, painted a deep green with a huge panel open on the side. The other two were luxury models, black and gold, sleek and shiny. I had never been in a helicopter before, and I nudged David.

"A helicopter ride to a castle? Am I dreaming?"

"Better than a carriage ride through Borga Pass," he whispered. "Better put these puppies on."

Once inside the helicopter, a thrill of adventure coursed through my body as we rose in the air, and the pilot smoothly turned the bird toward our final destination.

"Miss Crisan?" A voice broke through my introspection, and I jumped in my seat.

"Yes?"

Dragos peered around the side of his seat. "Do I correctly assume this is your first time in a helicopter?"

"Yes, it is. I was admiring the twinkle of the lights in the dark. It's enchanting."

"There are many advantages to the night. But perhaps you are disappointed not to drive in an ancient horse-drawn carriage through Borga Pass? You own horses and a splendid coach. We can replicate the scene from *Dracula* if it will entertain you." A half-smile shared, and he swung back forward and resumed his conversation with the pilot. I caught David's wide-eyed expression. Note to self: Dragos's hearing was superlative.

The ground lights became sparser until there was little illumination from below. A mammoth shape formed in the distance—a mountain that appeared to glow, high and alone. As we drew closer, I realized it was Castle Dracul, and the practiced pilot rounded the left tower and landed the instrument softly on the helipad.

We disembarked. The military vehicle had landed ahead of us, its crew at attention and awaiting orders. Ana came forward and took my carryon. Dragos removed his headphones, and we followed suit.

"Miss Crisan, will all three of your friends be staying with you?"

"Yes. Is there a cellar or a cool area for David and Ian's, um, boxes?" He nodded.

"Yes, there is a large root cellar next to the wine cellar. I am happy you won't be alone at night." My safety was a constant theme. Given Slade's threatening behavior I was encouraged by his zealous precautions.

"May I walk you to the gate?" Ah. The garden gate in my dreams existed!

"Thank you, yes, I am very tired." He offered his arm, and I admit I appreciated the old-world courtesy. His arm through the sleeve of the light jacket he wore could have been iron covered by cloth. David, Ian, and Arabella followed at a discreet distance.

The gibbous moon hung in a star-filled sky. I breathed deeply—the air was crisp and clean with a slight smell of the forest we had flown over.

"This garden path was at its height a month ago," Dragos said as we walked past hedges interspersed with semi-circular recessed cut-outs. The niches held sculptures, and I recognized the *Four Seasons*, exact replicas of garden sculptures I had admired at a magnificent country home in England that I toured with my Aunt Loretta. As a young woman I'd never wondered why the *Four Seasons* theme was of great importance to my aunt. I stopped in front of the Autumn Goddess, dressed in harvest garments. Art, music, sculpture—the *Four Seasons* had played an integral part of my education. Why? Did Aunt Loretta know about my aristocratic Romanian heritage? Was she sent to protect me? Was she really my aunt? Questions clogged my overworked brain creating a jumble of confusion and I felt the rise of anxiety.

Dragos and I walked silently. He had said he only became aware of my existence recently—was he telling the truth? I plucked up my courage.

"Voivode, there are questions which I need answers to before I can fully embrace my current situation," I said. "What do you know about my parent's disappearance? Why, with your legions of followers did you not find the descendants of your son sooner? Did my Aunt Loretta know I was related to a Romanian queen?"

He didn't answer immediately. The light breeze blew colder as we strolled, penetrating the light jacket I wore. Up ahead, many lights blazed from inside and outside my new home, the glow a warm welcome after the stresses of the day. The path ended, and we faced a scrolled iron gate.

Dragos gently released my arm. When he spoke, his baritone conveyed candor and a hint of vulnerability.

"I tried for decades to find my son. Natalia had devised an ingenious series of red herrings. Many died during my hunt for Prince Dragos. I failed in my quest to recover him.

"I regret to share that your parents were killed in the Dolomites, by all accounts a skiing accident. My best agents report that the avalanche was odd, but there were no obvious signs of foul play. Removing your father, a male heir, would be important to my enemies, so I have reserved my opinion on the findings." He paused, pursed his lips and continued.

"Your Aunt Loretta's story is murky. Your parent's Last Will and Testament established her as your guardian, but we could find no record of her before she moved in to take care of you; so, her exact relationship to you has never been established.

Your parent's attorney died shortly after your aunt came to live with you. I do not wish to sully your memories of her, I had suspicions of her alliances and have no proof to share. She raised you well and was kind and loving. I apologize if my statement causes you pain. It is possible that she was another level of protection arranged by my late wife."

I placed my hand on the iron of the garden gate. There was a ring of truth to his statements, except for the aspersions against my aunt, which I would never believe. But I had asked, and he had answered with great detail. Had Natalia been brilliant enough to shield her descendants from her husband? Could a game of chess play out through a century?

"I will leave you here," he said. "Tomorrow evening, I will answer any questions you have about the house, its contents, etcetera." He addressed my friends. "Westwoods, you have been given a great honor, and I appreciate your dedication to Miss Crisan. It will not be forgotten."

"Thank you, sir," I said. "Good night." He waited until I unhooked the gate and then moved swiftly toward his castle. The howl of an animal split the stillness of the night, and its call was joined by others. Wolves? Did the pack know that Natalia's heir had returned?

CHAPTER TWENTY-FOUR

I climbed the steps of my new home and turned to my friends, waiting on the other side of the garden gate.

"I'm not sure exactly how this works, but David and Ian Westwood, I welcome you to my home. And, of course, my dear friend Arabella Bishop, please enter my home."

"Thank you, Natalie." David, Ian, and Arabella stepped through the gate, latched it behind them, and proceeded to the front door. It was impossible to appreciate the unique architecture of the home in the darkness, but I recalled a conversation with the voivode aboard *The Natalia*.

"My wife wanted a non-traditional home designed to resemble a grand folly because she found our castle in the winter to be cold, damp, and dreary," Dragos shared one evening. "An architect designed the building to her specifications, creating from a dream, a building with eight exterior walls, exquisite crown molding and other finishes, and a glass conservatory for year-round gardening. She called it Le Refuge Bleu. I am delighted to have it occupied by her heir."

On the porch of Le Refuge Bleue, I reached for the doorknob and before I could turn it, the door swung open, and a mature version of Ana greeted us. Her brown hair was highlighted with sparkles of gray and pulled back smoothly into a low bun. Ana had her eyes, a soft kindly brown. They were the same height, and when she spoke it was Ana's voice I heard.

"Miss Crisan, I am Ana's mother, Maria. His Majesty asked me to open the house for you. Welcome to your new home." We stepped inside and it was love at first sight.

Natalia had embraced color. The foyer and center hallway walls rose upward in a splendid sunset of burnt orange. Above, a bronze-forged chandelier glowed with amber glass. The diamond pattern of the black-and-white floor tiles was partially covered by handmade rugs.

"Hello, Mama." Ana came up behind us dragging a suitcase, and Maria rushed to hug her.

"Sweetheart, the baggage must come in through the back entrance." Ana blushed.

"Oops, I forgot." With an embarrassed smile in my direction, Ana exited, and we heard her crisp footsteps cross the porch. Maria closed the front door. I couldn't have cared less about Ana coming in the front door. I didn't live in Downton Abbey, and although I adored the TV show I would insist on a modern approach to running my new home.

"Please excuse my daughter's mistake," Maria said. "She has told me what a lovely person you are and how kind you have been. My husband and I were worried since she has never been away from home, but my husband is dedicated to the voivode. Would you like to see the drawing room, or do you wish to retire?"

"I would love to see the drawing room, but have you been waiting up for me? It's very late." Maria smiled.

"It is my honor to be here to welcome you. Here is your beautiful drawing room." With a flourish of ceremony, she depressed the gleaming gold latches on the rosewood doors. In the center of each door, an inlaid vase of mother of pearl flowers beckoned us into the refined elegance of Natalia's drawing room. I gasped; could the art which filled the impressive room truly be mine? I crossed the muted rug to the hearth and held my hands out toward the cheerful fire in the grate.

"Would you like me to bring a refreshment?"

"Yes, thank you. For two, please." She smiled and hurried toward the sound of voices, no doubt belonging to the people delivering our luggage and my friends' boxes.

I had always given Ian and David complete

privacy when it came to their coffins, which they referred to as boxes. I didn't know what wood was used to create the resting place my friends returned to before dawn. A vampire must rest in the coffin he or she was buried in, that I did know. They had never offered more information or details, and I had no intention of prying.

"Nat, do you mind if we make sure things are set up properly in the cellar?" David and Ian's boxes had voyaged across continents, and it would be a disaster if I couldn't accommodate them properly.

"Sure, go get settled. I'm overwhelmed by the splendor and may faint onto the Louis the something sofa." David laughed and trailed Ian toward the conversation drifting from the back of the house.

Arabella had been quiet during the helicopter ride and the walk through the garden. She gaped at a painting.

"Natalie, this is an Old Master painting. My goodness, it's the Vermeer mentioned in Natalia's will. Do you see the faded letters within the herbs in the trug?"

I leaned closer to the painting, a composition featuring two matronly women at a kitchen table peeling potatoes. A dog lay under the farmer's table, and a trug of herbs spilled onto the far corner.

"I like the word trug; I would have called it a long basket," I said. "Let's see—it looks like an arrow under an upper-case M. Then, eer. . . No way. Dragos wouldn't have left an original Vermeer in an empty house. The painting must be a copy."

"Your inheritance included a Vermeer. Don't you remember?" Arabella shook her head. "Do you actually think Natalia would have a copy in the drawing room of her house?"

I jumped back as if I'd been chastised for being too close at The Met.

"The Vermeer and the contents of the house are worth millions, pet. Based on that and Slade Suit's stalking us in Lisbon, a solid strategy for your protection is crucial," she said. "Is there an alarm system?"

"Yes. Dragos told me there is an additional security panel in my bedroom."

Maria arrived with a tray of tea, finger sandwiches, and little cakes, and we settled on the sofa by the fire. Ravenous and nervous, I stared at the painting, annoyed. Would every day begin with complications from my new status as Natalia's heir? There was enough to deal with, and I wasn't sure I wanted to be responsible for a Vermeer.

We munched in silence. David and Ian returned presently and filled us in on the cellar. "We are settled, but will need to do a thorough clean tomorrow," David said.

David was a clean-freak and organization whiz, and if he took on a project, like my home in Bedford, New York the results would be fabulous.

"There are a few very old bottles of brandy in

the wine cellar, Nat. Otherwise, the wine racks are empty."

"Now that's a problem I will be happy to fix." I yawned. "Sorry. It's after two, peeps, and I'm wiped out.

"We're going to inventory the house tomorrow. Arabella thinks the painting over there is the Vermeer mentioned in the will."

Arabella rose with me. "Good night."

"'Night, ladies," David said. "We will lounge in this opulent room and ogle the accoutrements. I will not abscond with the painting of the poorly dressed women peeling potatoes. I never liked potatoes, even when swimming in butter. See you tomorrow night." In the hallway, Maria was arranging flowers on a table.

"Maria, can you please show us to our rooms?"

"Of course, Miss Crisan. This way, please."

The staircase to the second floor ran up the left wall to a landing. Maria pointed to a door on the left.

"This door leads to the third floor. There are rooms for staff and storage." We rounded the landing and headed straight toward an open door, spilling cozy light into the hallway. Maria paused at the door.

"Miss Crisan, this is the primary bedroom." I stepped into the feminine space and immediately felt a feeling of safety and contentment. Ana and her mother had already unpacked my suitcase. Ana had left a note telling me she'd made storage decisions based on where I liked my clothes in the ship suite aboard *The Natalia*.

"Ana is a marvel."

Maria beamed with pride at the compliment.

"Thank you, Miss. I hope you don't mind that I sent her home to sleep, but we'll be back early in the morning. There's so much to do! Would you like me to show you where we arranged your things? We can adjust everything tomorrow if our method doesn't suit your needs."

"I'm sure it's perfect, but please show me. And then I would like you to go home and sleep. We can chat about the running of the house tomorrow."

Maria opened drawers and armoires and then opened a paneled door to the left of the four-poster bed. She tapped a switch, and an immense crystal chandelier shimmered. A walk-in closet was inadequate to describe the sublime dressing room. Dragos had spared no expense, and I began to giggle uncontrollably. The room was at least as big as my living room in America. The pale pink walls were paneled à la Bridgerton. Several dress forms lined a far wall, and on the right cubbyholes awaited Imelda Marcos's shoe collection. Near the ceiling, lit shelves behind glass doors would display bespoke handbags. Several recessed cubbies of varying lengths would hold gowns, blouses, jackets and slacks. It was like a boutique, and I felt a sense of appreciation for Dragos's obvious desire to please me.

"David is going to faint," I said. "He designed the prettiest closet for me and it could fit in here ten times."

Arabella sighed.

"This isn't a closet, Nat, it's an heiress's lair to stash her stuff, like an Egyptian antechamber." I hugged her.

"Let's get you to bed. We can inspect the craziness after a good night's sleep."

Maria directed us to a bedroom on the other side of the dressing room. The guest bedroom was painted a sunny yellow and covered in floral chintz.

"My goodness, this is lovely."

"His Majesty insisted on refurbishing the fabrics, but all the furniture is original. He'll be pleased to hear you like it."

"Maria, thank you for welcoming us and getting the house ready. Now go home and get some rest."

"Thank you, I will see you around nine."

Arabella and I hugged goodnight.

"Nat, if I don't keep moving, I'll fall asleep standing up."

"Me too. Sleep well."

I perched on the edge of my bed and removed my shoes. If the drawing room was opulent, the extravagance of my bedroom was off the Richter scale. A huge four-poster bed dominated the far wall. The triple dresser appeared to be French, one of the Louis's, and the drawers which now contained my lingerie were lined with lavender-scented paper. Mirrors abounded, and tasseled lamps, crystal wall sconces, and a breathtaking Lalique, I think, chandelier dripped light onto the silk rug. Next to my bed, a carafe of water and a glass sparked gratitude for Ana's attention to my care. Another note mentioned there was a mini fridge in the bathroom should I need more cold water.

The overhaul of my home in the States had felt like the peak of chic, and I'd been grateful for David's amazing talent. These digs, however, were the private chambers of an aristocratic, sophisticated, discerning woman with no budgetary constraints. My phone pinged.

David:
We're retiring, darling. You can engage the alarm.

The alarm panel had a button that said *on*, and I pressed it. I texted a thumbs up.

Me:
👍
Goodnight, David.

I crossed the wide space to the bullion-fringed drapes and pulled them open. From my bedroom several windows of the castle sent pale beams of light toward the garden path. I checked the locks on the windows and pulled the drapes closed against the night. Safety first. I reopened the armoire; I even peeked under the bed. After carrying my nightgown to the bathroom, I removed my makeup and applied a sleep mask. The bedroom wasn't stuffy despite the home being closed up for decades. Dragos had maintained the home for a century since Natalia's death. The vampire king had mourned for his queen, keeping her home impeccable, as if he was awaiting her return. Had he anticipated the return of an heir?

A series of four paintings featuring bucolic nymphs cavorting in a garden hung on the wall behind the bed. The signature, Fragonard, was remarkable. I couldn't process any more largesse and switched off the lights except for the low glow of the bedside lamp.

I woke to birdsong. The bold songbird was serenading just outside my window, and I hopped out of bed to check out the little rascal. Parting the drapes slightly, I quickly spotted the nervy offender, a plump guy with orange around his face and soft blue across his head. His compact wings were blue with white stripes on top. I would later find out my little friend was a Common Chaffinch.

I released the heavy drape and snuggled into a robe. After using the bathroom, I disengaged the alarm and went in search of the kitchen. It was eight, and I hoped Ana had enjoyed a well-deserved lie-in.

I found the kitchen easily and followed the directions Maria had left, pushing a button on a fancy European coffee maker. The kitchen was a cook's space—efficient, well-lit, and sparkling clean. The aroma of brewing coffee was irresistible, and drew Arabella, clad in her brightly colored robe, to the cheery space.

"Good morning. How did you sleep?" The coffee brewed quickly, and I poured two cups. The fridge yielded what, hopefully, was half and half or cream.

"Really well. The mattress is a dream. You?" It was a joy to be back in my bestie's good graces.

"Wonderful. A cute bird sang me awake. Honestly, I'd love to wear comfies, pull my hair back and lounge around. But I also need to explore Natalia's house."

"You mean your house," Arabella corrected me quietly. "We have all day to roam around Le Refuge Bleue. I'll help you. I admit I'm dying of curiosity."

"Oh, thank you. We'll squeeze in naps later." A clatter at the back door announced Ana, off-balance due to the multiple shopping bags she carried. Her mother came in behind her, her arms overflowing with flowers.

"Good morning," echoed from mother and daughter. Ana moved straight to the counter and dumped the straw tote bags. "We have provisions for breakfast. And my mother ordered several bouquets of flowers from the village florist."

"If you don't mind me saying, a house is not a home without plants and flowers," Maria chirped, filling a side sink with the blooms. "There is a butler's pantry with vases and other china. You can choose the ones you like best if you wish."

"I trust your judgement. And breakfast would be welcome. Arabella is going to assist me in exploring the house."

Ana clattered two fry pans onto the cook top and then twirled to me.

"Ana, I want you to take time to see your family today. Okay?"

Ana smiled over her shoulder.

"Thank you. My mother plans to be with me all day to spruce up your home. We can chat while we work, but my father would like me home for lunch —if it's okay. My father requested that you stop by if it's convenient. It's important. . . in a good way."

"Sure. A walk this afternoon will do me good."

While we talked, Ana filled a hand-painted pottery bowl with fruit and Maria whisked eggs in a glass bowl. We were treated to a slice of freshly baked rustic bread, and featherlight omelets filled with a local cheese.

"Do you know if there is any stationery in the house?" I asked through a mouthful of eggs.

"The drawing room has a desk. Maybe there?"

After breakfast, the ornate Louis the something desk yielded sheets of paper. I had a pen in my handbag, and I could have used my computer, but I decided not to. It seemed more appropriate to handwrite the contents of the house with questions next to them.

Showered and dressed in my favorite jeans and a sweater, I met Arabella in the drawing room.

"I love the color palette Natalia chose; well, I'm assuming she chose it. The richness of the colors reminds me of a sunset."

"Romanian winters are probably gray and depressing. Brightly painted walls would be cheerful and keep the doldrums away. Color is one reason I love Jamaica. You never have to search for green, red, blue, yellow . . ." Her face was wistful, and I knew we had left her country too soon. She hadn't been back since she had shown up on my porch as a starving enchanted cat, under a curse from a malevolent witch. When the witch had died, she'd been released from the spell, but she'd stayed with me in the States out of loyalty. As soon as I was settled, I would insist she return to her family.

"Might as well start with the potato painting," I said, hoping for levity.

"I wouldn't call the Vermeer a potato painting in front of Dragos," Arabella warned with a chuckle. I wrote Vermeer at the top of the page.

There was a small, enameled box on a sideboard. A monogram with the letters NCD left no doubt as to the owner of the precious coffer. I picked it up and examined the stones inset in the initials.

"For heaven's sake, I think this box has diamonds on the lid."

Arabella inspected it and agreed with a shrug.

"Yeah, diamonds for sure. I suggest a greatest hits list. Nothing in the room is post-nineteenth century. Let's check the room across the hall."

The furniture in the dining room was also French, and the only item I added to the list was the quality still life over a buffet table. Etched glass hurricane shades enclosed heavy silver candlesticks. Did Natalia host dinner parties in this formal room?

Behind a closed door near the kitchen, we discovered a butler's pantry chock full of crystal stemware, china, and folded linen. The vases Maria had mentioned were against a wall, and I selected a Midori vase for a future floral arrangement.

"While we're in the kitchen, let's heat up the soup Maria left." A note on the counter said to text when we had time, and Ana would introduce me to her father. We demolished the soup and soaked up the broth with thick slices of the brown bread.

"I am definitely going to take a nap," Arabella said. "What is it about warm soup that makes me comatose?" Arabella returned to her bedroom, and I texted Ana. She showed up ten minutes later, rosy-cheeked and grinning with delight.

"Are you ready? We can't wait for you to see."

A soft breeze rustled the leaves on the trees and a stroll in the sweet country air was exactly the medicine I needed after yesterday's stresses. I latched the garden gate behind me, and we headed off toward the left of the towering hulk of Castle Dracul. A five-minute walk over a stone path led us to the working area of Dragos's estate. Ana's home, a cottage painted a charming shade of green with a red door, was surrounded by a potager garden. Late summer flowers thrived alongside herbs and vegetables. A security guard trailed us, smoking a cigarette.

"What a pretty home you have, Ana. And the garden is a marvel." We stopped to admire the pots and rows of veggies in the weedless soil.

"My mother loves her garden. We put up the vegetables and eat them through the winter. There are berries and mushrooms in the forest, and we preserve them, too. Romanian winters are long."

"I would love to walk the woods with you. Before it's too cold to go outside."

"It's never too cold," Ana chuckled. "Romanians love winter sports."

Up ahead, a gray-haired man waited, wiping his hands on a work apron, which he removed as we approached.

"Hello Miss Crisan, I am Boris Popa. Thank you for taking time out of your first day to visit the stables. I care for the horses of His Majesty and am a general handyman. Should you need any jobs done in Le Refuge Bleue." I extended my hand, and his firm, rough grip was a testament to his words.

"It is a pleasure to meet Ana's family. She is a treasure." Boris beamed.

"I am happy to hear she did her best job. Behind me are the stables. Do you ride?"

"Sadly, I don't." Olenka had asked if I rode. Ballet and horseback riding didn't mix. A ballet turnout was destroyed by the need to keep your heels down and toes turned in when your feet were in the stirrups. But I wasn't a ballerina anymore, and apparently, I owned horses.

"It would be an honor to teach you—if you're interested. You own several horses, and the voivode also has a few, although he seldom rides. Would you like to meet them?"

"Oh yes. How exciting!"

We followed Boris around the side of the barn and into a cleanly swept stable. Several horses whinnied, and one stuck her head into view.

"Hello, Diana. This is Natalie Crisan. If your new mistress is agreeable, we will take you out for a trot tomorrow. Here, give her this." Boris produced a carrot from his pocket, and he demonstrated how to feed it to the horse without losing a finger. The other horses poked their heads over the half door and demanded their treat, and we ambled along the enclosures until we arrived at the rear of the barn. Mewling and yips came from behind the left enclosure, and I peeked over the top.

In a far corner, a head raised—the white head of a wolf. The knowing yellow eyes bored into mine. Three pups rolled in the straw. She reminded me of Lupu, my mind-reading protector who graciously appeared when called. The she-wolf got to her feet.

"She is protective of her brood," Boris said. "She came to the back door one day about a year ago. You could see her bones, and my wife immediately fed her and led her to this unoccupied stall. She slept for a whole day. We think she was ejected from her pack."

"Aren't wolves dangerous?"

Boris scoffed at the question.

"They can be, but Hermione has become our protector. She comes and goes as she likes and obviously met another wolf in the forest. Wolves mate for life." The pups rolled and played.

"Can we pet the pups?"

"We'll see." Boris opened the stall door, and we waited in the doorway. Hermione emitted a soft sound, and the three pups rushed to her side. She approached tentatively, pups in tow, while Boris crooned in a singsong voice. I didn't move. Then she did a very strange thing. She bowed, and the three pups dropped gawkily to the ground.

"She is giving us permission to admire her new brood."

Before I could move forward, the largest of the cubs rose from the straw and approached me. It halted at my feet, and I reached down to pat its head.

"Ah, Decebal has chosen you. He will be a great protector when he can leave his mother."

Ana squatted down and the other two pups raced toward her. Hermione remained in the background, content to allow her progeny to be admired. Was Lupu sending me physical protection from the next life? Decebal rolled over, and I stroked his tummy. A wolf for a pet and protector and learning to ride horses in fresh country air would be as calming as a hot yoga class. I patted Decebal's round tummy and stood up.

"Boris, do you have time available tomorrow to teach me to ride?"

His face broke into a grin.

"I have the horses to take care of, but would ten work?"

"Ten it is." I patted Decebal's head. "Ana, I'm going to head back to the house." The word 'home' didn't feel right, at least not yet.

Outside, the security guard waited. Dragos wasn't kidding about twenty-four-hour protection.

CHAPTER TWENTY-FIVE

Natalia's color palette of choice for Le Refuge Bleue was audacious, reflecting the stages of a brilliant day flowing into a spectacular sunset. The rich blue of the drawing and dining room melted into orange and burnt sienna in the central hallway. Color was her canvas, masterfully employed to highlight the art and collectibles located throughout her home.

Natalia's love of flora and fauna was evident. The walls were hung with outstanding paintings depicting horses, birds, and nature. Unfamiliar with the artists, I noted their names on my list.

On the second floor, opposite the bedrooms, the music room caused me to blurt out,

"Arabella, am I dreaming? This is like the movie, *Amadeus*!"

"For all we know, Dragos bought the

harpsichord from the composer himself," Arabella quipped.

"Do you think Dragos is that old?" We howled with laughter. "I better ask Ian before I make a mistake and ask Dragos if he saw Mozart in concert." Giddy, I twirled in the center of the room.

"I am going to learn to play this gorgeous instrument." A gilded pianoforte centered the room, painted in shades of pink and accented with gold scrolls. I imagined Natalia playing for a close friend, fingers flying across the keys. I reached toward the intricate garlands of flowers intertwined with a large N, and Arabella grabbed my hand.

"Don't touch it," she said. "Something isn't right."

"What?"

"Trust me. There is dark magic here." I recoiled from the gleaming instrument, nearly knocking over a harp. Adrenaline jolted through my body.

"What should we do?" I backed up several feet to a window. Directly below, a security guard walked along the woods behind my house and disappeared around a corner. "There's a guard walking around the house."

"That's good. We may have discovered how Natalia was murdered."

"You think the pianoforte is cursed?" I felt sick to my stomach.

"I can feel it emanating bad energy. You'll need to tell the voivode." Devastated, I sat down on the closest chair, a gilded side chair with a needlepoint seat cushion. The charm of the music room paled under Arabella's suspicions. Her intuition had never failed me before, and if Natalia had died as the result of dark magic, Dragos should be informed.

"Nat, let's go downstairs and inventory the plants and statues in the conservatory. But first, we'll have a cup of herbal tea." In the kitchen, Arabella plugged in the kettle and steeped two cups of chamomile tea.

"Here Nat, drink this—slowly. It's very hot." I didn't really like tea, but chamomile was Arabella's favorite panacea.

"Do you think the. . . dark magic is meant for me?" I cradled the warm mug in my hands.

"Don't know, hon," she said. "Come on, bring your tea into the conservatory."

The conservatory, although not huge, was a multi-faceted glass structure reminiscent of a cushion-cut diamond, with a red brick floor covered by rugs. Several comfy armchairs faced each other, and a wood stove close to the interior wall guaranteed use of the room, except for the coldest winter days. Arabella perused the plants while I considered the quickest way to communicate Arabella's suspicions to Dragos.

"There are two plants I'm not familiar with," she said. "We need to have them identified. We aren't being paranoid, Nat. There are poisons that can go through the skin and are undetectable."

I shivered. "But if there is poison or a curse on the pianoforte wouldn't someone cleaning or dusting it be affected the same as Natalia?"

"I agree that's confusing. My recommendation is to dust down the keys with a damp cloth. David and Ian could do it. The poison won't kill them, obviously. I will say a few counter curses over the instrument and the entire room. They can give the cloth to Dragos to be analyzed."

The back door opened, and Ana and Maria arrived carrying bags and a large stock pot emanating a yummy smell.

"Good afternoon, I see you have discovered the conservatory."

"Yes, we're enjoying the light and the plants. There are two plants I don't recognize. Can you tell us what they are?" Maria set the tote bags on the table and followed Arabella to the pots.

"This is a cutting from a plant in the moonlight garden, a rare peony, the national flower of Romania. We're rooting it for planting next year. This is edelweiss, also being rooted." Maria waited. Did she suspect these were not idle questions?

"Thank you." We weren't going to air our suspicions. Slade's stalking and Mike's impending conversion were facts. If I was in danger, I had to bring the evidence to Dragos.

"Maria, how do I get a message to the voivode?"

"My husband can bring a message for you. The voivode does not have a phone in the castle."

"If I write it, can he take it up now?"

"Of course." I rose and went to the desk in the drawing room.

Your Majesty,

Is it possible to have a few minutes of your time this evening?

Thank you,
Natalie Crisan

I sealed the note in an envelope and returned to the kitchen. Arabella was slicing a beautiful black bread and chatting away with the Popa ladies.

"Nat, would you mind if I stayed here tonight? I haven't spoken to my auntie in days, and she wasn't feeling well when we left. And I'll do the other thing we talked about."

"Of course. David and Ian can come with me."

Boris arrived at the back door, and I handed him the note. Promptly after sunset, I received a response from Dragos.

Miss Crisan,
It would be my pleasure to answer any questions you have. Shall we meet at the

garden gate at eight? It promises to be a mild evening, and you can enjoy an inaugural stroll. I have a surprise for you as well.

Dragos Dracul

After dinner, we brought David and Ian up to speed on Arabella's reaction to the pianoforte. David reached for Ian's hand and then rose from the sofa in the drawing room.

"I'll dust it down, and we'll bring the cloths to the Big V tonight. He'll get them analyzed tout suite. Arabella's intuition may have saved your life. We'll need a plan to sweep the house for poison and any other . . . sorcery."

* * *

Despite Olenka's fashion edicts, my casual outfit of slacks and sweater would have to do for our appointment with the voivode; I wasn't changing into a skirt for a garden stroll.

After the setting of a weak sun, a damp chill had crept in with a ragged quilt of clouds. From the drawing room window, I observed Dragos pacing in front of the garden gate, the safety barrier Natalia had created. The gate had failed to protect Natalia. . . who had betrayed her trust? I put on a coat and exited the front door, Ian in my wake.

"Good evening, Miss Crisan. . . Ian." He appeared surprised at a chaperone, but accepted Ian's presence graciously. "The jasmine path is quite fragrant in season. Let us begin there. I am ready to answer any questions you have about your new home." He offered his arm.

"The night is unfortunately overcast. Natalia assured me that although the garden was lovely during the day, it was even more spectacular in the moonlight. When the moon is full, and the torches are lit, the statues glow and the white flowers, and snow in winter, reflect light like the stars above." I wondered at the romantic description of Natalia's garden spoken by a man who had led a bloody rampage after her death.

The recessed cut-outs I had noticed the night before were lit from within by votives. Torches, flames glowing red against the black night, brightened the perimeter path. Ian trailed us at a distance, and behind him the security detail's cigarette floated in the dark.

"Thank you for making time for me, Your Majesty." I'd decided to begin our conversation with the Vermeer, and then bring up Arabella's reaction to the pianoforte. "I hope it isn't a faux pas to ask about the paintings and other objects in the house. Arabella believes the painting in the living room is the Vermeer mentioned in the will. If so, shouldn't it be behind glass or something?"

"Yes, the Vermeer was a gift to my wife for our

first wedding anniversary. Art experts do not know of its existence. Do you feel unsafe with it in the house?"

"I don't know. I mean, I don't want to appear ungrateful or rude." Heat flamed in my cheeks, and I was glad he couldn't see it.

"The painting belongs to you, and you have the right to question its security," he said. "The Vermeer is wired to a separate alarm system which alerts my security guards. We are rather remotely located, and I don't think an attempted theft would be successful, or . . . advisable. Since it is an unknown painting, no one is looking for it, anyway."

Broaching the subject of Natalia's murder, I proceeded with delicacy, divulging Arabella's reaction to the pianoforte. Dragos halted and faced me, dropping my arm.

"The pianoforte? Cursed or poisoned?" His hands clenched into fists. "What treachery surrounded Natalia and me?"

"David is dusting the instrument, and we hoped the cloths could be analyzed."

"I could never solve how the poison was administered. Have David bring the cloths to me." We resumed our walk, the silence of our thoughts pierced by the gleeful animal shrieks of a successful hunt.

"Am I in danger?" If we were to be neighbors and spend time together, he had to share intelligence regarding my safety. Dragos didn't respond immediately, but let my question marinate.

"I would be negligent to say no. You are of interest to dangerous . . . people—but you know this. We can review the security of your home. I did not wish to be intrusive; I respect your privacy. However, we may be able to add a few additional layers for your peace of mind."

"Thank you." Once again, he offered his arm, and I accepted.

"Miss Crisan, I would like to celebrate your arrival in Transylvania with a ball. Perhaps in the next week? We can discuss the details tomorrow evening, if you would join me after you have had dinner." We had strolled the outermost path of the garden and stopped at the garden gate.

"A ball in my honor?" Olenka had declared a ball was required because of my ancestry and friendship with Dragos.

"It is the proper way for you to meet Romanian society. Do you object?"

"No, not at all, but I will need a ball gown, which I guess will take more than a week. Olenka had offered to share her tailor—she also suggested adjustments to my existing wardrobe." He didn't need the details of the pieces Olenka had specified.

"Olenka is occupied at the moment," he said. "I know a fine tailor from the village. If you send your availability for tomorrow, my valet will set the appointment."

"Thank you, that is very kind. Good night, Voivode."

"Good night, Miss Crisan."

Ian joined me and together we navigated the exterior of Le Refuge Bleue. Dragos had handled the mystery behind the pianoforte with admirable self-control. Why did he leave the mystery of Natalia's murder unsolved? Had heartbreak and loss overwhelmed him?

Ian and I stopped at the back of the house facing the wood. A light shone through a kitchen window, and I checked the door. Locked. The windows of the conservatory were dark. Completing our circuit, we crossed the porch and entered the front door. Natalia's sanctuary had been the scene of her murder, and someone she trusted had betrayed her. A shiver ran down my spine.

CHAPTER TWENTY-SIX

Before I retired for the evening, I joined my friends in the drawing room for a nightcap. Leaning back on the sofa, I stared at the Vermeer. I owned a Vermeer. Ridiculous. I sipped my port and repeated the conversation I'd had with Dragos.

"What?" David jumped off the sofa and propped his hands on his hips. He was less interested in a priceless painting than he was about the tailor. "Allow another human to affect the signature style we've developed? This tailer must arrive after sunset. Period." I hadn't meant to insult David, but he tapped his toe and huffed his displeasure.

"The voivode has also asked if I would come up to the castle tomorrow. He wants to plan a ball for like next week to introduce me to society."

"A ballgown in a week? That's insane. We'll have to delay him."

"Oh yeah, that will work." Ian pulled David back down beside him on the sofa.

"If Natalie needs a ballgown, Dragos will fly in the best dressmakers," Ian said. "And you will have to decide what jewels to wear."

I glanced at the ruby ring. The pebble sized stone's facets flashed in the light. I loved the opulence of the ring.

"He will probably want to show me Natalia's jewel collection," I mused. "I suppose I should choose the jewels first, right?"

Arabella, although in the room, was silent and distracted.

"I need to make a phone call, Nat." She sighed. "If I'm invited, I'd love to see the castle and help you in any way I can." She moved toward the door.

"Of course you're invited. I hope your auntie is feeling better."

"Me too. Good night, folks." She closed the door softly behind her.

In the black of night, I awoke from a restless dream, startled and in pain. A burning sensation stabbed my heart, and as quickly as it had engulfed my senses, it faded to sadness.

I lay in bed, listening to the hoot of an owl somewhere outside my window. Dragos had said Olenka was 'occupied at the moment'. The ceremony had taken place and sealed the contract between Olenka and Mike. I wept. Beach-loving Mike Endicott would never again bask in the sun.

* * *

First thing the next morning, I sent a note to the castle with my schedule. Within an hour, an appointment was confirmed for 7:00 p.m. I was to meet Boris at the stables at 10:00 for my first riding lesson.

"Ana, I have no idea what to wear to ride. Is anything appropriate in my wardrobe?" Ana giggled.

"Not really, Miss. Your wardrobe is formal dresses, yoga clothes, Caribbean resort wear, and the clothes I added from the ship's inventory on *The Natalia*. You need tweeds, riding boots, jodhpurs—but don't worry. My dad has clothes for you to borrow today. There are local craftspeople who would love to make your riding attire, and especially your boots."

I breathed a sigh of relief.

"I don't know what I'd do without you. Thank you."

"Just wear your jeans and the blue sweater you have, and you'll be fine."

At 9:45, I walked over to the stables. Arabella was sleeping in, having been on the phone to Jamaica most of the night because of the spotty cellphone coverage. Outside the stables, Boris joined me, a wide grin on his handsome weathered face.

"Good morning. Ready for your first riding lesson?"

"Yes, I'm a little nervous. I hope Diana likes me. She's beautiful."

"Be sure to tell her. She is very vain. Maria laid out a set of clothes in the office for you to wear until you get your own. I hope it wasn't presumptuous. You need to be warm and safe."

"Not at all. I appreciate your concern. Ana mentioned there are people in the village who can make what I need, and I definitely will order from them."

"They'll be glad to hear it," Boris said. "Online imports have cut into their business, and the local craftsmen do beautiful work."

In Boris's office, I shed my blazer and inspected the riding clothes. Lightly worn but immaculately clean, the boots, chaps, jacket and helmet would serve for my first lesson. The boots were a little tight around my calf, and the jacket was loose at the waist, but the leather and workmanship was excellent. I attached the chin strap on the equestrian helmet and took a deep breath. Hopefully, I wouldn't embarrass myself.

Boris gave me a thumbs up.

"You look like a pro," he said. "I'll let you lead Diana out of her stall."

"Good morning, Diana. How pretty you look today. Would you like to help me learn to ride?" Horses are intelligent, and she approached me. I stroked her head, marveling at her smooth white coat. Her mane and tail were a soft grey, meticulously combed and falling to one side over her neck. Boris hovered nearby.

"Hold the reins using two hands. She won't bolt, and she'll know you are in control."

I led Diana to the stable entrance to be saddled, and Boris did the work but talked me through the proper method of adjusting the English saddle.

"We'll bring her to the paddock, and then you can mount her." In the paddock, Boris directed me to stand on the horse's left side.

"Left foot in the stirrup. You'll swing your right leg over the top and land as lightly as you can. She'll appreciate the gesture. Hold the reins in both hands, like this, and we'll work on posting. Posting is when you see a rider go up and down with the forward movement of the horse."

Walking her around the enclosure was easy, but posting posed a challenge. I had a difficult time synchronizing my movements to Diana's forward motion initially, but finally we managed to circle the ring with the correct rhythm. Boris applauded.

"You got it! Now for the dismount. Make sure the left foot is even in the stirrup. You don't want it too far forward, but you also don't want it to slide out when you swing the right leg behind. Loosen up the reins a little. You don't want to hurt her head." I dismounted without falling on my butt, a major accomplishment.

"You are a natural, Miss Crisan. We'll have you riding in the forest in no time at all."

"I will accept the praise, although I think you're being kind. And please, call me Natalie." He smiled but ignored the suggestion.

"Tomorrow then? I suggest a soak in the tub to help ease the sore muscles."

I trudged through the path back to Natalia's house and directly to my bathroom. Dumping a ladle-full of scented Epsom salts into the tub, I submerged myself up to my shoulders and let the warmth of the water work on the growing stiffness. I had pushed Mike's conversion out of my mind during my lesson, but thoughts of him, in pain and fear, rushed forward. I couldn't help him; I'd tried. We were not a couple, and he could do as he pleased.

After my bath, I followed the aroma of sauteed onions to the kitchen, where Maria was teaching Ana a family recipe for dinner. I watched them conversing in Romanian, their heads together, discussing the method of the recipe. They were lucky to have each other. Aunt Loretta had filled the role of mother to the best of her ability. How different would my life have been with a mother and father to love and guide me?

"Keep stirring." Maria wiped her hands on a towel and crossed the kitchen to where I had plopped onto a chair. "How was your first lesson?"

"Fun. Diana was patient with me. And the

clothes worked out. Can you let the craftspeople know I will order immediately?"

"Certainly. Normally they are superstitious about coming close to the castle, but it is daylight."

"Oh, gosh, I never thought of that. A tailor is coming here after sunset. David, my bossy stylist, insisted."

"Yako has the viovode's protection. No one would dare to touch him." Arabella joined us and scraped a chair next to mine, her eyes red-rimmed.

"My auntie is failing," she said. "I didn't know she was seriously ill, and I don't know what to do. She may only last a week. My cousin said she is holding on to say goodbye to me." Poor Arabella. We picked at the lunch salads Maria set on the table. I had to help my friend return to Jamaica as quickly as possible. I set my fork down.

"Then you must go to her. I'll send a note to Dragos and ask the quickest way for you to get to Jamaica. He will know."

Arabella gave me a fierce hug.

"Thank you. I will come back as soon as I can, I promise." She pushed her salad away. "Sorry, Maria, but I'm not hungry—I'll go and pack."

I toyed with the rest of my lunch amid the aroma of dinner and Maria's watchful eye. I knew I was doing the right thing, but I felt my anxiety rising. I was losing my gal pal. I needed a project.

What activity would distract me from my pal's imminent departure? Organizing always worked for me. I climbed the grand staircase to my bedroom to coordinate a few outfits from my current wardrobe. The nights in Transylvania were cooler than evenings on the ship, and if I wore pieces from my Caribbean wardrobe into town I'd freeze amid the hoots of laughter from the villagers. I did not want to be known as the eccentric American heiress. Twenty minutes later, I threw myself onto the bed amid the linen and cotton. I needed David's help with a proper Romanian wardrobe, and losing Arabella gave me a pain in my heart. Someone knocked on the door.

"Come in," I called.

Ana poked her head in. Seeing me laying on the clothes strewn on the bed, she approached, a concerned expression on her kind face. "What's wrong?"

"I'm devastated that Arabella is leaving," I said. "And it sounds selfish and ludicrous, but I can't put a single outfit together—I'm stumped. Please, can we go into town? I'll wear my comfy sweatpants, they're warm." The look on Ana's face made me realize how ridiculous Queen Natalia's heir would look shopping in the village in holey sweatpants.

"Okay, I guess that's a no," I said. "I'll wear a pair of jeans and my other sweater. Could someone drive us?"

"I'll text my father, I'm sure he'd be happy to drive us," Ana said. "You can order your riding outfit and check out the shops. There are a few very nice boutiques."

Relief washed over me.

"Ana, what am I going to do when you go off to university? Let's leave as soon as possible." Ana scurried off to talk to her father, and Arabella poked her head into my room.

"I managed to get a seat on a flight to Tampa leaving this evening out of Avram Iancu International Airport," she said, a hopeful expression on her face. "How would I get an Uber to the airport?"

A lump formed in my throat.

"Ana and I were going into town so I could order riding clothes. Her father can drop you at the airport after he brings us to the village." Arabella reached out and pulled me in for a solid hug.

Ana's quick light step could be heard mounting the stairs and hurrying toward my bedroom.

"My father will drive us to town," she huffed. She leaned on the doorjamb, breathing deeply.

"Thank you, Ana. You didn't have to run." She was the sweetest person. I updated her on Arabella's plans. "Is the airport far from the village? Do you think your father could drop her off?" Ana pulled her cellphone from a pocket and texted.

"My father's friend owns a taxi service," she said. "He will meet us in town and take Miss Bishop to the airport. My father would do it, but the voivode would not like him to leave you alone in the village."

"I'm so relieved," Arabella said. "Thank you, Ana. I'll miss your sweet face." Arabella went back to her packing, and I closed the bedroom door to dress for the trip to the village. I felt so lost.

Seeing Arabella's suitcases in the hallway brought tears to my eyes, and I turned away so she couldn't see. I helped her bring her luggage to the garden gate, and she, Ana, and I rolled the cases without speaking to the road outside the garden. Boris was waiting in the black Range Rover, and he arranged Arabella's suitcases in the hatch of the SUV. A husky stranger in dark sunglasses sat in the passenger seat of the car as we settled in. He kept his face forward.

"Natalie, I'm sorry I have to leave you." What words of support would send her off without guilt?

"Family is most important." I squeezed her hand. "You have been the truest friend, and you are welcome to come back anytime."

She blinked in shock.

"You're staying? Even if the cloth David cleaned the pianoforte with contained poison?" I didn't answer immediately. She was right; could Dragos guarantee my safety in Le Refuge Bleue?

I gazed out the window. The road twisted and turned, and although I had never stepped foot in Romania before two days ago, the scenery seemed familiar. Planted fields bordered by thick forest and picturesque homes of farmers who worked them were something I might have dreamed as a child. Aunt Loretta had read me bucolic stories of princesses gardening alongside farmers working the land. She'd told me of Marie-Antoinette's fascination with simple country life and the pretend village she built called Hameau de la Reine. Those stories had touched me in a way other fairytales hadn't. Why?

"The voivode and I have a lot to discuss," I said, pulling my attention away from scenic views. "My decision will depend on those conversations. I honestly haven't a clue what to do."

"Trust your heart. And David and Ian will help you make the correct decision," she said. My insides ached because she knew me better than anyone.

When we reached the village, we pulled into a parking lot where a dark blue sedan idled. The driver's door popped open before Boris put the car in park. Rapid Romanian flew between the men, and then they shook hands.

"Miss Bishop, this is Dani. He is an old friend of mine and will take you to the airport. He speaks English, although not fluently."

"You make me like stupid idiot." Dani reached out to take Arabella's luggage. "We discuss food. I am a great cook and eater." The joke diffused a smidgeon of the tension, but I stared at Arabella like a baby bird being pushed out of the nest.

"I love you, Arabella. Safe trip. Let me know when you get home."

"I love you, too. You'll be okay; just remember to control your impulsiveness. David and Ian are here to help you. Ask them questions about their world and take their advice to heart."

We hugged, and I kissed her soft cheek. I turned swiftly and entered the waiting car. Leaning forward, I tapped the stranger's shoulder.

"Who the heck are you?"

The stranger removed his sunglasses and flipped around to face me. His closely cropped blond hair and direct eye contact telegraphed confidence and success in his chosen profession. The fine wool fabric of the sleeve of his bespoke suit suggested Dragos paid his security guards well.

"I am Mihai, Miss Crisan. The voivode has assigned me to your security team. I must accompany you when you travel to the village or other places, and I circle the grounds around your home in rotation with the other men during the day. I am to be like the trees; a part of the scenery."

Dragos had expanded my security. Considering the pianoforte might have been tampered with, it was a smart move.

"Nice to meet you, Mihai."

"I will enter the store first," he said with

firmness. "My orders are clear. Your safety is my responsibility." Orders—Dragos wasn't messing around.

There was a knock on the window and Arabella handed me a note.

"I'll call after I visit my auntie," she said.

We squeezed hands one more time, and she turned and trotted to the car. She rolled down the window and blew me a kiss. The lump in my throat felt like a golf ball.

"Miss, I made a list of the stores we should visit." Ana handed me a paper with store names and their best offerings. I lowered my sunglasses to emphasize my seriousness. "I insist you call me Natalie. This isn't the nineteenth century." Ana giggled, and I replaced my sunglasses on my nose.

* * *

When we entered the first store, Mihai handed me an envelope, which I opened in the dressing room. Inside was a handwritten note and an American Express black charge card with my name on it.

Dear Miss Crisan,

This card is attached to an account established for you. If a store does not take American Express, you can use your own card and pay the balance from your checking account.

Dragos Dracul

I slid the card into my wallet, and after presenting ID for the first time, worked it hard. Since Dragos continued to anticipate my needs and provide for my comfort, I would make him happy by supporting as many shops as possible.

I dozed on the ride home. David and Ian were in residence but who could I trust to be my confidant during the day when my vamps were resting?

Ana and I carried the boxes and bags up to my room. I had a present for each of my vampire buddies, and Ana had accepted a turquoise-colored scarf from a chic shop. We laid out all the items for my stylist's approval.

"My mother says you spoil me," she said, running her hand over the cashmere of her new scarf.

The enticing smell of dinner reminded me a visit from a tailor would follow the meal and then a maiden visit to Dragos's castle. I washed my hands and headed down to the kitchen. It was weird to eat without Arabella's familiar and comforting presence. Maria had gone home to eat with her husband, and Ana stayed behind. I made her sit.

"Ana, I can't eat dinner by myself. Please join me." Dinner was a traditional chicken and pea stew called mazare cu pui. After dinner I sent Ana home with her gift and compliments to the chef. Ana's footsteps faded, and Ian and David's voices rose from the cellar.

"Good evening, heiress." My vamps bowed.

"Wow, the kitchen smells wonderful," Ian said. "So, what did you ladies do today?" My face dropped, and he frowned.

"What happened?"

"Arabella has gone back to Jamaica." I took a deep breath and filled him in on the events of the day, starting with my first horseback riding lesson to Arabella's departure, ending with my insane shopping spree.

"I'm sorry about Arabella, Nat," David said. "This is a logistical problem as well. We can't have you alone all day. You might get into trouble, again." I accepted the last comment without ego and changed the subject.

"I realize manic shopping for sweaters and jackets can't fill Arabella's loss, but I think you'll approve of how I focused my mourning." David pursed his lips, and my skeptical stylist joined me in my bedroom. He reviewed my purchases like a general inspecting the troops.

"All your purchases will work for Romanian Natalie. We need to style an outfit for your first visit to the castle—and I think the tailor has arrived. Put on the cream silk blouse with those slacks, and I'll grab the tan pumps and the short leather boots you brought today. The craftsmanship is remarkable!"

"I'll treat you to a pair for creating Romanian Natalie."

"Deal."

In a small sitting room behind the dining room, Ian was with the tailor, who was setting up his tools on a pitted farm table. He greeted David and me with a smile.

"Miss Crisan, how lovely to meet you. My name is Yako Palade." He had arranged the folded fabrics along the table in neat piles, and I brushed my hand across a fine gray wool.

"Yako, this fabric is gorgeous. Please make me something with this."

"I'm glad you like it; I just received it yesterday. Slacks would work well in the fabric. Please stand on the pedestal and I will take your measurements." Yako rolled out a well-worn tape measure, and I was rotated like a mannequin. Ian, who had volunteered as his scribe, recorded the numbers he called out in a ringed notebook.

"Natalie, the pedestal suits you." Ian elbowed David in the ribs. David feigned injury but continued to select fabrics from the tailor's offerings.

"I have also brought a couple of pre-made

jackets." He held a hanger in each hand. The right held a dark tweed with a forest green line in it. I reached for the left, a soft camel and gray check with a muted red line.

"Oh, this is dreamy." He slipped it over my arms, and I buttoned the single leather covered button. The blazer cinched slightly at the waist. To my eye, the hem and sleeve length were perfect. David circled me. Stepping back, he made his pronouncement.

"It's gorg. One would think Yako already had your measurements." Huh? Yako ignored the coincidence and held forth a folded camel colored cloth. We chose the material for an overcoat and David chose a few ready-made items from the tailor's inventory.

"Yako, I can come into the village for the final fittings. Thank you for accommodating me." The tailor dipped his head.

"You are very welcome. Please extend my greetings to the voivode."

"I will."

David, Ian and I carried the new additions up to my bedroom, and David threw open the wardrobes.

"Let's get these clothes organized and into the armoires. It's already nine, and we shouldn't keep the Big V waiting." The three of us hung, folded, and stored the garments with precision. The amount of clothing I had purchased shocked me. Aunt Loretta's cultured voice played in my head.

"Natalie, buy high quality, and remember, frugality is a virtue." Oops. Sorry, Aunt Loretta, but there was nothing frugal about what I had spent on my Romanian wardrobe.

Finally, we stepped outside the locked front door, alarm engaged. The castle was a five-minute walk, and when I hooked the latch, a bird simultaneously screeched in the forest. I jumped like a scaredy cat.

"Relax, darling. Ian and I are here." I slid my hand through David's arm, and we started off to the castle.

Light shone from many of the mullioned castle windows, and as we trudged over the gravel, I wondered if my residence in Romania was an accident. Nothing in dear Aunt Loretta's will indicated she had been chosen as a guardian to educate and finish me for the unimaginable jump into an aristocratic parallel world.

With Arabella's hasty departure, and if Dragos wanted me to remain his neighbor, protégé, and Natalia's heir, I needed friends who wouldn't turn to dust in sunlight. But where would I find them?

CHAPTER TWENTY-SEVEN

The ominous hulk of Castle Dracul threatened. Little girls had hopeful dreams of meeting a handsome prince and spending happily ever after in his bright and shiny Disney castle. Castle Dracul was no Disney castle. Turrets anchored the corners of the walls of the façade, a bastion of local stone which desperately needed a pressure wash. Two immense stone gargoyles, pitted and covered with a creeping brown moss, flanked the impressive front door. Pea gravel and not a single plant softened the imposing presence of Dragos's residence.

Ian lifted the door knocker and let it fall with a clunk. We did not wait more than a few seconds, and the huge door creaked open.

"Good evening." The butler's reserved manner betrayed little as his eyes registered our faces. "Please come in. His Majesty has been expecting you."

The entrance hall was immense, and a stagnant chill made me long for the outdoors. The vaulted ceiling soared to a domed surface on which was painted a magnificent mural of Lucifer being cast out of heaven. We craned our necks upward, and I jumped when I heard Dragos's voice at my side.

"Welcome to my castle. The scaffolding took almost as long to build as the painters took to complete the mural. They wore harnesses, so even if a fall resulted in a few broken bones, they would survive and could continue to paint." He chuckled at his own attempt at humor.

"Good evening, Voivode. Thank you for having us."

"My pleasure. Come this way." The butler had gone ahead to open the door for us, and after about fifty steps we entered a yellow drawing room, furnished in an extremely formal style with heavily fringed draperies. Oversized paintings of hunting scenes hung on the wall, and rare objet d'art covered the tables.

"My wife yearned for a sunny drawing room to replace the dreary Romanian winters, and to remind me of the sun I will never see." The butler returned to serve Ian and David a blackened goblet. Dragos indicated a bar to the side.

"Miss Crisan, I have opened a fine bottle of Chateau Lafite Rothschild Pauillac. May I pour you a glass?"

"Yes, thank you." I sat stiffly on the edge of a

silk sofa and tried to compose myself. When I wasn't with Dragos I felt brave and determined to question his insinuation about my Aunt Loretta. When in his presence my nerve abandoned me. Perhaps a glass of wine would restore my resolve to get to the truth. Dragos handed me a crystal goblet filled with a pinkish red wine and sat in the chair closest to me.

"I hear you had a riding lesson." Apparently, he received written reports on my daily activities.

"Yes, Boris is a first-rate teacher. I enjoyed it, and Diana was patient with me. She is a beautiful horse."

"She comes from excellent stock. Boris tells me you will adopt a wolf cub? My wife was fond of her Lupu." I sipped my wine. The small talk and the libation worked a miracle, and I felt able to breathe. David and Ian remained quiet while the voivode and I chatted.

"As previously mentioned, I would like to hold a ball in your honor," he said, "and two weeks was suggested to enable proper time for a bespoke gown. If you would like to invite anyone, please organize a list. Accommodations, and if necessary, transportation for those who cannot travel commercial will be available. I will provide room for personal boxes in a secure area of the cellar. Perhaps the Westwoods can assist you with the guest list?"

"We would be happy to," Ian answered. Dragos nodded and reached for a folder on the side table.

"We have already discussed many particulars of my wife's estate and your inheritance. We did not discuss your allowance. This paper details the various investments which have been transferred to accounts in your name. There is an allowance amount specified. Will it suffice?" My eyes traveled to the line item marked monthly allowance, and I coughed. Where was I going to spend thirty-grand per month?

"It seems like an awful lot of money," I said.

Dragos scoffed. "Your position in the Dracul family requires you to serve as hostess for my events. Olenka has fulfilled the function for decades. Hostess duties will necessitate an extensive wardrobe. After the contractual year, you will travel, and if you visit an art gallery and admire a painting, you will have the funds to purchase it. You have your own home to run and staff to pay. You may find, in the future, the number is too low for your purposes, and it can be adjusted."

I slipped the piece of paper into the outside pocket of my handbag. The numbers on the page required a gulp of wine. Dragos continued.

"You have a suite of rooms at your disposal in the castle. They belonged to my late wife. There are also her jewels, which I have gathered in my study. I would like for you to inspect them while they are out of the safe." Dragos led the way through an enfilade of rooms. A broad-shouldered man guarded the final door, and he stepped sharply aside while Dragos unlocked it.

The study smelled of leather bindings and mellow, well cared for wood. On a long conference table to the left, a series of low boxes lay in a row. Without ceremony, Dragos snapped them open. I approached the first box and David and Ian followed me, their hands tucked behind their backs.

"These jewels belonged to my late wife. She had exquisite taste. All her jewels belong to you except the royal diadem, which can only be worn by the queen. There are other tiaras; they are in the vault for future discussion.

"This is the ruby parure," Dragos said. I leaned forward to take in the spectacular ruby and diamond necklace, tiara, earrings, and bracelet laid upon black velvet. "A ruby and diamond cocktail ring has been missing since my wife's death," Dragos said. "It was magnificent craftsmanship, a peony. Natalia wore it the night before her death and I never caught the thief, most likely also her murderer."

I reached toward the jewels, and the flash of Natalia's ring I wore celebrated its reunion with the parure. Dragos had referred to the ruby parure when he had given me the ring in Jamaica. The magnificent suite of jewels would be worn together at auspicious events. Now I understood Olenka's seemingly offhand mention of the rubies and her undisguised obsession with the ring I wore.

"The Burmese ruby parure are the partner pieces to the ring my wife left you. When you rode Diana, where did you store the ring?"

"I put it on a chain around my neck."

Dragos could not conceal his shock. It was a careless way to treat a priceless jewel.

"There is a safe in your bedroom behind the landscape painting–Boris supervised its installation. I will give you the combination. It is wired. Please use it in the future."

I blushed, embarrassed at my faux pas. Thank goodness Dragos, Ian, and David were unlikely to gossip about my lame move.

"These were her favorite pearls." Dragos, like a seasoned museum docent, described the collection of jewels with admiration. "There are more pearls in my safe, but the size and color of these make them the most valuable. She loved this necklace." He picked up an opera length Tahitian pearl necklace and handed it to me. I could twist it three times around my neck, and it would still drop to my chest.

"This is gorgeous," I said. "I love it."

"Then take it with you. Pearls are meant to be worn, and Olenka has been permitted to borrow the strand often. Here are the emeralds." The Emerald City in *The Wizard of Oz* burst into my mind. A tiara, diamond and emerald necklace, square cut ring, and a diamond pave bracelet topped with an emerald cabochon mesmerized me.

"And finally, the sapphires. My wife loved to wear this parure with dark blue gowns, which she favored over black. Our social set prefers black. Natalia felt it was depressing for a ballroom to lack color. I would like to keep the parures, and the loose stones in my safe, if you agree."

"I would feel more comfortable if you kept them, Voivode."

"Good. Let us go back to the drawing room and discuss your home security."

We retraced our steps. Dragos refilled my wine glass, and we reclaimed our previous seats. Ian cleared his throat.

"Voivode, I have taken the liberty to suggest the following upgrades to the existing security set-up. Also, has there been feedback from the lab as to what was on the keys of the pianoforte?" Ian handed Dragos a paper, and after a quick scan, he placed it on the table.

"Your suggestions are sound. I will post a guard to walk the property day and night. Miss Crisan, you must agree to security even at a distance when you visit town or walk or ride." I nodded. He rose and paced to a portrait of a dark-haired woman in profile. Her hand rested on the head of a white wolf. In the distance, Le Refuge Bleue beckoned. Natalia.

"The cloth had very minute traces of a powder of ground herbs. It could be absorbed through the skin, or if one touched a lip or an eye, a most efficient killer. I knew my wife was poisoned, but I never knew the method. After Natalia's death, the house was closed, and all the furniture was covered. Maria must wear gloves for now until we can clean the entire house. Westwoods, may I request that you wipe down the entire music room? Perhaps the poison was on the keys and that is why Maria wasn't . . ." Dragos pressed his lips together.

"Of course," David and Ian said simultaneously.

"Miss Crisan, I understand Miss Bishop has left. Her awareness saved your life." His voice softened. "After your home is inspected and cleaned, you must be circumspect about visitors. Who has access?"

"David, Ian, and Arabella. Maria, Ana and Boris," I said. "Ana is going back to university; I will need to replace her. The house is too big for Maria. And she insists on cooking."

"I'm happy to cook for you, Natalie. Whatever I can do to earn my keep." David was the sweetest friend.

"I'll take you up on the offer. You're a much better cook than me."

"And you will require a day companion, or you will be lonely." Dragos and I locked eyes and silence spread softly across the elegant room. He understood loneliness.

"Yes, with Arabella gone I'll be in the village blowing up my Amex. Seriously, I have to finish the manuscript I was paid to write. A little quiet time is desirable." There was a knock at the door and the butler entered.

"Anatole is here, sir."

"Tell him I will be with him presently."

"Chess is a great passion of mine, and Anatole is a master. When you are ready, Miss Crisan, we will play. I have enjoyed your company and will say good night." He pivoted smoothly and exited the room. We were shown to the door by the butler, who handed me a sealed envelope.

"We get kicked out of the best places," David said.

* * *

David liked nothing more than a project to demonstrate his command of all things haute.

"I nominate myself as your chef, interior decorator, and stylist. These rooms are begging for a fabric refresh; I could make Marie Antoinette wigs out of all the bullion fringe. Oh, and I will become an expert at building fires. You're not used to frigid winters."

Lounging on a petite sofa I drank a cup of chamomile tea and opened the envelope the butler had handed me. Inside were five numbers, the combination to Natalia's safe. Ian spoke up.

"From now on, I am the head of Natalie's security detail," he said. "No one steps a toe inside this house without a complete background check. Since you need a fabulous ballgown fast, I have a suggestion—invite Iris Lavender to the ball. She'd love it. One of us can be her escort. And you'll need to think about the guest list."

"Ron de Jamme would donate a canine to be there." David flung his hands in the air in a Bob Fosse flourish.

"As would the rest of our friends. It's Natalie's party, and her choice." With a pout, David dropped onto a sofa.

"I choose to retire to my bedroom with these pearls," I laughed. "I have no idea who I should invite. We'll talk tomorrow. Night, peeps."

I locked my bedroom door behind me and padded to the landscape. Running my fingers around the frame, I felt a latch and pressing on it, it emitted a soft click. The painting swung to the right, and the safe was revealed. It was the old-fashioned kind with a turn dial. I followed the directions, and at the stop of the dial, pulled back the safe door. Inside, a note leaned against a series of journals. Addressed to **HRH Dragos Dracul**, my great-great-grandfather, I hesitated for a nano second before breaking the red wax seal. I recognized Natalia's handwriting immediately.

To my son, or whomever is reading this,

I hope that my death was quick.

Tell my husband I will love him forever, and if our child hasn't been secreted away to protect him. Also, my darling Lupu will mourn my death. Show him compassion.

My journals and personal letters are in the safe. I could not bear to destroy them. Perhaps one day they can be read by my heir, and he can appreciate the love which knew no earthly boundaries.

Natalia Crisan Dracul

Behind the journals, several stacks of yellowed letters were tied with a faded ribbon. My great-great-great grandmother had provided for her heirs but reading her private journals felt an intrusion. I folded the note, slid it into the envelope, and inserted it in the safe. I slipped the ruby ring off my hand and laid the pearls on a white T-shirt, then closed and locked the safe.

Did Dragos know about the contents of the safe, and if so, why had he left Natalia's heart locked away for a century? Was there something in her personal effects he wanted me to find?

CHAPTER TWENTY-EIGHT

The conservatory was my first choice as a superb writing spot, at least until winter dictated otherwise. The vibe of the smallish space reminded me of my home office in the States. Grand rooms could be austere, and I agreed with David's desire to inject a bit of modernity into Le Refuge Bleue. The conservatory, however, was perfect and would remain untouched.

Getting back on a schedule was paramount. Strong coffee fueled an hour of writing, and the sound of the back lock reminded me I had a riding lesson at ten o'clock. Maria entered with Ana and a plain woman of nondescript age. She froze awkwardly just inside the door while Ana and Maria gabbed in rapid Romanian. Finally, Maria spoke gently to her, and she removed her worn coat and hung it in the pantry closet.

"Good morning, Miss Crisan. May I introduce

my niece, Mimi Popa? Since Ana is returning to university next week, I hoped you would agree to have Mimi help me with the housework several times per week." The woman raised her eyes for a nanosecond and dropped them instantly. Her hunched posture and lack of eye contact broadcast a deep lack of confidence.

"Hello, Mimi, it's nice to meet you."

"Good morning, Miss Crisan."

"Maria, Ian Westwood will want references for anyone who works in the house," I said. "I must insist that no one enters the house without my knowledge. There was a problem with the pianoforte which could have seriously injured someone." Maria blanched. "Also, you must wear disposable gloves while you are working in the house, and for the present do not go into the music room. These rules are for your safety.

"David Westwood will be assuming dinner chef duties, which will leave you time for other projects. It would be super if you could do the food shopping, at least until I know my way around. I plan on having groceries delivered, if that's possible." The three women had listened attentively, and Maria smiled.

"I don't mind the cooking, Miss, but an extra hour or two will give me time to get this house ship-shape. There are rooms in the attic we should check for leaks and storage. I will, of course, follow your rules about visitors, the cleaning gloves, and provide copies of Mimi's papers and references. She's a good girl and a hard worker."

Ana grabbed Mimi's hand and kissed her on the cheek. Mimi blushed but remained still. How kind of Maria to suggest her, but she would have to gain Ian's approval. Hopefully, she could fulfill the job requirements.

"For today, please stay on the first floor," I said, stretching Ian's guidelines a tad. "Once Ian is satisfied, I'd like to discuss a plan for running the house. It is much bigger than my last home and I welcome your suggestions."

I scooped up my computer and carried it upstairs to the bedroom, leaving Maria and Ana in the kitchen preparing breakfast and lunch, and Mimi vigorously sweeping the brick floor in the conservatory.

At nine forty-five, I left home and turned toward the stables for my lesson. The morning air held a brisk promise of winter, and I noticed a bulky man materialize from the darkness of the woods and follow me as I hiked to the horse ring. Once there, I focused on the joy of riding Diana and didn't notice my guard except when I trudged home.

After a scrumptious lunch, I boldly moved a delicate writing desk in my bedroom to face the windows toward the forest. Le Refuge Bleue was my home, after all, and the conservatory would only work for writing when there wasn't activity in the kitchen and first floor. Pleased with the change, I hunkered down and rededicated myself to the work-in-progress. Ian was handling an upgrade on Wi-Fi and instructing Dragos's butler on how to operate a cell phone. The image of Dragos attempting to send a text made me smile. A game of chess would, perhaps, set our relationship on the right path. Aunt Loretta always said you could tell a lot about a person after a game of chess.

The deep green of the woods behind Le Refuge Bleue intrigued me and would be explored before winter arrived. Motion below my window caught my attention, and the bulky security guard trudged along the path circling the house. He paused to scan the perimeter of the woods, sucked on his cigarette, and resumed his march. The top of his dark head disappeared around the corner.

There was a light tap on the door. I called "come in" and Ana appeared.

"Natalie, we are finished for the day, unless you need anything else." I stood, rolling my shoulders back.

"Thank you, Ana. My goodness, I feel like a creaky old woman."

"Horseback riding is hard work; you should have a long soak in the tub," she said. "We'll lock up downstairs. And Natalie," Ana whispered, "Mimi is the sweetest person on the planet. It is hard for her to find work because she has to be taught with kindness. Once she understands how you want something done, it will be perfect every time. Good night."

"I will pass your endorsement on to Ian." If Ana and Maria approved of Mimi, hopefully Ian would agree.

Despite the age of the home, Dragos had installed many modern conveniences. The bathroom featured a huge claw-foot tub, double sinks, a toilet, bidet, and a small stall shower. There was plenty of hot water, and I turned on the taps and plopped a luscious bath bomb purchased from a shop in the village into the steaming water. Twisting my hair onto the top of my head, I stepped into the tub.

I must have dozed off and jolted upon hearing heel hitting tile and a soft voice whispering, "Trust no one." I sat up with a start, splashing water onto the floor. The bathroom was empty. I must have imagined it.

I dried myself off. The mirrors were steamed up, and I rubbed a thick body cream into my sore muscles. I donned the terrycloth robe hanging on a convenient hook and opened the door to the bedroom.

"Woah!"

The bedroom temperature had plummeted while I soaked in the tub. If my bedroom was this cold in the fall, how would I survive a frigid Romanian winter? I dressed quickly in a navy cashmere lounge set I'd picked up in town and was pulling my hair into a ponytail when my phone pinged with a text message.

Mike:

Hey Nat, hope you're settling
in. I'm well—never better.
Seriously. I hear the voivode is
planning a fancy party for you.
You promised me an invitation,
remember? We'll show them
what real ballroom dancing
is. XOXO

Mike never missed an opportunity or forgot a promise. Dragos had requested a guest list, and I opened a file on my phone and tapped Mike Endicott into the first spot. David and Ian would have to advise me on the rest of my guests.

Voices rose from below. My vamps were in the kitchen, and I eagerly joined them. Two boxes of wine sat on the table.

"Well, hello, beautiful." David was at the cutting board chopping vegetables. "How was your day?"

"Productive. What's this?" Ian picked up a case of the wine.

"Sublime wine from the voivode. Let's store it in the wine cellar." I hadn't been in the wine cellar yet, and I eagerly grabbed two bottles and followed him down the wooden stairs.

The basement of Le Refuge Bleue had a packed dirt floor. A huge dusty chandelier with candle nubs centered a room with three walls of cubbyholes for wine. A pitted butcher block table under the chandelier had seen many years of service. Musty and cold, the wine cellar vibe breathed black and white horror film. How many times had Natalia descended the stairs and chosen a fine bottle of wine to enjoy with her dinner? A broom and dustpan leaned against the wall.

In the far corner, a door led into another room. Ian answered my unspoken question.

"David and I rest in there. We'd appreciate if the entire cellar is off limits to the staff."

"Of course. I'll make sure they know." Upstairs in the kitchen, David had tossed the veggies in oil and put a turkey meatloaf, my favorite, in the oven.

"I need to test the oven before I get fancy." David had serious chef skills, and he confidently opened cupboards and drawers to get acclimated.

"The kitchen pantry is sufficient to support my cooking genius. Ian, go outside first. When you return, I will venture into the wilderness." David wiped his hands on Maria's apron, which he wore with panache.

"Nat, why don't you pour yourself a glass of wine? The Big V sent the rest of the bottle from last night."

After dinner, we rearranged the furniture in the drawing room, angling our chosen seats closer to the roaring fire. My guest list was brief and included only my closest acquaintances in the vampire world. Ian and David approved, and I copied and sent the list to Ian's phone.

"The voivode will provide accommodations and travel for your guests," Ian said, a warning in his tone. "The vamps can't stay here, and you cannot invite them in. Remember, Natalie, it's dangerous for you. By the way, Iris texted that she would arrive in a few days. Dragos offered his plane."

David, who had been staring into the fire, perked up.

"Iris is honored you would choose her to make your gown. Can we pleeese gossip about the crown jewels? Nat, did you pinch yourself?"

I sighed and drank another sip of the yummy wine.

"If I pinched myself every time something extraordinary happened, I'd be black and blue. And speaking of blue, I'll wear the sapphires. I'd like the gown to be . . ."

"Silver. You'll kill it in silver," David exclaimed loudly, "Your gown will pop against a sea of black gowns and tuxedos. Vampires *never* wear silver. It'll be a bold style statement."

"David, you're more excited than I am about the ball. Let's get Iris's input on the color, but we know how much she loves silver." I finished my wine and set the glass on a gleaming side table. Iris would have to sew at lightning speed.

"And thanks for building the fire in my room, hon. It was positively glacial when I got out of the bathtub. I need to learn how for emergencies." Ian patted David's leg and rose from the sofa.

"I'm going to write out the guest list and walk it up to the castle. I'll confirm Iris's travel arrangements with the butler. Be back soon." We heard the door lock behind him. David got up to tend the fire and stabbed at the logs.

"Dragos is involving Ian in the alien problem. Ian says he can't beg off, but I'm worried. There's always collateral damage in a war." A cold shiver ran down my spine. I hoped David's concern was just a case of spousal protectiveness.

CHAPTER TWENTY-NINE

The next morning, two notes lay on the floor by my bedroom door. I broke the red wax seal on the first and marveled at the elaborate scrolls and swirls of the handwriting.

> *Dear Miss Crisan,*
> *I hope you have settled into your new home. In preparation for the ball, I suggest we resume your instruction in protocol. I will be at the voivode's castle this evening at nine. I look forward to our conversation.*
>
> *Olenka Dracul*

There was also a note from Ian. Oops, I'd forgotten to turn on the second-floor alarm.

Natalie,

Don't worry, I pushed the note from Olenka under the door. She left it at the castle.

Ian

P.S. The second-floor alarm wasn't on!

Although I believed strongly in a handwritten thank-you note, it was time Le Refuge Bleue entered the twenty-first century. Ian's Wi-Fi upgrade project couldn't happen soon enough. I hadn't called anyone since arriving in Romania except for a quick touch-base with my literary agent when Ana and I were shopping in the village. My agent was curious about my whereabouts, and I assured her I was safe and would meet my adjusted manuscript deadline of next month.

Mimi, the newest staff member, had passed Ian's background check, and the three ladies attacked the second floor and the attic with rubber gloves and cleaning supplies while I wrote in the conservatory. Boris was unavailable for a riding lesson, and I was content to let my backside recover. With the conservatory door closed, it was a glorious space to write. Surrounded by plants and relaxed décor, I corralled my thoughts about the impending meeting with Olenka. She had conducted her ceremony, and Mike was deeply in her debt. I couldn't honestly rail on him about becoming a vampire—Ian and David were the poster children for the advantages of the undead. They were kind and caring. I had to get over my judgement of his decision.

Beyond the glass walls of the conservatory, the mysterious layers of the thick forest were hypnotic. Boris promised me that I would be accomplished enough to ride through them on Diana. Natalia had walked the forest, and to know her I had to explore her favorite haunts.

Movement in the trees behind the conservatory caught my attention. I couldn't see an animal or person, but the shifting shrubs registered in the newly installed motion detection system, and the low beep of an exterior alarm sounded. In a flash, the bulky guard positioned himself between the conservatory and the woods. Three other dark-suited men ran into the forest. What had just happened? Moments later the security team returned from the woods empty-handed, and I observed the guards talking, perhaps to compare notes. Although I was nervous, I tapped on the window. The muscled guard met me at the backdoor.

"Hello, I heard the outside alarm go off. What happened?"

"Miss Crisan, I am Sorin, one of your security team." He made a show of dropping his cigarette butt to the ground and crushing it underfoot. Was he buying time before answering? He picked up the butt and put it in his jacket pocket. "I am sorry we disturbed you. We, um, have run a test of your motion detection system and a speed drill for our response. It worked perfectly. There is no need for nervousness." Hmmm.

"Oh, okay. Thanks. Someone should have let me know, I was frightened something was wrong."

"My apologies." He stepped back. "Please, remember to lock the door."

I did as I was told. I would ask Ian to explain why I wasn't informed before the security drill. Sorin's explanation was awkward. Had Slade or another evil creature tried to enter my property?

The rest of the day flew by. My suspicions were confirmed by Ian's shocked expression when I inquired about the security drill. He spent the next hour mad texting on his cell phone. David kept his head down and prepared a luscious dinner of Chicken Provençal. I ate, but stared at Ian, telegraphing my disbelief in the lame story I was expected to accept. He wasn't getting off that easy.

David and I chose my outfit with great care. Wool slacks, the cream silk blouse, and the jacket the tailor had brought with him.

"Wear the pearls," David had coaxed. "They belong to you, and it's a way of establishing your position. Jewels in high society scream power and status." We twisted them three times over my head, creating a fabulous layer of nacre, and set off for the castle. Ian headed toward Drago's study for a meeting with the voivode's advisors, and David was off to inspect the accommodations for my guests.

Olenka had commandeered the drawing room and placed her needlework to the side to greet me. Walking toward me, she assessed the sophistication of my appearance.

"Miss Crisan, how well you look." Her eyes strayed to the plethora of pearls, but she said nothing.

"Duchess, you get younger every time I see you." The compliment pleased her immensely, and she took my arm to guide me to the sofa. After gorging herself on human blood her glow was to be expected. The thought of Mike's blood flowing in her veins disgusted me.

"It is all about diet and self-care," she said. "How exciting to plan your first ball! You must allow me to help you. We want society to be dissecting the details and gossiping about the event for weeks." We sat, and she focused her startling beauty on me. Her skin was plump like an infant, poreless and smooth. Her golden hair cascaded over her shoulders, rippling halfway down her back.

"There will be a receiving line, of course. The voivode will welcome his guests, you will stand to his left, and he will introduce you. If a guest curtsies, you return the gesture. The line will move fast. Simply express what a pleasure it is to meet them." Her gaze once more fell upon the pearls Dragos had let her borrow. David was correct about the power of jewels.

"Your first dance is with the voivode. People will want to speak with you, and you must circulate. You only accept a dance with the senior aristocrats, or with someone you know well." Olenka's attention shifted to my hands and Natalia's ruby ring. She sighed—and examined her nails, caressing the unlined skin on the back of her hand. Pleased with the inspection, she continued.

"Have you decided on your gown and jewels? Your appearance must be immaculate." David had slipped into the room, and he arranged himself elegantly on a gilded chair. He jumped into the discussion.

"Natalie has two options, and frankly, we can't decide. Your Grace, what is the protocol of a tiara? Will the other women be wearing them?" David had smoothly deflected the question with one of Olenka's favorite topics, jewels denoting social rank.

"It is a sign of respect to the voivode on a formal occasion to wear a tiara, and they are worn by married women or members of the royal family. There are many brooches in the Dracul safe which can be disassembled and worn as hair ornaments. I am happy to help you choose either option, but we can confirm with the voivode his opinion on a tiara." The door to the drawing room opened and Ian, Bogdan, and Dragos joined the discussion.

"Voivode, Miss Crisan and I are discussing the details of the ball, and I have offered my assistance. The question was raised whether she should wear a tiara. I thought yes." Dragos seemed lost in thought. We waited, and he came to a decision.

"Yes, I think as a direct descendant of my wife, it is proper. Miss Crisan's Romanian citizenship will be finalized by next week." I hadn't taken a test or explored the history books Dragos had given me. My confused expression caused him to explain.

"Due to your status as my wife's heir, the process was expedited. You will only need to know a few important facts, repeat the pledge to our country, and to sign your name on the document. I will send the information to your home."

Bogdan had seated himself next to his wife, and they observed the gentleness with which Dragos spoke to me.

"Thank you," I said. "I don't want to embarrass myself and not know my heritage." My words affected Dragos. He sat taller in his chair, and an expression of pride crossed his face.

"Miss Crisan, Romania will benefit from your citizenship." Olenka coughed.

"Sadly, Bogdan and I must leave you. We have guests, and one has promised to teach me to tango." I blushed, and she grinned with delight. Ian had said Olenka required her concubines to remain until she released them. How long would Mike be beholden to her? Her dig ruined the evening, and we trudged back to Le Refuge Bleue in silence.

Before retiring, Ian had once again stated that the security test was a planned drill. I pressed my lips together in disapproval.

"I don't believe you." Ian sighed and shook his head in defeat.

"Okay, it wasn't exactly a planned drill," he said. "Something set off the motion detectors. They worked, which is the important thing. So did the quick response of your security detail. The team found no indication of a trespasser. No footprints, broken branches, animal tracks. We've added two more cameras pointed toward the woods." I was furious.

"Don't keep important information from me in the future, Ian. I have a right to know." I stomped out of the room before he could answer and slammed the door to my bedroom.

Lying in bed, I wondered if Mike was enjoying his newfound popularity, and the luxury that went with it. Were V cocktails enough to satisfy his blood lust or did he follow the preferences of his benefactress?

It took me a long time to fall asleep.

* * *

From the garden gate, Dragos watched the light go out in Natalie's bedroom. She was unaware that most nights he walked the garden and bordering property, ensuring her safety with his personal surveillance. The night guard, aware of the voivode's oversight, traversed the property in continuous motion. It was an honor to be entrusted with protecting the American heiress, and he would not disappoint his boss.

Dragos sensed the jealousy behind Olenka's tiara inquiry. His plan to bestow a title on Natalie Crisan would infuriate the duchess. She was troublesome when angry: what should he do to soothe her temper?

Ah. The answer came easily. He would take a piece of family jewelry from the safe for Natalie to give her as a gift. A brooch. There was an elaborate pearl and diamond cluster, not Natalie's style, but gaudy enough for Olenka's taste. Problem solved.

The night's meeting with his advisors suggested the larger alien front was quiet, but the security breach at Le Refuge Bleue confirmed Natalie was still of interest to . . . someone. There was no trace of the trespasser. He was not fooled.

Taking the matter into his own hands, Dragos had successfully installed a spy close to the slimy alien, and the latest intelligence was disturbing. Slade Suit had hoped to kidnap Natalie in Lisbon. Her security detail had handled that situation admirably.

His spy also confirmed that Slade had visited Natalie in Jamaica. Dragos congratulated himself for heeding his brother's advice which had spurred the transatlantic crossing to the island. He'd outflanked the interloper.

And then there was Mike Endicott, her former lover. Dragos exhaled in frustration. A lack of a strong father figure no doubt contributed to Natalie's poor choice in men. He longed for a close friendship and maybe more but must proceed with caution. A slow advance and building trust could work. It had worked with Natalia, his lost queen.

Natalie had chosen poorly in the past, but she was bright and warmhearted. Her lack of overt attraction to him was merely an obstacle to overcome; one day she would choose him.

The thought pleased him, and with a commanding glance in the guard's direction, he marched back to his castle. A fox darted into the bushes, and he caught it easily. Satiated, he tossed the carcass into the wood where an animal would find it and continued up the gravel driveway to the front door.

The Sicilian Defense had positioned the individuals exactly where he wanted them to be.

CHAPTER THIRTY

In the evenings, Dragos and I strolled Natalia's garden, and our conversations grew increasingly personal. The century he had spent in seclusion had been used in self-reflection and extensive reading. He'd studied the Greek classics and was fond of Aristotle and Euripides. His knowledge of theology and philosophy would impress an Oxford professor. More importantly, the heartbreak of Natalia's death had left a scar across his soul, if vampires have souls.

"After Natalia's murder I know I did terrible, unforgivable things," he said. "My seclusion forced me to see how I might use my position to help my country, rather than wage war with my brother over land and wealth. It took me decades to reach this conclusion." He sighed. Were his confessions merely platitudes to gain my sympathy? Could a warlord change his intrinsic nature? His admission had a ring of truth; grief can spark anger and a lust for revenge. History books are filled with examples.

I began to see Dragos as the Roman two-faced god Janus. The god of beginnings and endings, of war and peace. He could look backwards at his mistakes, and forward, planning for a brighter future for his people. Did I want to be part of his future? What life would I have in Transylvania? I didn't need to be hit over the head to guess at the possible intention behind his attentiveness. He was fascinating and I liked him.

Iris Lavender had arrived, bringing her fairy energy and incredible seamstress skills. She wasn't my best friend Arabella, but her support during last year's tango competition had established the foundation of what I hoped would become friendship. She agreed with David that I should wear silver.

"The vampires will lean toward black. Silver is a metal they shy away from. A gown of silver will pop against the expected black and red." Iris promised she would attend the ball, but when we went to the castle in the evenings, she was content to stay home to work on my gown and other orders, or she mysteriously disappeared on a date. I suspected the presence of Romanian fairies in the forest.

Several times David, Ian, and I strolled to the castle and Dragos instructed me in chess. He was patient and chuckled at my awkward moves. Ian confided his concern.

"Natalie, Dragos is a different man with you. Be careful. I think he is in love with you." Ian's protectiveness resonated and the warning gave me pause. Dragos was not a man to be trifled with; I enjoyed his company immensely. Did I want more?

One evening, a civil servant came to the castle to confirm my Romanian citizenship, and Dragos organized an impromptu celebration. Olenka, Bogdan, Marius and his wife Camelia attended with David, Ian and Iris, who surprised me by leaving her worktable at Ian's urging.

"Congratulations to Miss Crisan, a Romanian once again. Salut!"

The vampires raised their goblets, and Iris raised a sherry glass of orange liquid, most likely peach nectar, her favorite. My flute was filled with a heavenly champagne.

Dragos set his goblet on the table and slid open a drawer. He removed a black leather box worn at the edges and unfolded a thick striped ribbon from which hung a gold medal. The chatter ceased abruptly.

"As voivode, and king of our world, I have decided to mark this auspicious occasion by doing what my wife would have wished. Natalia's heir should carry the proper title. Miss Crisan come forward."

David snatched the champagne flute from my

hand, and I hesitantly advanced several steps toward the voivode. Dragos closed the remaining space between us and held the ribbon aloft for all to see. Gently, he slid the ribbon over my head. The gold medal hung heavily between my breasts.

"Today, I, King Dragos Alexandru Dracul of Romania proclaim that Natalie Sophie Crisan, as a blood descendant of my wife, Queen Natalia Crisan Dracul of Romania, shall be known as Princess Natalie Sophie Crisan of Romania. Congratulations." Stunned silence was quickly followed by applause. I knew my face was scarlet, and Dragos suavely placed his hand under my elbow and turned me to the room. Applause and several bravas burst from the attendees.

"The world is your volcano roll," David whispered in my ear. I pulled back the cackle and turned to receive sweet air kisses from Ian. Olenka stared at Bogdan, frozen like a Greek statue, and with a quick lift of his chin, he directed her forward.

"Your Royal Highness, congratulations." Ever the pro, she dropped into a flawless curtsy. Bogdan's dark eyes betrayed nothing, and he clicked his heels with a sharp drop of his head. Marius and Camelia, the perfect courtiers, mimicked their courtesy.

"The honor allows you to wear one of the family tiaras," Olenka announced in a high-pitched voice. Two splotches of red high on her cheeks were the only sign of her shock. "I hope you will allow me to see them when they are removed from the vault. I was permitted to wear one when I married my darling husband."

Bogdan slid his arm around her waist.

"I have never seen a more stunning bride," he said solicitously. Olenka smiled up at him and he leaned down to kiss her on the mouth.

On the surface, the remainder of the evening was pleasant. The other couples left together, and Dragos offered to walk me home. The medal clanked across my chest as I walked. At the garden gate, I attempted a curtsy and nearly toppled over.

"I'm glad Olenka didn't witness my awkwardness. She'd have me walking around with a book on my head." In the shadow, I think Dragos smirked.

"Yes, she would. Olenka has served as an excellent hostess since Bogdan, and I have ended our sparring. She can be useful, and her taste is superb. She would consider it an honor to assist you with the tiara options."

"Then I will seek her opinion. Good night, Voivode." He stepped toward me and reached out his hand; I remembered the formal custom of the elite of his world. I raised my hand. The chill of his fingers, the soft brush of cool lips across the back of my hand . . . I did not draw back. Time slowed and still he held my hand.

"I would like you to call me Dragos when we are alone." Alone. The word circled us, sealing his promise and desire for a future filled with my company. No man had ever made me feel as cherished as he. I gave him the answer I knew he longed for.

"Please call me Natalie. Good night, Dragos."

CHAPTER THIRTY-ONE

"My goodness, Iris, your gown will outshine the jewels of the guests at the ball." Iris adjusted the waist and stepped back to admire her work.

"Thank you. Silver will coordinate well with the sash you will wear. I would have given the gown a train, but since there is dancing, it makes no sense. Are you going to pick out your tiara tonight?"

"Yes, the voivode has invited a few people to play cards, and Olenka is coming to help me. He gave me a gift for her—she's been extremely helpful. She has a passion for jewelry; all the ladies are obsessed with jewels." Iris unzipped the back of the gown, and I stepped out of it.

"The other night I caught Olenka watching the voivode and me," I said. Iris and I were in my dressing room, and I slid my arms into the blouse I'd chosen to wear.

"The voivode was teasing me about thrashing

me at chess and we were laughing. Olenka had a strange, possessive look on her face, like jealousy. It's really weird, because she and her husband can't keep their hands off each other. Her husband worships her." I buttoned the blouse and reached for the black pencil skirt David loved on me. Iris registered the confidence I'd shared but deftly steered the subject back to fashion.

"What are you wearing tonight?"

"Not a ballgown, thank heavens. David insisted I wear red, so we compromised. I'm wearing a burgundy cashmere blazer over this blouse, and these gorgeous black boots a cobbler in the village made. I'll eat before we go. . . will you join me for dinner?" Iris smiled secretively.

"I have a date. I know he can't come into the house, and I'll meet him at the garden gate. He's a forest fairy. Very hot." She winked. Iris confiding about her dating life was a big step. She had no intention of settling down.

Mimi had left a simmering soup on the stove, fresh bread, and a green salad in the fridge. I helped myself and set up my computer to reread the day's work. My first draft was almost complete, and I felt confident my agent would approve of the changes.

"That smells wonderful, but how come Mimi keeps cooking for you? I'm the chef." David pulled out a chair and frowned at the soup.

"Maria told me Mimi loves working here, and

the job has boosted her confidence. I didn't want to disappoint her."

"Hm, well, your kindness is one of your best qualities. Maybe we can negotiate a couple of nights per week for Chef David?" Ian returned with a blast of fresh air through the open kitchen door and David slipped out into the night.

Did Dragos hunt to fulfill the need for fresh blood? Recently, the thought of a future with the notorious warlord had occurred to me more than once. Would he be content if I remained human? A vortex of scenarios swirled in my head and finally smashed into a wall of self-awareness; I was falling in love with the king of the vampires.

* * *

When David, Ian and I arrived at the castle, the butler escorted me to Dragos's study, while my friends were welcomed in the drawing room. A moment after I entered the study, the adjoining door opened and Dragos entered with Olenka.

"Good evening, Voivode, Your Grace." I dropped a brief curtsy to the voivode, and Olenka bobbed an almost imperceptible curtesy. "Good evening, Your Royal Highness. How well you look in red." While we exchanged greetings, Dragos retrieved a deep blue leather box from his desk and handed it to me. Olenka eyed it with anticipation.

"Your Grace, I am grateful for your guidance

and assistance. Please accept this gift as a token of friendship and thanks." Olenka's eyes bulged when she snapped open the box. The golden south sea pearl and diamond pin, ostentatious by any standard, suited her blonde hair and obsession with flamboyant jewelry; for herself. She drew a deep breath and exclaimed, "Absolutely stunning—why I never expected a gift, my sweet friend, but I accept it happily. Please pin it on my jacket."

I stepped closer and took the heavy pin from the box. Olenka's perfume was unlike any scent I'd ever smelled. It's intoxicating notes of jasmine and cream included an herb I didn't recognize. The pin required a few tries before I'd grabbed enough fabric for it to lie flat. Olenka curtsied once more, this time with a deep knee bend of enthusiasm. Dragos strode to the table and removed two dust covers from the tiaras I could choose from.

"This is the Flower of Romania. It has three different cuts of diamonds totaling 1,546 carats. It was crafted in Paris as a wedding gift for my late wife to celebrate her love of flowers, and our national flower, the peony."

"The second is older. The Russian court jeweler crafted the original tiara, and my wife modified it to make it more balanced. It can be disassembled to form three brooches. Diamonds were added to form a star at the top here, and Natalia named it Mintaka, from the Orion constellation. We spent many nights studying the sky from the north tower. .

." He raised his head and captured my gaze. "The night sky is best when shared with another." The distant sounds of conversation faded, and we three were caught in the profound revelation of his words. Why had he revealed himself in front of Olenka? Did he trust her with such an introspective observation?

Olenka cleared her throat. "Which tiara appeals to you, Your Royal Highness?"

Both of the tiaras were dazzling, and yet I felt drawn to the Flower of Romania. Both were opulent, but it was soft where the other was sharp. I reached for it and Olenka clapped.

"Exactly, princess. The Flower of Romania is younger and fresher, and appropriate for your first formal occasion." I picked it up, and the weight surprised me. Olenka laughed.

"Yes, tiaras can be heavy, but the headache one gets from wearing diamonds and precious gems is worth it. We will need to have it adjusted and perhaps add invisible padding here and here." Dragos cleared his throat.

"I will return these to the safe and meet you in the drawing room. We will coordinate a fitting with my personal jeweler." Olenka took my arm.

"Wait until the ladies see what you have given me. They will beg to be of service to you. Camelia would scrub your floors if she thought jewelry, was the payment."

I allowed myself to be swept into the drawing

room with the swell of Olenka's charm. David rushed to my side.

"Take a deep breath. Don't. . ."

"Your Royal Highness, may I present a new addition to our circle of friends? Michael Endicott, from America." My hand dropped to my side, spilling the champagne the butler had handed me. David grabbed the glass before I dropped it.

Mike as a vampire was Mike sculpted as he'd wished for in life and dressed down like a billionaire in not-off-the-rack clothes. He had the grace to incline his head and smile sheepishly.

"Hello Princess Natalie. You are looking well." Olenka's exclamation of shock deserved a Tony Award.

"Do you know each other? How odd. Michael was discretion itself on our transatlantic voyage. Bogdan, did you see the gift the princess has given me?" Everyone rushed to Olenka except Mike. He tilted his head, gave me the once over, and raised his eyebrows in approval.

"Living the swanky life isn't so bad, Nat," he whispered. Remembering his fealty, he pivoted and added his sycophantic comments to the worship spewing from Olenka's entourage. David handed me a fresh glass of champagne just as Dragos returned. Sizing up the two distinct groups, he chose.

"Princess, will you partner me in bridge? I fear we may lose badly, but I am game if you are." Still reeling from Mike's reappearance and Dragos's romantic comments in Olenka's presence, I baited him.

"Of course, Voivode. I'm well aware my skills at the games you play are sadly lacking."

"Then we will correct your shortcomings." A raised eyebrow and the shadow of a smile accompanied the tease. I parried.

"Sir, once I focus on a goal, I am stubborn." I was determined to make my point.

"Stubbornness is a highly underrated quality." Our repartee was observed with interest by his guests.

"What a fascinating conversation." Olenka had heard enough. "Are we going to play bridge or taunt each other? Let's play cards. Michael is new to bridge as well. He will balance our foursome."

CHAPTER THIRTY-TWO

In the nights leading up to the ball, Mike texted me hilarious photos of Liberace-style tuxedos for my approval. A blinking red and black catastrophe was my vote.

Olenka applied herself to the particulars of my coming out ball with feverish delight. Her attention to detail required an army of staff to scrub and shine every square inch of the ballroom, disused for a century. There was no electricity in the room, and the exquisite chandeliers would be candlelit.

"Candlelight is much more becoming," she announced. "It is also romantic, but your behavior as Romanian royalty must be above reproach. Remember, poise with a touch of reserve is paramount."

Gilt straight-back chairs lined the periphery of the immense room. The crumbling drapes were replaced with a replica of the former emerald-green and silver chevrons.

"I would have chosen a different fabric, but the voivode insisted on the original; Natalia's taste was often quite dull. Gold and black would have been more dramatic, don't you think?" Olenka attended the fitting for my tiara and, holding it her hands, ran her thumb reverently across the large center diamond when she thought I wasn't looking. I walked a tightrope—keeping her close but entreating Lupu to protect my thoughts. I would be foolish to forget Arabella's warning about Olenka's bad energy.

Finally, the day of my presentation arrived. The sun sank below the trees, and I posed in front of the full-length mirror in my dressing room. Maria, Mimi, and Iris stepped back to regard their combined efforts.

"Princess, you will dazzle your guests," Maria sniffed.

The gown Iris had created enhanced my curves with a confident subtlety. The silver beading was skillfully elusive and allowed the sapphire jewelry to pop. My hair, piled high in a twist to support the tiara, was very formal, but appropriate for the auspicious occasion, per Olenka.

"There must be no doubt as to your position in our society. Trust me on the hairstyle, Princess." This was her final counsel the previous evening before we parted.

Across my body, a sash with the Dracul royal shield proclaimed my position in the royal family. I heard a gasp and, reflected in the mirror, David and Ian peeked into the open doorway of my dressing room.

"Princess Natalie, you are stunning. Are you ready to knock'em undead?" He and Ian were immaculately turned out in matching black tuxedos. Mimi handed me the black wristlet evening bag David and Ian had gifted me for coordinating their wedding. Iris draped a lined black velvet cape over my shoulders.

"I'm excited to see more of the castle," she whispered as we latched the garden gate. At the end of the garden path, a black stretch limousine idled.

The windows of the castle shone, each one illuminated by a single candle, rising high into the infinity of the night. A red carpet led the way up the stone steps, the ponderous door thrown open in welcome.

In the great hall, the butler gathered our capes, and Dragos stepped from the shadows. He was regally handsome, a billboard of medals pinned on the left side of his uniform, and I held my breath waiting for his reaction. He stood motionless . . . and the moment lingered with significance; he was obviously overwhelmed. A peel of Olenka's laughter in the distance broke his trance, and I exhaled. He hastened to our group. I curtsied, and he snapped out a smart bow.

"Princess, the Flower of Romania has never shone as brightly as it does upon your head.

"Thank you, Your Majesty." As instructed by Olenka, I waited while he exchanged greetings with my friends.

"Shall we welcome our guests?" He offered his arm, and we glided toward the excited chatter behind a receiving room door. He smiled down at me. "Ready, Natalie?" My Christian name was spoken with an intimacy bordering on reverence. He wanted me to succeed, and succeed I would, as the descendent of Queen Natalia and a newly minted Romanian citizen.

"Yes, I'm ready and excited—and grateful for all you have done for me. Thank you." He leaned toward me, and I thought for a crazy second, he might kiss me. Instead, he whispered into my ear.

"There isn't anything I wouldn't do for you, my princess." The butler, at some secret communication from the voivode, opened the door, and the guests began to pour into the hallway.

Bogdan and Olenka were first in line, and her normally bright violet eyes, taking in the splendor of my jewels and the royal sash, clouded with envy. Borrowing a page from her own sermons to me about superior breeding, she pushed her shoulders back, resuming her elegant posture. I admired her control. The sapphire necklace I wore dripped with exquisitely cut gems set with diamonds. The chandelier earrings skimmed my shoulders. On my left wrist, the pavé cuff bracelet weighed a few pounds. I admit the privilege of wearing Natalia's jewels, now mine, was something I could get used to.

Olenka had chosen diamonds to complement a black gown with a deeply cut neckline. Her tiara dwarfed mine in carats, but it lacked elegance of design. Rings adorned every finger of her hands. She curtsied.

"Your Royal Highness, you look beautiful and are a credit to our country." I curtsied in return.

"Thank you. I'm grateful for your hard work and dedication to making this event a success." Mollified by the high praise, she entered the ballroom, and the long line of vampires greeted their king and me, curiosity evident as they were introduced to the wealthy heiress of their murdered queen. It warmed my heart to see my guests, Ralph, owner of Nuit Boutique, Ron my dance coach, and Tom and Jerri the enforcers. The last guest, my ex-Mike Endicott, bowed to Dragos and me.

"Good evening, Your Majesty. Your Royal Highness, thank you for the invitation. I hope we can share a dance, perhaps a tango?" All men improve in a tuxedo, and Mike wore his with the panache of James Bond. With a wink, he scuttled into the ballroom. No doubt it was time to pay Olenka a compliment.

Inside the glittering hall, Dragos ushered me to a raised platform where the musicians sat poised to play. He raised a goblet, and I shakily held a glass of champagne handed to me by a white-jacketed waiter.

"Thank you all for traveling to meet the rightful heir and descendent of my beloved wife. Princess Natalie will add much to our world and will help me with the projects I have earmarked for Romania. Let us all welcome her and wish her well. Salut!"

'Salut' echoed the voivode's toast, and hearty applause filled the room. The musicians lifted their instruments, and the guests parted as the king escorted me to the floor. His arm circled my waist, and I placed my hand on his shoulder. A slow waltz began, and I followed his lead, stiffly at first, but more smoothly as I relaxed in his arms. He did not move his eyes from mine, and I felt the heat rise in my cheeks.

"You're staring at me," I said.

He raised one eyebrow.

"We are dancing. Where would you like me to look?" I had no answer and pulled my gaze away from his fixed intensity. A handsome stranger on the periphery of the room caught my eye and bowed deeply. Dragos noted the gesture with a frown.

His hand tightened on my waist.

"Are other men permitted to admire you, but I must remain oblivious to your beauty?"

"No, I mean, thank you for the compliment."

"I only speak the truth," he said. "You are the most beautiful woman in the room."

The music ended, and we were approached by a couple who congratulated Dragos on an education initiative he'd pressed upon local officials. Someone tapped my shoulder.

"Your Royal Highness, may I have the pleasure of this dance?" The reclusive Portuguese vampire whose villa we had visited for a port tasting bowed deeply.

"Of course." I remembered Olenka's caste system of vampires worthy of my energy. "It was kind of your nephew to share your delicious port with my friends and me." My comment pleased him.

"Shall we?" A slow salsa began, and I followed his lead with ease.

"You are an excellent dancer, Princess. I noted you waltzed with His Majesty. Do you dance often?" The count's magpie eyes were curious.

"Not recently. I must admit, I have competed in the past." We completed a more complicated step, and he sighed with appreciation.

"Excellent. You will be a charming addition to our world. The voivode is fortunate to have you at his side." The music finished, and the count swept an air kiss across my hand.

"Thank you for the dance." I dropped a brief curtesy, and was immediately claimed by a high-ranking Russian vampire, a distant relative per

Dragos. The attention of the senior vampires deprived me of time with my pals other than sharing a dance with David, but my guests planned to celebrate at the castle with me the following evening.

I was surprised when the candlelight dimmed, and a group of senior vampires claimed the dance floor. Bogdan escorted Olenka to the center, and he, Dragos, and the Portuguese vampire formed a circle around her. The other vampires formed a circle around them, and they all raised their arms bent at the elbows, like the front paws of an animal walking on its hind legs. A kettle drum began to pound. Slowly, other drums and timpani joined the beat as the vampires twirled and performed a hunter's dance. Who was the hunter and who was the prey? They engaged with each other, and then separated, moving to another participant. I was frozen in place, hypnotized by the beat that drove the music, and I felt my breathing synchronize to the pulse of sensuality which filled the room. Dragos dominated each encounter before smoothly sliding to the next dancer. When the performance was over the vampires dispersed silently, returning nonchalantly to their previous conversations.

I had no idea if what I'd witnessed was a common occurrence at vampires balls, or if it was a rite reserved for auspicious occasions. Its meaning was yet another topic my vamps would need to explain.

The ball was nearly over when I noticed Mike politely waiting to speak to me behind a pushy vampiress from Spain.

"You simply must come to our holiday ball," she insisted. "We would be honored to provide a separate villa for you and to include any guests you wish . . ." The tiara had begun to give me a throbbing headache, and I ended the conversation.

"I will inform His Majesty of your invitation and your thoughtful offer of a separate villa for me. His secretary will reach out." She beamed, and I turned to acknowledge Mike.

During a previous lesson in royal protocol Olenka had emphasized, "A man should approach you. A well-bred woman does not cross a room to speak to a man except on very few occasions." As instructed, I waited, head held high, and Mike stepped to face me.

"Princess, is this dance available for a foolish ex-boyfriend?" I wanted to smirk, but I felt many eyes upon us.

"Foolish? There are a boat load of adjectives to describe your behavior, Mike. But, since we've moved past our differences, I would welcome a dance." He grinned and I motioned to a hovering waiter. "Please tell the musicians to play a tango." The waiter hurried away, and immediately the orchestra switched to a tango Mike, and I knew well. He pulled me to him with confidence, and a hush fell over the packed ballroom. His icy hand gripped mine possessively.

"Behave, Mike. And if this tiara falls off my head, Dragos will be furious. No dips."

"As you wish, Princess Gorgeous." We glided across the floor, one body, and when we reached the end of the room, Mike employed a smooth behind the back spin instead of bringing his hand over my head. My headache evaporated while I concentrated on the joy of dancing with the man who had broken my heart.

"Nat, your beauty eclipses every woman in the room. For real." My heart lurched, but I quickly remembered the nights spent crying over his betrayal and my utter humiliation when he left me. I lifted my chin.

"Don't let Olenka hear you." We laughed, and he spun me slowly, expertly reducing our steps to a halftime beat.

"Oh, she's stunning, but she is a vain, vicious witch. Don't trust her. She is determined to get very close to you. Beware. Trust no one." What did he say?

"It was you I heard in the bath. How did you do that?" Mike placed his arm around my waist, and we circled in one of our signature moves.

"I'm not sure," he said. "We have a connection. I overheard a conversation, and I knew you weren't safe and had to be warned. There was a strange, nasty looking guy she entertained one night when

Bogdan wasn't home. She kicked me out of the room where they were talking, but I hung around outside the door until the butler closed it. I heard him say, 'I have a plan, she will join us. Leave her to me.'" The music stopped abruptly. We'd hardly reached the edge of the room when Olenka approached.

"Aren't you the handsome couple?" Her eyes were wide with excitement, and her voice bordered on hysteria. "Michael darling, may I speak to you? There is someone important you must meet."

"Of course, Your Grace," Mike drawled. "Whatever you wish." I was alone for a second before Dragos approached. We both watched Olenka usher Mike out of the ballroom.

"Was everything to your liking, Princess?" His eyes held mine with a veil of tenderness.

"Oh, yes. It has been a marvelous evening. Thank you."

"You are a great success," he said. "Our guests will be leaving soon. Let us move toward the door so they may say goodnight." He took my elbow, head held high. One by one the vampires expressed thanks for the invitation to my first ball. Olenka and Bogdan were missing, and I noticed Dragos scan the room. He did not share his thoughts, but I sensed his annoyance. After the guests had left, his valet passed him a note. Anger erupted on his face.

"Princess, I am unable to escort you home. State business requires my attention." He bowed and followed the valet in the opposite direction of his study.

"Did I do something wrong?" Dragos's abrupt exit bordered on rude.

"No," Ian said. "He was angry and walked in the direction of the dungeon. David, we should get home."

The limosine brought us back to the path to Le Refuge Bleue, and David and Ian disappeared with a wave and a kiss, closing the cellar door behind them. Iris and I carried a glass of water up to our bedrooms, and we chatted while she unzipped my gown and helped me remove the tiara and jewels. I had noticed her dancing with my guests and with a couple of attractive vampires.

"Oh, it was smashing," she said. "I felt like I was on a movie set. Two vampires asked me to dance, and they were intrigued when they realized I'm a fairy."

"Wonderful. Good night, Iris. Or should I say good morning?" We hugged.

"Good night, Natalie. Thanks for the amazing experience."

I performed the nightly beauty rituals, locked the jewels and tiara in the safe, and wondered when the adrenaline would subside. I craved sleep, but my mind would not rest. The ball had fulfilled my Cinderella fantasies, even if the room was filled with undead.

A searing pain stabbed my chest, and a burning

sensation spread across my body. Had a phantom poisoner succeeded in doctoring my creams? I broke into a cold sweat, shaking with pain and fear. Was I dying?

The pain slowly receded, leaving me mildly dizzy. I inhaled deeply, relieved to see strong shafts of daylight streaming through the slight break in the drapes. The dizziness faded, and padding to the bathroom, I filled my hands with cold water and splashed it over my face. The mirror told me nothing—a normal version of myself stared back at me. Perhaps I'd had a panic attack.

I slid into bed and pulled the covers up under my chin. Nothing strange happened, and relieved by the comfort of my bed and the coolness of the room, I slept the sleep of the innocent.

CHAPTER THIRTY-THREE

Peals of laughter reverberated down the hall as I followed in the butler's wake. Olenka had suggested I host a card party at the castle, but why was everyone here early? Olenka's normally stoic, image conscious gal pals were calling out words and howling with glee. I heard 'crispy', 'ashen', 'blackened' and 'bruléed', which resulted in wild clapping. The butler knocked on the door and the snakelike sound of hissing and shushing died down as I was announced.

"Your Royal Highness, we're honored to be invited to your first soirée." Olenka greeted me with air kisses, a deep curtsey and stepped back to assess the elegance of my ensemble. I had dressed, knowing my appearance would be dissected under a fashion scalpel. I wore a bespoke pant suit of camel tweed, a peach cashmere sweater, and all the pearls I could layer. Olenka preened; her acolyte was a credit to her mistress and presentable to the vampire beau monde. All the ladies rose and curtseyed in turn.

"How lovely you look." Her hand strayed to the huge pearl and diamond brooch I had given her, prominently clipped on the lapel of her black satin jacket.

"I heard the laughter. Were you playing a game?" One of Olenka's loyal sycophants giggled, and Olenka flashed her a disapproving glance.

"Oh, we were playing a silly word game while we waited for you to arrive. Would you care for a glass of wine? The butler has decanted a bottle of your favorite Margaux." Addressing her minions with a pert raise of the eyebrows, she said, "Shall we move to the card tables?"

Although the ladies were charming and supportive of my beginner discards, Olenka's deflection of my question, along with a secretive undercurrent, made me suspicious. There was more to the earlier merriment than Olenka had revealed.

When I returned home that evening, I sent a text to Mike. I hadn't heard from him in a week. He didn't owe me for the invitation to the ball, but I had so few friends in Romania. Arabella had called the night before, and it was obvious she was in no hurry to return to Transylvania. Iris would leave eventually, and I shared my frustration with Ian and David.

"I know, I know. Mike is a vampire and was a

horrible boyfriend. We'll never be together, but he did warn me about Olenka."

Ian shut the book he was reading with a loud thud.

"Stay away from Mike, Natalie. Olenka is possessive and expects complete loyalty. If she thinks Mike spoke out of turn, it could be dangerous."

"Dangerous how?"

Ian sighed.

"Just stay away from him," he said. "Please. For your own safety. As your head of security, you must respect my advice, otherwise I can't protect you."

I wondered if Olenka would dare to insult me or worse if she felt a challenge to Mike's loyalty. Still, it was incredibly rude for Mike not to at least thank me for inviting him to my presentation ball.

At the next ladies' card night, a young vampire named Lucrezia was friendlier to me than the others. When I excused myself to go to the ladies room, she followed me, tipsy on whatever fillip was in the V cocktails Olenka was serving.

"Why have we never played the word game the ladies enjoyed the last time? It sounds quite amusing. What was it called again?"

"The synonym game?" She was confused for a moment, and then her eyes widened with fear.

"Um, well, no, you wouldn't want to play that game. I spoke out of turn. Please don't tell Olenka I spoke to you about it."

"Spoke about what?" I made a zipping gesture across my mouth and tossed the invisible key over my shoulder.

She visibly relaxed, but I had to know what Olenka was hiding.

David and Ian were watching *Casablanca* when I returned. I tossed my overcoat onto a chair and blocked the TV screen just as Humphrey Bogart was telling Ingrid Bergman what color she had worn in Paris.

"What is the synonym game?" Their heads shot up simultaneously.

David grabbed the remote and waved me to the side to pause the movie.

"Where did you hear about the synonym game?"

"The first time I hosted card night, the ladies were playing it and stopped when I arrived. I thought it was weird they were at the castle early." David grimaced.

"Do you remember what they were saying?"

"Yes. They were calling out words and howling like a pack of hyenas. 'Crispy', 'blackened', 'ashen', and finally Olenka's flippant 'brulée' produced clapping and hoots of laughter."

Ian rose and poked the fire. The crackle of the fire filled the silence until Ian spoke as he stared into the orange blaze.

"It's a nasty game, Nat. You don't want to know." I would not be put off so easily.

"If I'm spending time with these ladies, I need to know what they do before the time I am expected to arrive."

Ian replaced the poker and faced me.

"Fair enough," he said. "It's a disgusting vampire death game. If the ladies are playing the synonym game, I don't think you should go to Olenka's castle for cards next week."

I crossed my arms. It was my first invitation to her home, and I had already accepted. Mike would no doubt be lounging about, and I craved familiar company no matter their body temperature. Ian had conveniently neglected to provide details about the game.

"Does a vampire die in the game? Do vampires kill humans? I want to be clear."

David spoke up.

"Only the cruelest of vampires would enjoy the synonym game. It is played by describing in one word the manner in which a condemned vampire is. . . terminated."

"They were finding humor in describing a vampire dying by being burned?" I placed my hand on the arm of the sofa to steady myself and sank slowly onto the cushion.

David jumped to my side.

"Yes, hon. Burning is the most horrific manner of death for a vampire. It must be approved by the local vampire counsel and can only be overruled by the voivode. It is a rare occurrence in the States. Romania is more. . . old school."

"You mean Dragos permitted a vampire to be burned to death?" How could the man who spoke to me of music and gardens approve of cruel capital punishment? Once again, I had developed feelings for a completely unsuitable man. My stomach tightened and I tasted the essence of the wine I had drunk.

"There would have to be irrefutable evidence against the vampire," David said. "The Big V wouldn't have allowed it otherwise. He overruled the security panel's recommendation for Antonio to be burned after his multiple infractions and sent him to work on a Romanian castle restoration.

"We haven't heard anything about a vampire execution. I wonder why?" David and Ian shared a long look.

"I think I'm going to be sick." I ran to my room, locked the door, and vomited in the toilet.

CHAPTER THIRTY-FOUR

Sleep was restless and filled with phantoms of tortured vampires. It was late when I woke to the sound of tapping on my door.

"Princess Natalie? Are you okay? It's ten o'clock."

Maria's concerned voice woke me from a nightmare of fire and malicious laughter.

"Yes, I'm awake. I'll be down in a few minutes." After using the bathroom and dressing in jeans and a sweatshirt, I turned on my cell phone. A new text message slapped me across the face.

Unknown:
I'm sorry about Mike. He had a lot of potential.

The identity of the caller was blocked. Who knew my cell and would want to keep their number hidden? Our vampire friends had met Mike at the ball, so the text couldn't be from one of them. Whether Dragos liked it or not, he was in for a grilling that evening. A truly reformed king would never allow one of his subjects to be burned to death.

Iris and I had planned a trip into the village and although I knew the roads well enough to drive, Mihai, one of Dragos's security guards, insisted he chauffeur us.

"Mihai, I know how to drive. Iris and I are going to tour the historic part of the village. What will you do while we're in the old church?"

Mihai lowered his sunglasses and met my eyes in the rearview mirror.

"His Majesty requires me to keep you in my sight. Where you go, I go. I'll fade into the background. And, Your Royal Highness, please call me Ten. I am the tenth Mihai in my family, and the nickname keeps things simple." He pushed the sunglasses back up his nose.

"Fine, as long as we don't have to hold hands. I appreciate the escort." Iris made a silly face, and I shared my own version by rolling my eyes.

Iris and I walked along the center of the village and entered the hushed interior of the ancient church. The life of a village often centered around daily church services of prayer and reflection, and the murals depicted the typical scenes of creation and punishment. Light filtered through the stained glass and we both lit a red candle by the statue of

Jesus dressed in finery. I'd dreamed of a church wedding when Mike and I were together, even though neither of us were particularly religious. Organized religion had caused such angst and misery in the world, but I had wanted my moment in white, floating down the aisle to my forever after.

In a cute café on the main thoroughfare, we settled ourselves with our shopping bags in an open booth. Mihai slid into a booth in a far corner. Behind the counter, the waitstaff huddled over a tablet, and they groaned in unison.

"That is the grossest thing I've ever seen. Turn it off."

"It must be the trailer for a Halloween film. There's over a million views. The special effects are incredible. There hasn't been a decent vampire movie since Anne Rice's *Interview With the Vampire*. Did you hear the sizzle when the sun hit his skin? Crazy realistic." The manager came out of his office to disperse the group, and our obviously distressed waitress slunk to our table.

"Sorry for the delay. Would you like the drinks first, or are you ready to order?"

Something compelled me to ask.

"Miss, what were all of you watching? I overheard it was a vampire movie?"

She blanched.

"It's a trending video on YouTube, a vampire burning to death in the sun. Completely gross. I'm trying to unsee it. Disgusting. If someone tells you to watch it, run away." She forced a smile; we ordered and changed the subject to Iris's collaboration with a top French fashion house.

The speck of a thought nagged at me. We ascended the mountain, and the hulk of the castle came into view. Was it possible that the glee of Olenka's pals playing the synonym game related to the burning vampire video? Was the odd text message regarding Mike more sinister than I'd initially thought?

Mihai pulled up to the curb by the garden path, and I immediately realized something terrible had occurred. A battalion of security guards surrounded Le Refuge Bleue. Leaving Iris in my wake, I ran down the path to the garden gate. Before anyone could stop me, I charged up the front steps and burst through the front door, following the wailing to the back of the house.

In the kitchen, Mimi sobbed, head down on the wooden table. Maria rubbed her back speaking to her in a low, comforting voice, and when she saw me, she immediately rose from her chair. Iris took her place next to Mimi, and Maria pointed to the conservatory, closing the door behind us.

"What's wrong with Mimi?" Tears filled Maria's eyes.

"A terrible thing has happened. A man came to the door, and he looked exactly like my Boris, Mimi said. He told Mimi that you asked him to fix the flu in the fireplace in the drawing room. Boris is permitted to enter your home, and she didn't stop him from going into the drawing room. He was gone only a moment and then came running into the kitchen and out the back door." She paused to pull in a ragged breath.

"I can't . . . it's a disaster . . . please follow me."

In the drawing room I froze in disbelief. So much for Dragos's promise of security. The Vermeer painting was gone! Only the frame remained, a handwritten note thumb tacked in place of the priceless art.

My darling Natalie,
Nice digs. I am borrowing the Vermeer to hang in my castle in Italy. When we are reunited, I will prove to you that my ardor is sincere. You looked exquisite at the ball. Dragos cannot protect you; our union is a fait accompli, my love.
Slade

Maria wrung her hands and continued in a broken voice.

"Since no one is supposed to enter Le Refuge Bleue without your permission," she continued. "We waited for your return. The security team wants to search the house and post guards in your home, and until the voivode wakes up, they need direction. What do you think about . . ."

I sank onto the sofa. It was all a sham; I wasn't, nor had I ever been safe.

"Boris can come into the house, but no one else," I said. "Slade accomplished his goal. You and Boris can check the rooms. The guards must remain outside until I speak with Dragos. I'll stay here for now, but I need the laptop from my bedroom." Maria hurried off and I leaned back into the comfort of the sofa. If anything had happened to Mike because of our relationship, I would never forgive myself. I had become a danger to everyone I cared about. I had to know who was burned in the YouTube video.

After Maria brought my computer and hurried off to get Boris, I set myself up at the drawing room writing desk. Typing the search words 'vampire punished by burning' sent me to a YouTube video with 1.7 million views. I clicked on it.

A grainy video focused on a man chained to a pole in the middle of a brick courtyard. The frame got tighter, and the man lifted his head. My stomach lurched. It was Mike.

"Your Grace," he pleaded. "I would never betray you or the vampire world. You have been generous to me, and I am your loyal servant. Selena said she was permitted . . ." Olenka's scream reverberated across the courtyard.

"Lies! You agreed to be my loyal intimate until I

released you. I own you, fool. I know you spoke against me, behaved promiscuously, and consorted with the alien warlord. Selena confessed before her death. Betrayal and treason are unforgivable crimes. I denied you nothing—clothed you in bespoke garments and housed you in luxury. I've given you humans to feed your coltish blood lust. We will hear no more lies. The counsel has found you guilty, and the voivode remains silent. Burn, traitor. Scream Selena's name as the sun fries your flesh."

"Noooooo, please!" Laughter rang out, and a male voice said, "It's a pity we must watch a video. I prefer to witness justice live." As I watched in horror, shafts of sunlight shot over the brick wall of the courtyard briefly illuminating Mike's handsome face. Immediately, his skin began to bubble, melting as it fried amidst his screams of agony. I turned and vomited into the wastebasket. Resting my forehead on the desk, I focused on not passing out. After a few minutes of deep breathing, I struggled to my feet and stumbled into the kitchen. Iris flew to my side.

"Natalie, what's wrong?"

"Mike is dead—he was the guy in the video." She gasped and Mimi's sobs grew louder.

I would never unsee Mike's horrific death, and my body filled with a white-hot anger. Dragos was a liar and a murderer.

"The YouTube video the waitress told us about was Mike being burned in the sun," I growled.

"Slade was able to enter my home. I've never been safe and everyone around me is in danger. And worst of all, I'm in love with a monster." I burst into tears and Iris pulled me into a crushing hug.

"What are you going to do?"

"I'm going to tell the king of the blood sucking murderers what I think of him for not interceding like he should have." I crashed down the hallway and sprinted out the front door. Night had fallen and I wore only a sweater, but my fury was warmer than a fur-lined coat. The guards were assembled in a small group, and I pushed them aside as I ran toward the castle. Footsteps matched my frantic pace.

"Natalie! It is dangerous for you to be outside alone—and you aren't wearing a coat." I swung around and there he was. The ultimate chess player, a con man of the highest order. I despised the concern etched on his face, a face which had, to my pea brained naiveté, become handsome and kind.

"I know you allowed Mike to be murdered. How could you, Dragos? You haven't changed. You're still a cruel, heartless murderer."

He reeled, my words a slap across his shocked face.

"The evidence against Mike Endicott was damning. The council found him guilty of treason. He consorted with Selena Sidwell and Slade Suit, the alien leader. I couldn't justify overruling the verdict."

I stepped toward him and yelled with unhinged passion.

"You believed Olenka's evidence? Mike warned me about her at the ball. Did the warning make him dangerous? He told me she had a nasty visitor one night when Bogdan wasn't home." He stood frozen and I wanted to punch him. "Does caring for a friend justify a gruesome death? The video is on YouTube. It has millions of views. I overheard Olenka and her pals playing the synonym game using burn words. Is murder a form of entertainment in your world? And of course, you know about Slade stealing from my home. He was in my house. You promised me that I would be safe on your property. Liar!"

I ran to the barn and sank onto the floor, where the wolf cubs snuggled. Tears streamed down my face and Decebal lay his face on my knee.

Dragos was wise enough to leave me to grieve with the wolf family. Decebal was almost old enough to leave his mother, but she would always protect her pups, and they would be loyal to her. I wept, knowing Mike's unwise comments had precipitated his horrific death. There was a boatload of blame to go around, and I wasn't innocent.

Mike was dead and Slade had shown his hand. If I wasn't safe in Le Refuge Bleue under Dragos's protection I wasn't safe anywhere.

"Someone please help me," I whispered.

CHAPTER THIRTY-FIVE

Dragos paced his study. He needed to process Natalie's reaction to Mike Endicott's execution before reacting. Her accusations and anger had unnerved him. More importantly, despite the highest level of security, Slade Suit had entered her home and stolen the priceless Vermeer. The slimy alien certainly had inside help, and the traitor would be found and . . . punished.

Olenka would deny posting the video on YouTube, but the glee with which she viewed Mike Endicott's horrible death had been overheard by Natalie when she and her cronies played the synonym game. He believed Natalie. The inner workings of his kingdom were not for the Internet's consumption. He did not need to view the video to understand Natalie's disgust and outrage. Someone had released the video hoping she would see it, hoping the gruesomeness of her former lover's death would destroy his and Natalie's growing friendship.

Holding lovely Natalie in his arms, their faces had been inches apart when they danced at the ball, and she hadn't shrunk from the cold touch of his hand. She had held his gaze and commented on his staring at her. During their latest chess match, she had teased him about his obsession with the knights, and he had parried, accusing her of a weakness for the king. She had blushed.

The death of Mike Endicott had been calculated and unjust, and he would eliminate those responsible. It had taken many chess moves, and he was on the brink of unmasking Natalia's murderer. With the American's horrible murder by burning, the Sicilian Defense had been successful if cruel—Dragos controlled the center of the board, and the enemy was desperate and even more dangerous. So be it.

Blood for blood.

It was too close to dawn to command Bogdan and Olenka to travel to him. No matter. A rest would allow him to prepare his next move. He scribbled a note to his brother and handed it to his valet.

"I will retire for the evening and am not to be disturbed."

"Yes, Voivode." He drew the deadbolts across the doors of his study. Grabbing a flashlight, he opened the secret panel in the bookcase and pulled it shut behind him. Carefully, he crept down the hand-hewn staircase and toward his most precious possession.

The beam from his flashlight scanned the silent room for the candelabra and he recalled he had left it by the rear door to the private vault where his coffin lay upon Romanian soil. Across the tomb's windowless space, a golden sarcophagus, molded to her likeness, contained the corpse of his murdered queen. It comforted him to rest with her each day. Alone.

The match flared, and he lit the candles. He extinguished the flashlight and settled in his chair to absorb the glow of the Amber Room.

While the evil of the Third Reich raged across Europe, he had installed spies in key European cities. They were not to intervene in warfare, but to protect vampire castles and properties. Those who thought it a coincidence that particular castles were not plundered and survived unscathed were naïve. Hitler was superstitious, and wise enough not to take on a supernatural enemy he could not defeat. Vampire strongholds were avoided, and Dragos's spy network gained inroads into the German military.

Word came to him through a reliable source that the precious Amber Room of the Romanovs was being disassembled and shipped to a Nazi controlled location. His operatives successfully relieved the Nazis of the Russian treasure, and the world mourned its disappearance.

In the early morning hours before sunrise, he would relax in the absolute silence of the Amber Room and imagine his Natalia alive, voicing her strong opinions on history, art, music, or other subjects while she sipped a port. Natalia had never seen the Amber Room, but those were his favorite fantasies, ones he'd hoped would become reality with Natalie.

The Amber Room existed for his solitary contemplation while the mortal world created documentaries seeking to solve the mystery of its whereabouts. He had protected the treasure from forces which could have destroyed it. But what good is treasure if you had no one to share it with? Picking up the candelabra, he searched the amber for the fossil he admired the most. Entombed in the precious sap, the fossil resembled a tiny bat, an ode to his world, and to him, the flawed fossil culpable for Mike Endicott's murder.

Endicott's horrific death had, in the end, fulfilled two divergent purposes. In boldly removing an ally of Natalie's, the traitors had revealed a centuries-long game of treason. Slade Suit's bold theft of the Vermeer was a direct challenge to the voivode's power, and confirmation of the traitors' intentions for Dragos's ultimate removal for the new order.

Endicott's death also eliminated him as a

romantic rival, but Dragos's ego would have preferred Natalie choosing him freely. Her distress was hurtful to contemplate, and justice for Endicott's incineration would be swift. Endicott was collateral damage, a pawn sacrificed to move a knight.

If Natalie's accusations were correct, the heart of the treachery within his ranks had finally revealed itself. Check.

He blew out the candles.

CHAPTER THIRTY-SIX

The security guards eventually persuaded me to leave the stable. Grudgingly, I returned to Le Refuge Bleue and fell into a fitful slumber. The next morning, I woke up drenched in sweat, the horror of Mike's death temporarily muted by the vivid dream of Natalia's last minutes of life. I threw off the bedcovers and darted to the window. The sun was in hiding, shrouded by a veil of storm clouds. Sheets of rain pounded against the window. I had to record the dream before the details vanished. Opening my laptop, I typed with a ferocity born of fear and frustration.

Natalia fell onto the sofa. The slow burning sensation confirmed her worst fears— poison. How long did she have to live? She had to think quickly.

"Lana!" The housekeeper appeared instantly

and ran to her side, dropping onto her knees. *"What has happened?"*

Natalia held out her hands.

"Poison—don't touch me," she croaked, *"you can't help me. We are betrayed and must move quickly. Prince Dragos is in danger. Do as I say. Dress my son in the peasant clothes under his crib. Open the back door and call Lupu. Empty the contents of my jewel box into your washbag and take the prince to the address on the note with the clothes, ohhhhhh."* A hole, like a hot poker, burned in her stomach and she coughed up blood.

Lana began to cry.

"No crying. Do as I say. Dress my son and run. Use the forest. Lupu will guide you. Do not stop until you reach the safety of the address on the note. Now! Get Lupu."

Lana ran to the rear of the house. *"Lupu! Come!"* The sound of heavy paws and Lana's feet pounding up the stairs echoed through the house. There was little time to protect her and Dragos's son.

A tongue licked face. Lupu. She croaked out her final words.

"My loyal friend, I need you to leave me. Go with Lana. Protect my son. Guide her through the forest to the cabin. She will bring Prince Dragos to safety. She loves him. Listen to her—obey her. Good Lupu." Lupu laid his head next to hers and whimpered. Lana pounded down the stairs

in her hat and coat with the sleeping baby
wrapped in a thick wool blanket.

"Bring him here," Natalia whispered. The pain
was unbearable. *"My darling son. I love you.
Lana, Lupu will protect you. Go. Quickly."*
Natalia laid her head back and Lupu licked
her cheek one last time.

"Lupu, come," Lana commanded. With a final
glance, the wolf cub she had saved, the loyal
Lupu, exited his home to follow the dying
command of his beloved Natalia.

Exhausted, I staggered to the bathroom and
leaned on the counter over the sink. What should I
do? I needed a clear head and a plan. The boldness
of Mike's demise confirmed that I, and anyone
close to me, were in danger until the murderers
were caught. The dream of Natalia's strength as she
lay dying could only have come from the queen
herself. What should I do?

CHAPTER THIRTY-SEVEN

I drank a bucket of coffee.

I'd hoped for clarity and instead ended up with the jitters. The background hum of Iris's sewing machine soothed the heavy silence of Le Refuge Bleue. Since it was the weekend, Mimi and Maria were enjoying their families while I fretted alone with a detail of guards surrounding my home like the Gurkhas at the Tower of London. Wrapping myself in a thick blanket, I huddled in the conservatory, commiserating with the deluge of rain crashing into the glass panes. The day deserted me, cloaked in a shroud of desperation and frustration.

I had no doubt Dragos would confront Olenka that evening, and I wanted to hear her lies. But how would I breach the impenetrable phalanx of my heavy security and Dragos's gate-keeping butler? I had to do something which would confuse the staff so I could listen in on Olenka's trial. For it would be a trial, with Dragos as judge and jury.

In the kitchen, I toasted and buttered a thick slice of black bread and poured a glass of port. Caffeine to alcohol. At least I'd managed to feed myself. Finishing my snack and draining the port, I returned to the conservatory and closed my eyes while the patter of rain surrounded me. How could I get into the castle and witness Olenka's reckoning?

A spark of inspiration burst through my confused brain. If I carried Natalia's jewels in a tote up to the castle and said I wanted them stored in the main vault, it would seem a prudent request given Slade's theft of my painting. If I didn't hear Dragos and Olenka's voices on the first floor, I could insist I wait in Natalia's chambers for His Majesty. I was a princess, and although I had shown no interest in using the suite of rooms, my change of heart was no one's business. It might work.

Grabbing the carryon I'd used on the flight from Portugal, I carefully laid the boxed jewels and tiara in the bag and zipped it closed. The rain had slowed to a depressing drizzle and, not caring how I looked, I threw on jeans and a sweater, pulling my hair into a disaster of a ponytail. With boots and a lined raincoat, out the front door I went. The guards were frantic with my escape, running after me and shouting to each other in Romanian. A clap of thunder, bizarrely out of season, hastened my pace to the castle. Decebal appeared at the foot of the stairs to the castle and glued himself to my side as I mounted the steps.

Opening the castle door, the butler assumed his most impervious reserve. He glanced down at the wolf cub and then returned my determined gaze.

"Good evening, Your Royal Highness. His Majesty is unavailable at the moment," the butler said while water dripped from my raincoat onto the floor.

"Well then, I will wait." His face was a grim stone, and I decided to channel Olenka's attitude. "Do you think he will be pleased when I tell him you let me stand freezing and wet in the hallway?" My condescending tone worked, and, with a start, he helped me off with my soaking coat.

"If you will follow me, please. There is a cheerful fire in the yellow drawing room." Decebal stepped to my right, leaving a trail of pawprints to match my muddy boot prints.

"Would you like coffee or tea?" The main floor of the castle was eerily silent. Would tea or coffee take more time to make? I just needed Dragos's gatekeeper out of the way.

"Tea sounds lovely. Thank you." He closed the door behind him, and I set the suitcase on the sofa. After peeking out the door, I ran across the great hall to the staircase and climbed as fast as I could.

To the left, a light shone from an open door in the pitch-black hallway. Tiptoeing on the thick carpet, I heard Olenka laugh and knew I had found them.

Through a crack in the open door, I could see Dragos commanded the center of the room, and Olenka preened at her vanity. Had Dragos been swayed to believe Olenka's lies? Was my bold plan as foolhardy as when I had rushed to confirm Mike's presence on *The Natalia*? Dotia had paid for my last mistake, but this time, it could be me. Despite the danger, I was caught in the undertow of curiosity—I simply had to know the final act of the drama.

* * *

Dragos stood frozen, his eyes fixed upon Olenka's reflection in the mirror over her vanity, in the lavish rooms he had generously given her in his castle. She busied herself with her lipstick, avoiding meeting his steady gaze in the mirror. Before condemning her to painful extermination, and despite the physical evidence of her treachery, she was his brother's wife. She must admit her guilt.

"I will give you this opportunity to explain yourself. Speak."

She slid an embroidered handkerchief forward, attempting to cover the splendor of the ruby and diamond cocktail ring her maid had stolen from Natalia's jewelry box in her bedroom in the castle.

"And what if I told you I am innocent of the

ridiculous charges? Consorting with the shapeshifter Slade something in a treasonous affair? Coordinating Natalia's murder? Seriously, Voivode, you have been deceived by the paranoid American. Natalie has spun a tawdry tale of murder and intrigue." Olenka caressed her golden hair with smug satisfaction. Her lilt voice was ever confident in its ability to charm.

Her arrogance infuriated him.

"Innocent? You are the serpent who tempted Adam, cunning and vile. I allowed you unsupervised access to my castle because of my brother. He loves you, and you were given a license to amuse yourself because you didn't interfere in my business—or so it appeared. You pretended to enjoy Natalia's company. I imagined the four of us spending decades together building Romania, protecting our forests, celebrating our culture. Natalia wanted this, too." The memory of those dreams threatened to distract him from what he had to do.

"Making Romania strong. Is that what you tell yourself? Natalia was a conceited, entitled cow. Why should she live more luxuriously than me? Wear jewels better suited to my superior beauty? Have hordes of servants at her beck and call? Reign as a queen at your side?" Olenka fastened a ruby choker around her neck and admired the contrast of red against her ivory skin. "And Natalie is worse, a mongrel weakling. You need a proper queen, my darling." Boldly, she uncovered the ruby and diamond ring and slipped it on her finger.

Dragos removed the jeweled penknife from his pocket. She had almost admitted her duplicity, and he prepared to pounce. Light flashed from Natalia's stolen cocktail ring, missing for a century. He baited her with a laugh of derision.

"Bogdan has provided an extravagant lifestyle for you. He has ignored your indiscretions. He has been a loyal husband to you." Dragos let the point of the penknife rest against his palm, the prick of silver forcing him to ignore her plan of seduction.

Olenka chose a crystal perfume bottle, extracted the stopper, and dabbed at her wrist and décolletage. She rose and faced Dragos. This was the moment of reckoning, the moment she had waited for—dreamed of. She reached up and slipped the straps of her diaphanous slip over her shoulders. The garment dropped to the floor, and she met the eyes of the man she had killed for. She stepped closer and purred.

"Imagine how glorious it will be, my darling Dragos. You and me, ruling together. With Natalie and Bogdan dead, we can create a parallel world with the alien force and Romania can take its proper place as the most powerful country in the world. This magnificent body will be yours. I will be your queen." Could he really stand before her unmoved? The temptation of her bed was steps away. His inaction was maddening. No woman could equal her beauty.

"I repeat my question. Did you kill Natalia?" Dragos hadn't moved, and his eyes hadn't left her face.

In the hallway, a cloaked shape moved out of the shadows and grasped the doorknob.

"Fools," Olenka cried. "You and your brother, slaughtering thousands of your loyal soldiers when treason glittered on your doorstep. History will repeat itself and Bogdan will side with me, his wife and lover. There will be war, and I will see to it that the American mongrel, your adored Natalie, like Natalia, is the first to die."

The cloaked figure moved swiftly. There was a swooshing sound and two thuds. Check mate.

Olenka's head rolled to a stop next to the bed, and her headless corpse dropped at Dragos's feet. Shattered rubies from the choker scattered on the floor, the bed, and one gleamed on the toe of Dragos's boot. Blood spattered his face, and that of his brother. Bogdan released the hilt of the sterling silver sword and dropped to his knees. The polished metal of the sword gleamed through the deep red of Olenka's blood. Dragos ran a finger down his cheek and licked the blood from his finger. He exhaled and moved to place his hand on his brother's shoulder.

"That was a merciful death. I would have preferred the sun pit. You are a considerate husband, and a true son of Romania." Silence spread, inching its way across the floor like the blood that seeped from Olenka's severed neck.

"Bogdan, her blood is tainted and traitorous, it . . ."

"I understand the precautions. I will wash the floor and cremate her remains." He slipped the stolen ring from his wife's finger, rose, and with a sharp bow and a click of his heels extended the jewel in his blood-stained palm.

Dragos closed his fist over the ring and replaced the penknife in his pocket. He stepped forward and grabbed his brother in a crushing hug. Drawing back, they stared at each other. Bogdan, shocked by his brother's embrace and devastated at the destruction his wife had caused, suddenly remembered the other witness to Olenka's reckoning.

"Brother, Natalie is in the hallway—with a wolf cub." Dragos darted to the door, but his princess was gone.

CHAPTER THIRTY-EIGHT

When Bogdan burst through the door and beheaded his wife I ran. Was I to be the next victim of his murderous rampage?

I smashed the garden gate open and tripped on the front porch steps. Scrambling to my feet, I slammed open the door, nearly knocking over an elaborate flower arrangement. Decebal let out a howl and was joined by a chorus somewhere in the distance. I let out a primal scream and crumbled to the floor. Strong arms hugged me as I struggled to catch my breath. Ian closed the front door and he and David sat next to me on the foyer floor. Decebal stood at attention guarding the front door.

"Nat, darling, what's wrong?" The icy touch of David's hand comforted me. How many times had he and Ian warned me that all vampires weren't like them? The execution I'd just witnessed would join Mike's video as a horror I could never unsee.

"Olenka is dead." I choked the words out and David and Ian gasped. "She killed Natalia and stole the ruby cocktail ring from the Burmese parure. It was on her vanity in her bedroom in the castle. She is . . . was a traitor and wanted Slade and the aliens as allies in a new world order." Ian and David gently helped me up off the foyer floor and guided me into the drawing room.

Iris rushed forward to help me shed my wet jacket and I threw myself onto the closest sofa. Across the room, the empty Vermeer frame glowed under its museum lighting. Decebal abandoned his post to sit by the hearth, his yellow eyes scrutinizing the actions of everyone in the room. No one questioned his presence.

Ian stoked the fire and added another log. He replaced the poker and perched on the opposite sofa. Iris joined him, anger evident on her pixie features, her breath labored. David squeezed into the corner of the sofa next to me.

"You're safe, Natalie. We'll die before we let anyone hurt you." I didn't doubt David's words, but the beheading of Olenka was gruesome and unforgettable.

"I could summon the forest fairies to surround your house," Iris said. "They were fond of Natalia. She barred hunting in their part of the forest—she protected their homes. Do you want me to call them?"

I shook my head in confusion.

"I don't know what to do—Bogdan cut Olenka's head off with his sword. I can't believe I saw him do it." Ian's phone pinged as I started to sob again.

"The voivode wishes for you to meet him at the garden gate." I gulped back my tears. No—I couldn't and wouldn't see him. There was no gaslighting what I had witnessed.

"I'm afraid of him," I said. "I'm not leaving this house." Ian texted and his phone pinged immediately.

"He wants to assure you that you are safe."

Safe?

"No. Tell him I'm unwell. And petrified. I'm staying right here." Ian sent my message, and his phone pinged immediately.

"Since when can Dragos text?" I pulled out my ponytail and massaged my temples. Dragos had repeatedly stated his distaste for modern conveniences.

"His valet taught him, in case of an emergency, to protect you." Ian sighed. "Olenka's threat has been dealt with, Natalie. She's dead." Yes, but I was alive and terrified of the justice meted out in a parallel world by a man I had fallen for . . .

I lost it.

"So is Mike," I shouted. "Slade Suit is alive and well. How many other enemies are waiting to harm me?" Ian was speechless and David draped his arm around my shoulders and pulled me close.

"I agree with Natalie," he said. "The safest

place for her is in her home, not at the garden gate. The Big V can deal with the rest of the traitors first. He made a serious mistake with Mike Endicott, and I'm not letting him near Natalie until he routes out the rest of the Olenka's conspirators." Resigned, Ian shook his head and tapped my refusal into his phone.

David and I climbed the stairs together, his arm tight around my waist. Our friendship had survived incredible obstacles, and I loved and trusted him. Upon entering my room, he checked every corner and crevice. I laid a blanket on the floor in front of the fireplace, and Decebal settled himself on its warmth.

"Your room is safe, hon, but you should reconsider Iris's offer. Forest fairies are powerful and clever. Their magic is beyond a vampire's supernatural abilities." He ran his hand through his hair. "Keep the drapes shut and don't open the door tonight unless you hear my voice. Password is *Nuit Boutique*. I'll bring tea and soup before I rest. Don't leave the house tomorrow. Stay in your room and only let Iris in. We'll sort this out tomorrow night. Love you." He leaned forward and brushed a cold kiss across my cheek.

"Love you, David. On second thought, tell Iris I gratefully accept her offer about the forest fairies. Goodnight." I closed and locked the door. The drapes were already pulled tight, and I fell backward onto the bed. My phone pinged and without reading the text, I switched it off. In the silence of my bedroom in Le Refuge Bleue, the weight of Olenka's final words and the horror of her execution replayed over and over in my mind, the torturous repetition highlighting every gruesome detail.

I stared at the landscape painting which concealed the safe containing Natalia's journal and Dragos's love letters. I knew I wouldn't sleep, and perhaps it was time for me to read Natalia's innermost thoughts and understand the deep love she and Dragos had shared.

The room went ice cold and a woman's voice whispered, *"Yes, Natalie. Only by understanding the past can you survive the present and thrive in the future. Do not judge us too harshly. Love makes fools of us all."*

I sat bolt upright, adrenaline pumping madly alongside the burgeoning questions exploding like Fourth of July fireworks. Natalia had reached out to me from beyond the grave, sharing her most private moments in my dreams. It all made sense. She was my great-great-great grandmother, after all. She loved me and had protected me in my journey to Romania. I felt the swell of gratitude, and love.

Natalia had bestowed her permission. Before I could doubt myself, I squeezed the latch, and the painting swung to the right, revealing the safe. I inhaled deeply, entered the code, and withdrew a worn leather journal.

ACKNOWLEDGMENTS

A huge thank you to my editor Stacy Juba for shepherding this story and for asking all the right questions.

Thank you to Claudia O'Neill for her proofreading acumen.

My formatter, ML Tompsett always makes my books pretty.

ABOUT THE AUTHOR

Lois is a proud New Jersey native who lives in sunny Florida with her husband and fifty plus orchids. You can follow her on her Instagram @theorchidmadame or @orchidcottagelife